I0713536

RESISTANCE

Redeemed
Trilogy
2

RESISTANCE

DONNA M. YOUNG

Resistance
Copyright © 2017 by Donna M. Young. All rights reserved.

No part of this publication may be reproduced, stored in a retrieval system or transmitted in any way by any means, electronic, mechanical, photocopy, recording or otherwise without the prior permission of the author except as provided by USA copyright law.

Published by Donna M. Young
P O Box 76, Lawton, IA 51030
dmywriting@wiatel.net

Author photo by Elizabeth Rose Kahl

Book Cover and Layout by Christina Hicks Creative
christinahickscreative@gmail.com

Published in the United States of America
ISBN: 978-1-947143-00-5
Fiction / General
Fiction / Christian General

But in a great house there are not only vessels of gold and silver, but also of wood and clay, some for honor and some for dishonor.

2 Timothy 2:20

CHAPTER 1

Cage didn't have friends growing up, at least not in any conventional sense. He'd been too busy defending himself, and using enormous amounts of energy being angry, to spend time cultivating relationships. Angry at his parents, his circumstances, or his crazy childhood, he didn't know. Perhaps it was just his name that made him so angry. Radcliff Ansil Tiberius Cage IV. The very thought of the ridiculousness of it made his blood pressure rise. Who names their child Radcliff Ansil Tiberius Cage IV, whether it's a generation's old family name or not? Things like a person's name should be carefully thought out, shouldn't they? For the sake of future nicknames, and monogrammed towels, if nothing else. As far as he was concerned his parents intentionally sentenced him to a lifetime of ridicule and bullying. If they'd loved him at all, they couldn't have put that kind of weight on his shoulders. But, he didn't believe there was any chance of that anyway. At most, he was heir to the family fortune.

Cage's father, Radcliff the III, was forced; by his very wealthy, and very controlling family; to marry his innocent bride in order to produce a long awaited male heir. His duty, he was told, in no uncertain terms, as his father's son.

He'd been a spoiled child, and grew up to be a very spoiled, entitled man. His own peculiar preferences leaned in less traditional directions, as the world, outside his father's estate, was abundantly aware. But, those disturbing preferences wouldn't be considered, or even recognized, by his ultra conservative parents.

Dashing, handsome, and already in his mid-forties by the time he was required to marry; he never forgave his own father, Radcliff II for his meddling interference in his life, and affairs.

Never before seen in the company of women, at least in any romantic pairing, much to his dad's feigned confusion; his well connected parents made all the necessary arrangements for the strained coupling, and the upcoming nuptials.

Quite aged by that time, Radcliff II had, quite reasonably, become impatient to see his family's line continued before he died, and he single handedly decided his son's days of flitting about; in odd social circles, and without a purpose in the world; were over. However, once the serious, and, in his own thinking, unsavory, business of a successor had been accomplished, and he'd satisfied his parents demands, Radcliff III never shared his beautiful, young wife's bed again.

The minute Cage's mother discovered she'd been a pawn in the family's plan, and that her husband didn't have any interest, what-so-ever, in her, or their small son, she went into a deep depression for months and left his care solely to the family's eccentric, elderly nanny. Short visits to the garden, to snip flowers for his mom's numerous, daily bouquets, were some of the rare glimpses he had of his beloved mother, and sadly, they would have to do.

She was a delicate creature, always had been, and could now be found roaming aimlessly, with tear stained face and vacant eyes, about the vast estate. Usually tending to her favorite flowers. Servants, and visitors, alike, pondered her sanity, and the precarious future of the tiny, forgotten lad.

His mother, poor naive dear, never aware of her husband's unnatural proclivities, until after she'd produced the family's desired beneficiary; became society's pitiable, sweet darling ever after; and once she began, slowly, to come back to herself, never lacked for abundant companionship from any manner of interesting, well-to-do gentlemen.

Forever away, his parents were continually out on some world-wind tour, or involved in another charity event. Each to mask his, or her, own, private pain; which kept them far too busy for the little boy who ached to be their focus, even if just once. They were persistently invested in things they found more important than Cage, or his quickly fleeting childhood.

His grandparents, very advanced in years when he was born, died while he was not much more than an infant. So, they never played a significant role in the raising of this long-awaited grandson. Perhaps his life could have been much different if only they'd lived long enough to dote on their young descendent.

Radcliff IV was a beautiful child, hauntingly handsome in fact; but his appearance, though it garnered approving stares from others when he was paraded through the crowd, at must attend events, never seemed to puncture the veil which surrounded him in his parent's eyes. He'd never known a nurturing word, or loving embrace, from either of them in his life. They sent him away to boarding school as soon as it seemed remotely appropriate to do so, and they'd never looked back. He'd barely seen them, much less spent time with them growing up; only on an occasional, strained holiday. But, it didn't matter. Not anymore. The damage was done. He was mostly raised, and tortured, by first, his old, unbending nanny, who'd performed unspeakable punishments on the tiny, frightened lad, when he didn't hop to as quickly as she desired; and then the head master of the much respected military academy where he'd spent most of his young life. Until, of course, he went on to finish his college career at yet another, even more prestigious, armed forces institution.

The academy became his home, or as close as he would ever know to one until he grew. And though he never felt loved there, he quickly learned to adapt in the competitive, testosterone driven atmosphere.

He was only a small boy when his parents sent him away. He didn't really care. In his mind, the circumstances at his new place of residence couldn't be worse than in the big, drafty mansion; where they'd left him to languish in loneliness for five desperate years; or so he thought.

He started kindergarten at the academy, and right away became a target. Some of the older boys, bent on impressing one another with their evil exploits, began torturing him. He ran to the head master for help, and was whipped within an inch of his life for his efforts. "Don't be a panty-waste boy! Nobody likes a panty-waste." Head master yelled at him. He went off to hide, and lick his wounds. He would have to be strong. He would have to be brave; and he would have to take care of himself. That was simply all there was to it. He decided, then and there, he didn't need anyone in his life. He could do it alone. And Satan smiled.

As he grew, his anger, cultivated by loneliness, and his ever wretched circumstances, simmered continually in the background of his psyche, eventually developing into a force of its own. He became as devious and mean as his tormentors had ever been to him in his younger years. More, in fact, because he was an extremely bright and inventive young man. Instead of protecting new cadets who came in, he became their worst fear and their biggest enemy. Head master grew oddly closer to him the older he got and the meaner he became, and in fact, one day, told him he was proud of the way Cage had grown into such a strong, capable young man. That was the first compliment he'd ever received from an adult; well, besides being told, exhaustively, how attractive he was; and it made him all the more determined to be the best he could be at what he believed came naturally to him.

Understandably then, Cage's free time was spent holed away, in various dark corners; whispering quietly to himself, and planning his next attack; or in outside activities that could only be described as blatant sociopathic behaviors. Often setting small fires around the school's property, he was always careful not to get caught; and, extra cautious not to destroy anything too terribly valuable to the school. Frequently transfixed by leaping flames fashioned from his acts of arson, he came close to setting himself afire on numerous occasions, as he loitered too closely to his creations. Those budding embers, and intense heat, delighted him in ways he couldn't quite describe. If someone had stumbled across him in one of those moments, they would have witnessed the savage glee in his eyes, and justifiably thought him quite mad.

He loved walking the beautifully manicured grounds, finding the quiet solitude a centering force. During these times he searched for avenues in which to release his creative energies. Discovering small birds in their natural habitat; awaiting the return of their mothers; he would remove them, ever so gently, from their nests and very careful not to dislodge the flimsy structures from their branches. Then, he'd pull off their delicate wings and gouge out their eyes.

Afterward, he'd put them carefully; their tiny bodies trembling; back where he'd found them, to see the effect their deformities had on their unsuspecting moms. It thrilled him no end to see the returning mothers throw their wounded babies from the nest, squawking and chirping all the while. *"Perhaps all species toss their broken young to the dogs"*, he thought. He was certain that was the case with human beings. He was, after all, living proof of that.

One day as he walked the tree lined shore of a large, natural lake, which abutted the south end of the academy's property, he spotted a little grey and white kitten, shivering in a pile of autumn's fallen leaves. He walked slowly to the decaying, downed tree where the animal shivered in the cold, picked up the small quivering creature and gave it a couple quick strokes with his gloved hand. The kitten, grateful for some warmth, and any sign of affection, immediately began to purr. Cage looked at the tiny being in his hand, and marveled at its complete trust and total lack of fear. He removed his glove, and found that the kitten's fur was soft as a whisper in his hand. Its almost transparent, miniature eyelids fluttered closed as it relaxed in the boy's grasp. Cage walked to the water's edge, took another long look at the baby creature, and hurled the kitten as far as he could into the dark, cold water. He watched as it swam with all its might to the shore, to drag its small, soaked body onto the rocks. Picking it up again, he watched it gasp for air, and finally regain its breath. But, the moment it began again to purr, he threw it once more out to the murky depths. As he watched the kitten flail about and go down for the last time, he shook his head. "Not strong enough. Too bad. You gotta be stronger than that little guy."

Small cadets walked as quickly as possible, away from the young man they'd taken to calling RAT Cage.

One had only to look into his eyes to see the evil which lurked there. Simple frozen darkness filled him to the very depths of his depraved soul. And Satan smiled.

It would have been easy for an outsider, seeing the loveless childhood he'd been subjected to, to feel sympathetic toward the lonely, twisted young man; except that the last thing in the world Cage wanted was anyone's pity. He was proud of who he'd become, and would grow in his evil proclivities, throughout his assent into manhood, until he was indeed the master of torture who'd persecuted Josh for so many months, in a hidden militia prison, high on a secret mountain plateau.

• • • • •

Cage had indeed eventually inherited his family's fortune; which necessarily required his absence from the militia base where he was commander, over the most recent Christmas past. His father, after years of pointless encounters, with multitudes of suitors as confused as he, met his end at the bottom of a bottle of gin. His mother, still wildly beautiful after all this time, had given up her claim to the family riches years ago, to run off to Dubai with a wealthy gentleman who doted on her every whim. Sadly, when she'd gone, she'd left without a word to her son; cementing the feelings of abandonment he'd denied, but carried never-the-less, through from his warped childhood.

He kept the estate. Why, he wasn't certain. He hated the way it made him feel whenever he was forced to visit. It was expensive to run, especially since he normally wouldn't actively reside there, but he kept it. Perhaps, if his plans went as desired, he would soon be promoted to North Western Regional Commander and the place could make a very comfortable home base. That might even give him a bit of an extra edge in the mind of whoever made those final decisions, as it would ultimately be a money saver for the struggling new government.

They say you can never go home again, and that had been Cage's plan throughout his life, up to this point. But, in this case he would have to, if only to make his presence known, and to give the servants instructions concerning his future, and imminent, return.

Usually when returning to the place of our childhood, we are met with an extraordinary illusion. The place is seemingly never as large as we remembered it to be, now that we are in our grown up bodies. This was not the case with Cage's ancestral home. His return to the ominous mansion brought back many feelings from his childhood. Feelings, which manifested before he'd left that terrifying place, so many years ago. Feelings which left him angry to a point of, well, only slightly veiled, insanity.

Making his way up the agonizingly long, oak lined, cobblestoned drive; while bits of the hundred and fifty year old manor house peeked intermittently through trees which lined the path; ancient memories popped into his mind, haunting his psyche with flashes of past tortures, and long-ago fears. As he approached the mansion, and seemingly out of nowhere, black rumbling, storm clouds, like hell's evil omens, crept in overhead, chasing away any last bits of lingering sun, or blue sky. Then suddenly, there it was, in all its primordial, and horrific glory. The origin of his first self loathing. He thought it odd how a 'mere place' could have such a devastating impact on one's self esteem; especially when that person is otherwise, seemingly, very confident; yet there it was.

Gothic spires constructed along the expanse of the gargantuan, dark roof looked, at least in his estimation, like dead, black fingers reaching for the sky, struggling to be free of this wicked place. So many memories, all bad. So many rooms, all dark and foreboding. So big. Just so unnecessarily big. Well, he didn't have to remain for long, at least not on this trip. As far as he was concerned, his mountain militia base was his home, and he would be glad to get back there. At least there he was unwaveringly in charge of all he surveyed. No latent feelings of fear to haunt him in that place. There he knew what to expect and how to get exactly what he wanted. Thank goodness his stay here would end swiftly. A shiver danced down his spine as he exited the car and walked toward the enormous, carved mahogany doors. And Satan smiled.

• • • • •

Cage returned to his beloved mountain base a couple days after Christmas; hard on the heels of the worst blizzard of the year, so far; glad to be free from the oppression of the family estate. And, in plenty of time to witness the special surprise Jana had in store for the government militia camp. Of course he hid himself during the conflagration. He felt it was only his duty, of course; to keep himself safe; for the good of the men and all. After the attack, the traitorous resistance soldiers locked him, and what remained of his bruised and bloody men, in the very caves where they themselves had been held prisoner through the previous, bitter cold months.

With no radio contact to headquarters during, or immediately after, the battle he was forced to wait until a new replacement cycle of reinforcements were automatically sent from the head office, in order to mount a counterattack, which turned out to be one of the most frustrating periods of his career. As soon as back up arrived, ready or not, he was off on the chase.

Looking back, perhaps he'd been a bit hasty in escalating that attack. After all, it'd been an unmitigated disaster. In hind sight, perhaps he should've packed more provisions for his men, and even trained them better for the hazards of a mountain trek. But, he wasn't about to admit that to his superiors. No, he would never admit his own incompetence to anyone, forever laying the blame at someone else's feet. That is how he'd made it so far in his black and shady career. A trait that earned him much disrespect and animosity from the men in his personal command.

• • • • •

After the conclusion of the second mountain battle, it'd taken eleven long days for the PM rescue team to find and release Cage, and his men. It was a relief to be free from the prison cave where Josh and Jana left him; after his last dismal failure; on the snowy mountain pass. By the time help arrived with much needed supplies, the mountain was covered in several inches of new snow, and there'd be no way of tracking Josh's band of traitors to their ARM camp now. Angry, and frustrated, once they finally arrived back at home base, Cage stormed away to his quarters to plan his revenge, cussing Josh, his rescuers, and the situation in general, to anyone within earshot. His men could do nothing more than stay out of his way, or be sure to risk his imminent wrath; and none would be stupid enough to do that.

Residual feelings of inadequacy, left over from that brief visit to his ancestral home, and combined with irritation at losing the traitors in his charge, threatened to undo him. It would be imperative that he get it together, and soon, if he was to launch an attack on ARM when their base was finally located. And, he swore to himself, he wouldn't stop until it was.

• • • • •

After the loss of so many comrades during their last battle, several young cadets in his charge got together to discuss a plan for reporting Cage to the authorities. They were angry about the way he'd treated their fellow soldiers while out on that latest mission to overtake the resistance troops. With so many dead, a total of fifty-five in all on that ill fated mountain trek; and some by his own homicidal hand, in rampant fits of rage; they knew they had to make him pay. But, once they discovered there was no administrative path which did not go directly through Cage himself, their minds were changed very quickly. He was crazy. There were no two ways about it, and there wasn't a man on the base foolish enough to challenge him to his face. Several of those men put in for transfers, knowing they couldn't continue to follow this insane, maniacal leader, but the minute Cage found out the names of the individuals who'd requested transfers, they were in his sights and would find their remaining time in this man's militia something to dread. In the end, almost none would escape.

Cage easily covered his tracks, and the catastrophic losses that resulted from his lack of judgment and poor choices, when he returned from the prison cave on the pass. No one in command above him would ever know of his incompetence. Admittedly he'd been distracted when he arrived back from his visit to the mansion, before the brutal battle on the plateau. But, it never occurred to him that an attack could be launched from the back side of the mountain, so he'd been overwhelmingly underprepared for the carnage Jana managed to achieve. She was clever, Josh's woman, but he would never admit that out loud to anyone. No one would have believed one scrawny girl could create the kind of devastation they saw on the mountain that dreadful night. From the looks of it, she'd surprised even her own husband!

Once he'd arrived back on base, from his imprisonment, he'd had all evidence of her one woman show erased forever. The more he realized how easily he'd been bested, the angrier he became. He would get them both. He would destroy them. It was all he could think of.

Now the bodies of hundreds of dead militia had to be flown off the mountain. The plateau, where the original battle had taken place, was mostly stone and shale, and certainly no place to attempt to bury so many. Additionally, teams had been sent out to recover the fifty-five lost on their recent, unsuccessful march. Without their commander; as they had been for a significant period of time, while he flew off to chase Josh and his band; the base had been in a state of confusion, and disarray.

His hasty departure, to hunt the resistance soldiers, had been made without thought to his duties on base, and nothing at all had been done to clean up the devastation which was wrought there on that bloody night. Remaining PM soldiers did the best they could, without any meaningful orders, to round up body bags and treat their comrades with as much respect as possible under the circumstances.

So, for days now, since his return, the shiny, black transports had flown back and forth carrying their precious, frozen cargo in tagged body bags.

It was Cage's job to contact the families, who'd lost loved ones, but he shirked even that duty, and had his underlings dealing with that most unsavory chore. He wanted only to be finished with all the boring tasks keeping him from the one mission he longed to complete. The capture, torture, and slow killing of Josh Conyers and his crew of traitors. And Satan smiled.

For we do not wrestle against flesh and blood, but against principalities, against powers, against the rulers of the darkness of this age, against spiritual hosts of wickedness in the heavenly places. Therefore take up the whole armor of God, that you may be able to withstand in the evil day, and having done all, to stand.

Ephesians 6:12-13

CHAPTER 2

Sixty eight miles due North, as the crow flies, from the government's secret Militia base high in the snowy heights, was the very well hidden entrance to ARMs even more secret Northwest regional headquarters.

After the victorious skirmish with Cage, on the mountain pass, and his subsequent capture and imprisonment in the make shift prison cells; Josh's forward scouts, representing his rag tag group of one hundred and seventeen resistance soldiers and prisoners, finally joined up with ARM forwards from the base, who'd been sent out to search the mountain for recent government defectors.

When they discovered who was leading the band of resistance soldiers they couldn't get back to home base, as a large group, quickly enough to share the joyful news. So, they sent scouts ahead to headquarters post haste. The remaining scouts became Josh's escorts and led the larger group through dizzying heights, narrow ledges, fog, and falling snow, for many days, to a hidden miracle that defied all imaginings.

Through a well guarded, though virtually impossible to detect entrance they walked two abreast, down a long passageway. Lights hung on the eight foot tall passage walls every fifteen feet, or so, and were strung together by, from what Josh could surmise, actual electric wire. One might have thought fifteen feet between lights was an extreme distance, but the illumination they shed was multiplied a hundred fold by the luminescence of crystallized minerals in the rock walls, and their way was bright as day.

Josh was confused by the electric wire, especially so high in the mountainous heights, but didn't say a thing. So far, everything was too amazing for words. After walking at a downward, and constantly curving, incline for over fifteen minutes; and getting to a point where she was wondering when they would arrive at their destination; Jana was just about to ask if they were there yet, when they turned a corner and stepped out onto a large, stone ledge. Josh and Jana both gasped out loud and then looked at each other in total awe of their surroundings. Their eyes grew wide, and their mouths hung open in utter astonishment, as they tried to take everything in. *"How could this be?"* Josh thought as he looked about in wonderment. Jana, being a more vocal person simply said, "Wow, I mean, wow. I don't believe this!" Scott, Mike, Mark and Dr. Rose followed close behind and elicited their own gasps of disbelief at the vision before them.

The inside of the mountainous cavern, easily the dimensions of a good sized city, was an underground metropolis of activity. Deep enough in the mountain to thwart heat sensing satellites and weapons; their presence was masked to the outside world. Josh and Jana would certainly have to get to the bottom of how any of this was even possible, but for now it was enough to stand amazed. The whole enormous grotto was lit, with what appeared to be sun mimicking lighting units. Hanging from crisscrossed metal structures fastened into the rock ceiling high above them. In itself a feat of architecture beyond their understanding. The units lighted every corner of the vast space. Light magnified by the same luminescent metals in the rock walls of the entryway, left the inside of the caves as bright as a summer day. The place was eighty degrees, or more, warmer than the air temperature outside the cavern; which was currently in the minus teens; and felt extremely comfortable after so many days upon days in the frozen wild. Looking around, they saw individual dwellings sprinkled liberally throughout the immense space, and then other sectioned off areas with actively growing crops of all types. Even an orchard of young fruit trees off in the distance. Tents and other more sturdy structures for munitions, storage, group food stores, and medical purposes dotted one side of the massive cavern. And then, as the gentle noise of their surroundings began to settle in, even the comforting and familiar sounds of cattle, pigs and chickens filtered in.

Whoever had the insight to set up the diverse agricultural bounty before them, had Josh's respect immediately. They'd even had the insight to incorporate bees into the general plan. Two waterfalls, one quite close, and another clear over, and across the expanse of the secret grotto, appeared to be their water source. And, they would later discover, the basis of hydraulic power for what they could only describe as a kind of Shangri-La. What a magical, wonderful place. And, all so familiar somehow.

Josh couldn't quite put his finger on it, but there was something very memorable about this place, as if he'd seen it in a dream. No wonder the world lost track of ARM. They certainly seemed to have all they could possibly want or need in this mammoth place. Josh was filled with so many questions, and couldn't wait to begin asking.

"Hey, soldier, who's in charge here?"

"Well, you are sir. You and the group of elders. We've been waiting for you since we discovered you were still alive. I'll go get Mr. Conyers, but he'll tell you the same thing. He and the other council members have been keeping things going, and making decisions, up till now."

"My dad? My dad's here?" Jana saw her husband's eyes well up with unshed tears.

"Yes sir. Your mom too. We've all been praying for your safety, and that you'd be coming soon. They're going to be pretty excited to see you."

"Oh Josh. Your mom and dad. I can't believe it."

"I know Jana. They aren't just going to be excited to see

me. They're going to be astounded to see you too."

"Well, let's not just stand here then."

" Please, take me to them soldier." As Josh and Jana began to ascend the stone steps to their new amazing reality, and the other guys followed close on their heels, the rest of their traveling party came out of the passageway and into view of the amazing mountain base. They heard "Ohs", and "Ahs" echo from each and every one as they were faced with the impossibility of their grand, new surroundings.

• • • • •

The reunion was filled, as would be expected, with tears and many praises to God. "Dad, Mom, I can't believe I'm seeing you again. I should have known you two had something to do with this place as soon as I saw the layout of the crops. It's set out just like our farm back home. That's why it seemed so familiar to me."

"Oh, Josh, we thought you were dead for so long. To see you here, alive and well, God is so good and we are so grateful. And, Jana, how wonderful it is to see you. You look different, good, and stronger somehow."

"Thank you, Mr. Conyers. It's wonderful to see you too. We couldn't believe it when the soldier said you folks were here."

"We've just been helping to hold the fort down until we could get some real reinforcements in. Things have gotten pretty bad out there in the world."

"Well, Jana managed to dig up and save all the papers that Mark and I put together, Dad. But I'm not sure how much good they'll do anyone now. If things have gotten that much worse, who would we take them to?"

"That's a good question son. More and more the government has been corrupted, until only those hand-picked by the administration have been allowed anywhere near the seat of power. And, the few who would stand up to the administration have been silenced, in one way or another, long before now. We've had a difficult time staying connected to the other regional ARM bases from inside the mountain. But, we wouldn't give this place up for anything, it's been such a blessing. The last we heard, the other four bases were housing two, to three, thousand resistance soldiers and their families, in secret facilities. We've got about twenty-five hundred here now, with your group included.

"We've discovered we're not fighting a battle, just to take back our country anymore; but, in reality, to survive with those who've been able to escape implantation. We don't know in detail how far things have gotten, since we've been holed up in this cavern. We don't always have reliable communications with any source on the outside, but we know enough to see that our country is no longer our country as we knew it. Whenever we can get someone far enough down the mountain to get out of these clouds and get a signal, we find out a little more about how much ground the bad guys have taken, and how much further behind we are than we last knew.

"We tried antennas and even a satellite dish up here, but the clouds are so thick it interferes with reception, and we worry that installing one lower on the cliffs, with cable to our location, would be discovered, so it's hard to stay current. We try to send scouts down the mountain a couple times a week to get a better feel of things. At those times they listen in on radio broadcasts, and try to update what we know. We also send scouts out, often, to get information about families who might need our help, and if those people are implant free, they are brought here.

"The president, who you know declared martial law, when citizens began fighting against implantation; has recently joined with the United Nations Counsel. Our country seems to be functioning in some sort of a global government situation now, in agreement with just about every other world power that matters. With our president as commander of the North American continent. The Prime Minister of Canada and President of Mexico weren't very fond of the idea, but it didn't take much for the People's Militia to put them in line. Especially with all the special forces that were sent in to help. Those soldiers from the Middle East are especially effective at that sort of thing, and they seem to truly enjoy their work."

"Yeah, I can attest to that. But, we can't just give up, Dad. What can we do?"

"That's what we're going to have to try and figure out son, but we will. It's so good to see you. So good to know you're alive!"

"Well, I can't stay quiet one more minute! Oh Josh, Jana, praise God you two kids are safe and sound! I've dreamt about this moment for months!"

"Mom, I missed you so much." Josh picked his mother up and squeezed her tight. When he set her down she grabbed Jana and wrapped her arms around her daughter-in-law.

"It's great to see you too Emma."

"Oh, no, none of that Emma stuff from you, young

lady. It's Mom, do you understand?"

"Yes ma'am." Jana laughed and allowed herself to be mauled by the diminutive woman.

"Your mother really has had dreams about this moment for months, you two. After the third dream she refused to believe you were dead any longer. So, we increased our number of scouts out on the mountain, and she's been waiting to hear word that they'd found you ever since. You'll have to fill us in on everything. You can see what we've been up to, but we want to know everything the two of you have managed to pull off as well."

"Well, that's a story best told when we can sit awhile. There's quite a lot to tell."

"I have to say son that the counsel is very excited to talk to you. So, if you want to collect your group of elders, and follow me, we'll all sit down and talk awhile. Then you kids can get to your quarters, get cleaned up, and rest for a spell before supper."

"Just give me a minute, Dad. I know they're all out looking around, which Jana and I can't wait to do, so I'll have to gather them together."

Once Josh and Jana assembled their group of elders, Chuck led them into a large tent furnished with a beautifuly polished, wood table and chairs. Several smiling men, and women, already occupied some of the seats. And, as Chuck and Emma took their places, Josh and his group were urged to sit and relax. They were still wearing their gear and many protective layers, so they began to undo straps and zippers, removing some of their outer wear, and making themselves more comfortable.

"Hello counsel. Some of you know our son Josh from when he was driving families to safety for America's Resistance Movement, but others have never met him. Well, here he is! And, this is his beautiful wife Jana. Son, you'll have to introduce the rest of your party."

"Hi folks, we're all happy to be here, and out of the cold. We want to thank you for your hospitality, and we hope to be able to share some things that will make our combined experience a more productive one. God bless you all. Now I guess some introductions are in order. This gentleman to my far right is pastor Mike Anderson. Some of you already know him. He was left behind on the mountain, quite some time ago; by one of the ARM battalions;

to wait for my wife. He eventually began to imagine her dead, since so much time had elapsed, and when they finally met she almost killed him, thinking him to be a militia soldier. Then she nursed him back to health, and eventually rescued us all, but that's a story for another time. This fellow is Mark Randal, who was driving families out of danger with me. Some of you may remember him. He and I have been through a lot together. This young man to my far left is Scott O'Fallon. He is the newest member of our group, but without his blood donation, my wife would be dead now, also a story for another time. I think most of you know Doctor Rose. He has been invaluable to our group, and without him, Jana wouldn't be here at all."

"Doctor Rose, we have some folks out there who will be very happy to see you. We all thought you were dead, just like we thought Josh and Mark were dead."

"My family? My family is here? I didn't know if they were dead, or alive. Oh, praise God. Where are they? When can I see them?"

"We're going to track them down right now, Doc. Your kids are in school, but I think your wife is working in the fields today. And, Mark, there are some little ones who are going to be pretty excited to see their daddy too."

"My kids are here? Thank God, thank God. I'd love to see them. Josh, Jana, do you believe this? My kids are here!"

"Yes, Mark, your sister-in-law, Rachel, managed to fight her way here, after the tragedy with your wife. She knew the news of Tina's suicide was a lie and wasn't about to allow the government to implant your kids. How she managed her way up the mountain with those two little ones is beyond anything we can understand, but she got them here safe and sound. We are all so sorry for your loss. We'll send someone out to get all of them right now. Doc, Mark. Just have a seat, so we can get started. We'll let you know when we've rounded them up, okay?"

"Great. We can't wait."

Jana couldn't help but look over at Mark; whose lovely wife had been killed by the militia; as the conversation was taking place. Now he would have his children back in his life, and she was very glad for him, but with Tina gone, it wouldn't be the same ever again. She knew the feeling very well after her months, and months, of believing her own husband dead.

When Mark heard that Dr. Rose's whole family was safe, he smiled, and then his eyes grew misty and he lowered his head. She knew his heart was breaking for the loss of

Tina, and her own heart broke for him, and for his loss too. She gave her husband a barely perceptible nudge, which prompted him to put his hand out to touch Mark's arm. When he did, Mark nodded his appreciation and took a deep shaky breath before he relaxed into his seat.

"I have so many questions, Dad. I can't believe this place. How did you accomplish all this?"

"Well, much of it was done before your mom and I ever got here, Josh. Let me go back a bit. There were those who saw what was happening to our country long before we were smart enough to begin catching on. This man is Doctor Joseph Stevens."

"Just call me Joe. Happy to meet you all, Josh, Jana, Mike, Mark, Scott, Doc."

"Nice to meet you Joe. It's good to know we have two doctors on board."

"Well, he's not that kind of doctor Josh, but we do have another one of those too. I'll introduce you when we're done. Joe is a physicist, but he's also an electronics genius, and several other things we'll go into later. He was one of the first members of ARM, and was up here in these mountains quite a number of years ago in the spring, looking to set up a home base. This group could see where things were heading even then, and wanted to get a jump start on preparing a safe place. They tripped over the entrance to this cavern while looking for small caves that could be useful later on, for various reasons. Obviously, back then it was just a huge empty mountain covered in clouds, but they saw the potential and started doing some logistical calculations."

"Well, looking around, they had to be doing some pretty heavy calculations to come up with all this."

"I have to say, Josh, it hasn't been easy. But, what in life, that's worth having, is ever easy? We saw the potential here, but one of the biggest challenges was getting some of our equipment up this mountain undetected. God has been good. Much of it we had to chopper into a lower elevation during good weather, and then haul up, unseen, the rest of the way. It took lots of men, lots of hours, but after we got the main pieces in position, the rest has fallen into place much more easily.

"Once we had good lighting we discovered there were two underground, spring fed waterfalls, instead of just the one we'd originally known was here. Also, after we installed lighting; which was probably the most complicated feat; we also discovered there was a large part of the cave floor which was covered in rich, dark soil, instead of the typical rock you would expect to find, and the ideas began to flow. We started planting some test crops, but didn't have much success the first few seasons. About that time your mom and dad showed up. It wasn't difficult from there to begin growing our own food, with all the help and wisdom from your dad. "Now we have animals as well, and we can harvest crops for food, and for seed, and there is little we need from any outside source."

"I'm very impressed Joe. I would never have believed a society could be so self sufficient inside a mountain, but you have certainly proved me wrong. From here, we should be able to launch substantial missions, without being detected, and perhaps we can begin helping some of the people who were left behind when we were captured. I know there must be more who are hiding out, who avoided implantation as we did. Who didn't know how to find an ARM encampment. I'm willing to go find them and bring them to safety.

"I'm also hoping Doctor Rose will be able to crack the code on those implants. He's been working on it for awhile, and I know he's getting close. Once that's accomplished he can go with us, and perhaps we can save some of those who were implanted against their will. That's something we'll have to work on. We wouldn't be able to risk bringing them here. Not if their GPS systems are still functioning. I am grateful to God for His hand in bringing us together, safe and sound. And, I hope we will all be able to benefit from our shared knowledge. We're all hard workers. I can see from this place that you are too, and I know that together we will accomplish much. How often will we be meeting as a counsel?"

"We try to meet once a week, to share ideas and results, unless there is a reason to come together more often. Of course we all spend time together in community, and in worship as well, so you will get to know each of us much better."

"Great, now Jana and I would love to look around a bit and familiarize ourselves with our new home."

"You can come with us son. Your mom and I will show you around for the grand tour. Each of you will be taken to your own personal quarters. As I said before, you can clean up and rest before supper if you like."

"We're too excited to lay down, Dad. We can sleep later, but we'd like to get the rest of these layers off and clean up a little."

"Doctor Rose, Mr. Randal? I don't mean to interrupt, but I have some people out here who are pretty excited to see the two of you." The young lady who stepped in had a huge smile on her face and was ready to lead the two men to their families.

"Please excuse me."

"No, Doc, go, go. You too Mark. We'll catch up later. Enjoy yourselves."

"Hey, Josh, Jana, do you mind if Pastor Mike and me tag along? We're a little outta our element too."

"No, Scott, of course not, brother. Let's get our housing assignments, and get cleaned up a little first. Then we'll paint the town red. Sound good?"

"Sounds great to me!"

"Me too. Maybe Scott and I will share a space, if that's okay with you Scott."

"Sure, that'd be great Pastor! It'll be good to have company, especially in a new place."

"Well then, I insist you call me Mike, okay?"

"Okay, Mike, let's go get our rooms and get back. I can't wait to look around."

"Jana and I will meet you two back here in an hour, that should give us enough time to get settled in and cleaned up a bit. Is that doable for everyone?"

"Yep, meet ya back here in an hour."

"I'm anxious to see this place up close! See you in an hour."

The travelers were shown to their quarters and again they were amazed. Each living space consisted of bedrooms and beds equal to the number needed for a particular family unit; a small space for food prep, since most meals were prepared in the community kitchen, and eaten together; a bathroom which contained a composting toilet, small sink and shower, with real running hot and cold water; and a nice sitting area for visiting with friends. Josh had more questions already, and they hadn't even begun to look around. After they stripped off their soiled clothing, they showered. Jana thought she'd died and gone to heaven. A hot shower felt so wonderful. They dressed in the new garments supplied for them; which fit surprisingly well, considering Jana's petite frame and Josh's extremely tall and muscular one; and headed out to meet their group.

The grand tour was remarkable, and though it only covered the basics before everyone finally needed to rest, their minds were blown by all the innovative use of materials and modern conveniences that had been made available, even inside a cave.

"Why don't we call it an evening so you kids can have some supper and get some rest? We can pick up where we left off tomorrow when we're fresh. We'll all sit down to a meal first. How does that sound?"

"Sounds great Dad, but I have a couple of questions first."

"Okay, son, but just a couple. We'll save the rest for tomorrow, okay?

"Well, one of the first things I have to ask is, how do we have running water?"

"Oh, that's an easy one, Josh. With twenty-five hundred people in the cavern, we have a pretty diverse group of talents. All that particular challenge took, was a large shipment of PVC pipe, and a group of guys who knew what they were doing. Cooking is a bit more complicated, which is one of the reasons we do it in a community kitchen. We have to manage it in stone ovens and over open fires, with no natural gas stores available in here. The elders agreed it would be too dangerous, and in the long run very costly, to try to keep propane tanks for this many people inside of an enclosed space, even one this large."

"Yeah, yeah, I can certainly see that. But I have to ask.

So, we have running water, but we're using composting toilets. If we have plumbing and running water, why don't we have a sewer system?"

"That's an easy one too, though I had the same question when we were setting things up. Scientists among us determined that even though we have some natural vents out of the mountain, the methane gas which would accumulate from maintaining waste ponds would probably overwhelm the population. Especially as we add more families. Besides, the space the ponds would take would be excessive. We're already dealing with a certain amount of methane from the animals. We use the material from the composting toilets, along with animal waste, as fertilizer once it's been broken down and detoxified. And, waste water from showers and such is much more easily cleaned and circulated back to the population."

"Okay, I see what you're saying. That is very clever, and not something I would have thought of. Good thing we have people here who are smarter than I am. My last question, for tonight anyway, is why are there so many housing units? You've got dozens, and dozens, that aren't even in use yet."

"Well, that's just us being prepared I guess. Every time we fill one with a new family, we build another two so we will always be ready for the next group coming through. We feel God would always want us to be prepared to do the right thing."

"I like that, Dad, and I'm sure you're right. Of course He would want us to be ready. Now, where do we go to get something to eat? I'm starving!"

"Me too. I didn't want to say anything, since I didn't think it would make me sound very lady like, but I'm famished. Aren't you guys hungry too, Scott, Mike?"

"Sure am."

"Yes ma'am."

"Okay Jana, and the rest of you guys too, Mom's been cooking all the while we've been out looking around town, and I'm sure she's got a spread ready for us. Let's get going."

As usual, Emma had prepared a meal worthy of kings for her family. A succulent beef roast, with whipped mashed potatoes smothered in gravy, and piles of fresh baby peas with pearl onions. A big basket of Mom's famous biscuits sat in the middle of the table, with bowls of hand churned butter and freshly harvested honey. A bevy of golden crusted apple pies, and ice cold lemonade, waited just off to the side. Jana couldn't believe her eyes. She hadn't eaten food this delicious since her visit out to the Conyers farm on that long ago fall day.

"I can't believe this Emma! Is all this food from your own crops?"

"What did I say about calling me Mom, Jana?"

"Oh, sorry Mom."

"That's more like it. Yes, all this food is from our own fields, and animals, Jana. Considering that the weather is temperate all year round in here, and we know how to rotate our crop varieties, we have a new harvest, of each variety, about every few months; depending on the type of grain we're referring to. We keep bees as well, and the fruit trees are producing now. Which, I, in particular, am very excited about! You know how fond I am of my pies.

"It was quite something learning to cook in a stone oven, and over an open fire, but I think I'm finally getting the hang of it, if I do say so myself."

"I would say you certainly have gotten the hang of it. I'm hoping you'll teach me."

"I'd be happy to, Jana. Nothing would give me more pleasure."

Josh listened to the exchange between his two favorite women on earth and smiled. He'd always believed in Jana, and now his mom would truly get a chance to know her too. *"God is good and all is well."* He thought.

"Hey, can we eat? It'd be a shame for all this delicious food to get cold!"

"Yes, son, let's say grace and begin. I wouldn't want any of you to starve to death."

For the next hour the group ate, and shared stories of their adventures. After awhile Mark and his kids joined them, and then later, Doc and his family showed up as well. Finally, with exhaustion overtaking them, fires were banked and everyone went off to sleep, with promises of more sharing tomorrow. How good it was to be home with loved ones.

Back in their quarters, Josh and Jana crawled into bed and cuddled up close. Jana was no longer plagued by nightmares from her childhood. That situation was resolved after she learned how very much God loved her. And, Josh no longer had nightmares about Jana walking through fire, now that she was safe in his arms. So, for the first time in recent memory, secure in their own little home, wrapped in each other's arms, and out of the cold, they slept like babes.

While they slept, sheltered in their new community, the world continued to deteriorate.

For they do not sleep unless they have done evil; And their sleep is taken away unless they make someone fall. For they eat the bread of wickedness, And drink the wine of violence.

Proverbs 4:16-17

CHAPTER 3

Back in the people's militia camp; sixty eight long miles from a blissfully happy Josh and Jana; and completely unaware of the magnificent city built inside a peak, in the same mountain range where he resided, Cage tossed and turned in the throes of another nightmare. Peaceful sleep eluded him, had eluded him since he'd lost the resistance traitors in his charge on that fateful winter's day. Night after night he lay in a pool of cold sweat, and woke gasping for air, reliving the horrific battle on the plateau, and the subsequent losing battle on the mountain pass all over again. Complete with flashes of his haunting, ancestral home thrown in for good measure. On the rare occasion that he drifted off into a fitful slumber, the faces of that damnable Josh Conyers and his equally troublesome woman filled his dreams, until he woke again in a state of panic. He hated them. He hated them more than he'd hated anything, or anyone, in his entire life and he would make them pay, he swore he would.

He was clearly insane, that was a fact for certain, but the lack of any significant sleep for so long, was further clouding his already skewed, and evil, judgment. And, all things considered, he was becoming, with each passing day, more dangerous to everyone around him. His anguished soul twisted and churned inside him. Filled with a white hot rage he couldn't quench. A fury which wouldn't allow his tortured mind to quit focusing on past humiliations, at least short of torturing and killing his enemies. And Satan smiled.

• • • • •

Body bags containing hundreds of dead, frozen soldiers, recently killed under Cage's command, and stacked around the perimeter of the camp awaiting his orders, were thankfully, at last, removed from the highland. Their presence had been a constant reminder of his own incompetence. A reminder he didn't relish and was now free to extinguish from his selective memory. Families had finally been informed of the loss of their loved ones, by those subordinates tasked with that unsavory duty. And, after several short inquiries, his superiors were even satisfied with his version of what had gone down on the plateau, and then later, on the mountain pass. He was cleared of all wrong doing, much to the disappointment of the soldiers in his authority; who'd been subject to his poor decisions on those occasions and lived to tell about it; their hope of justice extinguished once and for all.

Those militia personnel, who'd put in for transfers after the battle on the pass, were finding themselves in more dangerous duty situations, day after day, and several had already lost their lives through carefully orchestrated 'accidents'. Those that remained feared for their lives, but there was simply nowhere to turn, no one to listen. The government entities in charge of militia, had after all, set these camps up as total dictatorships; to relieve themselves of the responsibility of taking care of their soldiers; and further, to give the insane leaders of the camps the autonomy needed to get jobs done without the worry of guilt, or retribution. In essence, what happened in the heights, stayed in the heights.

Everyone in camp knew the 'accidents' were being handled by the Middle Eastern recruits among them. The unit of Muslim mercenaries who kept themselves apart from regular militia; considering them unclean infidels; and who came out of their tents only to eat; to answer the call to prayer that blared over loud speakers five times a day; and to fulfill secret missions for the commander. What kind of pact they had was anyone's guess, but it was vastly effective. Their numbers appeared to be growing as of late, and the regular military soldiers on base were growing more uncomfortable, as the balance of power shifted drastically in the favor of total and complete evil.

• • • • •

As a 'One World Government' mindset evolved, and emerged, in a growing global society; where the president's power had once reigned supreme through martial law; Christianity was taking a major hit. United Nations leaders decided that religions, such as true Christianity, were not open and accepting enough. Those who'd yearned for the complete takeover of political correctness were finally having their day.

The administration was fine with that. ARM was, after all, filled with those troublesome Christians, and this would be the way to silence them once and for all. So, as a combined government, they fell comfortably in with those who could accomplish a new way forward. And, they trusted groups of Muslim mercenaries, more often now, toward that goal.

The UN, claiming the presence of so many different religions was a leading factor in the breakdown of humanity's communications, and the separating of people groups; and, that Christianity was by far the biggest culprit (though statistically that was far from true); meant to do away with anything which didn't present itself as all accepting and completely inclusive, pertaining to all other religions, and lifestyles.

Let's just never mind that all other major religions believe in exclusivity as well; and that most others have rules and regulations, regarding lifestyle choices. Right down to the fact that in some of those religions, such as Islam, certain life style choices are punishable by death.

On a day which would go down in infamy, the UN finally voted unanimously, to ban worldwide, the public practice of Christianity. Christians watched the vote, via government television, and sat stunned. Knowing that if they continued to practice what was in their heart of hearts, they would necessarily have to fear for their very lives.

Those in powerful positions, in other major religions, cheered the death of Christianity. For centuries the religion, which focused on the sacrifice and love of Jesus Christ had cramped their style, and proved itself to be the bane of their existence, so they basked in the glory of its demise.

As new authorities grew in command, their influence became a power unto itself. Soon, much sooner than many had anticipated, if a citizen was found worshipping in a Christian church, or was accused of 'leading others down a path to Christianity', they were immediately imprisoned, for 'inciting fracture in the global community'. Churches were closed by the thousands and many became afraid to express their beliefs to a progressively liberal, socialist and radical public. Not knowing who to trust could get you locked up, or even killed, as the haters grew in power, and control.

Underground churches sprang up by the thousands, but were discovered, and leveled, as quickly as they began. Fear was quickly the dominant emotion in the American experience. Rapidly then, new government controlled churches sprang up, and citizens around the world were 'encouraged' to attend services in the lavish, modern structures. These 'World' churches celebrated diversity, and the multi-cultural world experience as their gods. They emphasized complete allegiance to the growing, new 'World Order', which upset rulers in other countries. Countries where citizens were expected to give their allegiance entirely to their own country's leaders.

The idea of new 'World' churches also upset leaders of various faiths. Leaders who'd assumed that by turning Christianity over to the wolves, they would be free to do as they pleased within their own religions. Religions who insisted their followers adhere closely to certain laws, and worship solely, their own prophets and gods, such as Islam.

Muslims, Buddhists, Hindus and many others rioted over the insistence that they attend the government churches, but were mowed down by United Nations peace keeping troops, until the streets in numerous cities, of various countries, ran red with rivers of blood. United Nations soldiers invaded many dictatorships who would not conform, and gave them no choice, assassinating many in the streets as an example to others.

Islamic extremists, who held a 'Twelver's' ideology, began slowly to find one another, and to band together from the middle east and around the world, hiding, worshipping, plotting, and growing in strength.

Even the president was forced to answer to the new United Nations Global Counsel. Absolute power corrupts absolutely, and the world's leaders; in an attempt to gain more of it themselves; had unflinchingly handed their own power, and their freedoms, however minimal, or vast, over into the clutches of a power they would never understand or control again. Suddenly, as Islamic extremists rose up, the president discovered that making Christianity the world's whipping boy, and allowing his Muslim cronies in to the country in droves had availed him nothing, but the destruction of his own country's ideology, and the distain of his own countrymen.

When Cage found out about the shift in power going on in the outside world he became confused. As the decades of work he'd undergone to reach a place of control in this man's militia were being undermined by global influence, his treatment of the men in his charge became even more brutal. But, as long as his orders from those above didn't change; as long as he was still expected to hunt and torture the subversives who'd escaped government implantation, he would live with whatever other changes came down the chain of command. At this point, as far as the UNGC was concerned; since implantation was now mandatory on a universal scale; Cage and his thugs, along with many other militia groups here and abroad, were a necessary evil.

His entire focus became about eliminating anything in his path that came between him and achieving that goal. So far, his scouts hadn't been able to find any tracks which would lead him to Josh and Jana. No signs of his enemies remained on the mountain and he was more frustrated and filled with rage as the days ticked on with no evidence of their path.

Months passed and soon Spring would begin, slowly, to show evidence of new birth in the lowlands. Trees, surrounded by faint halos of misty green, from which new leaves would emerge, and bits of grass peeking through melting snow, would be evident. But, it would be at least another two to three months or so, before they could expect to see any signs of that new birth higher in the heights. And, there would be very little change at all in the dizzying altitudes where the ARM encampment was located.

Cage was relentless concerning his men and kept them

busy with war games and survival challenges, which slowly eliminated those who had been opposed to him in the past, and weeded out those too weak to follow him on his next perilous trek. He was determined that nothing would keep him from the plans he had for his enemies.

But the path of the just is like the shining sun, that shines ever brighter unto the perfect day.

Proverbs 4:18

CHAPTER 4

Jana was becoming a rather good cook, with Emma's motherly help and guidance. Josh smiled as he watched her intently forming a piecrust for the juicy, green apples she'd just cut; and mixed with sugar, cinnamon and flour. Her auburn tresses piled on her head were wrapped in a flowered scarf, and her hands were thoroughly covered in flour, as she pressed the rim of her creation into a perfectly crimped edge. So, he almost burst into laughter as she tried to scratch her nose with her shoulder, and then stopped to blow sideways at a piece of hair, which had escaped its bandana prison.

He was amazed at the domestic marvel she'd become,

and his parent's view of her had been completely altered since their surprise appearance here on the hidden resistance base. His eyes became misty as he remembered how close he'd come to losing the most important person in his life, this beautiful, spirited, strong woman who held his heart in her flour covered hands.

Josh had been out helping in the fields this season, and it felt good to have his hands in rich, dark soil again. The earth here was black as coal. Filled with all the nutrients needed to grow excellent crops. And, he was astonished at the insight and inventiveness with which the founders of their little colony had set all these things in motion. Happier in this place than he could remember being in his life, he would have been more than content to dig his heels in and settle down for good. But, he knew too that there were others out there in the world he was supposed to find and rescue. Those that God was impressing so heavily on his heart.

The weather would clear up pretty soon. He intended to lead a group out into the lowlands to find others who might have been hiding out from the authorities avoiding implantation. He hoped Scott, Mark and Mike would go with him, but he would understand if Mark wanted to remain with his kids. Of course Doc should stay here on the base. He was valuable to the larger group for his medical knowledge.

"Hey, are you in there, husband?"

"What? Sure, I was just thinking?"

"About what? As if I needed to ask?"

"You know me too well, babe."

"Well, before you go trekking off on another adventure in your mind, come have some of this roast chicken I've been working on all morning, and after that the apple pie should be about done." Josh sat at the table with his friends and family and felt richly blessed. Jana loaded his plate with succulent roast chicken, boiled baby potatoes swimming in herbs and butter and fresh green beans; then they topped their meal off with pieces of warm apple pie, smothered in fresh whipped cream.

"Well, if you keep feeding me like that I'll be too big to get through the passageway to the outside."

"That's what I'm aiming for. That way I can keep you all to myself!"

"You don't mean that."

"Well, I still think you should let me come with you."

"Jana, you are still healing. You will be for awhile. And,

Doc said you shouldn't be crawling around out on the mountain until he gives you the go ahead."

"I know, I know, but you know how antsy I get just sitting around."

"Yes I do my antsy pantsy, little wife. I am very aware of how much you hate to sit around, but I'm sure Mom can find lots of things to keep you busy while I'm gone, can't you Mom?"

"I sure can Jana. Too bad for you that you have shown yourself to be so capable and such a quick study. I can use you for all sorts of things while the guys are gone this spring."

"Okay, okay, I'll sit this one out, but not forever. Do you hear me?"

"Yes dear, I hear you, and I know how hard you are to hold off. As soon as the Doc gives us the thumbs up, we will take you along. I promise."

"I'm going to hold you to that. And I have plenty of witnesses."

"Yes, Babe, plenty of witnesses. Sharpen your bow skills and before you know it we will be back out on the mountain together."

"I can't wait! Not that I don't love working with you,

Mom, but you know that my first love is taking care of the rough stuff with the boys."

"Yes we do, Jana. What a difference from the young woman our Josh brought to the farm that fall day. We wouldn't have been able to recognize you if we hadn't witnessed some of the change ourselves. We feel truly blessed to have you in our lives, and we couldn't have asked for a better wife for our son."

"Thank you Emma. I mean, Mom. That means more to me than you could ever know."

"Anyway, the boys won't be heading out for a couple of months. The snow has to melt enough at the lower elevations for them to get back up the mountain with the families they'll be bringing back, so we still have a little time with them, enjoy."

"You're right Mom, and I will. You're going to get so sick of me, you'll be glad to get away for awhile, husband."

"Never, Jana. I could never get tired of you."

• • • • •

Their lives had settled into a pleasant pattern here in the cave. New friends and old ones all together as one. Community sharing meals, ideas, and lives. Jana's favorite day of the week was Sunday, which she found rather ironic, considering her feelings during the first years of her marriage with Josh. Twenty-five hundred people, give or take a few, all singing and worshipping together. It was magical and touched her soul as nothing ever had before. They didn't worship inside a church building, as they didn't have to worry about inclement weather in the cavern. Their celebrations were held in the open square and drew almost every citizen of the city each week. Every elder took a week, in rotation, sharing a message of love, Grace, and Jesus, while their congregation sat on blankets in the grass; and each week Jana felt as if she left the meeting with an even better understanding of her Savior. Nothing had ever felt so much like home.

One week she was asked to give the message. Surprised, and a little frightened, she prayed and prepared all week for her opportunity. She shared a bit of her life with the people, some of which was a shock even to Josh and her in-laws. She spoke of her parents, her grandmother, foster families, and her feelings of inadequacy and fear growing up. Then she confided that she'd never felt loved by God, not until her time alone in a cave when Jesus came to her in a dream and she chose to trust Him with her life. There wasn't a dry eye, as far as she could see, and she apologized for her candor, all to the protests of those listening.

She spoke of the battle on the plateau, and the way the Creator of the Universe had guided her hand; and her experience with a loving God in heaven, after her fatal injury, during that same battle. The people sat in awe as her story unfolded, and she knew she'd found her true calling. God spoke to her that day, in the looks on the faces of those to whom she ministered. She couldn't wait to share again, and felt she truly became a member of the family that day. Not just an onlooker, but a true member.

For the next couple months Josh and Jana lived an almost fairy tale life. Days of hard, honest labor and nights of sweet passion. Their relationships grew with people in the community and developed into friendships that would last a lifetime. Jana wished it could continue forever, but she knew God was calling them to a higher purpose. She continued to share her story on the Sundays which were assigned to her, and became more comfortable with each experience. Josh was a natural preacher, and his sharing Sundays were moments of learning, about God's unending Grace, for the congregation. His vast knowledge of the Bible, and his use of Scripture was inspiring. Jana could only hope that she would someday be as well prepared, so she studied every day. Josh was infinitely proud of his beautiful wife; the ways in which she'd grown during these past months astounded him.

• • • • •

Jana was mastering bread, with Emma's expert help, the day Josh came and told her he would be taking a group of men out on the mountain the following morning. The decision had been confirmed in the meeting he just left.

Weather on the behemoth finally cleared up enough that they thought they could make it down and up again in relative safety, even leading new comers. They planned to seek out a group of fellow Christians they'd been in contact with through a prior scouting trip. Those contacts knew of a group who'd been in hiding throughout the long winter months, in and out of attic, and basement, refuges; or squirreled away in the woods; and they were at the end of their wits and their supplies. Things were also complicated in the fact that they had young children with them, which would make the assent up the mountain a bit more tricky than usual.

Jana understood the need to rescue this frightened

group of fellow human beings. It must have been horrible for them surviving through the cold winter, especially with kids in tow. She didn't have a problem with what Josh was doing. Only that she couldn't go with him.

"How long will you be gone?"

"You know there's no way I can predict that, babe."

"I know, I know. I'm just going to be worried about you, that's all."

"Hey, you know God always takes care of me. There is no plot of Satan that He can't thwart, and as long as there is a purpose for me here, there is nothing He won't do to shield me."

"I am aware husband that you are definitely one of His favored ones. I just wish I was going with you, that's all."

"Maybe next time, Jana. You've been improving much faster than Doc ever thought you would. We'll see how he feels the next time we're going out. I'm going to go get my things together, so we can spend some quality time tonight, before I have to leave in the morning."

"Okay, Josh, I'm going to hang out here and help Mom finish up with supper." Her bread felt the full weight of her frustration as she began to knead the dough with fury; and the occasional tear rolling down her cheek, seasoned the loaf with just a little extra touch of salt.

• • • • •

Their evening was filled with good food, good friends, family and laughter. In bed that night they held each other tight, and tears once again ran relentlessly from Jana's eyes. She cried silently, so as not to upset her husband. She knew he was doing what he had to, what God would have him do, but she'd gotten used to seeing him each day and knew she'd miss him terribly. Sure, there was lots to keep her busy here, but it wouldn't be the same as being out on the mountain with her man, and she was terribly upset about that.

Morning came and Jana tried to look cheerful as she helped Josh assemble his gear. She'd made him several, thick cut, roast beef sandwiches, to start off the trip; using her fresh, homemade bread, and creamy, hand churned butter; adding them in with his regular supplies. The group would, after all, need to have enough return provisions to feed the people they were headed out to retrieve, and she knew how quickly things could change on the mountain. As near as she could figure, it would take them at least eight weeks to get down, make contact, and get back to base.

More, if things went awry. This promised to be a very long two months.

• • • • •

Jana barely held it together for her dutiful goodbyes, but again, she didn't want to upset Josh, so she put on a brave face and assured him she'd be fine. He was doing the right thing and she certainly didn't want to stand in his way. Josh held her tight and promised he'd be okay. That he'd return as quickly as he could. And, that he would think of her and pray for her every day. She, of course, promised he'd be in her prayers each day as well. Then, with chin held high, she walked him through the long corridor to the mountain's exterior opening, pulling her jacket tighter as she approached colder air. When they arrived at the well hidden opening, Josh turned to her, and brushed a strand of auburn hair from her face, tucking it behind her ear, before giving her a long, drawn out kiss. She waved goodbye, choking back tears, with a smile on her face, until he was out of sight.

• • • • •

Spring's subtle light had managed, somehow, to melt a

small amount, of the multiple feet, of accumulated winter snow. With each passing day, during the past couple of weeks, the lower mountain passes had become more maneuverable. The recent mild defrost should make the going a bit easier, but Josh knew they would still have quite a task ahead of them, especially at these heights, and they would have to be ever watchful of possible avalanche situations. However, if they waited longer, the folks they were meant to rescue might not have the resources to survive until their salvation came. They simply couldn't put off the inevitable any longer.

Jana stood in the sun, just outside the cavern's hidden entrance and basked in the warm glow of it; as she gratefully took in great gulps of bitterly cold, fresh air for a few long moments; in an effort to compose herself. She loved her new community, but she missed her mountain, and her heart already ached with the thought of two months without her Josh. She promised herself determinedly that she would be back out on the heights, with her husband, as soon as she could safely manage.

When she reentered the underground city she was in control and made her way back to her communal kitchen again. At least there she wouldn't feel so alone. She enjoyed her new relationship with her mother-in-law. Emma was an amazing teacher, mother, wife and friend. It was the best and most fulfilling connection she'd ever had with another woman in her life.

"Why didn't you tell him?"

"Tell him what, Mom?"

"About the baby."

"How did you know?"

"Never mind that, Jana. Do you know how far along you are?"

"Not very. Maybe four to six weeks. I haven't even confirmed it with Doc yet. I just didn't want to worry him, or make him feel as though he had to stay behind."

"You're a good wife, Jana. You are also a good daughter, and I'm going to be a grandma!"

"Please don't tell anyone yet, Mom. I don't want it to get around until I've had a chance to tell Josh. I think he'll be pretty excited."

"I know he'll be excited. Can't I at least tell Dad? I've never kept secrets from him, and he already knows that I have suspicions."

"Oh, go ahead. You look like you're about ready to bust if you don't tell somebody. But let's just keep it between the three of us, okay?"

"Good enough. No one will know from me until you have made the announcement yourself. Oh, I can't wait to see the look on Josh's face when he finds out he's going to be a daddy! He's been waiting practically his whole life for this."

"I know. We used to talk about it all the time, or I should say argue about it all the time, before he was captured by the militia. He was always up for the idea, and I was always against it. I didn't want any children of mine to suffer the stuff I'd gone through as a kid. And, I didn't know if I could love anyone that much, you know, the way Josh loves, the way you love, but things are different now. Now that I know about God's love for me I feel as though I can be the kind of mom my kids deserve, and I know Josh will be the best daddy in the world. I've always known that about him. When I thought he was dead for so long, I thought we'd never get the chance to be parents; like I'd robbed him of that; you know? And I couldn't seem to get over the pain and guilt of it. Now I feel as though God has given us a second chance in this and in so many other things."

"God is good, Jana."

"Yes, Mom, God is very good."

Evil shall slay the wicked, And those who hate the righteous shall be condemned.

Psalm 34:21

CHAPTER 5

Cage knew the Islamic fundamentalist mercenaries in his command didn't have any love for him, and, for that matter, didn't feel any loyalty to him or his cause. They were using him as much as he was using them. As long as he continued to give them jobs to do, jobs that satisfied their desire to kill infidels, they would be at his disposal. And, as long as they continued in their role as his hired assassins, he would be at theirs.

He despised ARM and all it stood for, but not because they were of a mostly Christian base, not any more than he liked his mercenaries because they were Muslim; all religions were meaningless to him. He didn't believe in a god of the universe by any name. He simply hated ARM because he believed them to be a danger to his beloved president and all he stood for; and because that loathsome Josh Conyers was one of their captains. Cage's commander in chief was as close to a god, in his mind, as he would ever get. But, now, with the new global rulings in place, power as he knew it had shifted, and he was growing more fearful for his future. For the future of the president he loved, and for the outlook of his own authority here on this mountain, or anywhere else for that matter.

As far as his working relationship with the mercenaries in his camp; he wasn't a threat to them, because he didn't follow any form of religion. Though they had no respect for anyone who did not bow to Allah, they also considered him a harmless, necessary evil. Conversely, they weren't a threat to him, because he didn't care what god they prayed to. Their demands for Halal foods to be made available in the mess hall, and for their insanely annoying call to prayer to be blasted over the camp's loud speakers five times a day, were just small irritations he dealt with, to have these expert killers in close proximity. He knew the rest of the camp were fearful of his middle eastern comrades, but he also believed that their presence helped him to control the troops who grew more dissatisfied with his leadership by the day. With that in mind, he sent them out on the mountain only when he felt he truly needed to. Compared to his own battered, and beaten down, troops; who he used, and abused, until they were fairly used up; they were treated like kings, and the militia soldiers resented them greatly.

Just this morning his most recent scouting patrol had returned from the mountain at large, with news again, that they still didn't have a clue where the resistance soldiers were hiding, and he was currently having them heavily disciplined for their failure. He was beyond angry. "*How can it be?*" He wondered. "*How do they disappear the way they do. It's as if they magically merge with the mountain every time I get close.*" Could they have vacated the area? He didn't think so, as extensive searches on the next range, and in the lowlands, hadn't uncovered any tracks either. He couldn't begin to understand why he was failing at every attempt to locate them. Absolutely sure they weren't smarter than he, and undoubtedly not as well trained as he and his troops, he was at a loss. The only reason they'd bested him before, he was certain, was that Josh's ever irritating woman had surprised them on the plateau. No one could have predicted that. Then later, they'd had a logistical advantage over him, on the mountain pass. He was sure that in a similar circumstance where the odds were more equal, he would be the superior soldier, and that he would vanquish them once and for all. That was the only thing that kept him going.

Recently, he'd managed to rid himself of two more eye witnesses to his epic failure on the mountain pass, through another 'unfortunate accident'; and he was sure those soldiers who remained were becoming more wary. He didn't think there would be much trouble from that camp going forward, but he kept his eyes and ears open. Anything which threatened his authority as base commander got his attention without delay.

• • • • •

News from the capital was getting worse. The UNGC had stripped world leaders of power; to a point that they were nothing more than mere figureheads in their own countries, and even that would soon end. Cage's orders had not changed, but he was no longer answering to the president, or his administration. The UN Global Council had actually gone so far as to set up their own member leadership representatives in each country, and they; along with a mediating council, who answered directly back to the

UNGC; were essentially in control of every facet of society, from food, to medical aid, to allowed religious practices; which were all centered around the 'World Church'; etc., around the planet.

For all those so quick to hand over their unanimity to the UN, and jump in to the idea of a one world government, they were finding out pretty quickly that what they'd considered fair in their previous life, was no longer an option.

Those world visions of socialism, held by the council, and so many left leaning groups, demanded that all peoples everywhere should have the same common degree of lifestyle opportunities, which certainly sounded great before the losses were tallied. Until the government began to take from those in wealthier countries, to give to those in poorer countries, to even the score in some unseen universal design of their own making.

This new order was agony for those who'd given their all, their sweat and tears, to build something, just to have it stripped away and awarded to someone else for their singular great feat of simply being alive. Taking from those who worked, to give to those who didn't. And, to wipe out all vestiges of a once rich and diverse nation, doing away, once and for all, with the so called American dream. It was a sad day indeed.

Government owned food distribution centers opened in every major city worldwide, and grocery stores, as this country had known them, closed. As did restaurants, and many other businesses, catering to any perceived notion of luxury, or the individual. Persons were removed from their previous work positions, and careers; evaluated, for their most valuable talents, and assets, in view of the council's most urgent needs; and given food vouchers for their families. Farmers and food manufacturers now turned over every ounce of what they'd produced, by the sweat of their brow, to the local authorities, to be portioned out to those in the community.

Those UNGC member leaders, who were assigned to each community to control new government allocated jobs, food distribution, and law enforcement, held a form of power that made them practically invincible, compared to the average citizen. If a leader didn't like you; or a citizen was being punished for some supposed breech of law; that leader could choose to withhold a food voucher, or worse. The country had quickly gone from a democratic republic, to a socialist dictatorship, and finally to an extreme communist state, simply by removing the people's choice, will, and religious rights.

Cage received a letter telling him that his family's ancestral home had been confiscated as a UN asset. Next would be his bank accounts. He didn't really care. Though he could certainly see how that would upset others who cared more about worldly things. His home was in these mountains; and if truth be told, he was relieved he'd never again have to go back to that dreadful place. As long as his mission stayed intact he was fine. He suspected that if the UN forces were as skilled as his militia soldiers were, at working these mountains, he would have been without a job long ago. He wasn't even hassled about the religious practices of his henchmen, with all that one world church crap, at least not yet, as long as they yielded results for the council.

His private prison cells, located on the back of the plateau, though empty for a considerable time after the infamous battle, once again contained prisoners. It seemed there were still those who refused implantation, and who sought protection from the same resistance soldiers who continued to elude him. As long as the council still considered him an asset, a way to contain the rebellion, he would be free to hunt the heights to his heart's desire.

Cage's last communication with his superiors, through the UNGC, had left instructions for him to continue to squelch the resistance, with extreme prejudice. He would do that with pleasure. He was also informed that the council had finally chosen a new UNGC leader, from Iran of all places. The man was reported to have a magnetic personality; charisma and charm, which oozed from every poor in his body; important connections; and had swayed those in power quite convincingly. The council was encouraged that this man could bring unity, in places where up to this point, had been only rage, strife, and discord. They also hoped, that since he was greatly esteemed, in the Muslim world, he might quell the uprisings, and attacks, coming from that quarter. Cage was sure that appointment wasn't going over well with most of the world's supplanted leaders, now that the last meager vestiges of their power were gone, but that was none of his concern. He would go about his duties, and ignore the world with its new global order.

His recent prisoners suffered most egregiously at his hands. He meant to gain as much information from this resistance scum as he was able. His orders no longer included instructions to keep the enemy soldiers, or their families, alive. So, he used every torture technique in his vast arsenal, to drain their resolve.

He thought nothing of inflicting pain on the wives and children of the men he'd captured, in order to get them to talk freely. Finding this to be a most effective tool, he resorted to this type of persecution whenever it suited him. Each day new prisoners were added, but there seemed to always be adequate room in the cells, as each day there were also multiple body bags carried from the detention center. Some of those body bags were very small indeed. And Satan smiled.

• • • • •

Most of the eye witnesses to his debacle on the mountain pass had been dealt with, in one way, or another. Cage was mostly free from the accusations which might have held him back in his chosen profession, and the powers that be were considering him for a promotion. He didn't want the promotion, or anything that might take him away from his mountain base command. And, he certainly didn't want to lose whatever chance he had to get even with Josh and his woman, so he would buck the system for now.

The torture of prisoners under Cage's command continued, though, as of yet, it had netted him no results what-so-ever. Those prisoners simply didn't know the whereabouts of the hidden ARM base, so there was no possibility they could share that information with him. From the outside looking in, one might wonder if just the sheer joy of inflicting pain on the weak and innocent was somehow enough to keep him satisfied.

He'd recently set security guards on the back side of the mountain, so they would never again have to worry about an attack from the rear. Jana had changed his perspective on many things. He was less confident now than he'd ever been in his illustrious, twisted, military career. That woman, and her husband, haunted every waking, and sleeping, moment of his life. He wouldn't rest, couldn't give up, until they were punished for the way they'd humiliated him. And, again, Satan smiled.

• • • • •

An early spring storm blasted the mountain. For now his hunt would be forced to a halt, until the weather could once again cooperate. He paced in his quarters, and ranted at no one. "This has got to stop! Now! I have to get out on that mountain, and I have to put them in their place.

I can't, I won't let them win. I will be the laughing stock of the entire base if I let a woman best me. It isn't going to happen! I have to eliminate Josh Conyers, and that woman of his, come hell, or high water, and I will not stop until they are both crushed and buried deep beneath my feet! Do you hear me?"

Anyone watching would necessarily conclude that he was insane, and they would most certainly be correct. His mental state deteriorated daily; and there was no one between him, and those he led, to buffer the destruction caused by his angry tirades. Those in his command suffered almost as much as those locked away in the cells at the rear of the plateau.

The salvation of the righteous is from the Lord; He
is their stronghold in the time of trouble.

Psalm 37:39

CHAPTER 6

After more than a week maneuvering through ice, then melting snow and mud in the descending mountain heights, Josh and his fellows found themselves caught up in the same massive Spring blizzard which halted Cage's frantic hunt for them. But, they managed to make their way to the large cavern that had been home to Mike and Jana, during last winter's long recuperation.

Josh never had the opportunity to set foot in Mike and Jana's cave; prior to the need for shelter from the current storm; but he'd heard enough stories from his wife, to assure him that his suspicions were in fact, truth. He had no doubt, as he looked around the organized space, that his wife's hand was evident here. There was still ample fire wood on the far wall, and fresh water continued, thankfully, to flow through the indoor spring. Even the remnants of their carefully built fire ring still dotted the cave floor, and only needed some slight repairs before a new blaze was dancing within its borders. He had only to pick up a few odds and ends; set awry by those soldiers who'd broken in to haul Mike away, or disturbed by curious animals; to make the place presentable again.

With a bit of luck, and a practiced hand, Scott bagged two unsuspecting rabbits, as they scampered for cover from the raging snowstorm. Now they were cooking slowly, over a hastily built fire; filling the space with the aromatic, mouthwatering smells of roasted meat and tubers salvaged from stores in the back of the cave.

Mike remained behind on this trip, with an impatient Jana, as he too was still healing. But, he vowed he would be with his comrades on their next rescue mission. Mark, though he hated the thought of leaving his kids behind, especially so soon after their recent reunion, had come along to help. He was currently, silently, regretting his decision to do so, as he sat in a cold, dark cave. Surrounded by other equally annoyed resistance soldiers, waiting for the Spring tempest to end, or the leaping flames to take the evening's chill out of the air.

"Josh, how long do you think this weather is going to last?" Mark paced back and forth in the space before the cave's exit.

"Don't know, Mark. Wish I did, because whatever time we spend sitting in this hole, is going to add to the back end of our trip. I don't want to worry the folks at home anymore than you do, and with no way to contact them, they will be concerned when we don't show up as expected. You might have forgotten that I left Jana, and my folks, back there too?"

"I know, I know, so, what are we going to do? Are you thinking we should turn back?"

"No, Mark. We've come too far for that to be an option at this point. We're going to go on, and rescue those families, just like we promised. This weather might be negatively affecting us, but I know it's hitting them even harder. Remember they have young children with them, and no supplies. How would you feel if your kids were out there in that same position, and the help that was promised didn't come?"

"You're right. Sorry I brought it up. It's just that we've

spent our share of time in caves over the past year, and I'm feeling antsy to get going, so I can get back to my kids."

"I know, my friend, and we'll get out of here as soon as it's safe to do so. I've got more than myself to think about on this mission. You and Scott aren't my only concerns. There are three other soldiers in my care as well, so I want to do whatever I have to do to keep everyone safe."

"Do we know where the families are, Josh? The ones we're out to rescue, I mean?" Scott sat with his fingers laced behind his head, lounging against a boulder, not far from the warming blaze. Close enough to turn the rabbits when the time came.

"We've only got a vague idea, Scott. I've got their last known location, but that will only be good if the weather, or local military forces, haven't given them reason to move. We'll pray that they've been able to stay as close to those first coordinates as possible. We're just going to trust the Lord. He hasn't let us down yet, has He?"

"Nope, I gotta say He's been pretty darned good to me! Just tell me what you want me to do, and I'll be on it."

"All we can do is wait at this point, Scott. You already got supper together for us, so our dried goods will last a little longer. You're getting pretty darned good with that thing."

"Thanks, whoever knew, when I was messin' with knives as a kid, that I'd get this good at throwing 'em, huh? You know I like to feel like I'm contributing."

"You are definitely doing that, Buddy, so just keep relaxing. The snow is coming down pretty hard right now, and we've got the cave entrance blocked against intruders, so we'll just hunker down, stay as warm as we can, and watch for our best chance to get out of here."

• • • • •

Not far away, Cage and his assassins waited for their opportunity to get back out on the mountain to hunt their elusive prey. Little did they realize that Josh and his men were practically under their noses.

• • • • •

Just outside the city; hidden safely from prying eyes, in the base of the trees in the same forest that had been Jana's shelter during her bold escape only seven months before; were the cold and starving families who awaited Josh's team of rescuers. It was warmer in the forest, than way up on the mountain; but with spring just begun, and patches of snow still evident in shaded parts of the woods, they were by no means cozy, or comfortable. Their food, all but a few dried items, and some canned goods, had run out a week ago, and though they rationed the packaged items in their possession, that would soon be gone as well.

It was too early, in the season, to find berries, or nuts, and hunting would do them no good, as they were unable to start a fire for cooking. The blaze, and the smoke which would accompany a fire, would give them away for sure. They were immensely grateful for the plentiful streams they found in the wood, and for their water purification filters. Those things, at least, were keeping them hydrated, and were also keeping them from the debilitating effects of tainted water. But, the children were becoming more hungry, and weaker, as each day of slim rations was imposed. All the group could do, was try to encourage one another, and pray.

The kids had been very good, so far. Far better than she'd expected. Especially for children so young. But, they had their limits, and they missed their warm beds, and their toys. Becca knew, absolutely, she would never see her sister again, but she'd determined that she couldn't allow her small niece and nephew to be implanted by the GHO that fateful day, months ago. And she did the only thing she could think of, to save them from that fate. She knew her sister didn't have the children's best interests at heart, she never had. She was more concerned with using the kids to get 'her share' of the free stuff the government was offering to citizens who dutifully presented themselves for implantation, and then signed a letter of allegiance to the administration.

Becca couldn't do that. Not the implants, and not the pledge of allegiance to the government. The whole thing sounded fishy, and just plain wrong. And, now, with the new world government situation looming over their heads; well, even though she'd never been a religious person before, she couldn't imagine being okay with someone telling her where she had to go to church. She knew she didn't want the ruling regime to be able to track her. And, she couldn't bear to let the little ones undergo that kind of future. Even if their mother didn't care, she did, and she would protect them with her very life, if need be.

Therefore, after she'd heard about a group of resisters, who were headed out to a secret ARM base on the mountain, she knew she had to follow them to safety, and, hopefully, a better life. She'd made contact, and on the morning in which she was expected to appear at the GHO implanting center with her sister and the children, she bolted. It was easy enough to escape her clueless sister.

Virginia, as usual, was sleeping off her indulgences of the night before, so she packed up a few things for herself and the kids, and high tailed it to the agreed upon meeting place in the park by the river.

Throughout the fall, and most of the winter, families who were sympathetic to ARM shielded the runaways in basements, and attic hideaways, but that wasn't getting them any closer to the fabled base they longed to find. Now that winter's worst was over, and spring had begun to breathe new life into the trees, and fields, around the city, she was anxious to be off in search of the resistance movement she knew would help her, and her young charges.

• • • • •

Virginia woke that Fall day, six months ago, and knew what her sister had done. She fully intended to go ahead with her scheduled implantation, and was angry about the privileges she would forfeit for not bringing her children forward. But, she could at least use Becca as her scapegoat, and would be free from punishment for the actions of her rebellious sibling. Maybe it was better this way. With the kids gone, she was free to live any way she chose, and she was having the time of her life. *"Let her be saddled with the responsibility for those brats,"* She thought, *"She'll see who got the better deal, and it'll be too late for her to do anythin' about it. She's stuck now."*

• • • • •

Now that Becca and the kids were holed up in the forest, with other renegade families, they had to lay low for fear of being discovered by the government's People's Militia goon squads. The situation was made worse by dwindling food supplies, and by the fact that they were trying to stay within the same general coordinates, per their initial contact, to help their rescuers find them. Spring rains weren't helping. They had acquired some plastic, camouflaged cover, but it seemed they were perpetually wet, and miserable.

From where they sat, there appeared to be banks of storm clouds covering the mountain's higher regions, enveloping the very area they hoped to ascend. The storm, which was causing blizzard conditions on the mount, swept across the grasslands in the form of a cold, stinging precipitation, part ice, and part rain. At the edge of the forest, where Becca and the kids took refuge, driving wind and rain caused the grasses to sway violently, making them appear as the green, foam covered, ocean waves on a rough sea. Becca swore to herself, as she wrapped herself around her young ones to impart whatever she could of her own body heat, that if they survived this she would treat herself to a hot bath, and some much needed rest, if they survived....

•••••

Jana, and the rest of the occupants of the ARM encampment at the top of the mountain, were oblivious to the stormy conditions further down the behemoth. After all, it was perpetually cold and snow covered up here in the highest heights, and warm as toast inside the resistance stronghold. As each day passed, Jana got stronger, and learned more from her mother-in-law, about the arts of housewifery. She was becoming more and more secure in her ability to make a house, a home. She also had a few surprises in store for her husband when he returned. She couldn't wait for him to come back to her. She missed him horribly, and so desperately wanted to share the news of their baby with him.

To her credit 'Mom' was doing her best to keep Jana occupied, and to help her overcome her anxiety about Josh's absence. They cooked together, and baked together. They sat, for hours at a time, sharing stories of life; and then they played board games for hours more. Emma learned a great deal about what made her daughter-in-law tick, and came to understand how difficult her troubled youth had been. Her heart ached for this young woman she'd come to love so dearly. And, as each day passed, she became more aware of how blessed they all were to count her as part of their little family. Emma could say with confidence she was truly glad Jana, this strong, Christian woman, would be the mother of her grandchild.

Jana was ever so grateful for the company of her mother in law, but it wasn't the same as having her big strong man by her side. The time until he would return, could not pass quickly enough to suit her.

• • • • •

The storm outside raged on for days, upon days, creating a winter wonderland of drifts so vast, it was difficult to see where the cliff's edges ended, and the chasms began. The danger of avalanches grew, and when the snow finally began to slow, Cage was hard pressed to find volunteers willing to go out on the mountain's passes. He didn't care though. He wasn't asking for volunteers. If they balked at his orders, he would simply shoot them for treason. No spring's tempest could rage more wild than his foul, twisted soul. And Satan smiled.

• • • • •

Time passed, and Becca knew the planned pickup date had come, and gone. She wouldn't let CJ and Angel know. There was no reason to worry them, when she had no earthly idea what was going on. She assumed the resistance soldiers had been held up by the weather, but couldn't begin to guess for how long. Her guides wanted to find better cover, and more shelter from the blowing gale; than was currently available; but she knew instinctively that if they moved, it would be harder for their rescuers to find them.

She and the children decided to stay behind, when the larger group moved on. Her guides urged her to follow, as they felt responsible for the young woman, and her two charges, but when she stubbornly refused, they did all they could do, and then left her a bit of the remaining dried food for the kids. She dug deeper into the base of the giant redwood tree, on the side opposite the blasting wind, and covered her small family with plastic, and pine tree boughs. Now, all she could do is comfort the children with stories, and hope she'd made the right decisions, until the help she prayed for might arrive.

In peace I will both lie down and sleep; for you alone, O Lord, make me dwell in safety.

Psalm 4:8

CHAPTER 7

Growing up, Becca had always feared her sister's odd temperament. Four years younger, and blessed with a gentle, loving spirit, soulful brown eyes, a spray of light freckles across the bridge of her nose, and hair the color of late spring radishes; she'd lived, in relative obscurity, deep beneath Gin's shadow, for as long as she could remember.

Forever at her older sibling's sparse, and sporadic, mercy; and first to endure her unpredictable, wild rages; she dreaded every waking moment of her harried existence. Along with the strange requests, and humiliating comments, which emanated from her sister's mouth.

At last, then, after so many years of abuse, she'd earned

the right; through her hard work, and diligence; to leave her parent's house, and attend college. And the idea of being away from Virginia, was liberating indeed. She was absolutely giddy with the thought of it, and the smile that lit her face was contagious to anyone who ventured into her path.

As part of her full ride scholarship, she was awarded living expenses, so she located and rented her own small apartment, and believed herself finally rid of her old nemesis. Little did she know she would eventually, though unwillingly, become her sibling's refuge in the impending storm.

Virginia, bossy, in charge; and without conscience, or, for that matter, even a working moral compass; was more apt to get herself into trouble, than her younger sister. She was a continual thorn in her parent's sides, as they spent her teen years, and into her twenties, trying to cover for her lack of judgment, and poor choices. Firstly, to protect their own reputations, and secondly, to protect her already questionable one. She was the pretty one, or, at the very least, the flashy one, and ended up in one precarious predicament after another, due to her less than honorable character and boundless selfishness.

Mom and Dad were angry, even hurt, that Becca was

so quick to take the opportunity to leave their home, the very moment she was able; but they also knew it was solely due to her sister, and couldn't blame her for wanting to be away from the craziness that surrounded their oldest child. Perhaps, if they'd been more strict with the girl, she might have grown to be a more kind, and respectable woman. And, maybe she wouldn't have decided that taking her clothes off in that sleazy dive downtown was the best way to earn a living.

But, it couldn't be just their own mistakes that led Gin in the downward spiral that seemed to consume her. They had the evidence of a very highly regarded, and productive daughter Becca to prove that point. If Virginia could only be as decent, and hard working, as her sister. But, it was much too late for that now, and they were paying the price for what seemed to be their lack of proper teaching, and attention to discipline in her developing years.

When the two girls were younger, her sister's whims controlled every aspect of their lives, so it was no wonder she was happy to shed that madness. All of Becca's life; as far back as she could remember; if Virginia wanted a certain food for a meal, a particular television show, a cookie, or an item at the department store, you'd better bet she was going to get it, or all hell broke loose. Once going so far as to tip over a large, costly, display case, and begin throwing expensive jewelry boxes, until the whole family was ushered unceremoniously out of the store. No one wanted to deal with her temper tantrums, so everyone in the house catered to her every demand, in order to keep peace, or so they thought.

When Gin wanted to go out with friends for the evening, she'd lie, and tell her parents she was headed to the library to study; because she knew they simply didn't trust her to be out roaming the streets. And, she would have to agree, rightly so. However, due to many past experiences where their eldest daughter was concerned, her folks didn't believe a word she told them anymore. They did want her to have access to the materials she needed for better grades, though; so, to ensure she was truly headed to the library, Becca was forced to accompany her sister on her 'study' trips.

Mom and dad assumed Becca's very presence would keep Gin out of trouble, since she was their good, sensible girl. Instead, Becca was forced to witness many, many things that a young teen shouldn't. Virginia dragged her to parties, and various other completely inappropriate venues. Becca never ratted on her sister, however, for fear of the threats which were leveled at her by the older girl. But, she'd sworn to herself that she would be free from the shackles of her sister's perverted desires, once and for all, as soon as she was able.

• • • • •

Looking back, Becca's memories included the time Gin took her to a party in a particularly bad part of town. She was only twelve years old at the time. There she was, sitting in a dark corner of the room, with a warm beer in her hand; so as not to look too un-cool to whoever might be watching; as she witnessed young people sticking dirty needles in their arms. Pot smoke hung so heavy in the air, she could barely breathe, and so strong it gave her a splitting headache. Couples, in the murky shadows of every room, writhing in the throes of passion, kept her eyes focused forward, for fear of seeing something too embarrassing to forget.

Occasionally, she'd pour a bit of the beer she held into a withered, potted plant which sat beside her, so it would appear she was grooving right along with the others. When in fact, every cell in her body screamed at her to get up, get out, and run for the hills.

The apartment, where they partied that particular night, belonged to the old deaf grandmother of one of the boys, who; by the way; was passed out on a beat up, old, green sofa in the corner. Becca tried to get her bearings, in case something went wrong; since something almost always went wrong when she was with Gin; and she saw that the space was a very dark and gloomy conglomeration of badly laid out rooms. Decorated with odds and ends of stained, torn furniture, and piles of trash, walls that were in desperate need of a coat of paint, and carpet so dirty she was loath to walk on its grimy surface, even with her shoes on. One uncovered light bulb hung in the middle of the cobwebbed ceiling, in the area where she sat, and was the only source of illumination for the combined, front rooms.

At one point, as it was getting a little later in the evening. She was humming lightly to herself, and rocking ever so slightly, to quell the growing discomfort in her gut. A long haired, bell bottomed, young man, with a thin wisp of red beard, fell to the floor in front of her, twitching, and foaming at the mouth. As he clutched his chest, and labored for breath, his eyes darted back and forth, finally locking with hers. Panicking, Becca tried to help him, but he convulsed over and over again, and then, finally stopped breathing. He died in her arms. Just as she was about to pass out, she took a great breath, and steadied herself.

She hadn't been aware she'd been holding her breath, until that moment. She sat for a time, who knows how long, staring at him; while his eyes clouded over, and changed from vivid green, to a milky white; watching the small yellowish bubbles around his mouth pop, and a strange, viscous liquid make its way slowly down his cheek. He'd wet himself, in death, and she gently laid him down, on the filthy carpet, to look around the room for something with which to cover him, not wanting him to be shamed in front of all these people. Yes, young Becca, ever the kind one.

She finally settled on an old newspaper, from a pile of garbage in the corner. As she covered him, she suddenly realized her face was wet with tears. Tears which were making it difficult for her to see. And, her nose was running. Wiping her eyes, and nose, quickly, with the sleeve of her sweatshirt, she noticed vaguely that she'd left a large wet spot, and a streak of clear snot, on the soft, grey fabric, so she absently rubbed it against her side.

Later that night; on the local news; and still very much in a state of horror, she would discover that the green eyed, young man's death was caused by an overdose of drugs.

And, though that wouldn't be the only death she would be witness to, in her life, it was the first; and was as deeply engrained into her psyche, as her own low self image.

From her shock induced fog she heard someone begin screaming, then someone else called an ambulance, and soon police sirens were screaming down the street toward them.

She snapped out of her daze, and yelled for Gin, knowing they couldn't be caught in this place, but she got no answer. Running through the hallway, crashing into walls, and throwing open doors; she found her sister naked, in bed with two boys, and very much unconscious. Due to the large amounts of alcohol, and drugs, she'd ingested. She dragged her sister to the nearest window, threw it open, and saw that on this side of the building they were about two and a half stories above the ground. She tossed out her sister's clothes, and shoved Gin unceremoniously over the ledge.

In her drunken stupor, Gin's fall was uneventful, and she ended up spread eagled, and moaning, on a pile of garbage beneath the window. Becca then took a deep breath, closed her eyes, and jumped out the opening. Upon landing, she sprained both her ankles. Dragging her sister, limping all the way down to the river's edge, she stashed Gin and her clothes under a bush, and waited for her to regain consciousness enough to get dressed and walk by herself.

Her own pain was quenched for now, due to the contact high she was experiencing from the pot filled room she'd just vacated. Not to worry though, the excruciating pain would return with a vengeance later that evening. Their return home that night took a great deal of time, and a lot of explaining; but the truth wasn't any part of it. Becca felt as though she slid farther down that slippery slope of deceit, right along with her sister, with each and every falsehood she covered up to her parents.

On another evening, as the girls walked down a dark alley to the 'library', Gin handed her a gift. Becca wasn't used to receiving anything of value from her sister, so she was touched by the gesture. She opened the small package, and lo, and behold, found that it held a stiletto switchblade, identical to the one her sister carried. It was a thing of beauty, with an ivory handle, black etching, and silver workings. She was thrilled, though a little intimidated by the power she wielded, as she held that deadly instrument in her hand. She pressed the button and a blade, sharp as a razor, and glittering in the moonlight, slid swiftly, and silently, from its holster. She had to admit, though not out loud, never out loud, that the mere sight of it caused a stirring in her; an excitement she couldn't quite put her finger on.

On a fall evening, later that same year, as they were returning from another party, where her sister had sown her wild oats yet again, they walked down the same dark alley, with gleaming weapons in their hands. This time, though, they heard the sound of footsteps behind them. They began to walk more rapidly, but the footsteps came quicker. When they broke into a run, they could hear their pursuer speed up as well. Finally, when Becca thought she would burst from fear, she turned, and the man who had been chasing them ran right into her outstretched arm, and the deadly blade she held. She knew she'd never forget the feeling of her knife penetrating human flesh. She screamed, and together, they ran. They watched the papers for days, waiting to hear of a man dead, in an alley, with a switchblade protruding from his gut, but they never saw anything of the kind. She often wondered about the man, and even to this very day, wondered if she'd taken his life.

On another occasion Gin arranged a date with a boy from the military academy down the road. When she discovered her parents weren't going to let her go to the 'library' without Becca, she made arrangements for the date to become a double one. Becca was terrified. Her sister was a buxom beauty. She on the other hand, had not, at twelve years old, been blessed with a figure. "Gin, I am not going out with a boy! I will not!"

"What do you mean, you ain't goin'? If you ain't goin', I can't go, so you better change your mind, or you'll be sorry."

"Nothing you say is gonna make me do what you tell me this time, Gin! I wouldn't even know what to do."

"If you don't come, I'll tell Mama, and Daddy, about the party, about the dead boy, and that you covered the whole thing up!"

"Then you'd be tellin' on yourself too, you stupid idiot!"

"Well, they won't be shocked by anythin' I do, baby girl, but they might be a little bothered to hear that their perfect little Becca, ain't so perfect after all. What do you think?"

"You wouldn't! You know I've never done anything wrong when they make me go with you!"

"Yeah, but they don't know that. It's fine with me baby girl. I don't care if you break their hearts. I do it all the time."

"Gin, you know the only reason I ever lied to them was

to cover for you. You threatened to kill me if I didn't".

"Hey baby girl, that option is still on the table if you wanna take it, but I will tell 'em about the party, and that's a fact."

"I hate you, Virginia, do you know that?"

"Yep, baby girl, I do. And I don't care, not one little bit."

Becca gave in, totally, to her sister's threats, and to her ministrations. But, how would they ever make her twelve year old zipper straight frame look like that of a sixteen year old, young woman?

Well, after Gin put one of her own bras on Becca, and filled it with wads, and wads, of toilet paper; she then applied way too much makeup to her twelve year old face, and dressed her up in some of her own slutty clothing. Becca had never felt so disgusted, or so disgusting. Her insides shook so violently, she was sure she'd throw up before the night was over.

Their 'date' consisted of the four of them driving up into the trees, in the nearby foothills. There was beer. The boys began by kissing them, and Gin started moaning. Becca, pulling away, was scared to death, and completely mortified, when the boy she was with touched her hard, toilet paper filled bra, and pulled back as if his hand had been burned with a hot iron.

He looked at her questioningly, and tears began to stream down her face. He knew, and she was so ashamed, and embarrassed, she could have just died right there.

She could tell at that point, and gratefully so, that he was either disgusted by her, or terrified to touch her; so they spent most of the evening listening to the sounds of her sister having sex, for hours, in the front seat. Her face blushed red, more than once, over the noises from the couple thrashing about before them. And, then she thought she just might have to fight, after all, when she looked at her escort and saw him gazing at her, as if he was ready to ignore her obvious lack of legal age and join in on the fun. At that point, she opened the car door and stepped out. Her sister didn't even notice her departure, and alone, she walked through the black night, back into town. She was sure her sister didn't leave her date wanting for anything, and had probably taken care of both of them. It wouldn't be the first time, or the last.

It seemed after that night; when years later she finally began to look more like a woman than a stick straight little boy; if any fellow showed the slightest interest in her,

Gin would swoop in, to steal him away. Not that she'd really wanted him for herself, as she had plenty of fellows grunting after her already. She just wanted to prove to herself, and the world, over and over again, that she still had 'it', whatever 'it' was, and her slutty ways left Becca alone many times.

Becca wasn't the only one who suffered at the hands of her selfish sister. Gin made it a practice, whenever the opportunity arose, to entice men away from their girlfriends and wives, for a quick romp in the hay. She was single handedly responsible for more break-ups in their town, than any other ten factors combined. Becca was sure that somewhere in Gin's life there must be a tally board, with an accurate number of her conquests, but if she were pressed for a guess it would be somewhere around five hundred or so. Never the less, Becca's love life, or lack of one, sucked, and she'd finally just sort of given up on the whole idea of having someone of her own.

• • • • •

Becca had been an excellent student her whole life, and graduated high school at only fifteen years old. She went on to college, and then a successful career as an accountant.

She loved her life, loved living alone, and loved her job. She enjoyed the freedom of having her own money, and now that she was in her twenties, she'd saved enough money to begin traveling. There was something missing though, and she knew, deep in her heart, it was a husband. Someone to love, and be loved by, to laugh with, to share her thoughts, and dreams with, to travel with, someone to have children with, and to grow old with. Just because her sister, and her parents were miserable, didn't mean she had to be miserable too. Meeting the right guy, however, might prove to be a bit tricky since she never left her apartment except to go to work, or the grocery store.

She'd decorated her little place all by herself. It was a hodgepodge of miscellaneous bits and pieces she'd picked up from flea markets, and rummage sales around the area. Anyone who knew her, and her ridiculously fastidious, meticulous, and organized personality, would have been shocked at the obvious contrary results of her decorating attempts. But she loved every piece, and the stories she'd make up in her head about each one. She was comfortable in her little home and she guessed, since she didn't feel she had much choice, content to wait until the man of her dreams wandered randomly into her life.

When Gin wound up pregnant, by that good for nothing ex-con, Scott, and ended up in their parents basement with her new, jobless husband; Becca was elated that she could turn off the ringer on her phone, and lock her front door. Gin's wedding had been a joke, and her husband a bigger one. He'd gotten so drunk he puked half the night away, and they'd had to carry him down to the old couch in the basement. She was ever so glad she wouldn't be there when he woke up. And, felt almost sorry for him. Knowing he'd have to endure the sarcastic remarks, and degrading comments, she was sure would be coming his way when he finally woke. After all, she'd been at the receiving end of her sister's evil wit on enough occasions to know the drill.

• • • • •

Scott turned out to be an alright kinda guy though, even if you counted his stints in prison. He never cheated on Gin, and never raised a hand to her, though, if truth be told, he'd probably had plenty of reasons to. He'd ended up with a descent job, and turned out to be a real hard worker. He'd even fixed up that broken down house, to be a cute little home for his family. And did a very respectable job at it, which, in Becca's mind, was way more than her fickle sister deserved. They'd had a couple of great kids to show for the time they'd been together, and as far as she could tell, he was a great dad to them.

Becca knew Scott didn't like her. Her sister, as usual, had used her as an excuse for her terrible behavior, when she didn't get home as would be expected. Scott sincerely thought that on those occasions, the ones where he was sure his wife was drinking, and sleeping around, that Gin was with her; when in fact, she had no idea what her sister was doing.

Every week she'd receive calls that went something like, "Hey, Becca, if Scott calls, I was with you, okay?" No wonder he didn't like her.

And, no wonder he didn't trust her anymore than he'd trusted her sister. Her usual response, to her sister, went something like: "Oh, Gin, why don't you just quit tramping around, and go home to your husband like you ought to?"

"Hey, baby girl, don't you get all judgmental on me! I got every right to live my life. He spent so much time in the joint that he ain't got no rights at all, at least not on me, far as I'm concerned."

"But he's your husband Gin. And, he's trying his best to be a good one, now that he's out. You know he's a good daddy to those two kids."

"You don't even have a husband of your own, Becca. You don't know nothin' about any of it. And if you think he's so great, then why don't you take him? I was doin just fine before he came back this time!"

"If only it worked that way, Gin. I'd probably take you up on that. Sometimes people don't know what they've got till it's gone. The biggest problem would be that if I did take him, and you could see for yourself that someone else thought he was alright, then you'd want him right back. I'm nothing, next to you, so what chance would I have? I don't have the energy to mess with all that anymore, Gin."

"Then just shut your mouth, and if he calls you, I was with you all night."

"Whatever, Gin. I hope you're proud of yourself. You know, you don't ever spend time with your children anymore."

"Hey, if they need me I'll be there. For now I got more important things to do."

"More important than your kids?"

"Never mind, just never mind, Becca. You just better mind your own business, if you know what's good for you."

"Okay, Gin, but mark my words. Someday this will all

come back to haunt you, and you have no one to blame but yourself."

"I'll worry 'bout that when 'someday' comes, baby girl. For now, I'm havin' a good ol' time. So, quit tryin' to rain on my parade."

Well, someday came, and now Becca sat in the hollow of a giant tree, on the edge of the forest, covered in camouflaged plastic, soaking wet, and freezing cold, with two small, hungry children. While Virginia was warm and cozy after a night of fun. Perhaps fate was fair, and perhaps it wasn't.

Becca was sure Gin didn't even miss the kids, was probably happy they were gone, so she would no longer be saddled with the responsibility of their care. But she also knew her sister was angry she'd cheated her out of the extra benefits she'd have received if she'd brought her kids in for implantation. So, she fully expected that the militia were after her. The fact that she was family, wouldn't have played into her sister's decision to turn her in to the authorities, any more than it had played in to her own kidnapping of her niece, and nephew. Her sister was doing whatever would suit her own needs, just as she was doing what she thought best for the kids, and they would be better off away from all the craziness.

For the wicked boasts of the desires of his soul, and the one greedy for gain curses and renounces the Lord. In the pride of his face the wicked does not seek Him, all his thoughts are, "There is no God."

Psalms 10:3-4

CHAPTER 8

As the weather slowly started to let up, Cage began pacing, ready to be on the hunt. Nothing in his life vexed him as much, or filled him with such excitement, as the thought of Josh Conyers. The idea of besting him, of capturing him, and his woman, of torturing him slowly, and watching him die. It consumed his every thought, and every waking moment; and, well, most of his non-waking ones as well.

He'd developed a noticeable twitch as of late, and the men in his close command started commenting on it among themselves. It made him appear more crazy than they already knew him to be.

Cage's Muslim assassins left the mountain for some time, before the weather turned bad, to travel back to their homeland. But they'd returned, and seemed more intent than ever on crushing every infidel in sight. Their zeal was becoming quite annoying. Where before they'd left on their pilgrimage, they were only concerned with maintaining their privacy, and doing their jobs; as long as no one interfered with their right to worship their god the way they saw fit. Now they seemed hell bent on making everyone around them bow to Allah. It was no longer enough that each keep to his own beliefs; now, in their eyes, there was only one faith allowed, and they were willing to kill for that ideal. Somewhere along the line, they'd gone from being Muslims, and excellent mercenaries; to becoming radicalized, extremist terrorists.

This was troublesome. Cage tolerated their excessive behavior before; the maddening call to prayer blaring over the camp speaker system five times a day; the need to keep the mess tent stocked with Halal foods, which had to be prepared, and cooked separately from all other foods; and their unreasonable expectation that everyone on base would be respectful of their holy days, while they were not the least bit respectful of anyone else's. But even he now thought they were taking things a bit too far.

Little did Cage know, the Muslims of the world were finding ways to come together, growing stronger, to prepare for what they believed to be the end of time. They were angered by the UNGC's 'One World Religion' ruling, the same as everyone else was, but were not about to hand their fate over to, in their opinion, a bunch of filthy infidels.

The UN council's ruling had done much in the Muslim world, to bring all factions of Islam together, as nothing else in history ever had. These were factions, which refused to live together, work together, or have anything to do with each other before that time, except to kill one another. And now they became silently united, as they, together, began to prepare the way for the elusive twelfth Imam.

Cage didn't believe in any god; theirs, or anyone else's; and he'd faced them off on more than one occasion, when he thought their demands were becoming vastly unwarranted. He knew they only tolerated him because he was a means to an end, but in all actuality, he only tolerated them for the same reason.

Upon return from their homeland, and with bad weather locking the base down, mysterious things began to shake the confidence of his militia men. Without a means to leave the base, they'd all been trapped together, for good, or bad, and tensions ran higher than ever. Soon, minds were twisting every sound into a crisis, until terror reigned supreme. Then, without warning, a new horror began. Each night, throughout the tempest, another heinous death among his non-Muslim troops, and by daylight each day, a new severed head appeared, on a pike, at the front of the camp. Obviously, they all knew who was perpetrating the crimes, but Cage was too much of a coward to confront them, so his men suffered.

Communications with headquarters had broken down, with the advancing storms, and Cage had no way of bringing in much needed help; wouldn't have, until the weather cleared.

Though his own sleeping quarters were in a solidly built structure, unlike most of his men who slept in tents. And he didn't necessarily have to be paranoid about someone breaking in to murder him in his sleep. He was still becoming frightened by recent events, and his men were rebelling at an alarming rate. Demanding protection from this new and imminent threat.

Cage, knowing nothing about Islam, wasn't aware of the reasons for the altered behavior of his Muslim recruits, but, indeed, their visit back to the homeland had put them in touch with several fundamentalist groups. Groups who were vehemently opposed to the UNGC's policy of a one world religion, and they meant to do something about it. They'd become part of a fringe group, with cells in every country, who were planning to overtake all countries, in the West; who they believed were becoming weakened by new 'one world' policies. The UN had actually done most of the difficult work for them, and they planned to finish the job by putting in place an Islamic Caliphate.

Through these small terrorist cells scattered around the world, working in unison, and growing stronger, they would eventually be in a position to dominate. Those Muslims believed by hastening the coming of the twelfth imam, they would also speed up the end of the world. Thereby gaining access to paradise, as jihadists of the Islamic state. They were sure Allah had orchestrated their positions, and access, to give them victory. Additionally, they believed it was their duty to remove all infidels from the earth to make the way clean and clear for their 'End Time' savior.

The people's militia, and UN troops, couldn't patrol every neighborhood in every world community at the same time. So, those Muslim extremists were combining their efforts to work with one evil purpose and the element of surprise, forcing all people into submission. What had aided most, in their ability to come together? The leaders of the world caving in and allowing the admission of tens of thousands of Muslim refugees into each non Muslim country around the globe, including America. At a time when the country was at his weakest, while that president was still at the height of his power. By the world's governments allowing, and even encouraging, mass migration, the influx of bodies created overrun refugee camps, and became breeding grounds for descent, and a growing hatred of the West. The very people who had taken them in.

Christians too, had been, and continued to be opposed to the government's 'One World Religion' plan, but were bucking the system a different way. By finding places to meet in secret, to worship God according to their own beliefs.

Muslim fundamentalists, who'd entered the country, continually, beginning several years earlier; at the behest of the president; had decided to take the law into their own hands and were deploying groups, large and small, to overcome infidels in their own communities, wherever they might be. Over the years they'd developed 'No Go Zones' in every major city all over the globe, and ran those zones under the auspices of Sharia law. No sane person would dare enter, or they would be put to death. And, strangely, while Christians were being punished for practicing their faith, no one attempted to breach the gates of these zones.

• • • • •

Snow finally stopped falling, and Josh decided his small group would head out at first light. With any luck they'd be able to find those they were sent to rescue, before they starved to death, or succumbed to the elements. He knew time was not on their side, and was filled with a sense of urgency, to find his charges, and get back home.

Mark was excited, because the sooner they could get on the road, the sooner he would get back to his kids. Scott was antsy, and eager to be out on the mountain. He'd realized the more he discovered about his own abilities, the more he wanted to press himself to learn everything available. He hadn't left anyone back home, and he was traveling with his best friend, Josh, so he was happy as a lark.

Morning dawned cold on the mountain. With a pink, and orange sunrise just coloring the sky, and sun beginning to creep in through the cave opening, Josh, and Scott started a fire. Rubbing their hands together over the flames, to get their blood moving they prepared to meet the day. Mark began packing up their things, to get ready for the trip, but it wouldn't take long, since they'd only brought essentials.

"How far out do you think these families are, Josh?"

"Well, if they stayed put, which is what I would have done in their place, they should be on the edge of the forest."

"What if they didn't?"

"Well, Scott, if they didn't, then we'll have to find them."

"We're going to be sitting ducks out there."

"Yeah, I know Mark. Let's hope they followed instructions, and stayed as close to the original coordinates as possible. Obviously, I haven't spoken to them, so I only have the word of scouts who were in touch with their advance group. There isn't much cover from the weather on the edge of the forest, so they might have found it necessary to change positions for the sake of the little ones. I have to admit, the children are my biggest concern. If we can locate them, I'll be satisfied with that."

"You want any more of this coffee, Josh?"

"Nope, let's get loaded up, and out of here. I've had about all I want of this cave for awhile. Gather around guys. I'd like to offer a prayer before we leave."

"Good idea, Josh, we can use all the help we can get."

"Father, God, thank you for providing all of our needs; food when we're hungry, shelter from the storm, and good friends to walk beside us. Help us, in your purpose Lord, to bring these families in from the cold. In Jesus' Name. Amen."

With Amen's ringing in, all around, they ventured back out into the crisp, frigid air.

• • • • •

Becca and the kids were still hunkered down; under their camouflaged plastic cover; cold and hungry, but alive. They were playing twenty questions for the thousandth time.

"Auntie Becca?"

"Yes, CJ?"

"Are we going to die?"

"No, CJ, we are not going to die. Not if I can help it."

"I don't wanna die."

"I know, Angel baby, I don't want to die either. I know that the men who are supposed to rescue us will be here soon. Please don't worry."

"Auntie Becca?"

"Yes, CJ?"

"If we die, will the wild animals eat us?"

"I don't want the wild animals to eat me, Auntie!"

"There will not be any wild animals eating us, kids. And, CJ, quit scaring your sister. Okay, I'm thinking of something. Who wants to ask the first question?"

"I'm tired of twenty questions, Auntie. Can't we play something else?

"I'm cold, Auntie, and I'm really hungry."

"Well, you come up with another game, CJ. And, I'm sorry Angel. There's only a little food left, and we have to make it last. Come here and cuddle closer. Let's see if we can warm you up a bit. We still have water. Why don't you take a big drink, it will help fill up your tummy for awhile."

"I'm tired of water, Auntie. Do we have anything else?"

"No, we don't, honey. We have to make do with what we have for now. I promise you, when we get to the base where we're headed I'll make you lots of yummy food."

"Pie?"

"Yes, pie."

"And chicken, and biscuits?"

"Yes, and chicken, and biscuits, and anything you want."

"Will it be warm there, Auntie?"

"Yes, honey, it will be warm, and you can soak in a nice bath before we wrap you up in soft blankets and furs."

"With bubbles?"

"Yes, love, with bubbles."

As Angel snuggled close to her side she felt her breathing grow slower, and more regular, and knew she'd finally fallen asleep.

"Here, CJ, you crawl in here closer too. Your sister is asleep, and I think we should all try to take a nap."

"Okay, Auntie. Do you really think they're going to find us?"

"Yes, little man, I do."

The nations have sunk in the pit that they have made; in the net that they hid, their own foot has been caught. The Lord has made Himself known; He has executed judgment; the wicked are snared in the work of their own hands. The wicked shall return to Sheol, all the nations that forget God.

Psalm 9:15-17

CHAPTER 9

The UNGC had chosen well, or so they assumed, at least to suit their own purposes. Dr. Amir Bahram came from a very prominent, and wealthy, Iranian family. His appointment would do much to calm the rattled Muslim community there, and in various other areas around the world. He'd attended a Madrassa as a youngster, learning the Quran, and reading many Hadiths recommended for his age group. But the Western world would be more likely to welcome him, with open arms, due to his university education, which began first at Oxford, and continued later at Harvard. Especially for those socialist types, who felt the people of Islam had been horribly downtrodden for centuries, the appointment was embraced with vigor.

He'd completed his doctorate in Political Science, early; and this particular line of study, served him well, as he came up through the ranks in an ever changing political climate in the U.S., and Europe. He'd recently found himself touted as the newest rising star on the political horizon by Time magazine. And, he'd thought the picture on the front cover of last month's issue almost did him justice; emphasizing his black wavy hair, dark smoldering eyes, and swarthy complexion.

Many outside the Islamic faith aren't well versed on the various sects of Islam, so the council members hadn't picked up on the fact that Dr. Bahram was a Twelver. This small fact would become a much bigger problem soon enough.

• • • • •

As a child Amir was raised in a strict, fundamentalist household; where men ruled supreme, and women were allowed to survive in order to give birth, and serve their men's needs. All girls were circumcised, to keep them from growing fond of physical, or sexual, relationships. Holy days, and five times daily prayer, were unquestioned pieces of his day by day schedule.

As a boy, he'd seen things that might cause a Western heart to skip a few beats, but these things were common where he lived. He vividly remembered watching, as his older sister was beheaded for her attempt to convert to Christianity; the ultimate offense in a Muslim world; the sound of her pleading for her life still rang in his ears even now. A female cousin, of only sixteen years, was doused with acid, for looking at a boy; and an aunt, who dared to leave her house, without a male escort, was stoned to death. He'd seen thieves relieved of their hands; adulteresses with their breasts ripped off, bound in stocks for the world to see; and babies, who'd been born to unwed mothers, left outside to perish in the elements.

When his father beat his mother, he cried, until his father beat him too, for showing weakness. Eventually, when he witnessed his father's inhumane treatment of his mother, he felt nothing. He was actually encouraged to punch, slap, or kick, the women in the household; to build his feeling of superiority over women; and though he didn't partake of that expression of dissatisfaction often, while in his father's household, he grew to believe that women were put on the earth for his pleasure.

Of his four wives, his father fancied the youngest when he was feeling amorous. Sadly, she was not always so inclined. It was common to hear her screaming. One day he beat her so badly that she appeared to be nothing more than a bloody pile of rags on the living room floor. To emphasize his power over her, he took her right there, as the other members of the family tried to discretely leave the room, or look away. Amir never saw her again, after that day. His father's anger was merely a part of daily life to him. If he ever decided to marry, he would do the same. It was his right, and was expected of the man, to show that he was leader in his household.

As a young boy, he'd had a good friend for many years, who, later on as a man, confessed to being gay. The Imam, from their mosque, assembled the community. And, when the young man was hung, from a meat hook, in the town square, Amir was expected to wield the strap right along with all the other village people. He struck out, over and over, and watched with detached interest as his friend's skin came off in bloody strips with each lash of the whip. He was actually surprised later, to find that his own face was wet with tears, and quickly swatted away the offensive expression of weakness, with the back of his hand.

This event haunted, and confused him; had for years; as he knew his uncle, and his father, also had sex with young boys, and girls. And, even he and his younger sister had not escaped the grasp of his father's friends. This, he was instructed, was perfectly fine, because it was not considered an act of homosexuality to have sex with a boy under the age of twelve. It was only a sin, once the act took place with someone thirteen, or older. He wondered if his friend had ever been one of those young boys, used by an older man as he had been.

There was much that confused him as a child, but he'd grown to be hard. Hard enough to live in, and through, those circumstances. And to grow, eventually, to have no empathy, what so ever, for any of those weaker vessels. Only the strong survived to rule the world. He was hard enough, now, to look down his nose at anyone lesser than he. He knew his place in the world. He'd been groomed for this his whole life.

Admittedly, he was treated like a prince, when he arrived home for visits. But, he was also comfortable living in Europe, and in the United States. There were many treats available here, which could not be obtained at home; and he'd acquired quite a taste for those forbidden fruits. At home he couldn't have his nightly brandy, because a good Muslim doesn't drink; a good cigar; or the occasional un-wed fling, though there were a few complicated loop holes around that one too, even for married men. He knew that if he chose to marry he could have more than one wife at home, but somehow that didn't seem as titillating as a romp in the hay with a bevy of beauties from around the world.

His precious Holy book prepared him for the role he would assume in the world. He knew that the writings of the prophet instructed him to lie to the infidels, until he was in a position to overtake them. If they would not submit, he would kill them; but first he would cause them to trust him. They would come to him like rats, drawn to the haunting melody of the pied piper, and he would slaughter them all.

Now that the leaders of all countries had been relieved of the bulk of their power, by the UNGC, they must look to him for direction. And he would gladly lead them down a path to their ultimate demise. The sheep had been hand-ily delivered to the wolf, and they were so busy grooming their wool in order to impress him they didn't see the dan-ger of their own decisions.

God is our refuge and strength, a very present help in trouble. Therefore we will not fear though the earth gives way, though the mountains be moved in the heart of the sea, though its waters roar and foam, though the mountains tremble at its swelling.

Psalm 46:1-3

CHAPTER 10

"Are you okay, Jana?"

"I guess so. I just miss Josh, and I feel like I've made a million loaves of bread since the last time I saw him."

"I know, Dear. It's hard waiting for someone you love. When Dad was in the service, I laid awake praying for him every night."

"I didn't know Dad was in the service. Why doesn't Josh ever talk about that?"

"Well, he wouldn't remember that time. He wasn't born

yet. I was a young wife, expecting my first child, waiting, and hoping that my husband would come back to me. And, I was one of the lucky ones. Many women weren't as blessed as I, and their men never returned. It was then that I first came to trust in the Lord with all my strength, Jana. I knew God had great plans for all of us. That He was going to use us for some greater purpose."

"Was Josh born before, or after, his Dad returned?"

"Josh was ten months old before Chuck returned. What a wonderful moment that was. I'd shown Josh pictures of his daddy, since the moment he was born. My own father died when I was an infant, so I never knew him; and my mother passed away when I was only two months pregnant with the grandson she would never meet... Cancer took her, and with Chuck gone, I felt very much alone in the world. That baby became my whole universe, and I relied heavily on my relationship with the Lord to get me through. When Chuck came home, and picked up his son; Josh looked at him for the longest time, smiled, and put his little arms around his dad's neck. When he said "dada", I saw his father's eyes fill with tears, and it was as if they'd always known one another."

"So he's always been close to both of you. I envy that.

You know my parents were killed when I was very young, and I grew up in foster homes. That's why it's so important to me for this child to have both a mom and a dad to grow up with, and to be a family who shares their faith together."

"He'll be home soon, Jana. Maybe they ran into weather. I'm sure they're okay."

"I hope you're right, Mom. I lost him once, and I don't know what I would do if I ever lost him again."

"Well, you'd go on, Jana. Just like all those women whose husbands didn't come home from that war. You'd go on for your child, and Dad and I, would be right here beside you. But, let's not borrow trouble. They are late getting back, but they aren't terribly far overdue yet. I'm sure they're all fine. We're going to pray, and know that God is in control, right?"

"Yeah Mom. I know. I just keep seeing those prison cells in my dreams, and Cage's eyes. Those eyes were just so filled with evil, and I can't help but think he will try to be very true to his word, about taking Josh down."

"Just remember that God is on Josh's side, Jana. That gives him a huge advantage."

Emma gave Jana a big squeeze, and a pat on her slightly expanded tummy, and then she went back to her quarters.

She was worried too, though she would never admit that to Jana. She wouldn't want to raise concerns in Jana's mind, especially in her delicate condition. She too had lost Josh once before, and the thought of losing him again was heavy on her mind. She would pray, and leave it to God to watch over the boys, to bring them safely home.

• • • • •

Josh and his men made their way slowly down the frozen slopes, and they were currently slogging through miles, and miles, of turkey foot grass. Making their way gradually in the direction of the forest's edge. With the ground still mostly frozen, there was nowhere for the spring runoff to go, so the recent deluge of rain had flooded the grassland. And, the water was cold indeed.

"Wow, Josh, I didn't remember the grassland covering this much acreage."

"Well, you'd have to remember that we were captured in the late summer, Mark. Just as Fall was coming around the corner. We didn't have to make our way through all this bloody grass. And we sure as heck didn't have to slosh through any freezing marshlands "

"Hey, I came in on my bike, guys. I think I must have

taken a side route. There were dirt paths. My machine is probably still under the pines along the way. Not far from a huge boulder that sits right under the base of the mountain."

"Well, you're lucky, Scott. Jana told me about her escape, and it included a path from the forest, through the grass, and up the mountain, with a sprained ankle no less."

"Hey, I think we'd all have to agree, that's one scrappy little lady you're married to, Josh."

"Don't I know it. I hope she's not too worried. We should be back by now. All that time in the cave, and the slow going in these infernal weeds, tiptoeing through the tulips, hasn't helped."

"Yeah, I hope my kids aren't too worried. I wish there was a way to let them know we're okay. I'm sure you wouldn't mind getting word to Jana, and your folks too."

"We'll see them soon enough. We just need to keep our minds focused on the mission at hand, and get out of this freezing water as soon as we can."

"Boy, a big ol' juicy steak sounds good right about now."

"Leave it to you, Scott, to have food on the brain, especially when there isn't much left. And, I can promise you, none of it is steak!"

"I'm a growing boy! And I know none of its steak, but you can't blame a guy for dreaming."

• • • • •

"Auntie Becca?"

"Yes, CJ?"

"I was sleeping."

"What's wrong, honey, did you have a dream?"

"Yeah, there was a field there, and more flowers than I ever seen in my life. On the other side of the field was a man. He had long hair, and he was wearing something that looked kinda like a long white robe. He waved at me, and I knew He wanted me to come to Him, so I ran. When I got to Him, He lifted me up, and held me. I looked in His eyes, and you know what I saw?"

"No, honey, what did you see?"

"Love."

"What a beautiful dream, CJ."

"That's just the thing, Auntie. I don't know if it was a dream. I think it might be real."

"Okay, honey, now lay back down, and try to get some rest."

"I'm hungry, Auntie."

"I know, Angel baby. I know. Hold on awhile longer. Help is coming soon."

"But my tummy hurts real bad."

"I know, baby girl. Here, have some water."

"I don't want water."

"I know. Come here and stay warm. Somebody will come soon. I promise."

• • • • •

Jana was aware no one would allow her to leave, if she asked permission, so she wouldn't. No one could dispute that she knew these mountains better than just about any-one, and she couldn't just sit here any longer. Not when her husband was so far overdue. Several more days had passed since that last, somewhat comforting, conversation with Emma, and she just couldn't get the worry out of her mind. Mom would insist she was being foolish. But her injuries were completely healed now, and she was as healthy as a horse, so she was going to go out and find the boys.

She'd secreted away enough supplies to make the trip, and extra, in case she encountered others who needed help. Her furs, which had been cleaned, folded, and put safely away in storage, for all these months, were out, and ready to go. Her hand gun was cleaned, and she'd stored extra ammunition, along with her bow, arrows, and extra fletching, a compass, water purifiers, and first aid kit rounding out the supplies for her trip. She would wait until everyone was sleeping, so she wouldn't encounter any unnecessary resistance, and then she would be off.

• • • • •

"Josh, My feet have gone completely numb. I can barely walk."

"Yeah, mine too, Mark. But, there isn't anywhere to rest around here. We'd be sitting in this freezing water if we stopped now,"

"Hey, guys, what if we cut enough of this grass to stack higher than the water level? I'd say the water's about a foot and a half deep, and this grass is pretty fibrous. If we alternate layers, to get a good solid foundation, I think we could make a platform high enough to get us out of the cold. We'd at least be able to rest for awhile."

" I think that might just work, Scott. Good man! You've been quite a blessing to all of us on this trip. Okay, let's get to work!"

In about an hour, the guys had cut sufficient amounts

of the sturdy turkey foot grass, and alternated it, layer upon layer, to make a platform big enough for all of them to lay on, if they scooted close together. That would help them conserve warmth as well. For the first time in days, they rested, dry, and hidden in the foliage. They'd removed their shoes, and socks, in order to dry things out; even though they would be just as wet and cold once they began their trek again; and they slept. Yes, they had folks waiting for them, but they wouldn't be any good to anyone if they were frozen, and exhausted. So they slept the sleep of the dead, for six hours.

• • • • •

Becca, who'd never prayed a single time before in her life, sat with her two precious charges tucked close by her sides, and began to speak softly. "God? If you're out there? I'm getting pretty worried. You can see I've got these two little ones to care for, and so far we have no one here to save us. I think you might have visited my little nephew in a dream, but now, if you're real, we need your help. If you are there, I'm really sorry I've never tried to talk to you before. I guess I just wasn't raised like that, you know? I mean, we never went to church, or anything, so I don't even know if

I'm doing this right now. Anyway, I'm asking you, God, to save us. Help me to get these kids to safety, so nothing will happen to them on my watch."

In the Lord I take refuge; how can you say to my soul, Flee like a bird to your mountain, for behold, the wicked bend the bow; they have fitted their arrow to the string to shoot in the dark at the upright in heart; if the foundations are destroyed, what can the righteous do?

Psalm 11:1-3

CHAPTER 11

Lights were dimmed, and it appeared the community in the mount was asleep. Jana rose quietly, and gathered her supplies. After making her way to the outside tunnel, undetected, she began to layer on her furs. Once she was set for the cold, she patted her slightly rounded abdomen. "Come on, little one, let's go find your daddy."

As she stepped outside, she shivered; and at the exact same moment, many miles away, Josh, opened his eyes, as a tremor traveled the length of his spine. He knew immediately, that something was terribly wrong. He laid still, so as not to bother the rest of the guys; but couldn't shake the feeling of concern filling his heart; so he began to pray.

• • • • •

On the edge of the forest, under a plastic, camouflaged sheet, Becca felt a sense of calm for the first time, in a long time. Somehow, she knew they would be okay. When the kiddos woke, she let them eat half of their remaining rations. She was that sure help was on the way.

"Is everything okay, Aunt Becca?"

"Yes, CJ, everything is great."

"Are you crying, Auntie?"

"Yes, honey, but it's okay, it's a good cry."

"But, why are you crying?"

"I'm crying, because I was praying to God, and I believe He's answering me."

"Is that why you let us eat most of the food?"

"Yes it is. I know that He is sending someone to save us, and they will have food with them, so I'm not worried anymore."

"Auntie?"

"Yes, honey."

"What does God sound like?"

"He sounds like all the joy, and peace in the universe, CJ. All packed in a big hug."

"I've never met Him before."

"Actually, I think you might have, CJ. I know I haven't, but even though He never heard from me before, He heard me today. I'm sure of it. I just know He is sending someone to help us, very soon."

"I like God."

"I like God too, CJ."

"I like Him too, Auntie."

"Yes, Angel, we all like Him. And, I think we might even learn to love Him, very, very soon."

• • • • •

After a night of fitful, but somewhat healing, rest, Josh and the guys were again slogging through the twisted grass, and freezing water. "Hey, Guys, I think I see the trees." Josh was taller than any of the other fellows, so it would stand to reason he could see over the tall grass, to the forest, easier than the rest of the men.

"I don't see anything. And my feet are numb again."

"I know, Mark, we all have frozen feet. But, there are trees. You'll just have to take my word for it, at least until we get a little closer."

"Let's go faster. If you can see the trees, we must not be much farther out."

"Okay, Scott. You take the lead. But, don't get tangled up in the roots, or you'll be face down in this freezing water."

"Right on boss. I'll be careful. Follow me boys."

Scott had been such a trooper on this trip, and what a great attitude. Josh could only hope some of that positivity would rub off on Mark. Though, if truth be told, he didn't blame him for wanting to be with his kids, back in a warm cave, versus stumbling through these hellish fields of grass. He was sure everyone would rather be home, but there were people out here that needed their help, so they would trudge on.

• • • • •

Emma dressed quickly. She wondered why Jana hadn't been by yet. Their usual routine was to walk to the community kitchen together, and begin preparations for breakfast. She hoped Jana wasn't having another bout of morning sickness. The girl was otherwise very healthy, but she'd been plagued by intermittent episodes of queasiness, since practically the beginning of her pregnancy. Maybe she was sleeping in a little this morning. It would be rare, but she certainly deserved it. Well, she would get over to the kitchen before her daughter-in-law, and make her a soothing tea, and if she still wasn't up yet, maybe she would take her breakfast in bed. The thought of this possible surprise for her very favorite, if only, daughter-in-law, caused her to hurry a bit faster.

When she arrived at the kitchen, several other women were already starting hot water for coffee, and rolling out biscuits. Jana wasn't there. She got to work slicing bacon, and brewing a nice tea. Once she had a tray ready, complete with flowers, and a special note, she set off for Jana's quarters, with a huge smile on her face, ready to bless her darling sleepy head.

She knocked lightly, at first, but then grew concerned, and rapped a bit harder. "Jana? It's Mom. Are you up, Dear?" When she received no response, she set the tray down, and opened the door. "Jana, are you okay? I'm coming in. Jana?" After a quick inspection, she concluded that the girl was gone. *"Perhaps she left for the kitchen already. Well, you'd think I would have passed her in that case.*" She thought. Once she arrived back at the kitchen, and didn't find her illusive daughter-in-law, she grew more concerned. Running to her own quarters, she burst through the door, practically scaring her husband to death. "Chuck, Jana's gone."

"What do you mean, she's gone?"

"I mean she's gone. I've looked everywhere, and I can't find her."

"We'll, she can't have just disappeared. Here, let me help you look."

They looked everywhere she might possibly be, and then they went back to her quarters. There, Emma noticed that Jana's backpack was missing from the corner where it normally rested. "Oh, my, Chuck, do you think she's left the base? Where would she go? She couldn't have gone after Josh, could she? Oh, Chuck, we have to find her. What about the baby?"

"Emma, where would we look? We don't know how long she's been gone, or what route she took. She knows these mountains at least as well as our best trackers, and she can certainly take care of herself. There isn't anything we can do at this point, but pray for her safe return."

"What will we tell Josh?"

"We'll hope she gets home before he does. She's a grown woman, Emma. He wouldn't have expected us to have her under lock, and key, would he?"

• • • • •

Jana made excellent time, since she'd left the ARM base in the middle of the night. She had a photographic memory, which made school, and her job, a major whiz. What's more, she'd memorized every step, of the return path, to the militia camp, where Josh had been held prisoner. Ever shifting, growing, and depleting snow banks, made her memories a bit less reliable, but she would manage.

She suspected her husband, and the rest of the soldiers, had been held up. Whether by weather, or by PM thugs, she wasn't sure, but she was going to rule the later out, before going on down the mountain to search further. There was still a good amount of snow, up here on the higher peaks; but she could see the levels diminishing, as she descended. She intended to get as many miles in, as humanly possible, before slowing down to stop for the night; but she knew she had to be mindful of the baby, so she stopped often to rest, and hydrate.

She'd missed her mountain; the crisp, fresh air; the profound feeling of being present on God's doorstep. She'd always felt so close to her Lord way up here on the heights. Her furs kept her warm, and helped her to blend in with her surroundings, at least in the snowy landscape; and as she eventually sat, to rest, a pair of snowshoe rabbits scampered by. Her knife flew so fast, she was hardly aware she'd thrown it. Survival was innately dependent on instinct, and she'd always had good instincts.

Field dressing the animal, in record time; she tied the small carcass to the back of her pack, to save for her upcoming supper. She dug a small hole in which to bury the entrails, and fur, of her kill and headed on her way. For now she would throw back some more water, and nibble on homemade granola; made with oats, dried apples, and honey.

That night would be spent in a tiny cave. She cut enough wood for a fire, and pine boughs to block the entrance. She didn't bother to build up a pallet for her bed. She wasn't planning on hanging around here that long. She roasted the hare, until the smell of it left her fairly drooling from the savory smells. Once it was cooked to perfection, she ate ravenously, and drank more water, then she pulled out her Bible, and read until the fire began to die down. Jana was too tired to stay awake tending a flame over night, as might be expected after so many months of reduced exercise in the cold. So she slept with her pistol on her chest, and hoped the pine boughs would deter any unwanted visitors.

• • • • •

Josh, and his men were getting closer to the forest's edge. And, though they might have to spend one more night in the grass, they would certainly be able to gain the tree line by sometime tomorrow. As they made their way, slowly, through the torturous foliage, they talked quietly. "I know we're out here to help a family, Josh, but is there any part of you that wishes we hadn't come?"

"Yeah, Mark, every fleshly part of me, exposed to this infernal grass, wishes I hadn't come. Every part of me that lives by feelings. My freezing feet, my raw hands, my tired bones, and my head that aches wondering if the folks we've come after will be where they are supposed to be. The thing is, we can't live by feelings if we're going to accomplish what God has put us out here to do. I know He will make all things right, so I just count on Him, and I forget about my feet, my hands, my bones, and my head."

"I wish I could do that as easy as you can, Josh."

"I didn't say it was easy, but you don't have to do it alone. Just ask Him for His strength, and He will pick you up and carry you."

"Well, I know you don't mean He will actually pick me up, and carry me, or you wouldn't be slogging through the same freezing swamp the rest of us are in."

"No, Mark, but He will give you the will, and the ability, to mentally overcome whatever you are enduring physically. It's gotten me through some pretty tough stuff."

"Is that what you did back in the prison caves, when Cage was torturing you every day?"

"Yeah, it is. I just try to focus on how much Jesus loves me, and all the great things He has done, and will do in my life. These days, I focus on how I know He is going to get me back to Jana, and my folks. Look at how long I thought I'd lost all of them. For that matter, Mark, look at how long you went, thinking you would never see your kids again, and now you've got them back. Try to focus on what you'll do when you get back to them."

"I will. Thanks, Josh. That's exactly what I'm going to do. Maybe that will help me to stop complaining so much. I'm sure I've gotten on everyone's nerves by now."

"Well, you said it."

"Oh, thanks, Scott."

"Like I said, you mentioned it first. We know you miss your kids, so we didn't want to say anything, but you were getting a little hard to take. No, hey, I'm joking with you, man. Just pulling your leg."

"Well, everyone, I'm sorry for being so negative this whole trip. I'll try to be better. Though, I will tell you now, I'd rather be home with my kids."

"It's okay, Mark, we're all sick and tired of being out here. And, we'll all be glad to get home, once and for all."

• • • • •

Becca and the kids sang songs, very quietly, and played every game in her arsenal as another day wore on. They drank plenty of water, and tried not to think about being cold, and hungry, stuck for another day, under the old camouflaged tarp.

• • • • •

Back at the ARM base, Emma and all the ladies, in the community kitchen, said another prayer for Jana's safety. They'd banded together, in intercessory prayer, ever since Emma previously brought them news of Jana's midnight flight from the cavern. Only Chuck and Emma knew about the baby, because they'd promised not to say a thing until Jana had time to tell Josh. But in the privacy of their quarters, they would pray for their grandchild as well.

• • • • •

Jana drifted from sleep, reluctantly leaving Josh in the soft glow of her dream, and prepared for another day. She didn't have any visitors during the night, but the small cave had gotten plenty cold with no actively burning fire. So she built up the flame as quickly as possible, brewed coffee, and pulled together a breakfast of dried fruit and granola. Boiling a little snow, and adding it to a bowl of cold water, she came up with enough warm water to take care of her morning ablutions. Face washed, teeth brushed, and thick, auburn hair pulled back in a sleek pony tail, she was set to clear out of the small space. Making sure her canteens were full, and all her supplies were in order, she moved the pine bow door, and headed out to another brilliant morning. Spring's gentle breezes were actively melting snow. And the sun created thousands of light pixies, which danced across the ice's surface, as if with glee for the dazzling sunshine. She breathed deeply of the freshest air in the world, and launched herself confidently out into another beautiful day.

•••••

Cage woke from an ongoing dream he'd been entertaining for the last several nights. In his dream, he'd found a cave. In the cave, there was a roaring fire; and there, on the floor, a prone figure bundled up near the flames. He'd awoken at this point on the first night. He poked the shape with his boot, to find out it was Josh Conyers' wench, Jana. He'd wakened on the second night, here. He successfully captured her, and now she was safely stored away in one of the cells on the back of his highland base. This is where he'd jolted awake this morning.

When he woke on this particular morning, he knew there was something more to his dream. Something he should know, but couldn't quite figure out. He had the notion that the universe was trying to tell him something. Something he would need to know soon. Could this be a foretelling of the future? Was Josh Conyers' wench actually loose on the mountain? He roused himself, drank an entire pot of coffee, and then began to prepare troops for a foray out on the slopes. And Satan smiled.

• • • • •

"Josh, I can see the trees! How far out do you think we are?"

"I'm not sure, Mark. Distances can be a bit skewed when your feet are freezing, but I think we can make it by sometime tomorrow. What do you think, Scott?"

"Yeah, I'm sure of it. If we keep going at this pace, we shouldn't have to spend more than one additional night out here. Believe me, Mark, we all want out of this grass. Just remember that after we get what we came for, we'll be right back out here, slogging through the ice water, isn't that so, Josh?"

"Yep, you're right, Scott. As much as I hate the thought, there isn't another way back up to the mountain."

"Wait, Josh. Maybe there is. Remember I told you I came in on my bike, over dirt paths, not through the turkey grass like the rest of you did. Maybe when we get to the tree line, we can follow it around until we find those same paths? They can't be too far away. I climbed up the same side of the peak that you guys went up. It might take us a little out of the way, but if it saves us walking through the damned grass, and all this freezing water, especially with a couple of little kiddos in tow, it might actually save us some time."

"You just might have something there, Scott. I think we'd all be up for a different route, if it will save us from this tangled foliage. What did I tell you before, buddy? You have been such a blessing to all of us on this trip. Keep those great ideas coming."

"Hey, I'm all for anything that might get me back to my kids a little quicker, and I think we'd all agree that less time in the freezing water won't bother anyone."

All the guys agreed, and they pushed ahead with a firm plan in mind, grateful for new ideas and the possibility of solid ground. They would set about to find the families they'd come to rescue, and then they'd walk the tree line to find a dryer route. They hiked until dusk; and then they cut enough of the tough, thick grass to make another platform, up out of the water, and settled down for the night."

• • • • •

As day flowed gently into evening; and a bright blue sky slowly transformed to a canvas of muted shades of pink, red, yellow, and orange; Becca gave her charges the last of their rations. They ate with a gusto, which belied their situation, and settled down to sleep. Becca knew, with every fiber of her being, that salvation would arrive tomorrow.

She didn't know why she was so positive, but she had no doubt that her saviors would come. With her own stomach rumbling, for lack of food, she snuggled down with CJ and Angel. As she slept, she felt herself wrapped in a blanket of peace.

• • • • •

Jana made excellent time again, throughout that bright, cold day. And as the sun was beginning to set, she bagged a surprisingly healthy, fat squirrel. Even commenting to herself, how heavy he was, especially for this early in the spring; and found another small cave in which to spend the night. She knew Chuck and Emma were surely worried about her by now, and she hated that she'd most certainly frightened them. But this was better than lying in bed each night with a cacophony of 'what ifs' dancing through her mind. At least out here on the mountain, she was in charge. Oh, she knew Emma was right. Right, in that God loved Josh. But, she couldn't just sit around, with all the rest of them, doing nothing. That's simply not who she was as a person. For now she would concentrate on making her way to the PM camp, and doing a little spying.

Cage stood before his freshly assembled scouting team in the camp's mess hall, and began his pre mission speech. For this especially detailed mission he'd recruited only Muslim mercenaries, and two loyal PM soldiers (who seemed immune to the tugging, of the heart strings, affecting the rest of the camp these days), from all the bodies on base. He intended to go out on the mountain and find out if his suspicions were correct. He believed Jana was in the heights, and if she was, he was going to capture her and use her as bait to bring his nemesis to justice, once and for all.

He continued to be confused by the tension on base. Why couldn't all the men in his charge see what a danger the members of ARM were to their cause; and therefore the cause of the entire country? He could feel the mindset of the entire regiment being swayed in the favor of those damned, radical, resistance soldiers. And when he walked among the troops he was not blind to the hateful, suspicious looks he received from those who were no longer loyal to him. Though, if truth be told, he tended to be a bit paranoid anyway, and might have imagined those looks even if they weren't actually there.

Through a series of planned accidents, he'd managed

to rid himself of some of the witnesses to his past, poor decisions. But there were still those who knew his secrets, and they had influenced others. Once he'd begun to receive inquiries from the head command about the constant and steady death rate of his soldiers, he'd had to discontinue those efforts to rid himself of witnesses, at least for now.

Cage requested a new influx of recruits, on several previous occasions; to replace the dead, injured, and less than cooperative troops in his command; but headquarters, it seemed, had grown tired of replacing his abused, and used up soldiers over, and over. And had become suspicious of the rate of loss, and attrition, among his regular forces. So, it seemed, he would have to figure this one out on his own.

The obsession surrounding the capture of Josh Conyers, had become so important, such a fixation to him, that new requests, which soon became unquestionable orders from headquarters, for an audience with the new head of the UNGC, had gone unheeded.

The two reasons that units, from headquarters, had not been dispatched to collect him thus far, were weather, and cost. He'd been largely overlooked, previously, due to his location, and extreme prowess in collecting and extracting information from those undesirables who were still on the run from the new government. With implantation now a global mandate, at least for the masses; and vast numbers fleeing every day; talents like his were greatly appreciated and sought after. However, Dr. Bahram was not used to being avoided, or put off, by anyone. And he was becoming more impatient over the lack of respect from characters like Cage, for his station and position. He simply would not be denied.

He'd heard good things about this Colonel Cage, up until a few months ago. But the man seemed to be breaking from convention as of late, and he needed to be sure they were both still on the same page. He could use good men. Men with the talents Cage displayed, on his UN military forces team. His particular strengths would be valuable, at least until they could sufficiently quell the world's panic over misunderstandings about the need for implantation.

Oh, he was aware that many regular citizens around the world were against the idea of a global government being able to follow their every move; and he even understood their fear, to a certain extent. If he'd been expected to undergo implantation, he would have rebelled with all his might. But, the truth of the matter was he didn't need anyone to direct his every move not the way those multitudes of mindless sheep did. Those of average, or less, intelligence needed that guidance and instruction, in order to orchestrate the fundamentals of their mundane existences. Of course, no one with his higher IQ would be expected to succumb to the same treatment as the average man in those universal masses. Well, it was neither here, nor there. Implantation was, and would continue to be, their way of controlling the hordes. So those who were considered, 'the masses' better learn to live with it, or face the consequences.

For now, the good Doctor needed to meet with his outlying base commanders, to go over strategies and to determine who was still loyal to the Global Council. He was a pretty good judge of character, and he was sure if he could look into the eyes of the men under his command, he would be able to see where their particular allegiance fell, once and for all.

· · · · ·

Josh and his men woke to a beautiful spring day. The air seemed a bit warmer, though, they were certain the water would still be cold. Birds sang, in the distant tree line, loud enough to be heard from where they were currently located, and that gave them a strong feeling of coming liberation. They all sat up, slowly, so as not to disturb their grass platform; and began munching on granola, while drinking fresh water from their canteens. All, very excited to be on the way to dry ground, they were smiling, to a man, for the first time in many days.

"Hey, Scott, you still the lead man today?"

"You betcha!"

"Well, then let's get ready to head out. I can't wait to find some dry ground!"

"You got it boss. Follow me."

"Good man. Remind me to put you in for a promotion when we get back to base."

"Promotion? You can do that?"

"Well, I can sure try. I'm definitely going to tell anyone who will listen, how valuable you have been to all of us on this trip!"

"Hey, man, you've got my vote too."

"Thanks, Mark, that means a lot coming from you."

"Okay, okay, let's get a move on. We can congratulate Scott later. Let's get out of this freezing swamp!"

• • • • •

Jana lay still, for some time, waiting for the light fluttering in her abdomen to stop. She was sure she'd felt the baby move, and that brought tears to her eyes. She'd so wanted to share every single piece of this experience with Josh, and he was missing it. Perhaps if she'd told him about the baby before he left; but, no, she knew her husband well enough to know the news might have altered his decision to go after the families he was about to rescue. And she wouldn't have wanted that on her conscience. No, it was better this way. They would be together soon enough. She would see to that.

Most of the queasiness had subsided now, but she still had moments. She was feeling guilty about not having any milk to drink, for the baby, so she filled up again on dried fruit, granola, and a cup of soothing tea. She would be back on base soon enough and she'd would drink all the milk she could get her hands on. Cleaning herself up, she pulled her hair back in her signature thick pony tail. Then, checking her weapons, and supplies, she readied herself for the day's travels.

• • • • • •

The ground was beginning a steady, slight grade, upward, out of the water to higher ground. Praise God, they would soon be out of the freezing marsh. Josh and the men were ecstatic about this turn of events, and you could see it in their faces, and hear it in their voices. They were all trying to remain quiet, knowing that PM squads still patrolled the area looking for recent defectors, but their excitement was palpable.

"We're just about there, Josh. I can see the scrub, at the base of the tree line."

"Yeah, I see it too, Scott. Listen guys. We need to remember why we're out here, and that there are soldiers who will stop us, if we let them."

"Right on, boss man, we'll keep it down. Won't we boys?"

All the guys chimed their agreement. They knew how serious their assignment was, and how vulnerable they were to discovery. So, from that moment forward, socializing came to a halt. As they drew closer to the tree line, and their cover became more sparse, until it was non-existent; they grew more vigilant and much more serious. Definitely in enemy territory now, they didn't dare attract attention for fear of putting the family they'd come to rescue in danger.

Cage had been on edge all night. Tossing and turning, not able to sleep. He'd never been more ready for anything in his life. And, the very second the sun began it's slow assent into the morning sky, he and his troops were off.

The mercenaries who traveled with him, did so of their own free will. They did not feel a loyalty to this obviously crazy man, and he had no love for them. But, having them along, gave Cage a greater sense of comfort, and security. They hated Josh's team as much as he did, though for different reasons. He for the embarrassment they'd caused him; they because Josh's team were comprised of the worst of infidels, those pesky Evangelical Christians. Cage didn't care that their reasoning for detesting their foe was different, only that their ultimate goal was the same. Death to them all.

It was a beautiful day out on the mountain. But, Cage didn't care about the blue sky, singing birds, cotton candy clouds, or any of the ridiculous crap others were gushing about. He only cared that the nicer weather might make his tracking of Jana a bit easier. He ached to capture this thorn in his side, and ultimately her husband, to bring them both to the justice they deserved. He would finally have his revenge.

Becca woke that morning to the most beautiful spring day since being on the run. Bright blue sky, warmer breeze whispering in from the south, and birds singing so loudly in the trees above her that they too seemed to be filled with joy over the nicer weather. "Hey CJ, Angel, time to wake up little ones."

"Are they here?"

"Not yet, CJ. But, I'm sure they will be here soon."

"Good. I'm hungry. You said they would have food, didn't you Auntie?"

"Yes, honey, I'm sure they will bring supplies, and then we can get out of here."

"I'm hungry too, Auntie Becca."

"I know you are, Angel. We'll have something to eat soon. Let's try to get ourselves cleaned up as much as we can before they come, okay?"

For the next hour they folded blankets and tarps; re-packed backpacks; washed up, and tried getting a brush through mounds of tangled hair. After securing pony tails, and supplies, they were set to go with their rescuers the very second they arrived. It was good to be out from under the camouflage tarp, and the fresh air felt wonderful on their faces, but they would need to be extra vigilant, in order to not be detected by patrolling PM troops.

• • • • •

The constant upward grade had finally placed the guys on dry ground. They weren't all the way to the tree line yet, but it felt great to be out of the freezing water. They would make better time now that the water wasn't a hindrance. "Hey, guys, as soon as we make it as far as the trees, we're going to dry our feet, and change socks. Being in the freezing water for so long can cause some pretty serious damages, so we're going to check ourselves for signs of frostbite, and trench foot, understood?"

"Yes, sir. I wouldn't mind a few minutes rest in any case, but we'd better find some cover first, don't ya think, Josh?"

"Yes, Scott, of course. We'll find cover, and then check ourselves over, before we find the folks we're supposed to be after."

"Man, it feels so good to be out of that water."

"I agree, Mark, I don't know the last time I was so happy about anything. As soon as we reach cover, we will say a proper prayer. God is good!" To which he received a symphony of "All the time. And, all the time, God is good."

It didn't take much longer to attain their destination, and once they reached the trees they looked for cover. Finding a secluded spot in the foliage, they kneeled, as Josh offered a prayer of thanksgiving. "Father, God, we are so grateful for dry ground, trees, a gentle breeze, and warm spring air; your loving, protective hand in our lives, and the Grace, which keeps us each and every day. Thank you Heavenly Father, for the opportunity to make a difference in the lives of others, and to be able to reach out with your hand of Grace to those who are frightened and alone. Help us, Lord, to touch others, in your Holy Name. Amen." To which, he received an echo of "Amen", from all around.

Now, to the business of checking themselves over. After so many days in the freezing water, there were sure to be a number of frost bitten toes, and some evidence of trench foot among the men; but after careful examination, there appeared to be no injuries whatever. This was truly the protective hand of God, and they all praised Him for their good fortune. Once they'd changed their socks, and hung wet ones on their backpacks, they ate a little jerky, drank their fill of water, and set out to find those who would be waiting.

Becca, and the kids, sat patiently waiting for their rescue to arrive. She was so certain, today, was the day, that she did not begin any lengthy games, even when the children begged. Her stomach was filled with, what seemed like, butterflies. She knew God was sending salvation, and she was ready to accept it with open arms. After what seemed like hours of sitting, she thought she heard voices in the distance. Was it her rescue? Or, could it be the larger group come back to retrieve her and the children? There was even a chance it might be PM soldiers, out on patrol, in which case, she and the children should get out of sight. At least until they could determine the source of the noise. Climbing back into the tree roots, at the base of the giant redwood, which had been their hiding place for all these days, they hunkered down to await proof of the intentions of those approaching.

• • • • •

"I'm sure these are the correct coordinates, guys. If the families we've come to collect aren't around here somewhere, I wouldn't know where to begin searching. We can't give our location away to the militia, but we've got to let our targets know we're here." The guys began with a series of soft whistles, to try to get the attention of the people they were sent to retrieve.

• • • • •

Becca heard a soft whistle, and peeked out of the foliage where she hid. The men didn't appear to be dressed as militia, but she was still initially afraid to give away her location. She had all she could do to keep the little ones quiet, so as not to make themselves known. She watched the men for some time, and finally decided they looked safe enough. One of them actually looked familiar from this distance. As they were passing by, not twenty yards from her position, and continuing to whistle softly, she popped her head up, and quietly made herself known.

• • • • •

"Josh, over there. Hey, don't be afraid. We've been sent to help you."

"Scott?"

"Becca?"

"Do you two know each other?"

"Yeah, Josh, that's my sister-in-law. Becca, where are

Gin, and the kids?"

"Virginia is still in town, Scott, but I've got the kids. CJ, Angel, come out here and see your daddy."

"Daddy? Daddy, Daddy, we missed you."

"Wow, you two, I missed you too! But, how, what is going on. I thought Gin took the kids in for their implants the day I left."

"Well, she would have, but I took off with them before she got the chance. I didn't want the implant, and I surely couldn't just sit around and watch her do that to the kiddos."

"My God, Becca, how can I ever thank you? My kids. I didn't think I would ever see them again. I guess I didn't even know you cared."

"There are lots of things you probably don't know, Scott. We'll have time to talk another time. For now, these kids are hungry, and I'd like to get them someplace safe."

"Where are the rest of the families that were supposed to be traveling with you?"

"I don't know, Josh? Is that what he called you?"

"Yes, Josh Conyers is my name."

"When we got here, and you fellows weren't anywhere in sight, the others got antsy and decided to try to find a way for themselves. I knew our best chance was to stay as close as possible to the originally planned coordinates, so we hunkered down, and waited."

"You're a smart girl, Becca. We got bogged down by the weather, and then spent a number of nights in a cave on the mountain. Thank you for bringing Scott his little ones. I'm glad to meet you. We're going to find another route back to the mountain. The grass is swamped in about a foot, or so, of freezing water, all the way to the base of the peak, and we didn't make very good time slogging, and tripping, through all those tangled roots. Why don't you hang back with your family, Scott. We'll forge the trail, and you can all follow." Josh sent the other three men on ahead, to scout, and he, Mark, and Scott pulled granola, and jerky out of their packs, to feed Becca and the children. Once everyone had full tummies, they loaded up their packs, and prepared to be on their way.

You O Lord, will keep them; you will guard us from this generation forever. On every side the wicked prowl, as vileness is exalted among the children of man.

Psalm 12:7-8

The fool says in his heart, "There is no God". They are corrupt, they do abominable deeds, there is none who does good. the Lord looks down from heaven on the children of man, to see if there are any who understand, who seek after God.

Psalm 14:1-2

CHAPTER 12

Well, that was it. He'd finally had enough of the infernal excuses, by some of his outlying commanders. Dr. Bahram made arrangements to have a unit sent out to pick up Cage, and a number of additional holdouts, for a long overdue meeting on his home turf. He was unaware that Cage had just left on a mission to track Jana; and that he would stay out on the mountain for any length of time necessary to achieve that goal. But, for his part, he was determined to meet this elusive Colonel, and several others who'd been avoiding his control.

His plans for change, within the United Nations Global Council, were taking shape. Most of the leaders of the combined countries, which would be and were being affected, were too stupid, in his estimation, to catch the real changes. Changes that would alter their lives, and the lives of their constituents, forever. And, for those who might catch on, their power had already been delivered into his hands, so they would be powerless to do anything.

Governing forces were having great success implementing the 'One World Church' idea, within countries where Islam was not the primary religion. They'd successfully closed down most of the institutions in North America, and Europe, which represented a Christian world view. And those few who followed the various Eastern religions, with anything less than a total commitment to their beliefs. Their biggest stumbling block, so far, had been those countries in the Middle East, and on the African Continent, in addition to a few holdouts in Turkey, and Indonesia, where Islam was the primary religion. And where deviating from that ideology, at least as far as the fundamentalists were concerned, was an act punishable by death.

How amusing it was to find that most average Christians, or at least that larger percentage of people who'd always claimed Christianity; though many were without proof of their claims; found it so easy to deny their so called faith in order to save themselves from punishment, or death. But, most of those of the Islamic persuasion would rather die than give up their Allah.

Amir, too, subscribed to Islam. But of the many sects of Islam, his was one followed by fewer members, than some of the others. And, even among Muslims, to be of a different sect than their own, was not much different than being an infidel of another religion. If he really acknowledged the truth, there were more killings committed by Muslim, on Muslim, than there were killings of infidels coming from differing religions. Many of those factions, and sects, were already coming together, as never before, to prepare the way. And, well, he could be pretty convincing when he put his mind to it; so he would persuade even those rare Muslim holdouts, if given sufficient time. Then he would help make way for the 'Twelfth Imam', as was his duty, being a true follower of the one and only Allah, and his true prophet Mohammad.

He knew, when it came right down to it, that it was his responsibility to pave the way for the Mahdi. He'd been groomed for this function his whole life. It even seemed to him that Allah had set up every step of his journey, to lead him here, at this time, and for this very purpose. His father had helped him to keep this secret. And he was grateful for his support, as those in the West, and even Muslims of other sects would never understand his role in these end times. Essentially, the only way to protect the way for Muhammad ibn Hasan al-Mahdi (believed by Twelver Shi'a Muslims to be the Mahdi), was to clear the way of all other religions and sects, through conversion, or elimination. The god these stupid Westerners followed and prayed to, was a false god, as was very clear. This Jesus was a mere prophet, if one could acknowledge him at all. Certainly, Mohammad was a greater prophet, and any one with sense knew that Allah had no son. To even suggest such a thing was blasphemy, and he would not allow their lack of knowledge, and understanding, to impede his mission.

Amir knew the Mahdi to be the ultimate savior of humankind, and the final Imam, of the twelve Imams who would emerge with Isa in order to fulfill their mission of bringing peace, and justice, to the world. All of this in the name of Allah, which is the only way in the minds of true believers, too achieve that world condition.

Twelvers, like Amir, believe that al-Mahdi was born in 869, and assumed Imamate (his duty as an Imam) at the age of five years old, following the death of his father. In order to understand his disappearance and loss of contact with the world, for all these centuries, they assume that times were too dangerous for him. So he went into a phase of Major Occultation, which is a time of purposefully not being in contact with his followers, until he is due to come back on the scene as the Twelfth Imam. Most Muslims, even many who are not Twelvers, believe in the Mahdi's coming universal Caliphate, which will require the total subjugation, of all peoples, to be ruled over by the Twelfth Imam, for, and in the name of Allah.

The only way to assure he would be getting the help he needed; when the time came, for total, and complete domination; was to make sure that all UN armed forces were under his control, and that the commanders of all outlying bases were in sync with his thinking. They would, first and foremost, have to be sure that the leaders of those other religions, of the world, especially Christianity, were completely, and irrevocably, squelched. Only then could they successfully launch an attack on any independent, free thinkers who might stand in their way.

So far they hadn't had any luck locating those hidden, resistance bases, around the country, and around the world, where there seemed to be pockets of opposition. Those infidels who seemed to be overwhelmingly Christian, and completely opposed to implantation. It would be paramount to their survival and victory, as a globally unified government, to locate those traitors, and clean up the mess that seemed to gravitate toward them. For this purpose, Cage and other commanders like him, who were in charge of the outlying PM bases, were essential to his well thought out plan.

• • • • •

Jana had another productive day out on the mount. She felt stronger by the minute, and her mind was clearer than she could remember; due to fresh air, and her one-on-one time with the Father. She couldn't wait to find Josh, but she also coveted the time she spent alone with Jesus, and reveled in this time with her Lord. Again, she managed to snag a large rabbit for her supper, so she cleaned the animal, buried its entrails, and tied the carcass to the back of her pack. She'd continue to get in a bit more mileage, before she secured a cave for the night.

• • • • •

Cage and his troops were out on the peak, and making pretty good time. He was glad he'd brought only those who were out to get the job done, and those few who were still loyal to him. It made his work much easier, when those traveling with him had no false compunction about taking out the enemy, and doing exactly what he'd come out on this mountain to do. Let all the bleeding hearts hang out on base, where he could figure out ways to make them slowly disappear one at a time. He'd had to pull back, a bit, on his efforts to be rid of the last of his witnesses; those who had been present for some of his worst failures, and biggest mistakes. But, he vowed, he would take care of them all, in time. And Satan smiled.

• • • • •

Becca couldn't remember ever feeling so happy. Here

she was, still fleeing for her life, wrangling two small children, doing without what most Americans would claim
were essentials, and so tired she could barely keep up. Yet,
when she watched the kids with their father, she had to
admit it made her glad in a way she couldn't describe; and,
as long as she was being honest, every time she and Scott
came within two feet of one another, her heart skipped a
beat. She hadn't remembered him being so handsome, or
so peaceful, and his eyes had lost that caged animal look
that made him so frightening before. Now, when she was
close to him, she felt safe, and protected.

They were making good time, even with the little ones.
The guys took turns carrying CJ, and Angel, on their shoulders, so the kids, weren't nearly as whiney, or tired, as they'd
been on the long trip to the edge of the forest.

They were scouting out the land, which followed the
edge of the forest, in an effort to find the dirt paths that
Scott followed on his bike, to get to the mountain. It would
save them wading through the freezing marsh of turkey
foot grass to get to their destination.

Meanwhile, Scott was feeling every bit as fluttery as Becca, every time she drew near. Perhaps it was a reaction to
the kindness she'd shown his children, or even that during

their conversations, so far, she'd proved to be a very different person than Gin had painted her to be, when she'd used her sister as an excuse to cover up her own debauchery. But, it could also be that she was very lovely, in a girl next door kind of way, and his heart was softening toward her pretty quickly. Besides, the kids loved her, and seemed almost to have forgotten their mother, who always tended toward cruelty in her dealings with them. He was still married to Gin, though, so he would have to be careful, not to let his feelings take over.

• • • • •

Emma had a dream. In her dream, she saw a cave. In the cave there was a prone figure, bundled in furs, lying by a fire. There was also a man, with the most evil eyes she'd ever seen on any human. He walked into the cave, and prodded the prone figure with his boot. The figure rolled over. It was Jana, and she looked to be about nine months pregnant (though Emma knew it was actually about four months, or so, in reality). In her dream, the man with evil eyes grabbed Jana, tied her up, and dragged her back to a stone prison cell, on the back side of a plateau, out on the mountain. Emma woke crying, and it took Chuck over an hour to calm her down and get her back to sleep, with the help of a soothing cup of Chamomile tea. The same dream woke her again the following night, so she sat in her rocker, praying and soothing herself with the chair's rhythmic movement.

• • • • •

Pastor Mike started an intensive Bible study, with many willing participants, as soon as he healed enough to be out and about. He'd become invaluable to the community in the cavern, and well beloved by all. He, also, for several nights in a row now, had a dream about Jana, and Cage. When the dream occurred, for the third night in a row, he came to Chuck, and Emma, with a question. "Is Jana expecting a baby?"

"Who told you that, Mike?"

"I had a dream. In the dream, Jana was in a cave, and Colonel Cage came looking for her. When she rolled over, she was obviously with child; and about to deliver; from the looks of it. Is there something we should know? I mean, I, above all, know that Jana can take care of herself, but it could be much more difficult if she's also pregnant."

"We weren't supposed to tell anyone, at least not until

Jana had a chance to tell Josh, but it looks like, perhaps, the Lord wants you to know. Yes, she's expecting, and Josh doesn't know yet. We've been hoping she'd come back before he got here, so she could do the explaining, instead of us having to do it. So, that was Colonel Cage?"

"What do you mean?"

"In the dream. Was that him, the man with the evil eyes?"

"Wait, Emma, did you have the same dream?"

"Yes, I did. But, I didn't know who the man with the evil eyes was. It honestly looked like it might be Satan to me."

"Well, there isn't much to distinguish between the two, I guess; but he is a very evil man, who wants nothing in the world more than to take down your son, Josh and his wife. That is why it is so imperative we don't let him get his hands on Jana."

"That would be fine, Mike, but we don't even know where Jana is."

"Then, we will pray. She is in God's hands, and there isn't a better place for her to be."

• • • • •

Jana was startled awake. She lay in an almost dark cave, as the fire dwindled to mere embers. Adding more wood, and collecting her thoughts, she tried to make sense of the nightmare she'd just experienced. In her dream she'd seen Cage's face, and his eyes looked more evil than she remembered, they could very well have been the eyes of Satan. There would be no more sleep tonight, so she pulled out her Bible, and began to read. "I love you, O Lord, my strength. The Lord is my rock and my fortress and my deliverer, my God, my rock, in whom I take refuge, my shield, and the horn of my salvation, my stronghold. I call upon the Lord, who is worthy to be praised, and I am saved from my enemies. The cords of death encompassed me; the torrents of destruction assailed me; the cords of Sheol entangled me; the snares of death confronted me. In my distress I called upon the Lord; to my God I cried for help. From His temple He heard my voice, and my cry to Him reached His ears." Psalm 18:1-6

Jana missed Josh, but the Word always seemed to be a comfort to her, and she drew strength from its promises. Covering her slightly rounded abdomen with her hands, she began to pray. "Lord, protect this child. I'm not sure why I came out here, and put us both in danger. I think

I just missed Josh so much that I wasn't thinking clearly. Please watch over Josh, and those he was sent to rescue; and please save this child you have given to us, to love. I will try not to do anything too stupid. Please get us all home safely. In Jesus Name. Amen."

What had she been thinking? Sure, she was more than capable of taking care of herself, but what right did she have to jeopardize the safety of her child? Josh's child. And, what would he say to her if he were here right now? He would probably be pretty disappointed in her. Actually, he would be very upset with her. Maybe she should turn around and go home? Josh, and the others, were more than likely already back, or just about there. He would be so distressed when he got home and found that she'd left to go find him. Especially after he found out about the baby. And, when he found out she'd snuck off the way she did, leaving his parents to worry, wow, the images she was coming up with were not pretty. Okay, so her mind was made up. At first light she would pull together some breakfast, and then she'd head back to the base. Forget all this nonsense about spying on the PM camp. She had no business putting other lives in danger.

Josh's group found the dirt paths that led to the mountain, and they were headed to the stair stepped wall that led them all to the same mountain peak. Scott was sure they would soon see the giant boulder where he'd hid from the chopper on the night of his wild escape. Perhaps he'd even be able to show them where he'd hid his bike, though, looking back, it was all a bit of a blur.

When the men finally stopped for the night, with their charges, they refrained from starting a fire due to the area's open landscape and serious lack of cover. With weather clearing, the militia would be out in force, looking for defectors. Instead, they chose to fill up on jerky, dried fruit, and granola, with lots of water, and then they slept close together; covered, for the most part, with Becca's camouflaged tarp, and dark blankets. In the morning they would start out fresh. Climbing the face of the mountain was a herculean task, at minimum, even for grownups. This would definitely prove to be a tremendous feat with small children in tow.

• • • • •

Cage continued to dream, and he knew that someone, somewhere out in the universe, was looking out for him, and helping him decide what to do. He continued to dream about Jana, and now his dreams began to include glimpses of Josh as well. He was sure that somewhere, out on the mountain, he would find Jana, and ultimately Josh. He was giddy with excitement. This would truly make his hopes, and dreams, complete. If he could just prove to the world that Josh Conyers was not a better soldier than he. He would show everyone that he was the better warrior, the better strategist, the better man! Then his men would respect him once again.

• • • • •

Becca was completely taken aback by Scott, and he by her. Gin had used her sister as a pawn for so long. Causing him to believe she was a big part of the reason Gin partied, drank, and fooled around with drugs. Now that he was getting the opportunity to know her better, he could see that had been another lie, by his less than honorable wife. Becca was wonderful. Smart, pretty, caring, with a huge heart, and a deep love for his children. Becca, at the same time, was absolutely smitten. She'd only known Scott vaguely in the past, but, since he'd been released from prison, she'd watched him prove to be a good dad to CJ, and Angel; and she'd seen him put up with things from her sister that most men wouldn't.

Though she hadn't really spent enough time with him, previously, to know anything else, she was seeing him for who he really was now. Strong, and caring, smart, and creative. He seemed to have developed a deep spiritual side; which she respected very much. He was handsome too, in a sort of bad boy way, with all his assorted tattoos and scars. Even the idea of him gave her butterflies, so she didn't want to seem too eager to get to know him better. Besides, whether or not either of them liked it, he was still legally married to her sister.

It took her a very long time to fall asleep that first night on the road with the men. Scott's face, and especially his eyes, haunted her. The confident way he walked, and moved. The way the other men seemed to trust him. Little did she know this was a new Scott. The Scott, who had come to be through the love of Christ, and the love and respect of his new brother, Josh. And, similarly, Scott had no idea; as he lay far as possible from Becca; that he was on her mind, but he was having a hard time finding sleep as well. Tripping over Becca, out here in the wilderness, had been a confusing turn of events, to say the least. Even as his children snuggled into his sides, and he fairly glowed with love for them, another part of his mind was moving at a pace faster than the speed of light. With thoughts of this enchanting creature who had suddenly dropped from the sky, as it were, into his life. But, he couldn't let his feelings get away from him. Like it, or not, he was still married to Gin, and he wouldn't allow himself to do anything that would cause him shame before the Father.

• • • • •

Cage was off like a shot. Sniffing in every crag, and corner of the mountain, looking for his prey. If Jana was on this mountain, he would find her. He couldn't wait to have the upper hand, for once, where it came to Josh Conyers. Those soldiers and mercenaries he'd chosen for this trip were along for the ride, and would be handy if Conyers had any fire power with him, but he would have done this on his own if he'd had to. Nothing in his life was more important to him than bringing these traitors to justice.

• • • • •

Jana hadn't fallen asleep again, not after being startled

awake during the night, so she'd kept the fire going inside the cave. Instead of sleeping, she'd brewed a soothing tea, and spent her night in prayer. Prayer for her baby, for Josh, for her in-laws, for their home base, for the weather, for the people Josh had gone to rescue, and for anything else she could come up with. She felt the baby move again, and talked quietly to the little one about her daddy. "You're a very lucky baby, to have a daddy like yours. He will always be there to protect you, just like he's been here to protect me. He loves the Lord, and he will teach you about Jesus. That's something I had to wait my whole life to learn about, little one. There is nothing in the world more important to know, than how much Jesus loves you, so you will start out way ahead of most children. You have a wonderful Grandpa, and Grandma too. They are so excited to meet you, and I have a feeling they are going to spoil you rotten! I'm very excited to meet you too. I can't wait to be your mommy, and do all the things with you that I wish I'd gotten to do with my own parents.

"You know, you may have met your grandparents, the ones on my side, while you were still with God in heaven. I hope you did, because they don't live here anymore. I lost them when I was a little girl. They were killed in an accident.

I want to have the kind of life with you, and your Daddy, that I dreamed of having with my own parents. Birthdays, Christmas, Sunday suppers, and worshipping together; we will love you, and teach you, and have so many great times together. I do love you so much, little one. I'm going to get you home now, safely, and we will wait for your daddy together, like I should have been doing all along. And, when we get there, I will drink plenty of milk. I'm sorry I put you through all of this. But one thing you will learn, quickly, about your mommy, is that I am a bit rash at times. Your daddy helps me tamp that down a bit. I'm sure I will get better, now that I will have you to consider. "

After cleaning up a bit, and eating a breakfast of granola, and more dried fruit, Jana packed her bag, and readied herself to leave the cave. This place which had been her safe haven for the night. It would take her several days of hard hiking to get back home. She was at least a little grateful she hadn't come farther before she was jolted to her senses. Perhaps she could still beat Josh and his men if she hurried. She owed a huge apology to Mom, and Dad, and anyone else she'd worried, back at home base.

• • • • •

"There. Over there, Josh, I'm sure that's where I hid my bike, before I climbed the mountain! See the scrub pines? It's just over there. Hurry, I'll show you."

"Whoa, Scott, If your bike is still there, and it hasn't gone anywhere, it probably won't go anywhere while I walk. I've got CJ on my shoulders, and jogging is out of the question."

"Oh, sure, sorry. Thanks for doing that. I wish I could carry both of them, but my shoulders aren't big enough for that."

"Hey, Pops, I wouldn't worry about it, your shoulders are plenty big, and getting bigger all the time, as I pile more responsibility on them, but hold your horses, I'll be there in a minute."

Sure enough, Scott's bike was right where he left it. No one had spotted it, covered as it was, in branches, and grass. It looked as if it'd served as a home for several assorted small animals throughout its stay in the brush; and the leather on the seat had served as somebody's chew toy. But, aside from that, it was pretty much as he'd left it on his mad dash to the mount. As things stood, he still wouldn't be able to take it with him, so he was comforted in the fact that it was getting some good use. Who knew if it would ever even start again. But, that was of no consequence now, so he threw a few more handfuls of grass over the partially exposed chrome places. Then he headed toward the boulder, which had been his hiding place once before, not so very long ago.

In the distance, and coming closer, they heard the distinct sound of a chopper, and they all dove for cover until the coast was clear.

Preserve me, O God, for in You I take refuge. I say to the Lord, "You are my Lord; I have no good apart from you." As for the saints in the land, they are the excellent ones, In whom is all my delight. The sorrows of those who run after another god shall multiply; their drink offerings of blood I will pour out or take their names on my lips.

Psalm 16:1-4

CHAPTER 13

Amir was in the middle of a very important state dinner, when news arrived that his retrieval units had been unable to secure all their targets. Of the thirteen outlying commanders he'd originally sent for, only two had been located. This was going to be a much larger production than he'd anticipated. He tried to smile, and continue to be charming; to those in attendance. They were, after all, essential contacts for his future plans, and necessary conduits for the huge amounts of money which would be crucial in order to pull off the world wide coup he intended. But inside, he was seething. He was continually surrounded by incompetent peasants, and it would be difficult to achieve his goals, in a country filled with so many idiots, if he didn't maintain control.

They should all be grateful to him. He was attempting to enrich their lives with his intelligence, and ideologies. After all, what did they truly possess now? They prayed to their trite, little, false god, this insignificant Jesus, and their country was falling apart in every conceivable way; morally, economically, and politically. Once the Mahdi was among them, they would see what true divinity looks like, and their pathetic little lives could begin to change for the good. If only they would convert their minds, embrace the truth, the only truth, and come to know the peace of Allah; before they had to be snuffed out like the irrelevant bugs they are. Now, of course, he would be forced to send his retrieval units out again, to secure Cage and the rest of his elusive outlying commanders. In order to conduct their very necessary, if somewhat unsavory, business. He would then find a satisfactory way to make them all pay for holding his plans hostage, with their uncooperative actions, and for their inconvenient lack of availability. They would all soon learn that Dr. Amir Bahram was not one to trifle with, or ignore. The world would soon come to know of his ultimate importance.

$$\bullet \ \bullet \ \bullet \ \bullet \ \bullet$$

The guys stood before a giant boulder. It was the lone sentinel protecting the approach to this side of the behemoth they would soon attempt to scale. Wondering how they would manage to climb the sheer rock wall, with kids in tow, no less. "Well, obviously the children won't be able to climb. We're going to have to rig harnesses, for a couple of us to wear. We'll strap the kids into the harnesses, and do the climbing for them."

"That's a very good idea, Scott. And, you're right, of course. That's the only thing that might work. Now, let's start going through our supplies to see what we have. I'm sure we can come up with plenty of rope, so let's figure out what else we've got that we can utilize."

"Sure enough, Josh. This is the part where we can all pitch in, so I'll see what I can come up with. I just can't believe it."

"Can't believe what, Mark?"

"Well, you know Rachel, Tina's sister, climbed these rocks with my kids. How in heaven's name did she do it? I wish we had her here, right now, so we could pick her brain for ideas. I sure have a whole lot more respect for her now."

"Yeah, that was definitely a feat all right. And, truthfully, I can't imagine how she did it with two children either. We will have to pin her down, and ask her lots of questions, once we get back to base. I'd be very interested in the answers to that one."

"Now, of course I'll carry one of my kids; and, I'd carry both if I could, Josh."

"Yeah, Scott, I know you would, and I'll carry the other one. It only stands to reason, since I'm the biggest guy here, that I would carry the biggest child."

"Thanks, Josh, you know I love ya, and I appreciate everything you do and have done for me. If you'll carry CJ, I will climb with baby Angel."

"Glad to do it, brother. I know you would do the same for me, though, in all sincerity, I hope that never needs to happen. So, let's get set. We've got some building, and finagling, to do before we can be on our way. I don't know when the militia choppers will be back out on another run, so we need to work fast."

All the guys pitched in, using their combined knowledge and ingenuity, to come up with some pretty amazing tools to use on the climb. They all wore fitted, leather gloves, made by hand back at the base, which would help to save their fingertips; and they all had good, solid, hiking boots; a definite plus. It was a bit warmer for this climb, than Scott could remember for his previous assent. Josh, and Mark, for their part, had never actually climbed up this side of the mountain. Their trip to the top had occurred after being captured; while taking a family to safety; so they'd ascended, the first time, by helicopter. That lovely trip, provided by the United States government, ended with a lengthy stay in the prison cells on the plateau. But, both Josh, and Mark, were pretty skilled at just about anything they did, and they were both excellent climbers, so there really wasn't a worry about them getting to the top. The three additional soldiers traveling with them had all made the trip more than once.

The bigger problem would be, Becca. She was not equipped for the climb, and she was tiny enough to guarantee that none of the gear, worn by any of the guys, would have a chance of fitting her. They would adapt gear, as much as possible, to accommodate her. And, they would attach a rope to her jerry rigged harness, of course. But they would almost certainly spend a great deal of time saving her from plummeting the entire length of the cliffs.

What the guys didn't realize, was that Becca was actually in pretty good shape and very flexible. She wouldn't end up being even a small part of their upcoming difficulties.

· · · · ·

"Chuck, I'm really worried. Josh and his group are so terribly overdue; and after that dream I had about Jana, what can we do to help them?"

"You know the answer to that question as well as I do, my dear. Here, sit down with me, and let's pray." Emma sat with her folded hands, enfolded within her husband's folded hands; and a lone tear trailing its way slowly down her ageless face; as her husband began to pray. "Dear Lord, we come to you knowing that you already have our loved ones in the palm of your hand. Please help Josh and his fellows to complete their assignment, and help those families to find their way home to us, and home to you. And, Lord, please bring Jana and our grandchild safely back to us. We know, Father, that you have so many plans for all of us, and that you already have everything under control. We also know that you are still firmly on the throne. Help us to be in your peace, and in your will, Lord. In Jesus' Name, and in His Grace. Amen."

"Amen. Thank you, honey. I shouldn't ever fear when I know God is in control, and I can always come to you for comfort. Thank you for your prayers, and for your confidence in the Lord. You're a good man, Chuck. I'm glad you're my husband, and my best friend."

"Emma, you know you have the same faith I do. You are just allowing worry to creep in. Just know that He loves us, and has plans for us, and that those plans don't involve any of us dying anytime soon. There is just too much for us to do, to mess with all that dying stuff. And, I'm pretty glad you said yes all those years ago, too. You are the best woman I know, and I'm confidant God put us together for a reason. Thank you for all your years of love and respect. You have made it easy to be a good husband. And, just so you know, the members of counsel met to discuss what to do about our little escapee. We were all concerned, and knew how worried you were, so the counsel sent a scout out to be on the lookout for Josh and Jana. His orders are to help Jana, in any way he can, to get back home safely. And if he finds Josh, he is to tell him of his wife's outing on the mountain, so that our son won't have to come clear back here to hear about it. Perhaps there is even some way he can help her."

"Oh, Chuck, thank you for that. You can't imagine how much better I feel knowing that someone is looking for her. Tell the counsel I am grateful, though I don't know why you all felt the need to keep that meeting from me."

"Well dear, you were pretty upset, and we didn't know if you could be objective. However, there were enough others worried that we knew we had to do something, so here we are. Now we'll have to see how it all works out."

"Well, good, I'm feeling better, so I'm going to go help with supper. One of the men brought some freshly harvested beef roasts to the kitchen this morning, so we've got potatoes and carrots to peel. Everything should be ready by five thirty, so don't be late, okay?"

"I'll see you over there. Love you, dear."

"Love you too, Chuck. I don't know what I'd ever do without you."

"Well, then, let's not try to find that out, okay?"

"Very funny. See you for supper."

• • • • •

Jana was exhausted. After her hellish nightmare, and lack of sleep the night before, she already knew she wouldn't have a problem getting a little shut eye when she packed up her little road show tonight.

After polishing off a light breakfast and then taking care of her routine morning wash, Jana made her way outside to one of the most beautiful sunrises she'd ever had the privilege of witnessing. The pre-dawn sky was swathed in pastel layers of lavender, blue, and purple. As the sun rose higher in the sky, she watched it transform to shades of yellow, orange, pink, and red, before it converted to a brilliant, spring blue. The sparkling sun's rays, which filtered through the branches of the scrub pines, danced and twirled ahead of her along the mountain's twisting path like bright fairies. She breathed deeply of the fresh air, and wished with all her heart that Josh was here, this very minute, to share this gorgeous day with her.

Throughout the day, as she hiked, she prayed. "Lord, I know you love me, and that your hedge of protection surrounds me. I ask you to keep Josh safe in his travels, and to keep your hand on this child that I carry. Bring Josh and I back together again. Give Chuck and Emma the peace of knowing that I'm fine, that their grandchild is fine, and that we are on our way home to them. Protect those on the resistance base who are living and moving in your name, against the principalities and powers who would act to destroy them, this nation, and all who would worship you in word and truth. Thank you, Lord, for your never ending love and Grace, at all times. In Jesus' Name. Amen"

Sunlight, reflecting off of glistening ice and snow, which still covered the heights in large mounds, caused a magnificent, dazzling display; but also made it difficult to see, even through her skier's grade sun glasses. So she was mindful of her position at all times, and took special care to watch her steps. Ledges could be especially dangerous this time of year, with ice and snow pulling away from cliff edges, and plummeting to the depths below.

She'd awakened, still plagued by an uneasy feeling, which did not depart with the coming of morning. Knowing it was simply residual discomfort, from that horrible nightmare the night before, she tried to dismiss it and go on with her assent. But in the back of her mind, the tension was very real. She would attempt throughout the day to be extra vigilant, but didn't want to be paranoid. She knew that Cage was a coward of the highest degree, and he wasn't particularly fond of being out on the mountain, so that left very little chance he would ever come knocking on her proverbial door.

Throughout the unusually long day, Jana heard the distinct sounds of giant ice flows cracking, and breaking apart. Followed by great avalanches of actively melting snow falling from cliffs around, and below, her. Some sudden landslides so great they reverberated through the air, like claps of thunder from heaven frightened her, and set her nerves on edge.

Spring thaw hadn't managed to work its amazing and devastating magic, quite as well, this high on the mount, where the permafrost went much deeper. And, as she rose higher, she was sure there were small streams of frazil ice, from those melting ice flows, running down the mountain, in slushy, frothy, almost lava like rivers. She could imagine spring runoff collecting in foaming streams, from all parts of the great mount, to be washed away, eventually, with the last vestiges of winter.

She would spend the night in another cave, and as evening crept in, she narrowed her search to an area around the next bend. After finding a suitable location, she filled her pots and canteens, and cut pine boughs for her bed and door. Just as dusk fell, a pair of rabbits scampered in her path, and her knife flew with an accuracy which would assure her prey felt no pain. She skinned and gutted her supper, and prepared a fire. She was bone tired. More tired than she could remember being in a very long time, and she wondered at the extreme exhaustion. Sure, the night before this kind of fatigue made sense, because the night before that one, her attempt at a siesta had been filled with Colonel Cage's evil eyes, and subsequently, no slumber. But last night was different. She'd slept soundly last night.

Well, she was expecting a baby after all, and she had been driving herself pretty hard. Perhaps a few extra hours of sleep tonight wouldn't hurt. It was settled. She would roast her rabbit, eat her supper, read her Bible, and curl up by the fire for a good night's rest.

She'd decided long ago, out here on the mountain, that roasted rabbit was one of her favorites, and she reconstituted some dried fruit to accompany her meal. Eating every bit of the succulent juiciness, including sucking the marrow from the delicate bones; and licking her fingers afterward; she cleaned up her mess, and brushed her teeth. She was looking forward to an early night even more than she'd imagined. As soon as she curled up by the fire, and opened her Bible, she dropped off into a deep sleep, and was soon in the arms of Jesus.

• • • • •

Harnesses were set, and packs loaded. Night time was the only safe time to ascend the cliffs, and stand a chance of not being seen by militia choppers. Once they were covered by sufficient darkness they began their long climb. Scott insisted that he be able to climb near Becca, in case she needed some extra help, and though Josh wondered how he would help Becca with a small child strapped to his back, he didn't argue. He was carrying CJ, who began to whimper quietly, as soon as the climb began. Josh understood. The kid was hanging from his back, farther, and farther up the side of a mountain, and had no way of catching himself if he began to fall. So, Josh tried to comfort him, "Hey, CJ, you know what?"

"No?"

"I'm an expert mountain climber. I'll bet you didn't know that, did you?"

"No."

"Well, I am, and I've never, ever, fallen off of a mountain!"

"You haven't?"

"Nope, not one. And, you know what else?"

"What?"

"Up at the top of this mountain is a wonderful place. It's a place filled with good food, and warmth, and kids to play with, and my wife, Jana. And I can't wait to see her again. So, I'm not going to fall. Do you understand me?"

"Yes, Sir."

"Also, and this is the most important thing. Jesus is holding us up."

"Jesus?"

"Yes, He's our Lord, and He will keep us safe."

"Okay."

"So, don't be afraid, okay?"

"Okay, I won't.

"Thank you, Josh. For those words of comfort. I think we all needed to hear them."

"You're welcome, Scott. Now, we need to climb."

Scott remembered this climb, and how it had torn up his hands the first time. The gloves were a help, but he was still having a heck of a time finding good hand, and foot, holds, between the stair step ledges. Each time they reached a small ledge, they stopped to rest for a short while, and then they pressed on. They'd been at it for hours, but Josh could see the edge of a plateau above them, and he knew that on that level they would be able to find some small caves. Josh reached the ledge first, and was helping some of the guys over. Scott was reaching for his last hand hold before the ledge, and his foot slipped. He hung by one hand, and Angel screamed. The next thing he knew, a strong hand was helping him back to the rock, and up to the ledge. "Thanks, Josh. Thanks for catching me."

"That wasn't me, Scott. That was Becca who caught you and the baby."

"Wow, Becca, thanks. I had no idea you were that strong. Remind me never to think of you as 'just a girl' again, okay"

"Will do, Scott. Happy to help. I told you I would never let anything happen to these kids, and I meant it."

"Well, praise God for that!"

• • • • •

Cage woke in the night. He could feel her near. He knew it was Jana, but he also knew there was something different about her. The evil, that was filling him with these new snippets of knowledge, wanted Josh and Jana dead as much as he did; and it wouldn't stop until the deed was done. Cage woke his troops, and readied himself for a midnight trek.

• • • • •

While Cage was out on the mountain earlier that day, a transport had come to take him to an important meeting with the new head of the UNGC. The transport left, but gave instructions that Cage be notified to report to head-quarters as soon as he returned. The militia men who'd been left behind were confused by the urgency of the request, but wondered if there might be any chance of their own extraction from this impossible situation through this odd turn of events. Cage was right, not to trust them anymore.

Those who had not been murdered yet, should, by all means, be fearful for their lives. The 'accidents', which had taken the lives of countless of their comrads, were obvious in their intent and outcome. These men had witnessed the insane will of their commander, on so many occasions now, that they knew full well he intended to do away with them all if he was given half a chance.

Of course he no longer had their loyalty. Why should he? And, further, they would do all they could to thwart his plans, and those of his Muslim mercenaries. They had, in-deed, begun to see that the resistance movement's platform made sense. And, if this world was ever to have a chance to get back to a place where regular people could live, and worship, as they pleased, then people like Cage, and those he answered to, must be stopped. This might require them to make a stand, which would put their own lives at even greater risk, but they were through groveling to a man like Cage.

• • • • •

Entirely spent, Josh's group sat on the first substantial ledge they accessed, gathering enough energy to go on. They would find a cave in which to spend the night, and then they would get their bearings in the morning. Mark was the first one to get sufficient breath back to begin a search for shelter. The first opening turned out to be so small it wouldn't come close to accommodating their group; though he was sure he saw evidence of previous use by someone in the past. But the second cave he found seemed large enough, to provide protection from the elements, for all of them.

Once everyone was safely packed inside, the guys ventured back out. They collected fire wood, and water, and then took their finds back inside and built a large, warming blaze. A pair of hapless squirrels met their death, at the end of Scott's swift knives; and were quickly cleaned and readied for the roasting spits, before anyone knew what happened. A couple of the guys pulled out dried fruit, and grains, to add to the meal. Once they were boiled together, they made a delightful sweet mash. The canteens were refilled, and a pot of tea was simmering on the fire ring. Josh said a prayer of thanks giving, and after a hearty meal, and a time of cleaning up, the group sat around the fire for Bible study.

Becca felt a little uncomfortable. All the guys had their own Bibles, and seemed to know what Josh was talking about, including Scott, so her lack of knowledge was as plain as the nose on her face. Scott could see her stress, so he scooted a bit closer. The children climbed on their laps, and he opened his Bible to the appropriate verses, in order to share with her in a way that would make her more at ease. As she heard the message of God's Grace, and the sacrifice of Jesus; for the first time in her life; she sat stunned. Nothing in her time on this earth, had ever made her feel more accepted, and valuable, and now she began to understand the enormous change in Scott; from the man she'd known; to the man he clearly was today.

Josh said a prayer, and advised that everyone turn in. It was late. Since they'd scaled the heights after dark, and taken care of their supper, and Bible study, well into the night. So they all got comfortable, and did their best to get a good night's sleep.

• • • • •

Satan was working overtime in the hearts and minds of Cage and his crew; and the man fairly salivated at the idea of finally getting his hands on Jana and Josh. He couldn't sleep, or eat, and the look in his eyes was more deranged than ever before. Even those couple of subordinate officers who had, up to now, been behind him; no matter the twisted decisions he made; were loath to follow his every command as he descended further into madness.

To the degree they did follow, they followed simply because they believed Cage to be their best route to a command of their own. But, even with that, they grew more uncertain about his ability to make rational decisions each day.

And, the Muslim mercenaries who followed, or, more accurately, went along for the opportunity to kill more infidels, spoke among themselves of the lunacy which seemed to have engulfed this madman so completely. Currently, they waited. As soon as they received word from their command, about supplies they were expecting for missions coming up; and they were in a position to strike more terror in the lowlands; they would be off. They owed Cage no more loyalty, than he owed them. For now they would help him capture this Christian traitor and his woman, and maybe even get an opportunity to take part in the humiliation of these non-believers. That remained to be seen. The Colonel seemed pretty intent on saving all that excitement for himself.

• • • • •

Scott would have to be careful. Just the nearness of her made him uneasy. He knew he was still a married man, but her huge, brown eyes; the way she flipped her hair, to get it out of her face; and her musical laughter, were enough to cause him serious anxiety. He knew the children loved her too, and that made it even more difficult to remain at a distance. He laid in the darkness of the cave, after a great Bible study and time of fellowship, and wondered if God wanted him to stay faithful to the woman who had cheated on him, and turned him over to the authorities. He would have to ask Josh about that one. For now, he would need to keep a lid on his feelings.

Scott felt he didn't dare risk letting Becca, or anyone else know how he was feeling. Little did he know, however, that the woman of his deepest desire, who lay just feet from him, was suffering from the same dilemma. Becca thought Scott was just about the greatest guy she'd ever met, and she already loved his kids, heck, they were her own nephew, and niece. And, let's face it, she'd already had a great deal to do with raising them for these past few months.

Becca felt safe and special in his presence, and that was something she'd never felt with anyone before, not even in her parent's home. Without any experience concerning men to look back on, she still guessed it took more than feeling safe around someone to grow a lasting relationship. And she also knew the man she was currently dreaming about was married to her own; though, admittedly, very undeserving; sister.

• • • • •

Jana was deep in the throes of a terrible nightmare. She'd dropped off early, still holding her Bible in her arms, wrapped up like a burrito in front of a blazing fire. And, just after she'd fallen asleep she'd found herself enfolded in the arms of Jesus, sharing a beautiful time of fellowship. But, while she slept, a dark cloud of misgiving collected over her head, albeit entirely in her dream. If one had happened to be in the cave with her, they would have seen the look on her face change from peaceful, to deeply troubled, and then terrified, as she slept. She'd been filled with regret, anxiety, and doubtfulness since coming to the realization she should never have left the safety of her community; at least not in the condition she was in; that those familiar old feelings of self loathing were crossing over into her psyche, even in her sleep.

The dark cloud in her dream, grew in intensity, until she was fairly blinded by its presence. In the middle of the fog, she saw a pair of eyes. They were glowing red, and so filled with malice, that she felt quite literally frozen in place. Lifting her legs proved difficult, as her feet seemed stuck to the ground. She twisted and pulled, and managed to get them free. Turning to flee she fell to the ground directly at his feet, which changed before her eyes, from military, hiking boots, to cloven hooves. Opening her mouth to scream, she found it instantly filled with the awful fog. It was hot, and bitter, and she began to choke. Struggling to move, she found herself encased in a cocoon. Just then she opened her eyes, and realized she was still in the small cave where she'd fallen asleep, wrapped in her own blankets. She shuddered in relief, as she realized it was only a dream. But, then, she felt something nudge her back, and a chill ran the length of her spine. Turning her head, she found the same evil eyes from her nightmare, staring down at her.

• • • • •

Cage couldn't believe his good fortune! He and his men had been out on their midnight patrol, when he'd seen the reflections of a fire, coming through the pine bough barrier, of a small, recessed cave. He'd crept to the opening, and saw a figure bundled up, by the fire. He felt a surge of excitement, as he realized that the picture in front of him, was exactly like that of his dream. He knew he had found Jana. He quietly removed the pine bough barrier, and snuck into the cave. For a long while he just stood and watched the young woman sleep. She seemed to be disturbed, and he relished the idea of her waking to see him standing over her.

Savoring every moment of his exhilarating triumph. He almost didn't want to wake her up in order to make the moment last longer, but then the exquisite joy of seeing the look on her face as she realized it was he awakening her, would be so rewarding he had to nudge her with the toe of his boot. He was right. The look on her face was priceless, and he would do it all over again, if he could elicit the same response. There was something different about her. He couldn't quite figure it out yet, but he would. All he knew for now, was that his greatest dreams were about to be fulfilled.

She looked truly horrified to see him, before covering her feelings of fear, with a look of defiance. She struggled at first to release herself from the fabric cocoon in which she was encased, and then finally she was free, and gained her feet. Yes, there was most certainly something different about her. What was it? Her eyes still flashed confidence, and total hatred, even in this compromising position, but there was something about her stance. He took a step toward her, and her hands instinctively dropped to cover her abdomen. "Oh, my word, Jana. You're with child. How could this get any better?"

"Stay back, Cage. Keep your hands off me. Josh will be here any minute, and he will never let you get away with this." How could she have slept through his entrance into the cave? She usually had the instincts, and reflexes, of a cat.

"My dear, you are a very bad liar. Your Josh isn't anywhere around. We've been canvassing the mountain for days, and you are the only one we've found. Now, why would you be out on this mountain alone? And, in your delicate condition no less? Is your base close by? Or, are you out searching for someone? Well, my sweet young lady, I can tell you right now, that you should never play poker. Your face is as easy to read as the Sunday paper. So, you are out here alone, searching for someone. My guess is that your Josh is the only one you would risk your current condition to find, so he must be out here somewhere too.

"Certainly he would never let you out to traipse these mountains in your delicate state, so he must be unaware of your present condition, or your travels. Oh, this is even better than I thought! I actually know of this impending blessed event, before your dear husband! How divine. Well, we will take you back to camp, and await the arrival of your wayward soul mate. I can't wait to see the look on his face when he arrives to find out about the upcoming birth. I will allow him to revel in his impending fatherhood, for a few moments, before I cut the brat from your belly as he watches. He can see you both die, before I kill him slowly. What fun! I don't think I've ever looked so forward to anything in my entire life."

"You wouldn't dare. Even your evil commanders would never allow you to do something so heinous. And, remember how I bested you before. What makes you think I don't have a contingency plan? I'm telling you now, you wicked man, you will never get away with any of this."

"Oh, my dear, I will get away with this, and much more. You will tell me the position of the ARM base; you will turn over your husband, and all your friends, and relatives, and more. You will do whatever I say, if there is even a chance of saving the life of the little monster you carry."

"I would never tell you a thing, Cage. You can stop your little guessing game right now. I'm not searching for anyone. I'm simply out on the mountain because I missed the fresh air. And, no, there is no base, so you may as well give up right now."

"Men, get in here, and tie her up. Be careful with her. I don't want anything to happen to the brat she carries, until I have her husband safely tucked away in the prison cells on base."

Jana didn't try to fight. There were too many of them, and she didn't want to risk hurting her child. Was Cage right? Would she sacrifice everything, and everyone, she knew to protect her baby? And, what if she did? Wouldn't he still kill her, and the child? For now she would go without a struggle. There wasn't anything she could do alone, and she needed some time to think.

• • • • •

In a small cave, on a lower level of the mountain, Josh and his team slept. He'd spent most of the short night tossing and turning, regardless of the exhaustion he felt from the day's activities. At the moment Jana woke, to Cage standing above her, Josh woke gasping for breath, and drenched in sweat. He knew there was something wrong, and he knew it had to do with Jana, but what could he do? Tears ran freely, from his tired, bloodshot eyes, as he broke down in earnest prayer, for his beloved Jana.

The Lord is my light and my salvation; whom shall I fear? The Lord is the stronghold of my life; of whom shall I be afraid? When evildoers assail me to eat up my flesh, my adversaries and foes, it is they who stumble and fall. Though an army encamp against me, my heart shall not fear; though war arise against me, yet I will be confident. One thing have I asked of the Lord, that will I seek after; that I may dwell in the house of the Lord all the days of my life, to gaze upon the beauty of the Lord and to inquire in His temple. For He will hide me in His shelter in the day of trouble; He will conceal me under the cover of His tent; He will lift me high upon a rock.

Psalm 27:1-5

CHAPTER 14

"Private Phillips, move the existing prisoners from the last cell. I want her to be kept alone, until we can lay our hands on that traitor, Conyers."

"Yes Sir, but what should we do with the prisoners from that cell? The other cells are all up to capacity. We have two women, and their four children, in that last cell right now, Sir."

"You can walk them right over to the back of the plateau. That will take care of the problem quickly, and without a mess."

"Sir? I don't think I can do that, Sir. I know you and your mercenaries regularly dispatch women and children when you're in the process of interrogating them, but I've never actually had anything to do with that. They're just innocent women, and children, Sir."

"You will do as you are ordered to do, soldier, or you will be marching off that cliff with them. Do you understand me?"

"Yes, Sir, right away Sir."

Phillips knew he couldn't murder these mothers and their blameless children, but wasn't sure what to do after receiving such tough orders. He, along with most of the troops left on the PM base, knew Cage was the epitome of evil; and that he had absolutely no regard for human life; but he'd never been put in the position of having to carry out those unsavory orders himself. It was one thing to kill another person in combat, to protect your life, or your country. Every soldier had to make life and death decisions on the field of battle. But, these prisoners were guiltless, and had already suffered quite enough, at the hands of this tyrant. Cage, along with his merciless cronies, had murdered plenty of them. He knew he couldn't be party to taking the lives of these innocent souls, whose only sin, that he could see, was the desire to be free from the government's tracking chips.

He quickly located a length of rope, and took off to collect his charges. Coming up with a plan, he opened the cell, and whispered to the women. "Listen to me very carefully. Cage has ordered me to kill you by dropping you off the back side of this plateau. If we are going to have any chance of saving you, you need to do exactly what I tell you."

"Yes Sir. What do you want us to do?"

"First, I'm going to tie this rope around you, one at a time, as if I'm trying to keep you from escaping. I want you to scream, cry, and plead for your lives. This is very important. This has to be convincing. Do you understand?"

"Yes, but what, exactly, are we doing?"

"I happen to know that there is a narrow ridge about eight feet below the top of the plateau. It's dark, right now, but there is a full moon tonight, and I'm going to try to lower you to that ledge. From there you will have to find your way. That's all I can do to help you."

"Thank you. I don't know how we can ever repay you."

"By screaming as if I've pushed you off of a plateau, which is thousands of feet above the abyss where you are supposedly being thrown."

"God bless you. We will do you proud. Anyone listening will think you have carried out your horrible duty."

At that, Phillips took the prisoners, one at a time, and lowered them off the plateau to the ridge below, as they screamed bloody murder, and pleaded for mercy. He lowered the women first, and then their children, so there would be someone to guide the little ones along the narrow way. As they sought safety in the trees once they had cleared the ledge they waved to him, and he watched them go until they were around the bend, hoping they'd found enough solid ground to get them to their destination. All he had to do now was look as though he was devastated about having to kill those women and children until Cage saw him. This would be his greatest test.

Once the cell was empty, he reported back to his commander. "The cell is empty Sir."

"Good, you did as I told you to do?"

"Yes Sir, all prisoners from that cell are over the cliff, Sir."

"Good man. Now that I know I can depend on you, I will be calling on you more often."

"Yes Sir. Very well Sir."

The soldier shuddered as he turned and left Cage's quarters. There was something tremendously unsettling about being in the presence of pure evil. Soon, Jana was locked safely away in the cold, dark cell. She told herself she wouldn't cry; couldn't give that maniac the satisfaction of knowing he'd gotten to her. But as she sat alone, and began to remember all the ways she'd messed up by leaving the safety of the resistance base, the tears began to flow. She curled up, and began to rock herself, just as she had when she was a small child. And then she began to pray.

• • • • •

Josh knew something was wrong with Jana, but what? All he could do was pray. His night passed slowly, and without any significant sleep. In the morning he wasn't his usual self, and all the guys wondered what was going on. "You okay, Josh?"

"No, Mark, I had a nightmare last night, and I'm sure Jana is in some kind of trouble. I just don't know what I can do about it."

"Hey, man, the people back on base aren't going to let anything happen to her. Your folks would watch over her, if nothing else. You know that like you know your own name."

"I know, Scott, and yet I can't shake this feeling. I know she needs me. We have to get some miles under our belts today. Let's take turns carrying the kiddos, okay?"

"Sure, anything you say. But, if you need to scoot, the rest of us guys can take care of things. I can get Becca and the kids safely back home. One less man won't make that much difference now. The climbing is a lot easier from here on out anyway."

"Okay, I think I'll take you up on that, if you're sure you guys have got it."

"Yes Sir, Boss man. We can handle it from here. We will keep you in prayer, and hope you get to Jana as quick as possible."

"Thank you. All of you. I will keep you in my prayers too. Travel back the way we mapped out. It will get you home the safest. Love you all, and God bless."

"God bless you too, brother. Now, get a move on. Your lady needs you."

Josh emptied all but the smallest rations, from his pack, to leave for his friends. Then, throwing the bag over his shoulder he was off. He would take a more dangerous route back up the mount, one he and the guys had decided would never work with the children. But, by himself he could move more swiftly, and would be able to handle obstacles that the kids couldn't have managed. His heart was beating so fast, and so hard, that he prayed for God to reach inside him to calm him down before he had a heart attack. He knew his wife needed him, but not just that she needed him, that she needed him badly and right now.

• • • • •

Emma woke crying. She knew Jana was in trouble. She'd seen those same evil eyes that haunted her previous dreams, and knew that Satan had Jana in his sights. When she woke, a heavy cloud hung over her, and threatened to suffocate her. Chuck held her, and tried to reassure her, but to no avail. She would not be comforted. Her first grandbaby was in danger.

• • • • •

Cage was simply walking on air. Glee filled his black soul to a degree he'd never experienced before. He began to plan, to fantasize really, about the tortures he would perform on Jana, while Josh watched. He would make the pain last as long as possible; pull the child from her very womb, and crush it to bits before their eyes. He would break Jana's limbs, one by one, put out her eyes; and when she couldn't live through one more assault on her body, he would have his Muslim friends remove her head and mount it on a pole at the entrance of the camp.

He knew Josh wouldn't care much about any tortures he committed on him, once his woman and child were out of the picture; so a simple disemboweling and beheading would do. The two heads, on pikes, at the front of the base, would stand as a warning to those who might question his prowess and authority. He knew how many troops in his camp would like nothing more than to see him relieved of power. Well, they would be waiting for a long, long time for that to happen.

• • • • •

As predawn light began to peek through the bars in her cell, Jana looked over her surroundings to get a better feel for the predicament in which she'd placed herself. Of course she hadn't slept at all, from the moment she'd been captured, but she was much too filled with anxiety to think about sleeping anyway. The cell was rather large, and could probably accommodate up to ten men, comfortably; or more, if they were packed in like sardines. There was a natural stone ledge, about two feet off the floor, that ran two thirds of the way around the room. A bucket, for taking care of necessities, was stashed in the back and reeked with years of use; no matter how many times it had been emptied; blood stains colored the stone beneath her feet, and caused her to wonder at their origins; names, dates, and various personal notes, were etched in the rock all around the cave. Scripture verses, last letters to loved ones, countdowns to important events, or tallies of days spent incarcerated, abounded. One that broke her heart read: "Please tell my wife and daughter I love them, and that I will see them again in heaven. Mike P." She would have to check when she got back to base, to see if anyone knew a Mike P. Perhaps he was one of the men she'd freed, that snowy day so many months ago. She would like to think so anyway. The pain and despair; of prisoners come, and gone, those who couldn't stand up to the torture even one more day, and those who'd died of starvation, or exposure; fairly wept through the stone walls around her, but she couldn't let it defeat her. She had her child to consider.

As she sat and prayed, or to be more accurate, begged for her life and the life of her child, a voice came to her. It was so loud, in the mostly empty cave, that she was positive anyone standing outside the door could have heard. She knew the voice belonged to Jesus. Because, though she hadn't been listening very attentively as of late, she had come to know His voice quite well. "My child."

"Yes Lord."

"Do not despair. I am with you."

"Thank you, Lord. I know I'm not supposed to worry, but I'm afraid for the life of my child."

"Don't fear for the child you carry, Jana. I have great plans for your son."

"It's a boy? I'm going to have a son?"

"Yes, and you shall call his name, Alec, which means 'Man's defender, warrior.'"

"Alec, I like that. Yes, Lord, his name will be Alec."

"Now, don't be afraid, my sweet child. You have been through much in your years on this earth, but I know you will be strong for Me and for your family. Help is on the way, and will be here soon. Just believe in Me."

"Yes, Lord. I'm so sorry I didn't listen when Emma told me it was foolish to go out in search of the guys, and I'm sorry that I put my baby at risk."

"I know, child. For now, just be secure in the fact that I am with you. I will never leave you, or forsake you. Lean on me. Don't give Satan the satisfaction of seeing fear in your eyes."

"Yes, Lord. I will lean on you. Thank you for loving me, Lord. I love you too."

Nothing that Cage, or his mercenaries could think, or do, could frighten her now. She knew Jesus was on her side, watching over her, and keeping her safe. She couldn't wait to tell Josh about the baby, her conversation with the Lord, and the baby's name. Alec. She liked that name a lot. She hadn't really thought very much about names, since she and Josh hadn't had a chance to talk about the upcoming birth. But, now that she'd heard the name out loud, she thought it was a strong name. A name worthy of a soldier of God.

She wasn't frightened anymore. Cage couldn't do, or say anything which would change that now. He had no power over her. Satan had no power over her. All the negative thoughts and feelings, which had been plaguing her since Josh left the resistance base had vanished with those few comforting words from her Savior. She felt refreshed and renewed in God's love. Now, she just had to remain confident in Him to the very end.

• • • • •

Josh ran through the night. Covering vast amounts of ground in his haste to get to Jana back home. He was sitting under an old scrub pine, rehydrating and eating a piece of jerky, when he saw a soldier from home hustling by on the path beneath him. "Hey, soldier, is that you, Jack? Why are you out here so far from home?"

"Josh?"

"Yeah, it's me. If you're looking for the guys and the family we rescued, I sent them another way. This path would've been too hard on the children."

"No, no, it's actually you that I've been sent out to find."

"Me? Does this have anything to do with my wife?"

"Yes, it does. Jana left the base many days ago. We think she was looking for you, because your group was so late getting back."

"Yes, we got held up by weather, but why didn't someone try to stop her?"

"Your mom did try to stop her, but she lit out in the middle of the night, and no one knew she was gone until the next day."

"So, this is what my dreams have been about. You know, Jack, I knew she was in trouble, but I couldn't figure out what the problem was."

"Well, that's not the half of it, Josh. I guess your parents have known for some time, but none of us knew, because she wanted to be the one to tell you first."

"Wanted to tell me what?"

"She's pregnant, Josh. You're going to be a dad. The problem is, no one knows where she is, but your mom has been having dreams about a man with evil eyes."

"Cage. He's got her. I knew something was wrong. That's why I've been having these nightmares. Jack, you can stay with me, but I don't expect you to. I'm going to have to go to the militia camp, and see if I can find my wife before that madman does something to her, or my baby. There's no way for me to let my parents know you've found me, or that I'm headed out to get Jana back, so I'd prefer if you would head back home and tell them all what's going on. I'll see you shortly. With God's help. I need to save my wife."

"I'll get back as quick as I can. Good luck, and God speed, my friend."

"And, you too, Jack. Tell my parents I love them, and I will be bringing their daughter in law, and their grandbaby home soon."

"I will. You will be in my prayers.

• • • • •

Cage could sense things coming together. He knew Josh was near. He could feel it. He'd waited so long for this moment, and he would savor it. He and his mercenaries were out on the mountainside day, and night, waiting for Josh to show. They were quiet as mice as they waited. He would never know what hit him. Everyone had orders not to kill, though no one had been told not to injure. Josh would be his to toy with. The colonel could see his Muslim friends were not happy about his most recent orders, but, at least for now, they all answered to him. So long, it had been so long. Nothing would stand in the way of his fulfilled fantasies this time.

• • • • •

The baby moved again. It wasn't just a flutter anymore. Now she could feel solid kicks, and whenever he was especially active, she talked to him. "Whoa, baby Alec. You're going to bruise your mom from the inside out, with all your line dancing. Alec, do you like your name? I do. I think it sounds very strong. The Lord told me He has special plans for you, son. And, I'm here to tell you that when God has extraordinary plans for your life, you'd better buckle up and hold on tight. He and I have been friends for awhile now, and He has kept me pretty busy. He also told me that help is on the way, so I don't think we're going to have to stay in this cold, dark place much longer. When God makes a promise, He always comes through."

• • • • •

He wouldn't be able to make it all the way to the militia base in one day. It was too bad he'd run all those extra miles, expending so much energy; headed back home to the resistance base; before he discovered Cage most probably held Jana in his prison cells on the plateau. He'd have to make up time, but he was going to have to get a little sleep tonight, or he wouldn't be any good to anyone. He continued throughout the day, headed in the direction of his love and life, Jana. Nothing on this earth could keep him from her side.

He bagged a rabbit, and then field dressed it, knowing it would make an excellent meal. As dusk fell, he discovered a small cavern, found enough wood to last the night, filled his canteens, built a fire, and put the hare that would be his supper on a spit over the fire. He munched on a handful of granola, and pulled out his Bible, as he waited for the rabbit to finish cooking. Reading, in Philippians, he came across a verse, which was always very comforting to him. "What then? Only that in every way, whether in pretense or in truth, Christ is proclaimed, and in that I rejoice. Yes, and I will rejoice, for I know that through your prayers and the help of the Spirit of Jesus Christ this will turn out for my deliverance, as it is my eager expectation and hope that I will not be at all ashamed, but that with full courage now as always Christ will be honored in my body, whether by life or by death. For to me to live is Christ, and to die is gain. Philippians 1:18-21

Josh knew he would gladly lay down his life for Jana and his baby, just as Jesus had laid down His life for them all. A baby. A little baby. His baby. He was going to be a dad. Even in his current predicament, he couldn't help but smile.

• • • • •

Scott and Mark had their work cut out for them. They thanked the Lord they had three more strong soldiers with them on this journey home. The children walked some, but mostly the men took turns carrying the little ones. In the lower regions the snow had become slushy, and then at night when the temperatures dropped, it refroze and created furrows and ridges, which would have been too difficult for kids to navigate. As they continued, higher on the mount, the slush was replaced with deeper snow, and colder temps.

Thankfully they'd been able to find caves and caverns, large enough to accommodate their whole group, so they could build fires for warmth. And they were grateful they continued to find small game along the way to add to their staples. Meals were actually quite nice, including: grains, dried fruits, and herbs; and hydration was more than adequate, as their canteens, and pots were always filled with clean, cold water. If Scott had one complaint, it would be that some of the caves they'd occupied were a bit on the snug side, and required very close quarters. It was becoming harder to stay at arm's length from Becca. At times he was so flustered he couldn't remember his own name. And, at times Becca mistook his uncomfortable demeanor for an aversion to her. She liked him a great deal, and when it seemed that the feelings were not reciprocated, she felt a deep sadness. He wished he could tell her the feelings were, indeed, shared, but he didn't want to paint them both into a corner, from which there would be no escape.

· · · · ·

Josh hadn't slept well. He tried to rest, but was haunted by the thoughts of what Cage might be doing to his wife and baby. He'd prayed off and on throughout the night, and finally came to a place of peace. He knew Cage wanted him. He would go to the militia camp, and turn himself in. Perhaps he could bargain for Jana's release. Maybe, once Cage found out what Jana's condition was, he would allow her to leave. Then he could do whatever he wanted to do with Josh. Obviously he didn't want to die. He'd never even met his own child. But, if his death meant his wife and child could live, then it was a sacrifice worth making. He should be able to make it as far as Cage's base before the day was done.

· · · · ·

Jana was grateful for her furs. They were the only things between her and the cold. She hadn't been given any supplies with which to make a fire; and only meager food and water rations. She had no extra water with which to wash up, and certainly nothing to make the hard stone easier to lay upon. Well, she reasoned, she was after all in prison.

Cage hadn't tried to make further contact with her, since she'd been locked away in this cell, and she wondered at his whereabouts. All the threats he'd made. Why hadn't he tried to garner any information from his new prisoner? Overhearing the guards talking a bit, she wondered at their loyalty to their commander. One of the fellows had been relating a story to another about some women and children he'd helped to escape, after Cage ordered him to kill them. She heard one of the guards repeating what Cage told him he planned to do with Jana and her unborn child. And the horror in his voice, was apparent with the telling. It didn't appear there was much allegiance to their commander, from hearing the men who were posted as guards on the prison cells, and that might be a very good thing for her.

●　●　●　●　●

Dr. Bahram was growing impatient. He'd had meeting after meeting with the UNGC, and was anxious to get going on some more personal pursuits. Some of the outlying commanders had been located, and he wanted to begin wooing them with his plans. But, so far, no one had produced Colonel Cage. The man was one of the principle keys to his plan, and once again he sent a retrieval team to gather him. He would have his meeting. It was imperative he begin working with these men, to help them understand the importance of his mission, for the return of the Mahdi, on this earth.

Amir knew; since these men had been relegated to commands at outlying bases; that their assignments were made, in large part, due to their inability to follow orders and get along with others. And for their unconventional, but proven, practices when dealing with resistance runaways. Due to these things, he was more likely to be able to appeal to their baser natures. Further yet, that every single one of them was more involved in his own interests, than with the state of the nation they served. So, he would have a very great chance of winning them over to his side, offering enough wealth, power, and personal gain, to make their heads swim. He wasn't sure about this Cage. He'd not had the opportunity to talk to the elusive colonel.

The prior administration had been foolish in many ways. Their goals were focused on their own personal gain, similar to the goals of these men, but without any greater purpose in mind. They had nothing to offer these outlying commanders, that was not already available to them, just for the simple taking.

Throughout the whole of the government before him, there was not a single great hope, nor a solitary noble plan for humanity to rally around. So, of course they'd all strayed from any righteous intention. Intentions, which might have sparked the ideals of those great men of old, those fearless and faithful leaders who had fathered America. Winning the respect of the world would be easy, if he could give them a cause to gather around.

He was certain once he had a chance to explain the future world, in light of the arrival of the coming Mahdi; to those who seemed worried about the current direction of their failing nation: that everyone who thought there was a grand design for the universe, by any means, or any god, would sign on.

So many people were simply looking for something to believe in. Something larger than themselves to look to. Something magical, supernatural. And, it appeared they were tired of the results brought on by their half baked attempts to call themselves Christians. He would show them his better way.

Contend, O Lord, with those who contend with me;
fight against those who fight against me! Take hold
of shield and buckler and rise for my help.

Psalms 35:1-2

CHAPTER 15

Cage couldn't believe his luck. He was about to take into custody the man he'd been after for months. And, the absolutely crazy thing was, Conyers was walking right into the camp with his hands up. This was priceless. Cage and his men had come back to base to replenish their supplies, completely unaware of how close Josh was at the time. If they'd been further out in the field, they wouldn't have been available to witness the miracle; but here it was, his wildest dream come true.

Suspicious at first, Cage sent scouts out to comb the surrounding area for signs of rebel forces hiding outside the camp. Perhaps Josh had brought troops with him, and was using his surrender as a distraction. It was certainly a good one. What else could possibly be the reasoning behind a blatant, mindless surrender to one's enemy? They searched for hours, but found nothing. "Well, Conyers, what has brought you to me? What would cause you to turn yourself over to a man who will surely torture and kill you, without a second thought?"

"I was told you have Jana, Cage. I've come to get her back."

"And you thought I'd just hand her over to you, like that?"

"You and I have been at odds for a very long time, colonel. This fight has nothing to do with my wife."

"Perhaps you've forgotten that your innocent little wife blew up my base? She killed three quarters of my men that night, and left me with a lot of explaining to do. What makes you think she is any less valuable to me than you are?"

"Listen, colonel, I've recently discovered that Jana is expecting. No matter what you've done in the past, or what you think you are capable of, I don't think you're the kind of man who could hurt a pregnant woman. So, I've come to trade myself for my wife."

"Well, you certainly have me figured out all wrong, Conyers. I don't have a problem in the world doing away with your spawn, right along with your deeply annoying wife. And, you gave away any bargaining power, you might've thought you had, the minute you walked into my house with your hands in the air."

"Certainly the honorable thing to do would be to let her go, Cage. You can't seriously think that these men, who take orders from you, will stand by and watch you torture and kill a woman with child."

"These men have watched me kill hundreds of your rebel ilk, Conyers. And most of them have been women, and children. I just dispatched two women and their four children, off the back of the plateau a few mornings ago, to make room for your pregnant wife. And one of my men did the dirty work for me. My troops will do whatever they are ordered to do."

At that moment Josh realized he'd made a terrible mistake. By believing there was a single compassionate bone in this demon's body, he'd probably gotten himself and Jana killed. Cage likely wouldn't have laid a finger on Jana until he'd found Josh; and now that he'd handed himself over to the lunatic, what chance did they have? In the heat of the moment, he hadn't thought this through very well, and this could ultimately be the death of his wife and child.

"Private Phillips, get over here."

"Yes, Sir."

"Lock him up, right there in the cell with his wife. I want her to know that his thoughtless act is what finally caused her death, and the death of their child. This is rich. What fantastic luck! We will begin the fun tomorrow. I've been looking forward to this for a long, long time, Conyers. Who'd have believed it would be you, who would give me the best gift I've ever received? Well, Phillips, get on with it!"

"Yes, Sir. Right away, Sir."

• • • • •

Jana's cell door opened, and someone was shoved roughly in to the space. He landed on the floor with a thud, and the landing was followed by a loud grunt. There was something familiar about the man, who was not yet facing her. As he rose, and turned, she gasped. "Josh?"

"Jana."

"What are you doing here?"

"Well, it may not exactly look like it at the moment, but I came to rescue you."

"But, Josh, Cage was using me for bait. Why would you put yourself in this position, just because I did something so stupid?"

"Because I love you, that's why. I was on my way home, when I ran into Jack. You know, one of the new soldiers from the base. He told me you'd come out on the mountain. Likely to look for us, since we were running so late. He told me they thought you might have been captured by the enemy; and since I'd had some very disturbing dreams myself, I was sure it was true. He told me something else, Jana."

"What?"

"He told me that we're expecting a baby."

"Now, why did he go and do that? Chuck and Emma weren't supposed to tell anyone, until I'd had a chance to tell you first."

"Well, I'm sure they decided that the current circumstances warranted a slightly different approach. I thought by coming in here, and appealing to his humanity, especially where a pregnant woman is concerned, that he would let me trade myself, for the two of you. What I hadn't counted on, was that Cage doesn't have any humanity to appeal to. So, now, here I am."

"Yes, I found that out the hard way too. He told me he plans to kill the baby first, and then me, with you watching. I wish there had been a way for me to get word to you, but I got myself in a pretty terrible position, and our baby right along with me. I know the situation looks most dire, Josh; but God spoke to me, and I believe everything will be okay, somehow."

"I'm not sure how you came to that conclusion, but I'm always open to the workings of God in our lives. You know that. What did He tell you?"

"He told me that we are going to have a son, and that we're supposed to name the child Alec. He also told me He had great plans for the boy, so obviously Cage can't kill me, if God has plans for our son."

"Okay, I know God watches out for us, so even if I can't see a way out of this right now, I will keep an open mind. We serve a God who can make a way, where there is no way. He must have a plan. We will have to be vigilant. I can't believe I'm here with you now. I missed you. And, I am so happy about the baby. I'm going to be a daddy."

"You'll be the best dad in the world, Josh. This is something I didn't know we'd ever have, after some of the poor choices I'd made along the way. We are so blessed, and I love you so much."

At that, Josh came to her, picked her up, and held her tight. He buried his face in her hair, and breathed in the magic of her presence, here, at this moment, in his arms. They stood like that, with their arms wrapped tightly around each other, for what seemed like hours; and for the first time in days, they both felt completely warm, and at peace.

• • • • •

"Colonel Cage, we've been ordered to collect you, and to transport you to headquarters. From there you'll be taken to a meeting with Dr. Amir Bahram, the new leader of the UNGC. We have been instructed to allow you to pack your personal belongings, enough for a one week stay."

"I can't leave now. I've just captured one of the most wanted heads of ARM, and his wife; and I was set to interrogate him first thing tomorrow."

"I apologize, Sir, but that will not be possible. We are expected back at headquarters today."

"No, no, no, I have spent months tracking this man, and I will not be denied! What is the name of your supervisor? I will not go with you!"

"Yes Sir. Our superior expected this response. We have

been instructed to allow you to contact him. However, we are not to let you out of our sight."

Cage went, sputtering, and spewing obscenities, immediately to the communications building, and made his call. When he contacted headquarters, he was told in no uncertain terms that he was to board the transport, with his escorts, and come to home base immediately, or he would be locked in the brig forthwith. He acquiesced. If he allowed himself to be arrested, he would never have his revenge on Conyers and his annoying wench. He would simply put them both under heavy guard, and then he'd have his fun on his return to the camp. He gave orders to his most trusted man, Phillips, to double the guard on the prison cells, and he grudgingly boarded the waiting transport for his eventual meeting with Dr. Bahram.

You have seen, O Lord, be not silent! O Lord, be not far from me.

Psalm 35:22

CHAPTER 16

Cade Phillips was an okay kind of guy. He'd joined the People's Militia for all the right reasons; love of country, patriotism, a desire to keep his family safe; before he found out the extent of the organization's hatred of his own country and people. All the commercials on television made the PM sound like a force for good. He would be a hero, helping to win the war against rebels who were ripping the country apart. It wasn't until later that he discovered the 'criminals' he would be hunting, those folks who were part of ARM, were simply human beings who didn't want a global positioning chip in their hand.

At first he didn't understand their aversion to the implant. After all, this was the new currency, so a guy couldn't buy anything, see a doctor, or travel, without the darned thing. But, later, when he found out the chip was also used as a tracking device, to keep Americans; and later the world's population; in line. And that the administration could remove money from a guy's bank account, without his permission; or flip a switch and get somebody put on a list, so they couldn't travel, buy, or do anything; his opinion began to change dramatically. He'd been implanted himself, as a prerequisite to service. As if it was some kind of honor. And, now that he knew the extent of the damage the device could cause, he wasn't so pleased about it anymore. One of the guys in his barracks decided, awhile back, that he couldn't deal with Cage anymore, and was planning to go AWOL. He knew he wouldn't get very far with the tiny little GPS device in his hand, so he attempted to remove the offensive device.

Cade found him dead, on his bunk, the next morning. There was something very strange about the body. It smelled of burned things, as if it had been set afire from the inside. His eyes were not just dead, but strangely vacant, as if he'd never actually lived there. And, his mouth, tinged red along the opening, looked like a bloody gash in the middle of his face. The look of him haunted Cade's sleep;

made him feel more trapped than ever. How could he ever leave? Was he doomed to this existence forever?

He had no respect for his commander, having seen the madman kill hundreds of women and children. Even being on the same base with the man made him feel dirty. He also had no more respect for any government, which would not only allow these things to happen, but encourage and reward them. The world had very simply gone to hell. He still loved his family, his parents, and sister, and he loved his country. But he couldn't really see any vestiges of the America he once knew, except in the faces and beliefs of those resistance fighters. Everything he'd loved and fought for was gone; turned into this global alliance of money grubbing, soul selling, quasi leaders. All bowing down to an ultimate leader; who obviously didn't have the best interest of Americans in mind. He didn't know much about politics, but he knew the decisions that had been made for him in these past years, were all the wrong ones. And, from what he'd heard most recently, the man who'd taken over as UNGC leader, was a complete screwball. Yet, even despite his crazy ideas, the governments of the world were blindly following. He was at a loss, for what to think, or do.

He knew though that he couldn't allow Cage to get away

with killing another woman with child, so he determined to do something about it.

The two dozen Muslim mercenaries, who occupied the tents on the East side of the plateau, farthest from the prison cells, were another concern. With Cage gone at headquarters for a week, there would be no controlling them. They clearly hated all infidels, which accounted for everyone on base, PM, or resistance. And Phillips didn't know if he would be able to fend off any attacks toward his fellow troops, or the prisoners they held, if these guys got riled up.

He made up his mind. He would free the prisoners. He'd been left in charge of the camp during Cage's absence, and he would make those decisions which seemed best to him. He knew he'd be a candidate for court-martial, as soon as the colonel arrived back on base, but he couldn't, in good conscience, allow one more innocent to be slaughtered for no good reason. He didn't know for sure how the other troops felt about the state of affairs they faced, so he determined to make this happen on his own. No one else would shoulder responsibility for his actions. He felt good about what he was determined to do, and could only hope his actions would help America to be great once again.

The mercenaries prayed to Allah five times a day, inside

their tents, with much chanting and noise; so that would be the most reasonable time to accomplish an escape. Cade decided to make his arrangements with the prisoners, and get things set to go.

Instead of doubling the guard, on the back of the plateau, he relieved the one guard posted there and told him he'd watch the prisoners while the young man had a bite to eat, and a cup of coffee. Then, he went from cell to cell, and shared his plan with every captive. Telling them all that Josh, and Jana would lead them to safety, and freedom. Once he reached the Conyers cell he opened the door, and entered. Jana, who was closest to the door, took two steps back, and turned to Josh with an anguished look on her face; sure that it was time for her torture to begin.

"No, Jana, my name is Private Cade Phillips. Please don't be afraid. I'm here to tell you my plan to set all the prisoners free."

"And, how do you plan to do that? Cage will never let you get away with any of this."

"Cage is gone. He's been called away to headquarters, and won't be back for a week. I'm not expecting any resistance from the other troops on base. You might have noticed that Cage doesn't command much respect around here anymore. However, I don't plan on involving any of the other soldiers in this treasonous act, which will give them the option of denying that they knew anything about it. Now, the Muslim mercenaries, on the East side of camp, are a different story. They would kill us all in a heartbeat, so we simply cannot let them know what's going on. Agreed?"

"How are you going to manage that?"

"Well, Josh, and by the way, it's an honor to meet you, both of you."

"Thank you soldier. It's a pleasure to meet you too."

"Okay, what we will do is wait for the evening call to prayer to begin. When they pray they chant, and sing so loudly that they can't possibly detect an escape; if it's done quickly and quietly enough. That's why we all have to be ready at the drop of a hat. I will come to relieve the guard about ten minutes before their call to prayer. I will unlock all the doors, but no one is to try to make a break for it until I give the signal, which will be four loud coughs. Do you understand?"

"Yes, we've got it so far. Have you given the same instructions to all the other prisoners?"

"Yes, I've given everyone the same directives. I've brought your things. Jana, here is your pack, and I think this is your gun and your knives, and bow. Josh, your bag, your guns, and knives. I checked, and made sure there were some extra provisions stowed in each pack, and plenty of ammunition. I also packed some extra rations for the rest of your party, and they have those bags already. Blankets, food, and water. I know it's going to be a long hard trip to wherever you're going, and I just wish I could accompany you, but this will have to be my one contribution to the cause."

"But, why, Cade? Why are you doing this? I can't imagine the trouble you're causing for yourself. Why would you put yourself in jeopardy for us?"

"Well, all I can say is, when I first joined this fight, I thought I was fighting for a noble cause. I've found out recently that I'm on the wrong side, and that if there is a noble cause at all, it is the one you fight for. I know I can't come with you, because of my chip, so I won't ask. I wouldn't want to risk the safety of all these women and children."

"We don't know how we can ever thank you enough, Cade. You are a true hero. God bless you."

"Oh, I don't know about any blessings. I never really had much to do with God, and He probably doesn't care much for me now."

"Cade, you're wrong. God loves you. He died to give you freedom, and salvation. Even if you never taste liberty again in this life, He will give you that freedom in the next. All you have to do is believe on Him, Cade. Believe that Jesus, who died and rose again, is the Son of God, and you will have life eternal."

"Thanks, Josh, I'll think on it. For now, please hide these supplies as best you can, so the guard who is coming to relieve me won't see them. I'll be back in time for the escape. I'll bring enough rope, so you can help me lower everyone to the ledge behind the cells. You'll be on your own from there. Keep everyone as quiet as you can. We won't have much time to get this done."

"Thank you, my friend. You have our eternal gratitude, and our prayers."

• • • • •

"Josh, we're going to make it out of here. I knew it! God is so good, and He has been watching out for us all along. I just wish I'd had more faith back at camp, before I went out on a wild goose chase, and put us all in this terrible position."

"Jana, you can't keep kicking yourself forever. God always had a plan, and if we hadn't ended up here, there's a chance that all the other prisoners in these cells would be dead. Now, God is using these circumstances to bring about a greater thing, for all of us. We have a long trip ahead of us, so lay down a get a little rest before Cade comes back."

"I love you husband."

"I love you too wife. God is good,"

"Yes, God is very good indeed!"

• • • • •

Scott, Mark, Becca, and the others were making good time up the mountain. They stopped each night, to take shelter, and usually found caves big enough to accommodate the lot of them. But, when they couldn't, they slept under the stars, huddled together under blankets and tarps. Those were the hardest nights for Scott. The nearness of Becca was difficult for him. The more he got to know her, watching her kindness with the children, seeing her selfless nature, first hand, and hearing her sweet voice, the more he found himself falling head-over-heels for her.

Though he didn't know it, those were the hardest nights for Becca, as well. When she was close enough to see his muscles move beneath his shirt, could hear the gentle way he dealt with his children, and saw the fairness and compassion, with which he spoke to the men they traveled with, she felt more and more drawn to him. This trip had been wonderful, and awful. She couldn't wait to get to the ARM base, and put some distance between herself, and this man who was unwittingly pulling at her heartstrings.

She enjoyed helping with supper preparations. The guys could almost always bag at least one, or two rabbits or squirrels, as they trekked the behemoth. Small game seemed to abound plentifully on the mountain. She could also usually count on finding a few dried berries that the birds hadn't gobbled up, as they made their way during the day. Evenings normally wound down by finding lodging, cutting pine boughs for beds and doorways, and wood for a fire, and then the cook fires would be started. If they were occupying a cave, she could warm water to wash up a bit and then clean up the children, as she was prepping for the meal. This night the boys presented her with four plump rabbits, already skinned and cleaned, so she decided to roast the meat. There was still grain, and she'd found a few handfuls of dried, wild, berries along the way, so she made a nice mash. The smell of rabbits cooking slowly over a fire was intoxicating, and everyone settled down to wait for the meal to be done as they pulled out their Bibles.

Scott and Mark had taken over the study, after Josh's hasty departure, so the first thing they did was say a prayer for Josh and Jana still believing them to be safe at home, on top of the mountain. "Lord, thank you for our successful journey. We long to be home with family, and friends, but we are grateful for our new family and friends. We pray that Josh has made it safely home, or will soon be, and that all is well with Jana and everyone else back home. Thank you for keeping your hand on our lives, to keep us in your will, safe, and sound. In Jesus' Name. Amen."

Becca had begun to learn more about the Grace of God, as they studied the Bible each night, and she already had a favorite scripture. "I can do all things through Christ who strengthens me." Philippians 4:13. She was coming closer to asking Jesus to be her Savior, but still suffered from what holds many people back. She had a good old fashioned case of the, 'I'm not good enoughs'. For so many people it is difficult to understand that salvation has nothing to do with how good we are, but only how good He is, and the sacrifice He already made for us. Scott understood her dilemma, as it was the same one which held him back for so long, so he continued to mentor her. On this night, as she watched her new family share a meal, a meal that she had prepared, around a warm fire, she felt a wave of gratitude so strong that it brought her to tears, and she willingly and trustingly turned her life over to a loving God. Becca was saved by Grace and she would never be the same again.

• • • • •

Emma and the ladies in the kitchen back at the ARM base were deep in prayer, when Chuck came running into the communal area. Jack had made it back, and he had some disturbing news. He'd run into Josh, out on the mountain, and told him about the baby. And Josh, who was sure Jana had been taken by Colonel Cage, had last been seen heading to the PM camp to get her back. The women were shocked that Jana was pregnant, as this was the first they were hearing of the situation, and they began to pray again. Emma's heart broke, as she thought of Jana, and the fate of her little grandchild in the hands of that monster. Chuck sat with the women, and they all held hands as their prayers rang out.

Your steadfast love, O Lord, extends to the heavens,
your faithfulness to the clouds. Your righteousness is
like the mountains of God; your judgments are like
the great deep; man and beast you save, O Lord.

Psalm 36: 5-6

CHAPTER 17

Josh woke Jana, quietly, with a kiss. Private Phillips was unlocking their cell, and the planned departure would begin in about ten minutes. Josh and Jana knew, from their previous conversation with Cade, that four loud coughs would be their signal to leave the cell behind, and head for the back of the plateau. They gathered their gear, and waited just behind the door. As they waited, Jana took Josh's hand and guided it gently to her slightly rounded abdomen, where young Alec was, again, practicing his line dancing. Their eyes met, and Jana watched as a smile blossomed on the face of her husband. "Is that the baby?"

"Yes, Daddy, that is your son. He is quite an active little fellow."

"I think he's an adventurer, like his parents, and he can't wait for this new chapter to begin."

"Well, I'm sure you're right, Dad. I'm sure he feels my excitement, and a little fear, quite honestly. I wasn't pregnant the last time I had to go up and down over the back of the plateau. I'm hoping I'm in good enough shape to manage it."

"Don't worry about that, Jana. I plan to lower you all the way. You'll just have to guide the rope, so you end up on the ledge. I'm going to have to ask you to guide the others as well. Do you think you can do that?"

"I'm sure I'll be alright, Josh. Don't worry about me. I have my big, strong husband with me this time around. I'm sure God has got everything planned out for us already."

"Good. Then we'll just do what we need to do, and leave the rest up to Him."

They heard four loud coughs, and opened the door. Looking around to be sure the coast was clear, they saw Phillips waving to them from the side of the cells, and shushed all their charges. Jana led, and Josh urged speed from behind. When one of the women started talking to her little one, he put his finger to his lips, and gave her a stern look, which shut her up right away. They had very little time to get everyone over the cliff, to the ridge below, so they would have to move swiftly.

Cade had already gotten several lengths of rope together, and had them stowed behind the stone prison cells. He gave a two minute tutorial on the proper way to tie a knot, and they began attaching ropes to bodies. Jana went first, so she could be at the bottom, for guidance, but the others followed quickly. Soon, Jana had an entire line of women, and their children, hugging the underside of the plateau. Right before Cade helped Josh, over the ledge, he stopped him, and held out his hand. Josh moved his hand aside, and pulled him in for a huge hug. "I want to thank you for all your help. We are all grateful to you. But, especially for Jana and I. You have saved our child's life, and we can never thank you enough for that."

"No, Josh, it's I who should be thanking you. You've introduced me to a Jesus I never knew, and after I went back to my bunk last night, I had a long talk with Him. I asked Him to be my Savior, and I've never felt so complete."

"I know you're going to be in a lot of trouble, for helping us, and I feel terrible for that. What if they lock you up? I don't want you to lose your freedom, just for helping us."

"Don't worry about it, my friend. I feel more free right now, than I've ever felt in my life. There is nothing they can do to me that could ever take that away. Take care of that wife of yours, and safe travels."

"God bless you, Cade. You will be in our prayers every day for the rest of our lives. And our son, whose name was foretold to us, by God, will now be Alec Cade Conyers. Good bye friend."

At that, Cade held the rope, while Josh made his way over the gnarled roots and jutting earth that was the edge of the plateau. Josh held on tightly to both cliff, and rope, and made it safely to the ledge where Jana and the rest of the captives stood. Almost all the women and children came from families which used to include a husband, and dad, so these fractured families would need healing and help. Things would get better for them, once they were back at the ARM base, and didn't have to be frightened anymore. For now, Josh and Jana would have to lead them to safety, and it would be a long hard trip, especially for the children.

• • • • •

After Josh and Cade said their last goodbyes, Private Phillips walked back to his tent, and wrote a long letter to his parents and sister. Telling them everything he'd learned about Jesus, and freedom. Then he walked the letter over to the communications building, and buried it; way down in the middle of the outgoing mail; to make sure it wouldn't be intercepted. After that he walked back to his quarters, and straightened up a bit. Once that was done, he stopped, and looked around. The bleakness of his life here in this place of war and death, was magnified in the olive drab walls of his tent. He had nothing to show for his years on earth. Cage had stripped them all of anything which would distract them from his own personal goals.

He pulled out his pocket knife, and sharpened the blade, slowly. Next, feeling around on his hand, he found the small nodule, injected that day long ago during his appointment at the GHO office. He carefully cut around the small device, and when it was exposed, he took hold of the chip, and pulled. The results were instantaneous. His brain, and heart were both overloaded with electrical current, causing a burning effect, which would take his life in less than five seconds. As the light left his eyes, and turned them to vacant sockets, he smiled. His last look at this world, was through the lenses of a free man.

Josh and Jana would never know what happened to their friend. The instrument of God, who had freed them from Cage's prison cells. But, that was okay. He left this world, to go to a better one, and his life had meant something. He would be remembered.

As the next shift began, and Private Phillips' relief came out to the cells, he noticed something amiss. It appeared that the cell doors were ajar. Upon further inspection, he found that every cell was empty. Frightened, he ran back to the communications building, where he sent out an urgent message to headquarters. The prisoners, every one of them, had escaped. There would be no contacting Colonel Cage, as he was meeting with Dr. Bahram, but perhaps they could tell him what to do. Cage's cronies, who'd been left behind, and who were angry when Cage left Phillips in charge of the prisoners, would have hell to pay when it was discovered that they'd been on base the entire time, and witnessed nothing. They just might be better off throwing themselves off the back of the plateau.

Cade's fellow troops were in the clear. He'd been sure to make it evident, in every way, that he was the one and only perpetrator of this act of treason. His friends, thought him the bravest of the brave. They'd all talked about Cage's torture of innocents, and how heinous it was, as they sat in their tents and shared each night. Each one had come up with scenarios whereby he might be the one to free them all, and be hero to many. But none had the guts to carry out an act of hope, the way Phillips had. None of the men were loyal to the lunatic who commanded them anymore, but they all feared for their lives. And, because they feared necessarily for their lives, if they didn't continue to obey his orders, they continued to commit atrocious acts of war; the memories of which, they would carry with them for the rest of their lives.

Once the call had been made to headquarters, there was nothing else to be done. Some might argue they could have taken off from camp, to try to capture the escaped prisoners. But with their commander gone, there was no one there to give those orders.

The mercenaries on the East side of camp could do as they wished, but they didn't feel this was a mission worth their time. No one knew how long the prisoners had been gone, or what kind of head start they had. As much as they loved killing infidels, and torturing women and children, this felt a little beneath them, so they sat. All anyone could do, at this point, was to wait for Cage's return, and hope the base survived his wrath. It wasn't until the next day, that anyone found Phillip's body. His friends enclosed him in a body bag, which would go out on the next transport. There was nothing that even Cage could do to him now.

• • • • •

Scott, and the rest of the men, were busy rigging a series of ropes to help Becca and the little ones get across a large chasm they'd encountered late in the day. The guys could navigate the opening, but didn't want to lose those with shorter legs, down the gaping hole. They'd been making pretty good time; up until this latest snafu had set them back; but they were hoping they could get back on track soon. Instead, as the next day progressed, they were plagued by one mishap after another. The near disasters were not of their doing, but were becoming problematic at the very least. Tempers were on edge, and a couple of the guys were getting sharp toward each other. Scott and Mark sat down with the other soldiers, and tried to make sense of the issues.

"You know, Josh always says that if something continues to stop you in the plan you've devised, God might be trying to get you to go another way. Now, I'm not saying that this is God, but what if it is? What if we're supposed to be slowing down, or rethinking our strategy? I say that if something is slowing us down, it might be for a reason."

"I know what you're saying, Scott, but I have kids to get home to, and the folks back on base are worried about us. What if Colonel Cage has more scouts out on the mountain? The longer we stay out here, the more chance we have of being caught."

"I agree, Mark, and I'm not saying that we should turn around and go back. I'm simply saying that if God wants us to go slower, and the things that we're running into are making that a non issue, then maybe we should be paying attention to those signs. Do you agree?"

"Sure, maybe we should even stop for the night. The kids are exhausted, and there are a couple of good caves on this level of the mountain. I'll rustle up some fire wood, if someone else wants to fill all the water containers. Hey, you guys want to bag some meat? Let's tell Becca what's going on. I'm sure she'll be glad for the rest, before she tries to tackle the gulf."

"Great. Let's get going guys. The sooner we get our chores done, the sooner we can settle down for the night, and maybe even get time for a Bible study."

Cage was in awe of this great man; and completely under his spell. Why was it again, that he'd been so adverse to coming in for these very important meetings? Dr. Bahram was easily the most intelligent, and charismatic man he'd ever met. He sat rapt at every meeting, soaking up each word of wisdom. Some of the other outlying commanders were nothing but ignoramuses, as far as Cage was concerned. And they proved their foolishness every time they opened their mouths. Cage reverted to, almost, ridiculous fan girl status, every time Amir aimed any attention in his direction. This, coming from a man who had been one of the president's biggest fans, and loath to be involved in politics, of any kind. But on a scale of one to ten, he would have to rate the president at a one, and the new UNGC leader at a fifteen. He could certainly see why this man was chosen to lead, and why the world was flocking to him, and hanging on his every word.

The good doctor informed all the men that he intended to close all outlying bases; transferring all current prisoners to one large detention center, in the Plaines region. He didn't see as much productivity coming from the camps in the mountains as he would like. And, he felt that all future missions could be handled, logistically, from one central location. He intended to promote Cage to general, and place him as head of operations, over all the other commanders. The looks, coming from the other colonels, all around, were intense; and if Cage were the scared type, he'd be fearful of retaliation from those officers. But, Cage was not the fearful type, and he took the hateful gazes in his direction, as a challenge of sorts. He asked for a private audience with the leader, and was granted that interview.

"Thank you for meeting with me, Doctor Bahram. I am very honored by the appointment."

"You are welcome, General Cage, but you've earned this, so I won't accept any credit. Now, what can I do for you?"

"I would like to ask a special favor, from the council. I have some very special prisoners in my cells back at the base that I would like to deal with personally. I understand that our meetings will last until the end of the week, but when I go home, I would like to interrogate these traitors. Upon the completion of those interrogations, I will pack up, and be wherever you would like me to be post haste."

"I will grant you an extra two days, for your personal interrogations, but I expect you to have your base, and your troops, packed up, and back to the afore mentioned, central base, in nine days time. Do we have an understanding?"

"Yes Sir. That should be plenty of time for what I have in mind. Thank you for the extension, Sir. And, Sir?"

"Yes, General Cage?"

"I have never felt so confident, in the direction of our world, as I do with you at the helm. I believe the UNGC, and all their voting entities, made the right choice in appointing you."

"Thank you, General Cage. I appreciate your frankness, and your loyalty. I look forward to working with you, on a grander scale, but for now, let's get all of the mundane business of these meetings completed, so we can be off to bigger and better, things."

"Yes, Sir."

Cage sent word back to the mountain, that they were to begin packing up the base. That everything would soon be relocated back to a more centralized location, down off the heights. But, he warned them not to touch the prisoners. He would deal with them upon his return. Whereupon he learned of the great escape, and Private Phillips' apparent suicide. He dropped the phone, and stood for quite some time, before the soldier at the other end of the line assumed they'd been disconnected, and hung up.

He dropped to his knees, with his head down, and rocked back and forth for a long moment. When he lifted his gaze, the evil in his eyes could be seen to have grown to a whole new level. His fists clenched, and unclenched, over and over; and his face twisted with rage over the unexpected news. This was not the end of it. It couldn't be.

• • • • •

Josh and Jana's group, was moving at a pretty good clip; considering the large number of children they were leading. Moms were taking charge, and the bigger ones were helping the little ones. Jana had taken to doing the hunting for the group. With forty two mouths to feed, she tried to supply twelve rabbits, or squirrels, a day. She was an excellent hunter, and equally good with bow, knife, or gun. But she knew gunshots would bring unwanted attention, so she used her exceptional bow skills to get the job done. If she fell short of her goal, the night's menu usually featured soup, or stew; but if she met, or exceeded that goal, then roasted beast was the featured entree. Phillips had supplied them with plenty of staples, so their meals were rounded out with grains, dried fruits, and nuts, granola, jerky, coffee, tea, powdered milk (which made Jana especially happy), and lots of clean, fresh water. As long as they continued at this pace, and watched their rations, there was no reason why the supplies wouldn't last until they reached safety.

Josh was happy they hadn't seen signs of PM troops following, but a little wary too. Why weren't they following? Cage must not be back from his trip. That was the only explanation. Boy, was he going to be mad when he returned to find all of his cells empty. Josh hoped he hadn't caused too many problems for Cade. He knew the young man had made a huge sacrifice for them, and he would be eternally grateful.

Evenings were spent readying supper; eating together; cleaning up; both dishes, and bodies; and socializing. Josh knew lots of Bible songs for kids from his youth, so they would quietly sing, and then as the children were put down to sleep, the adults came together for a Bible study and time of prayer. Many of the women had questions, and Jana was pleased to be able to help answer them. There was a time, not so long ago, that she wouldn't have been able to do that. She felt at peace, and as she watched her husband interact with all the little ones, she was reassured once again that Josh would be a very good father indeed.

As they lay side by side, in the fire warmed cave, they

spoke very quietly. "You know what?"

"No, what, Josh?"

"I think I'm almost glad you are so stubborn."

"Wait a minute. Who's stubborn?"

"Well, we're both stubborn, but if we hadn't ended up back in those prison cells, all these women and children, would be dead."

"Yes, I know, and now that we've gotten to know them, that seems especially horrible, doesn't it?"

"Yes, I believe God put us there to rescue these precious souls for Him. You know I don't believe God does terrible things to us, but I do believe that some of the things we think of as terrible, perhaps, aren't so bad in the larger scheme of things. I mean, what are we willing to go through, if it will help to save one more for the kingdom?"

"I agree. When I see how those women and children were living in that prison, and how long some of them had been there. I mean I was only there for a few days, and I was cold, hungry, and terrified, so I can only imagine all that they endured. Especially with Cage torturing them every day. I really believe that man is the epitome of evil."

"Yep, without a doubt, one of Satan's special demons. But, now, here we are with all these new friends. I hope

Mom has lots of supper waiting for us when we return.”

“How much longer do you think it will take us to get back, Josh? I’ve never been so anxious to be home.”

“I’m estimating another week. We’ve been moving pretty fast, and now that we know a few shortcuts we didn’t have under our belts the first time we traveled to the base, we’re beating any old records we might have set. Besides, the last time we were on our way to ARM, with guides, you were pretty bad off, and not moving very fast. Do you remember?”

“How could I ever forget? But, even pregnant, I think I’m doing pretty well this time around.”

“Yes ma’am. Speedy as a rabbit. How are you feeling? Is the pace too hard on you, or the baby?”

“No, I think we’re doing just fine. I’m glad to have healthy rations, and milk, back on the menu, but I think the exercise is actually good for us. I’ll let you know if any-thing changes. You know I want this baby to be healthy, just as much as you do, Daddy.”

“Yes, Mommy, I know. I love you. Now, we’d better get some sleep. These kiddos will be climbing all over us before you know it.”

After another full day of unusual events and obstacles, Scott and his group were settling down for the night. Rabbits were roasting over the flames; a sweet mash, with dried fruits, and nuts, was staying warm on the fire ring; a pot of tea simmered on the hot rocks; bed rolls were already spread around the blaze; and the cave entrance was blocked by pine boughs. "Auntie Becca?"

"Yes, sweetie."

"Are we almost there?"

"Almost where, CJ?"

"At the good place. You know, the good place you told us about. I'm getting tired of walking every day. Can we be there yet?"

"Well, darling, I've never been to the ARM base where we're going. Your daddy knows way more about that than I do."

"Well, Dad, are we almost there?"

"I'm estimating about another week, CJ. As long as we don't continue to run into everything under the sun, to set us back. When you say your prayers tonight, why don't you say a prayer, for safe travels, for all of us?"

"I will, Dad. I love you."

"I love you too, CJ."

"I love you too, Daddy."

"And, I love you my little Angel baby."

"I love you too, Auntie Becca."

"I love you, CJ. And, I love you too, Angel."

"Me too, Auntie Becca. You know what?"

"No, Baby, what?"

"I wish you were my mommy."

At that, Scott and Becca's gazes met for an instant, and then they both quickly looked away, as little Angel, a little confused over the exchange of looks, snuggled into her daddy's arms.

• • • • •

The base was packing up. A steady flow of choppers from headquarters were coming in empty, and leaving full to the brim, with ammunition, and supplies. Communications, mess hall, and men, would be the last to leave. Overnight one of the two troops, still loyal to Cage, came up missing. Whether he was murdered, and buried somewhere on the mountain; or had decided he didn't want to face consequences for the loss of every prisoner on the plateau; and jumped off the back side of the cliff; no one knew. If he'd waited a while longer, he would have found that Cage was much more calm about the escapees than anyone would have imagined he'd be. Upon his return to base, men expected to be punished, and even court marshaled. But, where once he would have blamed every man in camp, though it was widely known that none had been involved besides Phillips; now, he seemed content to live with the explanation given to him by the troops who'd found Cade dead in his tent.

Those surprised soldiers didn't know it then, but they were witnessing a miracle. Cage would figure out a way, through his new position, to capture Josh and Jana again. He would make them pay for their treason, but for now he was trying to present himself as a cool head. A decision maker who could be trusted; a rational leader who deserved respect. He cared about what Bahram thought of him, probably more than he'd cared about anyones opinion in his life, and he wanted to present himself as someone who could be relied upon and sought out for council.

When he'd arrived back on base, he'd commanded the troops to take down the heads, which adorned the front entrance to the camp. They had become an embarrassment. Many were relieved, and even more were reassured

when they were told they'd be assigned to a new commander once they arrived back at headquarters.

Cage no longer needed to worry about those who could
remember his poor decisions, as he seemed to be trusted by
the man in charge. So, it stood to reason, those who were
once a threat to his career didn't need to be concerned either. He had almost everything he'd ever wanted.

Back in his quarters, he started sorting through his belongings. It dawned on him, as he pulled items from draw-
ers and closets, that he didn't own anything truly personal.
Oh, he had clothing, and shoes, and even hygiene items, but
there were no pictures, no collectibles, no little keepsakes on
tables, to spark a conversation with visitors. It didn't really
matter. He didn't have visitors, and he didn't have anyone
to impress. It took very little time to place all he owned in a
couple of boxes, to go on the next helicopter. He wouldn't
be the last man to leave the PM base. He would leave others
to clean up, as he usually did. He didn't feel the need to 'go
down with the ship' as it were. He owed nothing to these
traitorous, disloyal, men in his command. They'd been ready
to stab him in the back for months. He was ready to go onto bigger, and better, things. He felt as though he'd finally
discovered his calling. He was ready to belong.

Fret not yourself because of evildoers; be not envious of wrongdoers! For they will soon fade like the grass and wither like the green herb. Trust in the Lord, and do good; dwell in the land and befriend faithfulness. Delight yourself in the Lord, and He will give you the desires of your heart.

Psalm 37: 1-4

CHAPTER 18

Jana woke, and noticed a faint light coming from outside the cave. She removed the pine boughs, which were blocking the opening, and made her way outside. The morning was chilly, but the sky was alight with a hundred different shades of pink, and orange. It took her breath away. As she stood, silent, in the cold, she suddenly felt a large, warm hand, encircle hers. She looked up, and saw the face of the only man she would ever love, looking down at her, and realized that she had everything. "You okay, Babe?"

"Yep, just realizing what a lucky girl I am. God has been so good to me, when I don't deserve a bit of it. And, I'm sure glad He loves me, just because He loves me, because I could never warrant all this."

"And, just think of it. Soon we get to have our baby, on top of it all! I can't wait, Jana. I think about it all the time."

"You used to think of me all the time, big fella."

"Oh, you know what I mean. Of course I still think of you all the time. But, this is different. My son. I'll be able to teach him things, like how to throw a ball, how to hunt, how to be the man of his family, you know, guy stuff."

"Well, you are definitely good at the guy stuff, but you've taught me a few things too."

"You've gotten to be a pretty quick learner. I would never have imagined we'd be where we are today, would you?"

"No, actually not, especially after some of the stupid decisions I made. I was pretty sure we'd lost each other forever, when I thought you were dead. I'm really glad you're not."

"Yeah, I'd have to agree. I'm pretty glad I'm not dead either. And, I'm sure glad you're not dead. You are such a different woman than you were before all this began, and I love the way God has worked in your life. I'd have to say you are my favorite person in the world."

"Why, thank you husband. And, without a second thought, you are mine. Well, we'd better start breakfast, and get everyone up and at it, if we're ever going to get out on the road."

• • • • •

Mark was already sitting up in the cave, when Scott rolled over, and rubbed the sleep out of his eyes. "You okay, man?"

"Yeah, I just miss my kids. Sometimes I dream about them. It's hard to sleep through the night when they're on my mind."

"You'll see them soon, bro. We'll be home within the week."

"You mean if we don't keep running into problems. What if we don't make it back? You know there are a million things that can go wrong out here."

"Hey, let's not go there, okay? We're all going to be fine. God is watching over us."

"Is He, Scott? Or is He only watching over Josh? Doesn't it seem strange, that one thing after another has gone wrong, since Josh took off to find Jana? Does He really watch over all of us, or does He watch over a few, more carefully, than the rest?"

"I already told you what I think is happening, Mark. I believe that God has been saving us from something terrible that could have happened if we were farther down the road at that moment. I know He loves me, and I know He loves you too man. Just keep it together, and hang in there. You will be with your kids soon. You can hole up in your house for awhile, and play board games till the cows come home. We'll get some of Emma's good old home cooking. You can rest, and get reestablished in a good solid job. Then, maybe you shouldn't take any trips for awhile."

"You're probably right. I shouldn't have come this time. I've done nothing but bring everyone down on this whole expedition. Thanks for your positive energy, Scott. You have grown in the Lord so much since I first met you. And, I'm sure you're right. God is good, and I know He loves me. We will get home safely."

Becca had lain awake, listening to the exchange between Scott and Mark, and her respect grew for this man she admired, even more. She couldn't wait to get 'home' to this base they talked about endlessly. It sounded wonderful, and she needed to rest herself, perhaps for a good long time.

She sincerely hoped Josh had found his lady, and that they were safely on their way home. The stories she'd heard of their love, were inspiring, and she hoped to have that same kind of relationship one day. Perhaps, with Scott.

Chuck woke to see Emma sitting in the predawn light of their cabin, eyes wide open, with a grin on her face. "Are you okay, Em?"

""Yes, Chuck. I'm much better. Josh, and Jana are on their way home, and they're bringing a lot of company with them. We're going to need to get some of those cabins ready, and the girls and I are going to have to start cooking."

"Okay, my dear, whatever you say. I'll get the guys on it first thing this morning. Are you going to try to get a little more sleep? It's only five a.m."

"No, I think I'll get up, and go over to the kitchen. I wouldn't be able to get back to sleep now. I'm too excited."

Chuck knew better than to argue. He'd seen her dreams, and predictions come to fruition too many times, to doubt her. God had given her the ability to see things that others couldn't see, which came in pretty handy without a trustworthy communications system up here. And he was glad her visions were good ones this time. Well, now he was wide awake too. Maybe he'd go over, and start getting cabins ready for awhile before breakfast.

Emma made her way to the kitchen, and started planning meals for five dozen more people than usual. She sang, and hummed, as she looked over her supplies, and then went out to dig up potatoes. They would be here in a few days, and she'd have to make lots of loaves of her famous bread. She thanked the Lord, over, and over, that they would be home safe. Her grandbaby would finally be home safe.

• • • • •

Breakfast for so many was always a challenge. Coffee, and tea; milk for the kiddos, and some for her; hot cereal for almost four dozen people, made from the grains they carried, or granola, and dried fruit. Cade had been generous with the camp's supplies, so they weren't likely to run out of food, but the logistics of prep and clean up were frustrating. Jana enjoyed cooking with Mom in the base kitchen, but this was a completely different situation. When she found herself becoming so flustered, she couldn't help but wonder if she would be a patient mother. Self doubt was, admittedly, always her biggest downfall. She could see how wonderful Josh was with children. Would she be as gentle, and natural, a parent as he, or would she be like so many of the foster parents she'd known? Once they got everyone out on the trail, she found herself praying as she walked.

Josh was in his element with this many children. He

kept them marching on, by giving them goals to hit, items to find, or songs to sing. All the moms loved him, and Jana couldn't blame them. He kept their children safe, and busy, at the same time. This journey could have been a miserable one for so many reasons. Instead, it seemed more like a day at camp. And, as he looked after the kids, she hunted. But, why shouldn't she hunt? She was very good at it.

While they walked, a small boy came and walked beside her. She looked down, and saw him staring up at her with large, brown, unblinking eyes. "Can I help you?"

"Can you teach me how to shoot your bow?"

"Perhaps, when we get to the place where we're going, I could give you some lessons. But why do you want to learn to shoot a bow, and arrow?"

"I want to be a hunter, like you. My mom says she has a lot of respect for you."

"Oh, she does, does she? Well, I'd be happy to teach you, if you really want to learn, and if you'll practice very hard."

"Yes ma'am, I will. I promise."

Off he ran, to hop, and skip, along with his friends.

"Thank you, Lord, for that. You always know when I need a reminder of who I am in you. Yes, I was feeling a bit sorry for myself, and a little jealous of my husband; but

I guess we all have something positive to add to the mix, don't we? I'll try to remain a little more receptive to your urgings. I love you, Jesus."

Throughout the day, Josh and Jana both had a feeling that something was about to happen. Good, or bad, they weren't sure, but they discussed it at length as they walked, and they both kept their eyes and ears open for anything out of the ordinary.

When they stopped to rest that night, there were no caves big enough to accommodate their large group, so they built a fire, and set up their camp out in the open. Josh hoped they wouldn't attract any unwanted visitors, but he wasn't just concerned about wild animals. He was sure that Cage must be looking for them by now, and wondered if a week's head start had been enough to stay out of his grip. There was no way he could know that Cage was already safely back at PM headquarters, waiting to go out on a transport to his new duty station with Dr. Amir Bahram. Jana was concerned as to whether or not they had enough blankets to keep everyone warm, out in the open. But as the evening progressed, and they settled down after supper, she saw the mothers pull their little ones close and wrap them all together.

As dusk approached, Scott was sure he saw the glow of a fire, not too far in the distance. He knew there was a chance that Cage and his men had made it this far up the mountain, but he didn't feel this circumstance was a dangerous one. Still, they would approach slowly and assess the situation, before getting too close. They probably should have already settled down, for the night, someplace, and usually would have by now, but they hadn't found a suitable cave, and decide to push on for a bit longer. After all, they'd lost so much time on this trip already. And they felt a need to make it up somewhere. As they drew closer to the flames, they heard the sounds of soft conversation and muffled children's laughter, wafting on the breeze.

• • • • •

Jana was sure she'd heard something, out past the circle of light their fire was casting into the night, and motioned to Josh that she was going to investigate. He held his finger to his lips, and the children went suddenly silent, as they'd been taught. Now, as she listened more intently, she was sure there was someone on this part of the mountain with them. She hid behind a rock, with her bow ready, but something told her she wouldn't have to use it.

If this had been Cage and his men, they would have crashed through the camp site already. But, as the outside group drew closer, they seemed to be as wary as she was. Then, through the shadows, she recognized Scott. As she stepped out from her hiding place, Scott drew his knife, and readied to throw. But, he recognized Jana, even in the waning light. "Jana? What the heck, girl. What are you doing up here?"

"The better question would be, what are you guys still doing out here? Shouldn't you be home by now?"

"Well, that's a whole other story. Are you with Josh? Did he find you, or do we need to go rescue him?"

"No, he found me in Cage's prison cells, where he then decided to join me for awhile, but that's a whole other story too. Come, follow me. I'll take you to him now, and we can all get caught up."

"And, that is what I call a God thing, Mark!"

"Yes Sir, Mr. Scott. I'd have to agree. Let's go get some coffee."

The wicked plots against the righteous and gnashes

his teeth at him, but the Lord laughs at the wicked, for He sees that his day is coming. The wicked draw the sword and bend their bows to bring down the poor and needy, to slay those whose way is upright; their sword shall enter their own heart, and their bows shall be broken.

Psalm 37:12-15

CHAPTER 19

Cage covered his emotions well, at least in front of those faithless troops back at his mountain camp. He knew Dr. Bahram was looking for stable men to fill in the empty seats of his upper council. He hoped to be one of the voices, closest to the ear of the most powerful man in the world. From what he'd seen, so far, Bahram was well spoken, capable, intelligent, persuasive, and charismatic. He'd always thought he would spend the rest of his days hunting rebels in the mountains, but found that this man changed everything for him. Just being around him gave Cage a sense of power. Of course he still wanted to find a way to make Conyers pay, and he would do that, but for now he'd be satisfied to spend his days in the shadow of a true, proven genius, like Amir.

Stepping off the military transport, into his new life, he looked around and took everything in. A small piece of him shuddered at the thought of spending his existence in this place. Everything he looked at, seemed to be encased in concrete, or metal. Stone buildings, holding archives of the world's most precious items; cars, with their horns blaring, filling the endless roads with noise, and pollution. People walking by, bumping into him, but never raising their eyes from the electronic devices in their hands; police on every corner, wearing bullet proof vests, though he was sure he'd heard the gun laws were very strict here in the nation's capital. So much to take in, so much to process, and he felt overwhelmed already.

A limousine pulled up. The young driver jumped out to open his door, and take his minimal luggage. He was delivered to a large, brick house with white trim, which had been prepared especially for him. The neighborhood was a bit more quiet, than the downtown area where the military transport had dropped him earlier, but it still seemed to be comprised of mostly stone, brick, and concrete.

Making his way up the steps, to the carved mahogany entrance (very reminiscent of the portal to his ancestral home), he started to reach for the handle, and the door was flung open before him. Surprised, he took a step back and stumbled, almost falling down the entryway stairs. A homely, but neat, housemaid, of about thirty years or so, stood inside the door and offered to take his coat. She was dressed in a customary black, and white, costume; wearing no makeup; with her thinning, mousy brown hair pulled back in a severe bun, at the back of her neck. Her eyes were cast down, and she wore a slight smile on her lips.

Her hands appeared slightly raw, probably due to her cleaning chores, and were absent any signs of a wedding ring. She stood demurely before him, hands appropriately folded in front of her apron, as she awaited her orders.

A young man came running, and took Cage's suitcase. He noticed as the fellow sped by, that it was the driver from the limo. He was certainly used to servants, from his years of growing up in his ancestral home, but this had taken him aback, and he wasn't sure, yet, how to act. "Can you show me to my room, young lady?"

"Yes, Sir. Just follow me, Sir. That was James, who took off with your suitcase. It will already be up in your rooms. My name is Sally, and you can call me that, or whatever you'd like. I sort of come with the house. I've been here for two years."

"Who lived here before me, Sally?"

"General, Taylor, Sir. He got on the wrong side of some important people, from what I heard, and we haven't seen him for awhile. With you moving in, I guess that means he won't be coming back."

"You're probably right, Sally, but if you are going to be helping me, I won't tolerate any gossip, especially about me, to the world at large. Do you understand?"

"Yes Sir. I just thought you'd want to know, since you'll be living here and all."

"I appreciate your candor, Sally, but you will find that I live a very quiet life, and there isn't much to talk about anyway. What do we do about meals?"

"Well, that's where cook comes in. Her name is Mrs. Adler, and she's in charge of the kitchen. I can take you down to meet her, before I show you your room, if you'd like."

"Yes, I think I'd like that. We can get the supper menu taken care of at the same time."

Mrs. Adler looked over the top of her glasses, as Sally and Cage walked into the room. She was working on crust for a peach pie, which happened to be General Cage's favorite, so perhaps they would get along just fine. The kitchen was warm, and bright white, with yellow accents. Bowls of shiny red apples, lemons, and whole garlic, rested on the counter. The work surfaces were made of stainless steel, and a large farm sink, big enough to wash a human in, covered half of one wall. An eight burner stove top, and four ovens, made this kitchen a cooks dream. Looking around he didn't see a refrigerator right away, and then realized that the fridge, and freezer, were both the walk in variety. The previous occupants must have hosted many parties, in order to have needed so extravagant a kitchen. And, as he gazed around, with an appreciative smile, he could see that Mrs. Adler certainly kept everything ship shape. He heartily approved.

He held his hand out, and she quickly stopped what she was doing, to wipe her hand on the front of her apron. "I'm pleased to meet you, Mrs. Adler."

Blushing, and stammering, not used to being treated with respect by the men she attended, she held her slightly cleaner hand out, as Cage came in for the grasp. "And I'm very pleased to meet you, too, Sir. Goodness gracious, I certainly wouldn't expect you to come all the way down here to meet me, Sir." And then, he really turned on the charm. After all, he'd learned in his years growing up, these people would have access to his food, his daily schedule, and his very life. It was best not to bite the hand that feeds you. At some time, or another, he would need to use these people to cover something up, or to do him a favor, so he would cultivate them along the way.

"Well, of course I want to meet all of the very important members of my staff, Mrs. Adler. We will all be working together, after all. And, every member of the team is just as necessary as the rest. So, why don't you tell me how you run your kitchen, for meals, and otherwise, and I will respect that."

"Well, none of the generals I've taken care of before, ever asked me that. So, how about this, Sir, you tell me the things you like, so I can keep them in stock, and if you let me know your favorite meals, I will be sure to prepare those for you as well. How does that sound?"

"That sounds spectacular, Mrs. Adler. And, if supper isn't planned yet, Salmon, with baby potatoes, and asparagus, would be lovely."

"Yes Sir. That will be no trouble Sir. And, Sir?"

"Yes, Mrs. Adler?"

"Do you like peach pie, Sir?"

"Mrs. Adler. That is my absolute favorite pie. I will make up that list for you, and pass it along through Sally, if that's alright?"

"That's just fine, Sir. Now, you go get settled in, General Cage, and I'll get to the store for some fresh salmon. Good to have you here, Sir."

"Good to be here, Mrs. Adler. I think we will get along just swimmingly."

James popped his head into the kitchen, and Sally asked him to take the general up to his room, so she could help Mrs. Adler for a moment. James agreed. But, as the door closed, Cage overheard a snippet of conversation, which he was sure wasn't meant for his ears.

"He is very nice, don't you think? Way nicer than General Taylor was."

"And, so handsome! His eyes are almost hypnotic. What a gentleman too."

"What a relief. I was afraid we were going to have to live through another one of those snooty officers, who thinks his stuff don't stink. I really like him, God bless his soul."

James led him up the formal staircase, and down a hall, past several doors, which he would have to inspect at a later time. At the end of the hall, past beautiful wall art, and lovely table sculptures, was a set of double doors, which led into a suite. His accommodations consisted of a sitting room, with an inviting, white stone fireplace; a small dry bar; rugs that looked to be of oriental origin; more expensive looking art; and big, over stuffed, arm chairs.

A big screen television adorned one wall, and would most likely not be used, as he'd never spent a second of his life watching television. The previous occupant had excellent taste, if a bit opulent; and from the looks of it; he probably wouldn't change a thing. The bedroom was finished in masculine tones of browns, and burgundy, with a huge, carved mahogany, four poster bed. Another fireplace, done in dark stone, graced the wall opposite the bed, and with the drapes wide open, he could see that the gardens, behind the house, had probably been a retreat from all the concrete, for General Taylor. He was sure he would take advantage of the serene looking space, in the very near future.

The master bath was a work of art in itself. Heated, grey, marble floors; white, marble vanity tops; a soaking tub, which was quite literally large enough for four people; separate water closet; a shower that covered half of one long wall; and even a sauna. He wasn't sure what he would do with all this extravagance, after living on a military base in the mountains for so long, but he wouldn't say no to the offer either. Bahram's team, or whoever had chosen this house for him, was obviously out to woo him and as far as he was concerned, they could woo away. He would have joined Amir's team for nothing. The rest was just frosting on the cake.

As he sat in the magnificently appointed dining room, completely alone, enjoying some of the best salmon he'd ever eaten, and admiring the beautifully polished table, and gleaming chandeliers; he wondered where Josh and Jana were, right this minute: he began to mentally prepare for his meeting with Dr. Bahram. Tomorrow would be a very big day.

• • • • •

All concerned had agreed that the two groups meeting on the mountain, was very much a God thing. The trek would be easier with more hands on deck. Scott and Mark were amazed when they heard the story of Josh and Jana's capture, and subsequent escape. And, Josh, and Jana sat open mouthed as Scott, Mark, and Becca, recounted some of the more dangerous, and baffling things they ran into after Josh's departure from their group.

Jana decided to get to know Becca a bit better, and sat near her at the fire. She saw the furtive glances toward Scott, and watched how gentle she was with CJ, and Angel, and it didn't take long to ascertain that there was a longing there. She also watched Scott, and the way he tried very hard not to look at Becca. She was always amazed at the workings of God, and was thrilled that Scott had his children back; somehow, in madness of capture, and escape, Josh hadn't mentioned this; but she wondered what the answer would be for these two, who obviously had feelings for one another. This would be something they could discuss with the council, upon their return.

They were all puzzled over the fact that Cage, and his militia troops, hadn't tracked any of them down yet. But they weren't going to push their luck, so they determined to get some rest, and take off at first light.

Jana was the first to wake, before dawn, and she could feel that the moisture had frozen on her face. It was colder, especially at night, as they rose higher on the mountain. She wiggled her nose, to knock loose the tiny icicles lodged there, and snuggled closer to Josh. When he turned to her, she giggled at the icicles hanging from his beard, and mustache. He tickled her, and kissed her neck with his frozen whiskers. She jumped from the bedroll, and got away clean, to go do her business; which was a more frequent event, as her pregnancy advanced; before he could untangle himself from the blankets.

She woke Becca, who was completely buried under her blankets and seemingly free from any facial ice. And, after they cleaned themselves up a bit, they got started on breakfast. Even on their first day together, they made an excellent team, and Jana found she really liked this spunky, young woman. It was easy to see why Scott was enamored of her. And, since she knew Scott as well as she did, it was equally easy to see why Becca was charmed by him. She and Josh would really have to see what they could do for these two.

Coffee, and tea, for the adults; she couldn't drink coffee anymore without having acid reflux for the rest of the day; and milk for the children, and pregnant ladies. They boiled water, and made a nice hot cereal with millet, and dried fruit, which seemed to fill everyone up nicely. Once the cookware was washed up, they packed their gear, put out their fire, and headed out.

Their journey was uneventful for most of the day, until one of the children, getting too close to a cliff's edge, slipped, and was hanging on to scrub trees ten feet down a precipice. Her mother was screaming, she was crying; and Jana tried to calm the lady, as Josh, and the guys rigged a series of ropes to retrieve the child. It took a bit, and in the end Josh was forced to risk his life to scale down the cliff to retrieve the little girl, but the rescue was a success, and all the children were admonished to stay close to their mothers, and away from cliff edges.

Jana was getting tired. A part of her wished she'd never left home base, and another part of her was glad she'd come out on this mission. If for no other reason, than to spend time with her man on their favorite mountain range. She knew, though, that once she got home, into her own comfy bed, she probably wouldn't be going on any trips for awhile.

• • • • •

Emma, and Chuck, along with others in the community, readied several dozen cabins, and stocked them with personal hygiene items, blankets, and quilts. Each little family would have their own space, and they would all be integrated into the thriving society. There would be school for the young ones, farm work for some, and community kitchen help for others. Many people in the population, had special talents, and those were utilized in whatever way might best help the whole, so everything worked quite well together.

The council knew there would come a time when their men would be on missions more dangerous than the rescue of other rebels, who'd decided they didn't want to be implanted with a GPS chip. From intercepted communications, they'd discovered the world stage was becoming more dangerous by the day.

From recent scouting forays, over the past months, they'd discovered the UNGC had appointed a new leader, who hailed from Iran, and had many ideas that were opposite the views of the conservative Christians abiding in the ARM bases hidden around the country. At some point they would be forced to fight for the country they loved, and most likely, for their very lives. It was just a matter of time.

Even people around the world, who had opted for these changes with open arms, and supposedly open minds, were beginning to wonder what they'd gotten themselves into. Average Americans, who'd once lived in decent houses; who worked at jobs, which paid a livable wage; who'd eaten decent food, and were able to take care of their families; had found themselves in recent months, living from hand to mouth. Government stores were out of necessities, more often than they weren't, as the country's warehouses were emptied to send supplies to other nations around the world. Those that didn't work, were given the same rations as those who did work, so there was no real incentive to work at all. Medical care had become almost non-existent. The country had simply fallen apart around the ears of the liberals, who refused to see the destruction their own ideals spawned.

It was early in the lowlands now, but it was pretty obvious that once need began to raise its unforgiving head across the land, there would be an outcry from the people. Even those people who'd thought they were simply voting for equality for all; as they blindly agreed that Christianity was somehow an evil thing. When they agreed that all humans deserved the same of everything, despite the fact that many weren't willing to work for it like their counterparts. When they decided that political correctness was essential to the governance of a people, even at the expense of the freedom of others. When they agreed it was a good idea to hand over their freedom to a government who didn't care, in hopes of a system that would simply take care of them.

Yes, there would come a day.

The salvation of the righteous is from the Lord; He is their stronghold in the time of trouble. The Lord helps them and delivers them; He delivers them from the wicked and saves them, because they take refuge in Him.

Psalm 37:39-40

CHAPTER 20

Walking into the great council hall, dressed as he was in full military regalia, Cage felt very deserving of the honor he'd been given, and silently gave himself a huge pat on the back. Dr. Amir was on the other side of the room, but upon noticing Cage's arrival, he left his conversation and came toward the General with a smile on his face. "Welcome, General Cage! Welcome to council. I trust you found your accommodations comfortable?"

"Yes, Doctor, everything was exceptional."

"Well, I understand that when the last government was forming, it took possession of your vast holdings and massive wealth as its own. I decided this was the least we owed you, after your sizeable contribution to that failed cause."

"I was glad to do it. I never really cared for my ancestral home, and felt that the money would help in the country's attempts to set up a new way. The fact that it didn't work out, is of no consequence to me. I believe the government coming together under the UNGC, has a much better chance of making a difference. I'm glad to help in any way that I can."

"And, that is just one of the many reasons, General Cage, that I am happy to have you as a key player in my upper council."

Cage had been pretty sure this would be his appointment, but hadn't actually heard the words until this very moment. He wanted to shout, and jump up and down; but settled for, "Thank you, Doctor. I will do my very best to provide you with good council and unwavering loyalty, until my last breath."

"Thank you, General. Now, when we are in public, obviously I will expect you to call me Doctor, but when we are alone, I would like you to call me Amir."

"Yes Sir, I'm honored. You may call me whatever you'd like. I've never gone by my first name, which is Radcliff, as I didn't really care for the family name, but you may do as you wish."

"Well, how about if I just call you Cage, unless we are in public, and then I will call you General. Is that acceptable?"

"Yes Sir, anything you'd like Sir. I appreciate your faith in me, and I will do my best for you."

"Yes, Cage, I believe you will. I think we will even become good chums along the way."

Cage might have been surprised to find out how much research the good doctor had done into his past. Bahram was completely up to date on his childish exploits, the secrets of his family, and his deeply engrained cruel streak. He knew how much pleasure Cage derived from the torture of others, even women and children, and about his complete lack of conscience. He'd even gone so far as to question some of those who were present on the night that hell broke loose on the mountain; and those who'd gone out for the failed mission on the pass; to bring back the escapees. Yes, he knew all of Cage's secrets, but he wasn't upset about his findings. He was delighted. This would be a man he could truly use in the coming days. The man wasn't Muslim, that was for certain. But he had no ties, no affiliations with any religion, so he would be useful in crossing important lines of communication. And, it seemed he'd gotten along, passably well, with the mercenaries in his camp; who were now in the employ of the doctor. This was essentially a man with no conscience, no moral compass, and no compunction to rectify past deeds. They would be perfect together.

Cage was simply thrilled to be in the presence of this great and influential man. He felt lighter than he had in years. First he would concentrate on the job at hand, and then he would figure out how to get his hands on Josh Conyers again. He'd been so bogged down, back on the base, with the knowledge that his secrets might be found out. Now, here he was, free of those secrets, and when he walked, the bounce in his step proved it.

His situation at the house was working splendidly. It seemed he had Mrs. Adler, Sally, and James, wrapped around his little finger, and that would make his life very comfortable indeed. He'd never felt the need to garner the affection of his troops. They were soldiers, and so was he. They were there to follow his orders, or pay the consequences of their actions. But, this situation was different. He knew, from being around the servants in his parent's household, that the 'help' gossips. And, depending on where their loyalties stood, they would either be gossiping about someone else, or they would be gossiping about you. He decided to endear them to him, so that would not be a future concern.

Mrs. Adler proved to be an excellent cook, and the peach pie he ate for dessert last night was the best he'd ever tasted. Sally kept everything neat, and clean, and he believed, would lay down and die for him if he asked her to. James was quick as a whip, and a good driver. He felt that over time, and increased trust, he might be able to depend on him for additional tasks. So, his life, here in the city, was turning out to be not as horrible as he'd imagined it would be. Amir asked him to lunch that afternoon, so they might have a more private discussion, than they were afforded working in the council chambers. Cage was probably more excited than a grown man should be, about going to lunch with another grown man, but he doted on every word that came out of the doctor's mouth.

Over lunch, Amir asked Cage a number of questions that might give him a little more insight into what kind of changes he would be open to.

Cage ordered the baked chicken, and sautéed vegetables; Amir, the Cobb salad, with dressing on the side. They both drank white wine.

"So, Cage, did you grow up a religious man?"

"No Sir. No one in my family was ever affiliated with any particular religion that I know of. Though there was a small chapel at the family estate, which had been in use a couple of generations ago."

"You do know that I am a Muslim, do you not?"

"Yes Sir. I was made aware of that."

"Does that bother you?"

"No Sir, why would that bother me? I had a team of Muslim mercenaries, that I worked closely with on a number of missions, back at the mountain base."

"Yes, I'd heard that. Did any of their customs offend you?"

"I think they were probably much more offended by me, than I ever was by anything they did. Can I ask why you want to know?"

"Well, Cage, I have some very deep, personal beliefs. Beliefs that are central to who I am, and to what I intend to accomplish in my position. I have to know that you will support me, in whatever I need to do, to make certain things happen."

"Sir, I will do whatever you ask of me. I am your man, and I am here to do your bidding. I have no ties to anyone but you. I don't have any preconceived notions about anything. And, I am here to carry out your will. If you just tell me a little bit about your beliefs, I'm sure I can get behind anything you find important."

Amir told Cage everything he knew about Muhammad ibn Hasan al-Mahdi, the ultimate savior of humankind, and the final Imam. He explained the 'Twelver' movement, and their duty to make a way for the twelfth Imam. He also explained to Cage that Allah had made a way for him to be in the highest government position in the world, to accomplish his ultimate purpose. And, further, that Allah had arranged for Cage to be his right hand man through it all.

Cage was honored, though a bit doubtful. All this talk about Allah 'making a way' for him was a bit humorous, but he would never let on that he had that kind of doubt about his boss's beliefs, or plans. And, truthfully, he didn't really care about any of it. None of the extraordinary things Amir had just discussed seemed unusual, or blasphemous to him, because he'd come in with a clean spiritual slate. He was on board, and ready to do whatever it took to bring Amir's dreams to fruition. After all, what could it hurt?

Josh's group was almost home. They were higher on the range, and, therefore, colder because of it, so they were careful to find empty caves for their overnight stays. Finding caverns large enough for five dozen people wasn't easy, but God had been good. Jana continued to supply enough meat for everyone on their journey, and their staples, with conservative use, had lasted through their entire trek. Jana couldn't wait to get home. Her time out on the mountain had been nice, but she knew she'd enjoy being warm again.

Josh couldn't wait to see his folks, and have some of his mom's hot biscuits. He was tired, and needed a place to unwind. He knew the time was coming, quickly, when the men of the resistance bases around the country, would have to come together for a greater purpose. So, he intended to enjoy his time with family; and his hands in the rich, black earth; for as long as he could. His child would be coming soon, and he wanted to get to know his son. With war looming on the horizon, who knew how much time he would have to do so. He'd worried, before, about how he would force his wife to stay on the base, when the time came to fight; but with a baby to take care of, if that time happened anytime soon, he knew she would be safe at home with the little one. Obviously, he didn't know Jana as well as he thought he did.

Mark couldn't wait to see his children. He'd barely gotten to know them again, when he'd been asked to accompany Josh and Scott on this mission. He felt bad that he'd been such a negative influence the whole way, but he was sure the guys understood. When he got home he would spend every waking moment; when they weren't in school, and he wasn't at work; playing games, and loving on them. No one would ever replace Tina, but he was grateful for Rachel, and her love for the children. And, his mouth watered every time he thought about getting his hands on some of Emma's hot biscuits, with lots of butter, and honey.

Scott was excited about arriving back on base, to get his kids settled in to their new home. He would also be happy to get out of these close situations with Becca. He'd become so frustrated with his feelings for her, and was sure they were wrong, on every level. He didn't want to make God angry with him, so he was sure it would be better once he could separate himself from her presence. And, he too, couldn't wait to get a plate full of Emma's piping hot biscuits.

Becca wasn't sure what her new life, on the resistance base, would be like; but she was looking forward to being somewhere warm. She had many talents, and was sure she'd fit right in, especially with some help from Jana. She hoped Scott would continue to let her see the children, as she'd loved them for so long now. She didn't know if she could stand being without them. And, she'd heard so much about Emma's famous biscuits, she couldn't wait to get her teeth around a couple of those things, covered with lots of red eye gravy.

Jana was looking forward to so many things; a hot bath; group services, filled with singing, and testimonies; a cup of hot chocolate; and one of Mom's hot biscuits, for starters. It would be good to be home with family, and friends. She wouldn't blame Mom, and Dad, for being angry with her, and she would gladly face their disappointment, if it was followed by some really good hugs.

• • • • •

The kids would be home soon, she could feel it. Checking to be sure she had all the ingredients for a couple big batches of her biscuits, she continued working on dough for bread, and a big roast for sandwiches. A few apple pies would be in order too. She wanted to make sure she had enough food for all the hungry travelers. Emma cooked her whole life. Living on the farm as a child, she helped her mother, and grandmother, get three meals a day on the table, for dad, papa, and a good handful of farm hands. She figured she probably knew how to make biscuits, before she learned to read. She also believed that Chuck married her for her light, fluffy biscuits; and, whenever she teased him about it, he would neither confirm, nor deny.

She and Chuck had tried to have a baby for several years, with no luck, and thought they would remain childless; until God blessed them with Josh. She'd always wanted to be a mom, and did her best to be a good one. Her error, if you could call it that, was that she doted on him, and probably indulged him a bit too much. But, he'd become such an exemplary young man, that she could hardly be faulted for that. Her husband was a good man. Hard working, kind, and a strong man of faith. They'd been together for over forty years, with an anniversary coming up soon. She couldn't imagine her life without him. God had been good to them, in their previous life on the farm, and now, here, in this amazing place. She didn't know where they would be without all of the great friends they'd made on the ARM base.

The PM base was cleared. One of ARM's scouts, hidden in the rocks outside of the enemy camp, sat watching, in stunned disbelief, as the last of the communications equipment, mess hall supplies, and troops, were loaded into transports. Was this some sort of ploy to confuse their enemies, or to throw them off track? He didn't know, but he would glean the area for any remaining items, which could be useful at home, and then he would hightail it back to the cavern, with his stunning news. This would be the first time in years that they weren't sharing a mountain with those who would destroy them. Perhaps this move foretold of larger coming events?

• • • • •

Sitting in his backyard garden, Cage could hardly remember his previous life. He'd made up stories, for his staff, as to his former position; since he found that telling someone you were the commandant of the best darned, torturing, and killing, prison camp on the mountain, and very good at your job, didn't usually go over very well. Mrs. Adler, Sally, and James, thought he'd headed up a training facility, and had done so well that Doctor Bahram invited him to join his high council. They were very proud of their boss, and bragged him up all over town. And, Mrs. Adler made him special treats every day. So many, in fact, that he was in danger of growing out of his suit pants, if he didn't start watching it a bit.

Holding a glass of chardonnay, and soaking up the sun; he took in the sights, and smells of the gardener's efforts. The fragrance of cherry blossoms, so intrinsic to the area, filled the air with their perfume. He saw he was surrounded with several varieties of tulips, and crocus, pasque flower, Virginia bluebells, Russian iris, and daffodils. The roses looked just about ready to bloom, and would be just in time to replace the scent of cherry blossoms, with a heady aroma of their own. Later there would be tall lupines; delicate columbine; fleeting iris, and peonies. Sturdy daylilies; daisies, his mother's favorite; oriental lilies; bee balm, fragrant lavender, asters, and blooming trees, and shrubs in several varieties abounded. His mother's love of flowers, and the short time he had with her in the garden, were some of his favorite memories. Sounds of several fountains, throughout the strategically landscaped space, offered just enough distraction to drown out noise from the local traffic. The eight foot, white, brick, privacy wall, made the garden seem as though it existed in a different time, and place, and that was fine with him. He'd never been one who liked busy streets, or crowds.

His meetings with Amir had become more frequent, and seemingly, more urgent. He had no interest in politics, or religion, but the more frequently they got together, the more emphasis seemed to be put on both of those topics. He wasn't sure where he fit into this plan of Doctor Bahram's, but he wanted to be part of whatever this great man wanted. As long as he was free to enjoy the privileges he'd been allotted, he really had no thoughts, one way or another, on how the UNGCs rulings and practices were affecting the rest of the world. Let the masses fight over the scraps.

• • • • •

Josh led his dozens up the last slope, to the cavern's hidden entrance, and as they filed into the entry he heard gasps all around from the new comers. "Pretty amazing, huh?"

"Wow, you guys, I had no idea."

"Hey, this is nothing yet. Wait till we get inside."

They walked the long, well lit corridor to the cavern, and stepped out on to the landing. Oohs, and Ahhs abounded. The children, who'd seemed devoid of energy just fifteen minutes ago, were suddenly bouncing off the walls, and anxious to get down to the first welcoming place they'd seen in months. "Hold on, you little tornados. We're all going down together, in an orderly fashion, so no one gets hurt. Then we're going to get some food, before you run off to play. There are rules here, just like you had rules back at home, so I want you to know what those are before you take off. While you're playing, we will show your moms to your quarters, and they can see to cleaning you up, and getting you into some new clothes. Tomorrow, we will all get together for a worship service, to thank God for delivering us safely home! Everybody got it?"

He was assailed with a chorus of "Yes Sir". Then they began their descent into the place, which would be their new home.

Jana could barely believe what was before her. They were home at last. Her eyes grew misty, as she started down to the cavern floor, and she had to stop several times to wipe them away with the back of her hand.

"You okay, Babe?"

"Yes, I just can't believe we're finally here."

"I want to find Mom and Dad first, and let them know that we've made it safely home."

"Yes, I need one of your mom's hugs, and several of her biscuits, before I even think of cleaning up."

"I agree, with lots of butter, and honey."

"The hugs?"

"No, the biscuits. I think that would make the hugs way too sticky."

Vindicate me, O God, and defend my cause against an ungodly people, from the deceitful and unjust man deliver me!

Psalm 43:1

CHAPTER 21

Bishop Nathan Graham had been chosen by a unanimous vote of the UNGC, as the high priest of the new 'World church'. He was chosen to lead this new vestige of sanctity, for all the right reasons. Those being that he was blind to the real meaning of Christian faith, and he was completely compliant to the 'New World Order', right down to turning in congregants of his own previous church, for gathering together to conduct Christian services.

Former members of his congregation, who'd been turned over to the council, suffered punishments ranging from prison time; to agonizing death, for the leaders of the underground church movement. And, he was actually proud of the work he'd done to get those so called lawless troublemakers off the streets.

Graham had been head pastor of his own church for over two decades, but had never really bought in to the whole, 'Jesus Saves', rhetoric. His reasoning was that if there really was a God, and hence, a Jesus who died for all of us, why was there so much suffering in the world? So, he'd made the church collection plate his own personal petty cash fund, and ran the place like a downtown social club. Due to that mind set, those members who were true believers, had slowly left the congregation. Saddened by the state of their pastor's heart. Which, didn't bother him at all, and in the long run, left plenty of room for new members.

The church filled up almost instantly. Sadly, as it happens, the world was filled with people who weren't really looking for a relationship with a personal God, but were in fact, just looking for a place to hang out, have a good time, and socialize, on Sunday. A place that would afford them the right to call themselves members of a Christian church, but wouldn't come with any of the annoying moral ties and obligations.

He'd grown up in a tight knit community, where his father was pastor of the local church. Mom took care of the kids; and he came home to freshly baked cookies and family game night, throughout his young childhood. It wasn't until later; after college; once he had his seminary degree, that his world, and everything he'd ever known came in to question. His mother was diagnosed with stage four breast cancer; and died an agonizing death; no matter how much they all pleaded with God to heal her. Then he found out his father had been having an affair with his church secretary for several years. He wondered if his mom had known, and if that had made her give up hope. His father died in a fiery car crash, just one year after his mother's death, and before Nathan had a chance to forgive him. They hadn't spoken for the whole year, and he'd taken his time coming forward with the words which might heal their relationship.

Graham's church garnered quite a reputation, over time, and was filled to capacity every Sunday. It even became known as the place you wanted to go, if you were looking for some real good Sunday entertainment. And, soon grew to be categorized as a mega church, with tens of thousands of members. Hence, when the government crackdown began, Nathan was one of the first pastors to comply with the cease, and desist order. And one of the first pastors to begin reporting those who met in secret. Since he'd already made a fortune, off the broken lives of the world; and his own heart had never really belonged to the Lord; it was easier for him to deny Christ, than it was for many others who sincerely loved their members and their lives as fathers of the faith.

His name became well known to UNGC officials, in charge of stomping out Christian churches, for two reasons. Because he was well known in Christian circles, as the leader of a mega church, and therefore might lend credibility to the whole phony 'World Church' phenomenon. And, because he was loyal to the government order, to a degree that he was willing to throw others under the bus to comply. They needed men who were so malleable.

He was very proud of his appointment, and truly believed he was selected due to his successful mega church. He had no idea the council had chosen him mainly for his wishy-washy attitude, and broken soul. He wore his collar and robes with pride. And, people who filled the state run churches each week, acquiesced to him. Pride goes before a fall, and the bigger they are, the harder they will fall.

• • • • •

When Cage met Graham they looked each other up

and down, and saw through the facade immediately. But, since they were both as phony as a three dollar bill, and couldn't come up with any fault in the other, that wasn't already hiding in their own evil intensions, they nodded and carried on.

• • • • •

Amir prayed five times a day, in private, while attending the state run church on Sundays. He was expected to keep up appearances and would do so, until the last days when he could rally all the 'Twelvers' around the globe, for their triumphant Caliphate.

He usually dreaded Sundays, as it meant he would be surrounded by fawning women, and mothers who wanted to entice him into marrying their daughters. He also hated the glitz, and glamour of the new buildings, and the thought of how much money had been taken from the council's coffers, to make them the gaudy spectacles they were. But, he had to admit, at least Graham had made sure to include lots of entertainment.

Major, world known, stars came to perform each week. Which really drew in the numbers, and made the council happy. He knew if the Imams of his faith were to witness the entertainers, especially the scantily clad women who came to perform, they would condemn the entire mess. And they'd probably order all the buildings to be burned to the ground. So he didn't invite them. There would be plenty of time for that sort of thing later. Once their time had come, and the Mahdi arrived, they would do away with all the filth of this culture; though he'd enjoyed his share of it; once and for all.

As the council met, Cage could see new resolutions passed each week, which were moving the world society closer and closer to a place of no return. A place where Amir would be able to play his hand, and place his groups of 'Twelvers' in positions of power. America's previous administration had brought in so many Muslims and Islamic groups, while shaming the people into thinking their fear was a type of racism, that the deck was already stacked substantially in his favor. All he had to do now, was to make sure those groups had the tools and funding they needed to accomplish the tasks before them. And as they accomplished their awful takeover, Christianity, still refused to die, as it sparked anew in the underground churches of the world.

• • • • •

The feast was magnificent! Emma and the ladies in the community kitchen had outdone themselves, working for days, making pies, and breads; roasting meat, and preparing side dishes enough to feed their usual, plus five dozen more. They had created a vast culinary masterpiece, and people were still trying to fit one more bite into their already full stomachs. There was a fair amount of groaning going on, as men loosened their belts, and women patted their bellies. Moms began herding children off to baths and bed, and Josh and Jana wandered off to clean up, and get some sleep, after agreeing they would meet with the council in the morning. There was plenty to talk about, since a scout had arrived only hours before, chattering about the PM base, and how it had been evacuated and cleaned out.

As far as Josh was concerned, that didn't make any sense. He was sure Cage wouldn't have just given up on capturing him so easily. There had to be some pretty huge incentives for him to give up the chase this way. But, if it were true, what a difference it could make in their rescue missions, and their forays out onto the heights. It would definitely be interesting to hear all the news from the young scout. Perhaps they would even be able to put two, and two together, and come up with some answers for why the withdrawal had taken place.

The scout also spent some time going through items left on the plateau by the exiting troops; and there might be things that they could get some use out of. These would all be topics of discussion, in the morning.

Josh and Jana made their way back to their quarters, for a hot shower and some much needed rest. After getting cleaned up, they lay in bed, snuggled together, with Josh's large hand covering his wife's rounding abdomen. "I wonder what he'll look like? Who he'll be?"

"Well, I hope he looks like you. You are a very handsome man."

Josh tickled her until she begged him to stop, and then he kissed her neck. "I just hope we can help him to know who he is in Christ, Jana. I want him to be a strong man of God."

"I don't think that's anything you need to worry about, Josh. He will have you as an example. Remember that God has plans for him, so he already has an in with the best teacher of all. He will grow up here, with others who know the Lord. He will be a strong man of God."

Josh wrapped his arms around her, gave her a deep kiss, and they were both sleeping within thirty seconds.

Mark didn't think he could remember ever being so happy. He was exhausted, but after the children bathed, and he took his turn, Rachel came over with homemade cookies, and they played board games for hours. He knew he would have to sit through a council meeting in the morning, but listening to his kids chattering on about everything that happened since he left, just made him smile. Being a husband, and dad, had always been the most fulfilling piece of his life. And though he missed his wife, with a pain that cut to his soul, he still had his two great kiddos to love, and a wonderful friend in Rachel.

Forever grateful to God, for bringing them all together again, he was thinking he'd probably skip the next few rescue missions; and work full time here in the cavern; already knowing he didn't want to be away from his children for that long ever again.

Becca had been assigned her own quarters, while CJ, and Angel were bunking in their dad's cabin. It was strange being alone, after so long. She took a hot bath, and pampered herself with salves, and ointments, to remove the rough skin from her heels, elbows, and wind burned face. By the time she was done; with her thick, beautiful hair feeling soft, and smelling clean for the first time in weeks; she thought she just might be able to get used to this. She would be working in the community kitchen, with Jana, Emma, and some of the new moms they brought with them. And she was looking forward to some bonding time with the women on base. But having her own space would be very nice too.

Scott was having quite a time, wrangling his two little ones in and out of a bath. He finally achieved clean kids, and felt very accomplished. He decided to take his own shower, once he had the children in bed, so he wouldn't have to worry about them getting into trouble while no one was watching. They played games, and rolled around on the floor playing tickle monster, and they laughed until they couldn't laugh anymore. Later, some ladies from the community kitchen, brought fun quilts for the kids, similar to ones they'd made for the other children in the camp, and Angel fell in love with the pictures of kittens, and puppies on her new blankie. CJ, on the other hand, thought his quilt, covered with pictures of trucks, and cars, looked very grown up.

The ladies also made popcorn, and hot chocolate, for all the new children on base, to help them feel more at home. So after they ate their snacks, and brushed their teeth, Dad tucked them in to their brand new beds, with their brand new blankets. He crawled into a hot shower, deeply tired, but happier than he'd felt in months.

• • • • •

Nathan Graham was as scheming, and phony as they came, but Cage had seen through his guise right away. He knew the council was using the Bishop to draw in all those folks who enjoyed calling themselves Christians (while it was still legal to do so), in order to belong to a large social organization, but who never really knew Jesus at all. It was easy to get them fully on board with the new "World Church', with its socialist agenda, and its pat yourself on the back ethics. In fact most of those types were actually more comfortable in an organization, where they were not expected to go about 'evangelizing', and 'getting involved' in different aspects of church life.

For the most part, those who were so easily duped into thinking this was a 'real' religion, were also the type that frequently supported charitable activities, which were completely against anything the Bible, or true Christianity, stood for at all. In a world where it was cooler to be liberal, than it was to stand for Jesus, they fit right in. And now that it was illegal to read the Bible, or call yourself a Christian, their "I told you so" smug expressions, said it all.

Cage didn't mind. He'd begun attending Sunday services, with Amir, at his request, simply to present a united front. He knew that Amir, and probably hundreds of millions, of his Muslim brothers, continued to pray five times a day, to Allah. He also knew that their punishment, if caught, wouldn't have been nearly as severe, as that saved for Christians. He didn't really care, none of it made a bit of difference to him. The church, in their district, was a sight to behold, and it made him want to laugh every time they were dropped off at the gilded stairs, by their long, silver limousine. Huge golden doors opened, and led into a vestibule made of imported marble, and gold leaf everything. Crystal chandeliers hung every ten feet, or so, and once you passed through the equally golden doors, into the sanctuary, there were golden, and bejeweled statues of members of the UNGC. A fitting statement for a church that didn't stand for anything.

Cage didn't think he'd ever seen so much gold leaf in his life, not even in his parent's ostentatious home. The idea that so much money had been spent, on such an obvious farce, was laughable. It reminded him of Scientology, and the mess that had become. And, if it had affected him, in any real way, it would have made him angry. But, as it was, most of the people it affected, were already dirt poor, and probably wouldn't be able to tell the difference. He supposed it would have been nice, if the money spent here, could have fed people and their children, but that wasn't his concern either.

Today the entertainment came in the form of some young rock star he'd never heard of; and couldn't possibly care less about; but the place was packed, so the publicity seemed to have worked. The noise was excruciating, and he noticed the equally strained look on Amir's face, so he knew he was just as ready to leave. At the end of the nonsensical, meaningless service, they worked a path through the throng of young people, standing in line to get autographs. And made their way out to the waiting limousine.

On their way to lunch, Cage thought to ask a question. "Do you ever get tired of showing up at this fake church, and putting up with all the noise, and nonsense?"

"Of course I do. But, until everything is in place, this is what I will do. We have been placing our followers in strategic places and positions, for years now. But we must follow the plan, or it will blow up in our faces. The Mahdi will wait, until the appropriate time. He has waited all these hundreds of years."

"But how will you know when that time comes?"

"We will know, because the Mahdi will appear. It is as simple and yet divine, as that."

"Well, I'm not as spiritual as you are, Amir, so I'll follow you, if that's okay."

"That is just fine, Cage. I will lead you gladly."

• • • • •

The girls came together to prepare breakfast. Jana, couldn't wait to begin, she'd missed her time with Mom. But, more than that, she couldn't wait to begin tutoring Becca. She was such a willing and eager student, and caught on very quickly.

They would cook, eat, clean up, and then prepare for the huge worship service, which had been planned to welcome home the weary travelers. After services, the council would meet, and go over lots of new information.

Breakfast consisted of thick slabs of juicy, smoked ham; heaps of crisp bacon; piles of buttermilk pancakes; light, fluffy biscuits, covered in spicy red eye gravy; mounds of home fried potatoes; scrambled eggs, sprinkled with cheese;

bowls of fruit salad; pitchers of ice cold milk, and orange juice; and steaming pots of coffee. Bowls of hand churned butter, golden honey, and whipped cream, dotted the table, along with warm maple syrup. Becca had never seen so much food, and she'd certainly never helped to make so much food before. Chuck said a prayer, and they all dug in. So much deliciousness in one place. And, just like the evening before, everyone fought to make room for just one more bite, before the clean up began.

As the women washed dishes, the men set up for worship service in the city square. Most would stand, or bring blankets to sit on, but there were also chairs set up in various places, for those who were elderly, or who grew too tired to stand. Instruments were brought out, and the musicians began to tune. Jana urged everyone to hurry, so they wouldn't miss the opening song. She'd missed worshipping with these wonderful people, and couldn't wait to get started. As everyone assembled, and the music began, she could feel the Holy Spirit descend on His people. They sang, shared testimonies read Psalms and other scriptures, and sang some more. Chuck said a prayer of thanks, for bringing the soldiers home, and for the addition of new families. Jana moved over to the chairs half way through the service, and Josh was concerned. "Are you okay?"

"Yep, just a little tired, I guess. I am pregnant you know."

"Yes ma'am. I do know. I think Doc Rose should take a look at you tomorrow, just to see that everything is alright."

"That's fine. I haven't seen him yet, because I wanted to keep the whole thing secret, until I could tell you."

"Well, the cat's out of the bag now, so let's get you looked at."

"Yes Sir."

"Are you up to an elders meeting?"

"I think I can handle that, but I might need a nap afterward, if that's okay."

Their meeting was mostly comprised of well wishes, and welcomes home. Some time was given to deciding what to do about the items left on the PM base by the vacated militia. A consensus was reached that several scouts would go out and bring back whatever looked to be of help to the ARM camp. Then, Chuck brought up the fact that they'd received word about the UNGCs appointment of a new council leader. He relayed what facts he had about Dr. Amir Bahram, and the meeting took on a serious twist. Josh turned to the group, "I know it's difficult to talk about, because life in this cavern is so great, but at some point we will have to fight for our lives.

Some of the other ARM camps aren't as well hidden as this one, and to be honest, I don't know how they haven't been found out yet. But, when they are, the able bodied men from all the camps will have to come together to fight for our right to live, and to worship as we please. Does everyone understand, and agree?"

"We know, Josh. I think we've been putting it off as long as possible, even as the world raises its army of Muslim radicals. We've gotten a bit complacent here, in our comfortable homes, just like we did outside these walls, before the government became our enemy. We're so tired of war. But, we also know we can't stay hidden forever."

"I know how you feel, Dad, Jana and I have loved our time here, but we want our son to grow up in a world where he is free to worship Jesus, wherever, and whenever, he wants to. The idea of our men going off to war again, is something that many of us have been trying to avoid, but I'm afraid we're going to have to prepare for it anyway."

"As usual, Josh, you're right. But, not all the men here have been in battle before. We're going to have to train them. And, though we have some weapons, I know we are not as well armed as the militia, or the UN troops."

"You know, we can fight too. Don't count the women

out. And there are more of us than there are men in the camp.”

“I know Jana, but most of the women are older, sorry Mom, or have small children. I won’t have them fighting. And, in your case, let’s concentrate on having a baby, before you go save the world, okay?”

“Fine, but the time will come when you will need me, and I want to be ready too.”

“Okay, we will begin training, but first let’s train those men who are not experienced in battle, and later we can concentrate on training the women. It would be good for them to know basic self defense anyway, just in case.”

“Are we all in agreement? Let’s take a vote. All those in favor?”

Every hand on the council raised; Chuck, Emma, Scott, Mark, the doctors, and every single other member.

“Okay, since all were in favor, I won’t ask for those opposed. We will begin on Monday.”

“Wait a minute, I have to see Doctor Rose on Monday, I don’t want you to start without me.”

Doctor Rose laughed.

“We’ll save the good stuff for when you get back, okay?”

“Thank you, husband. I know you love me.”

"Yes, Jana, I do love you, but let's all remember that we will win nothing by our own hand. God is our shield, and protector. It is by His mighty hand that we will prevail."

O God, we have heard with our ears, our fathers have told us, what deeds you performed in their days, in the days of old: you with your own hand drove out the nations, but them you planted; you afflicted the peoples, but them you set free; for not by their own sword did they win the land, nor did their own arm save them, but your right hand and your arm, and the light of your face, for you delighted in them.

Psalm 44:1-3

CHAPTER 22

"So, how does everything look, Doc?"

"So far, so good. I want you to watch yourself though, Jana. I know you fancy yourself as strong as the boys, and I'm the first one to admit that you are one heck of a scrapper, but you are a tiny wisp of a thing, and you're carrying a growing child inside your body."

"Well, I think I had that one figured out, Doc, but if

everything looks good, I don't know what the problem is."

"There isn't a problem, Jana. Not yet. But you are underweight, and if you don't eat right, the baby will take the nourishment he needs from your bones, and that could leave you in a very bad place. I also want to keep an eye on your blood pressure. It was a little high."

"Well, if you remember, I did just get back from an extended hike, and I'll have to admit I got lots of exercise on that little outing, but I'm back now, and I'm eating right, so don't worry about me."

"Okay, I won't worry, if you'll promise me that you're going to take your vitamins, and get some rest."

"Yes Sir. I will take care of myself, and I'll make an appointment in a month."

"Make that two weeks, Jana. I want to keep an eye on you."

"Okay, okay, two weeks. You're a hard man, Doc."

"And, you're a stubborn woman, Jana."

Jana rushed down to the city square, where training was going on, and saw that Josh had everything completely under control. They'd agreed, with the council, that the men would train for an hour a day, so they could still get all their duties taken care of in a timely manner. It was pretty easy to see which men had trained previously, and which ones had not, but it would just be a matter of time, before they all had a handle on the basics. Jana's job would come later, as she would be helping with archery lessons and knife throwing. They probably still had quite some time to train, really, before things in the world got bad enough to pose a threat to them. But it could seriously be at any moment that one of the other bases would be discovered, and they'd have to assemble and go to their aid.

Communication between bases was hap hazard, at best, with only intermittent scouting missions bringing in any intelligence at all. But, if they got word, that one of their fellow ARM strongholds needed help, they wanted to be able to mount a team to assist them as quickly as possible.

Scott became one of the resistance army's best soldiers, and Josh was proud of the man he'd become, so he decided to assign him as top drill sergeant. The look on Scott's face, when Josh presented him with the honor, was priceless.

"I will do you proud, brother. I'll get these men whipped into shape, in no time, for whatever comes next."

"Well, don't be too hard on them, Scott. Just do the same bang up job on this that you've done with everything else I've handed you, and you will be my hero. You really have proven yourself to be my strong right hand man, and a valuable asset to the team."

"Thank you, boss. Having you as my friend, and Jesus as my Savior, has been the best thing that's ever happened to me. And, now I have my kids back. I seriously have everything."

· · · · ·

It started many years ago, when political correctness became the norm, and wondering about our country's safety became a hate crime. The attacks came less frequently then, but were usually, stunningly effective. Great towers felled by terrorist's planes; vans plowing through Christmas markets; bombs exploding at sporting events; and people shouting "Allahu Akbar", as they wielded knife, or gun, or beheaded a three year old girl. Those attacks grew in frequency, and severity, until they became a way of life all around the world. For the most part they were a distraction from the real issues, and Doctor Bahram was angry every time he heard that another attack had been executed.

It was much better, for his strategies, if those radicals would lay low, and allow their numbers to build. America's last president had been a brother, if only secretly, and had opened the doors of every segment of government, and society, to his Muslim friends. This made Amir's job much easier. But, complete discretion was needed to pull off the other pieces of the puzzle, which would materialize over the next few years. Patience was the key.

Cage was finding out, first hand, what it took to be the kind of charismatic leader he knew his friend to be. He watched as Amir won over every single person he talked to, either friend, or foe. No one that he'd ever known was as good at bringing a room together, and a vote to his liking, as this dynamic man.

Everywhere they went, people bent over backward to accommodate his every desire, and he never lacked for beautiful women to wear on his arm. Of course, Cage was no slouch in that department either, though he'd not dated much in his life; never finding the time, or the desire to think, or worry about someone else's needs.

He was a strikingly handsome man, with eyes that sent women into a tizzy. And, now that he was Amir's right hand man, it happened that when he and Amir went out on the town he was supplied with his choice of women. And he found, with this arrangement, that he still didn't have to worry about what they wanted, or needed. These women were as disposable as an old pair of socks. Before he knew it, his face was on the society pages of the paper, right along with the good doctor, and he began to get used to it, even liking it to a certain degree. As long as he didn't have to be in a relationship with any of these women, he was fine with using them for an evening of pleasure.

Amir was good at hiding the fact that he was a radical, fundamentalist Muslim. It had been essential to his being selected to head up the UNGC, and it was imperative to his future stratagem. He hid the fact, by being very non-Muslim in his actions, when non-Muslims were watching. After all, a good Muslim wouldn't have sex with a different woman every night, drink the evening away, or be seen in a church every Sunday, but it was all part of the plan. The Quran was very clear. Telling the followers of Allah and his prophet, that they should work their way into a society, with lies, and deceit, until they were totally accepted, and in a position to take over before they strike. So he was doing his job very well.

Mrs. Adler and Sally were worried. They saw the trap in which General Cage had become entangled. They'd witnessed it a million times, while serving various generals. And they could attest; that the old adage was true; absolute power really does corrupt absolutely.

He'd been so kind to them from the moment he'd first arrived, so they assumed he just wasn't that kind of man, and was only getting caught up in Dr. Bahram's world. When he'd turn up late at night, smelling of booze, and floozies, they would wag their heads, and look at each other meaningfully.

Cage still needed them, so, for his part he'd play on their sympathies for special treatment, and they'd fall for it every time. He was playing both sides against the middle, and it was working out for him in a big way.

• • • • •

Bishop Graham was getting a bit full of himself. His 'World Church' had grown to be the largest in the country, with tens, and tens of thousands of members. The council was forced to build an addition on the sanctuary, and later, overflow rooms around the city, with life sized screens, so more watchers could be witness to the meaningless displays. He knew this new religion was supposed to be about worshiping diversity and multi culturist values; as opposed to deities, or individuals; but as more members were added to the rolls each week, he saw that his charismatic personality was the real reason they came. He was correct, in part, because everyone needs something bigger than themselves to look to in times of trouble. It helps, though, if that something has the power to really do something about the problems. Nathan was just a man, and had no such power; but many discovered it wasn't healthy to try to remind him of that..

The more often that Cage, and Amir, attended Sunday services together, the more Cage grew to dislike Graham. Amir urged him to get along with the charlatan, because in the future, they would be expected to work together. So Cage decided he would have to pretend, for the doctor's sake. He truly despised the man's duplicitous nature. He'd rather hang out with Muslim mercenaries. No matter how dangerous they were, at least he knew where they stood.

There were those, in the general public and in different branches of government, who had suspicions about Amir's loyalties and his plans for the population. And many who questioned the purpose of the 'World Church', in the larger scheme of things. But they were powerless to do anything about it. He always stayed in places where he was surrounded by armed guards and personal supporters, so no one had been able to get to him for serious questioning, or for more powerful means of disagreement. Besides, many of his detractors reasoned, if they did away with him, who was to know if he would be replaced by someone even worse. Better the devil you know, than the devil you don't.

Meanwhile, the underground Christian church was beginning to thrive again. God was still on the throne. They'd finally found some safe places to meet, and were growing in numbers. These were those poor souls who had not escaped the GHOs thugs, and had been implanted with the dreaded government chip. They would rather have gone in search of an ARM base, but knew they couldn't risk exposing all those fellow Christians, by showing up with an active GPS. Therefore, they would wait it out. Due to their known political leanings, even if they were not publicized, they were at the bottom of the government's list for everything: food, medical help, clothing, and decent housing. But somewhere out there were brothers and sisters in Christ who would someday, need their help.

As the church grew, persecutions mounted. Doctor Bahram had found appropriate positions, for those outlying base commanders, who didn't fit into his cabinet; and their talents were being put to use. In any case, it was getting more terrifying, and more dangerous, to be a Christian. There was word, out there, that a large church cell had been discovered, right in the center of Chicago. The results were devastating, and poignant. Every member had been publically whipped, and tortured; the elders of the church had their eyes put out with hot pokers, simply to make a point; and the pastor was crucified upside down. A sign was attached to his cross, which read, "The future of all who choose Christ".

While the Christian church suffered distressing blows, right along with its growth spurts, other religions got away with a slap to the wrist. For instance, with Doctor Bahram's help, new underground mosques abounded, and terrorist cells multiplied. However, when one was discovered, it was simply ordered to disband. Once the authorities left the site, services continued as before. As the checks, and balances continued to weigh in the favor of Islam, and terror attacks abounded; authorities and council members scratched their heads, and wondered what in the world the problem could possibly be, and where they'd gone wrong.

Ordinary citizens grew more upset with the balance of power, and the unequal division of goods, and services. How unfair it all seemed.

So many, even many of those who called themselves

Christian, when they'd had the option voted for socialism; thinking it the perfect solution for taking care of the world's ills. The problem is, true socialism can only work in a perfect world. This form of government requires that everyone live equally, in all things. And if we are at all honest, there will always be those who don't want to do their share of the work, and others who want to be king of the world, which is exactly how the situation evolved. There were those who had it all, like Bahram, Cage, and the rest of the UNG council, to name a few; and there were those who had nothing, being forced to scratch for an existence. Then there were those in the several tiers in between, who see the unfairness, and decide they want to do something about it.

Conditions had gotten so bad in the world, in just the past year, that those tucked away in ARM encampments wouldn't have recognized it as the world they'd escaped. Still, there was much more to come; and America's citizens hadn't seen, by half, the devastation their UNGC could perpetrate.

• • • • •

Jana was helping to train the camp's men, in the fine art of archery. She was the best qualified, as she was the best archer on the base, and had an abundance of patience when it came to explaining her discipline. Most of her trainees were doing well, but there were others who didn't seem to have the coordination to achieve a mastery of the exercise. There were women in the camp, who were chomping at the bit, to train with Jana. But, an agreement had been struck, to train the men first. Becca was one of the women who desperately wanted to learn, but she would have to wait. When Jana showed up at the community kitchen, to help the camp's women with the evening meal, the young woman peppered her with questions. "How was training today?"

"It was good. I think we made lots of progress."

"How is Peter doing? He didn't seem to be catching on, the last time I stopped to watch."

"I believe he did a bit better today."

"I don't get it, Jana. If there is a man, who can't catch on, why are they so insistent that he learn that particular form of combat? Maybe it isn't his thing. Perhaps he would be better at something else. Everyone should be trained at something where they can excel, don't you think? We might have a better army, if each one is doing something they do well."

"You might have a point, Becca. It's something I can speak to Josh about."

"I know I'd be great at archery. I can feel it."

"I'm sure you will, Becca. We will begin training the women later. The elders want to keep women out of combat roles, as much as possible."

"I can certainly understand that for pregnant women, and moms, but for able bodied women, who are capable of fighting, that doesn't make sense."

"And though I might agree with you, to a certain extent, I'm sure you can also see the point of the council, can't you? For instance, you help out with your niece, and nephew, don't you?"

'Well, yes, though, not as much as I used to. Scott usually has them, if they aren't in school."

"How are things with you and Scott?"

"Why. What do you mean?"

"Oh, Becca, it was pretty obvious to most of us that there was an attraction between the two of you. Am I wrong?"

"Well, I know how I was feeling about him, but I don't think he ever felt the same way about me. Besides, he's still married to my sister, so it wouldn't be right."

"You might not have seen how Scott looked at you, Becca, but the rest of us did. That's why he avoids you now. You make him uncomfortable. But, from conversations he's had, with Josh, the only thing that makes him uncomfortable about the situation, is that he is attracted to you, and still married to your sister. Josh, and I are going to talk to the elders. Since Virginia was perpetually unfaithful to Scott, and chose not to accompany him here, we think there might be a way we can perform a sort of divorce proceedings, which would free him to marry anyone he likes. I'll let you know what they decide."

"Thank you, Jana. I guess I didn't know how obvious it was to the world."

"Yep, pretty obvious. Obvious that you're human anyway."

"Then I'll wait to see what the elders say, but I still want to train."

"Okay, okay, the subject is dropped for now, understand? Let's get these potatoes peeled, or they won't be done before supper."

"Yes ma'am. Subject dropped, for now."

Emma had always been famous for her great cooking, but she also had a keen eye, and a soft shoulder. She was determined, after the conversation she'd had with Jana, that she would talk to the elders on Becca's behalf. There was enough suffering in the world. Scott's wife had been unfaithful to him, and Biblically, that gave him the right to divorce her. They would do the right thing by these two young people. Jana was going to bring it up at the next council meeting, after she'd had a chance to confer with Josh.

• • • • •

There was a problem. Mrs. Adler and Sally had been caught at an underground church service, right here in the city. Cage was contacted first, in order to keep things out of the news. Amir was on his way over, to see if they could get things straightened out. He wasn't angry with Cage. Cage had nothing to do with vetting these people, before they were placed in his employment, but they would have to get a few things under control. Cage, on the other hand, was very angry. He couldn't figure out what in the world was so important, to these two women, that they would be willing to risk their lives. Mostly, he hated that this would be an embarrassment, and an inconvenience, to him. Another woman was sent over to cook his meals, until they could find replacements, but she didn't know how he liked his coffee, or his eggs. He was livid.

He wanted to speak to the women. Amir didn't think it was a good idea, but he was adamant. He had to know what was so damned essential to them, at this underground meeting, that they were willing to put their necks on the line, risk everything they had, and cause him such inconvenience. Amir said he could arrange it, but it would all have to be done in secret. The UNGC would be meeting tomorrow, to decide what to do with this latest batch of heretics, and if the vote went as expected, the generals who were handling torture these days, would have a real field day.

• • • • •

Josh agreed with Jana, that Scott and Becca should have the opportunity to be together, that is, if they wanted to be. The Bible was clear about a spouse's unfaithfulness, and the rights of the injured party; where that was concerned; so Scott had every right to divorce Virginia. The Bible was also clear, about what was allowed, if an unbelieving spouse deserted a believer; and Virginia had clearly deserted Scott, when she picked up and moved to her sister's house. Scott, and Josh discussed all of this at great length, so he was aware of the 'new business', which would be voted on at the meeting today. He was a little embarrassed that he would be the topic of discussion, but he also cared enough about Becca, to live with it, and keep his mouth shut. Initially he'd actually felt guilty about his feelings toward Becca, and thought he was fated to stay married to Virginia, his cheating, unfaithful, deserting wife, for the rest of his life. So, he'd tried to avoid the woman he cared about, instead of doing something that might anger God. Now that things had been made clear to him, he was hopeful Becca would feel the same way about their chance to be together.

Josh and Jana were in agreement that, if the two young people wanted to pursue a relationship, they should be able to do so. But, now they would have to present their opinions to the elder's committee, and hope they were all in accord. Jana stepped forward, and presented their case. Josh, Mark, Emma, and Chuck were there for backup, and offered a number of Bible verses, which supported their thoughts. The council discussed the matter, for quite some time, before coming to a conclusion.

The elder's council decided, that since they considered themselves a separate entity, and no longer part of the 'World Organization' which had recently been formed, they were also totally self governed, and had the right to set new rules and laws, which more closely adhered to their shared views of the Bible. They were thankful to Scott that he'd not acted on his feelings and impulses in an irresponsible way, and had instead decided to wait for a ruling from the council. The council, therefore, concluded that, as a God imbued, self governing entity, they could grant Scott a divorce from his wife, and that Scott could pursue a relationship with the young lady of his choice.

After the meeting, Jana went to find Becca, to give her the good news. And, Scott decided to ask her out for the evening, which would require finding someone to watch the children. Emma quickly agreed. "It will be good practice for this soon to be Grandma."

Becca was thrilled, and of course she said yes. But, now, the problem was that they didn't exactly live in a location with romantic restaurants, or nice clubs. Though other romances had been sparked in the ARM base, and there had been several weddings among occupants already, Jana wanted these two to have something to remember.

The ladies made them a special meal, complete with a lovely carafe of wine, and arranged to have a table set in the orchards. Candles made the entire area glow, as if lit by moonlight, and soft music followed. At the end of the evening Scott even got a small goodnight kiss, as he dropped Becca off at her quarters. Going forward, the two of them were seen together at all gatherings, and the kids couldn't have been happier. When Scott proposed, she said yes.

Of course Josh and Jana were asked to serve as best man, and matron of honor. "Well, Becca, all I can say is, we'd better not put this off for too long, or you will all have to roll me down the aisle."

"We do want to have the wedding as soon as possible, Jana, if that's okay with everyone."

"I don't think you'll get any arguments from anyone on that, and I can help you plan. I'm sure Emma, and the rest of the ladies, will help with a dress, flowers, and even a cake."

"Oh, Jana, I'm so excited. I've never been happier about anything in my life, and I have you to thank for this."

"Don't be silly, Becca. I think this was a God thing from the start, and everyone agreed that it was the right thing."

Pastor Mike was notified, and he began to make plans to conduct a wedding.

The ladies got together, and a lovely, borrowed dress, of cream colored satin, and lace, was altered, to fit Becca's small frame. She opted for swept up hair, and small white and yellow flowers worked into her shining, red locks, versus a cumbersome veil. A bouquet of daisies, and buttercups, tied with cream colored ribbon, and a pair of satin slippers, completed her ensemble. Becca didn't wear makeup, she never had, but her face was radiant, and her eyes sparkled with all the hope of a new life with the man she loved.

Scott wore a borrowed, brown suit, and cream colored shirt. The whole thing was very uncomfortable, as the thighs and biceps were so tight, he thought they might rip as he walked down the aisle. A boutonniere of daisies, and buttercups, decorated his lapel, but the only shoes he owned were the hiking boots he'd worn on his escape to the mountain, so, thankfully the pants were a bit long.

Josh and Jana also borrowed dressier items than either of them owned these days, and Jana spent the day of the wedding pulling, and tugging on a blouse, which tried continually, to creep up her rapidly expanding baby bump.

Little CJ proudly held a specially fashioned pillow, which was designed specifically for the ring bearer to carry; and Angel dropped white, and yellow petals from a small wicker basket, as she twirled and danced down the aisle. Both were thrilled that Becca was to be their mom, even though both Scott and Becca had thoroughly explained to them that Gin would still always be their mother. They'd loved Becca their whole lives, so this felt less like a tearing away, and more like a gathering in.

Several members of the community took part in the ceremony, from offering prayers, to special vows, to sharing of musical talent; and when Scott kissed his bride, the whole community cheered, much to Becca's glad embarrassment. She'd been welcomed into the fold, with open arms, and had never felt as comfortable, anywhere else in her life. The wedding supper was superb. Roasted chicken; mashed potatoes, with gravy; baby peas, with pearl onions; Emma's homemade bread; and a fresh salad of various lettuces, cucumbers, tomatoes, olives, peppers, and nuts, all drizzled with a sweet, peppery vinaigrette. Dessert would, of course, be wedding cake, but the ladies had also made hand churned ice cream, and mints, because who can have a wedding supper without a good mint?

It was an evening to remember. Josh, and Jana, took the children for the night, so the newlyweds could have some time to be alone. And, if Jana thought she knew what it was to take care of a couple of little ones, she'd thought wrong. By the time she got them bathed, and tucked in, after Josh read them a story, and they all said prayers, she was ready to collapse. She couldn't wait to get into some comfortable clothes, and decided that evening, that she needed to start figuring out something different for maternity wear. She lay in bed that night, with Josh's hand on her rounded tummy, and wondered out loud. "Am I even cut out for this? I absolutely did not know what to do tonight. You knew more about those children than I did. What am I going to do? And, what kind of mother am I going to be?"

"Remember, Jana, I babysat my cousins when I was a kid. You grew up rough. This isn't something we are born knowing how to do. That's why God gives them to us as little babies, who can't run around and jump on the furniture. We will figure it out as we go along, okay?"

"I'll take your word for it, Josh, but I'm probably going to need all the help you can give me. So, promise me you will be there to help all the way."

"Of course I will. And, without even asking, I can assure you my mom will be there every step of the way too. She will be way more valuable than I will, especially in the beginning. Remember, she's been waiting a long time for this. We will probably have to pry Alec from her fingers, if we want to spend time with him."

"Yeah, you're probably right. You talked me into it. I guess we'll go ahead and have this baby then. I love you, Husband."

"I love you, Wife. And, I love you too, baby Alec."

God is our refuge and strength, a very present help
in trouble. Therefore we will not fear though the
earth gives way, though the mountains be moved
into the heart of the sea, though its waters roar and
foam, though the mountains tremble at its swelling.

Psalm 46:1-3

CHAPTER 23

"What were you two thinking? Mrs. Adler, Sally, why
would you put yourselves in that kind of predicament, and put me in that kind of position, just to
check out something new?"

"Oh, General Cage, we weren't checking out something
new. We have always been Christians. We were just going
to church like we do every week."

"But, I don't understand. The state has provided perfectly good churches for you to attend. Why would you
risk your lives to go to an unauthorized church?"

"Well, the state churches are okay for some people, if you don't mind that sort of thing, but we go to church to worship Jesus. That's something we can't get at the state churches."

"What is so great about this Jesus? Is He worth dying for?"

"The miracle is that He died for us, General Cage. He died to make us free. No state church can do that. We will live with whatever the consequences are, just like He lived with the consequences of taking on our sin. Don't worry about us."

"I don't know what's going to happen when the council convenes tomorrow. I've been told that they will probably make an example of everyone who was caught today, and that would include the two of you. I'm in a bad position, and I don't believe there will be anything I can do."

"If that's what happens, then we will be fine. Whatever they do to us, won't be half as bad as what He endured for us. And, if we leave this place, we will be in the arms of Jesus for eternity. It's okay, General Cage. Don't worry about us."

Cage was furious. "How can you take all of this so lightly? What is wrong with you? Do you understand they are going to torture you, and most likely kill you? I've seen lots of people tortured, and killed. I've even done my share of the torturing, and killing. But it's never been someone I know. All they want you to do is renounce the underground church, and renounce this Jesus that you pray to, and they will go easy on you."

"General, we can't do that. The Bible says that if we deny Him before men, He will deny us before the father. We would never deny our Savior."

"But, this may be your only chance. I've tried to intervene, but the arrest was too public, so even Doctor Bahram can't do anything. If you won't renounce your faith, there is nothing anyone can do."

"It's okay, General. Really. We appreciate you coming down here. And, we appreciate you trying to help, but we will be fine. We hope this doesn't cause you too many problems. We appreciate your actions on our behalf. We have been praying for you. Praying that you will come to know how much He loves you. It's been nice to know you, and to serve you. God bless you."

Cage truly could not understand. What kind of hold did this Jesus have on these two women? What kind of hold did He have on all the Christians of the world? And he'd met plenty of them in his prison cells; including that infernal Josh Conyers; that they would be willing to die, rather than renounce His Name? He was tearing his hair out trying to come up with a way to save these women. A big part of it was that he knew they worried about him, so he could always trust that they would do a good job, and take care of him. But was there something more? Is that all it was? Had he become attached to them? Were they his friends? No, that was impossible. He hadn't had any kind of personal attachment to anyone, not since the sick relationship with Head Master at the academy. And, then, just recently with Amir. Was he going soft?

Things moved very quickly. A hearing was held to determine the fate of the thirty who were captured in the raid of the underground church over the weekend. The UNGC had decided to make an example of these, since they'd been caught, red handed, in the middle of the most important city in America. They'd grown more annoyed, by the day, with these underground churches; and especially infuriated with the Christians who continued to pop up, like an irritating rash.

The authorities didn't understand the whole Christian concept. Though their prisoners had tried to explain to them that true Christianity wasn't about a religion, but instead, about a relationship with the God of the universe, they still didn't get it. So, as far as they were concerned, the refusal of those Christians to denounce their faith to save their own lives, was ridiculous.

Punishment would begin the next day, and was to be televised worldwide. Cage was ordered to attend, and would be seated beside the doctor, for the whole sordid fiasco.

Special seating was arranged for UNGC members and their top staff, in the middle of the city square. The prisoners were brought out, and stood close together, in a single row. A few were visibly shaken, but most looked resolute, including Cages two ladies. His stomach clenched, which was an unusual reaction from a man who'd tortured, and killed thousands of Christians. Most of the prisoners looked to have already endured some abuse, as they were covered with bloody lacerations and bruises, and wore clothing that was dirty and torn. One by one, the prisoners were brought forward, and asked publically if they would renounce the Christian church, and Christ, and vow fealty to the World church. And, one by one, their answers were an adamant no. They would not denounce their Lord and Savior, Jesus Christ. Then, one by one, judgment was pronounced.

Death, by burning at the stake. Cages insides roiled. Death, by burning? These were not insurgents, who had fled implantation; or rebels who might have directions to an active ARM base; these were people who had worshipped in the wrong place, at the wrong time. This whole situation had turned into a witch hunt.

He turned to Amir, with a look of shock on his face; and Amir's own look was stern, warning him with his eyes not to make an issue over the council's judgments.

Cage attempted to rise, and Amir's hand shot out to stop him. He lowered himself back into his seat, and looked up. His eyes met those of Mrs. Adler, and he couldn't look away. Her face looked so peaceful. A large ring of debris, with thirty posts, and cords, had already been set up; as if the council had known all along that every prisoner would refuse the opportunity to save his own life; and the thirty prisoners were led to the posts and strapped securely.

Thousands had come to watch. They seemed to be drawn, like flies to a rotted carcass, or attorneys to a car accident. The event was having an effect on the crowds, just as the council had hoped, but probably not the effect they'd planned. Those who already attended the 'World' church, vowed silently to themselves never to seek out an underground congregation; but those who attended Christian churches became more resolute than ever, that they would not let the government tell them who, how, or where they could worship.

Cage's eyes were still locked with his cook's. Suddenly the group of thirty began to sing. "Onward Christian soldiers, marching as to war. With the cross of Jesus going on before." The prisoners were ordered to stop singing. "Christ the royal Master, leads against the foe; forward into battle see His banners go." Again, they were ordered to stop. "Onward Christian soldiers, marching as to war, with the cross of Jesus going on before." A signal was given, and the fires were set, but the afflicted still sang. "At the sign of triumph Satan's host doth flee; on then, Christian soldiers, on to victory!" Cage's eyes, still linked with Mrs. Adler's, began to tear up, as by now the look on her face was one of agony, but still she sang. "Hell's foundations quiver at the shout of praise; brothers lift your voices, Loud your anthems raise." As the singing continued, and the smell of cooking flesh filled the air, another signal was given, and the troops guarding the prisoners pulled out their guns. The singing grew softer, as one by one the voices were extinguished. "Onward Christian soldiers, marching as to war, with the cross of Jesus.....”

As the blaze engulfed his friend, Cage felt a strange sensation. He reached up, to touch his face, and found that his cheeks were wet. Were these tears? He couldn't remember crying, not since he was a small child. He didn't know he still could. He'd watched as her hair caught fire, and then her head dropped forward. He was glad she could no longer feel the pain. The smell of burned hair, and skin, was so heavy in the air, that some in the crowd were vomiting in the streets. This would be one heck of a mess to clean up, and he hoped the UNGC had gotten all the bang for their buck they'd hoped for, because he didn't think this was something he wanted to sit through every day.

“Are you okay?”

“Yeah, Amir, I'm okay. That was just a little close to home, and a bit more real than I was expecting.”

“I want you to know that you have to be careful. We are always being watched, and you got a little shaky today.”

“Well, those were two of my staff roasting out there. How did you want me to act?”

“The council doesn't want you to ever be close to a Christian. So your reaction today leaves your own actions suspect, as far as they are concerned. We know that our vetting system failed, or those two wouldn't have been in our employ."

"That is ridiculous. I was overcome by the sheer volume of it all, that's it. And, they can track me, and look into my past all they want. I am not now, nor have I ever been a Christian. Enough said?"

"Enough said. Now, why don't you take the rest of the day off, and I'll see you tomorrow. We have some meetings, and I'd like to help you select your replacements for the ladies."

"Sure. That's fine. I'll see you tomorrow."

· · · · ·

Jana was having a blast teaching her favorite discipline. She'd gotten permission to begin training Becca, who turned out to be a natural. Pretty soon they were having competitions, and though Jana always won, she guessed Becca was a close second, against anyone else on base.

Jana's tummy continued to swell, and Alec was so active, in the womb, that she went many nights with very little sleep. Her next visit with Doctor Rose was a bit strained. "I thought I told you that I wanted you to get plenty of rest? You look like a zombie."

"Thanks for that Doc, but you need to tell the little guy. He kicks all night long, and makes it almost impossible for me to sleep."

"Okay, but when I said rest, that didn't just mean sleep. You need to spend time sitting, and giving your body a break. I see you out there training all these guys, but never slowing down. Jana, your ankles are swollen, your weight is down, and the bags under your eyes are big enough to pack for a Caribbean cruise. I'm getting more worried about your blood pressure too. You have to take it easy, or you will be sick, and then you will jeopardize your chances of having a healthy birth. I know you love what you do, Jana, but you need to do less of it. Do you understand?"

"Yes, Doc, I'll take it easy."

"Why is it that I don't believe you? I'll tell you what. We are getting closer to your delivery date. When you come back in two weeks, if I don't see improvement, I will talk to Josh, and we will get you restricted from all activity. Are we clear?"

"Wow, Doctor Rose. Sure, anything you say. I promise, I will take it easy."

This would be tough, but she didn't want to be put on bed rest, so she was determined to follow doctor's orders."

Back in the training area she ran into Becca, and sent her off to practice alone.

"You okay?"

"Yes Daddy. I'm fine. Doc just told me he wanted me to take it a little easier, so I'm going to cut back on some of my activity, okay?"

"Why haven't you said anything before? Do I need to be going to your appointments with you?"

"No. Like I said, he just wants me to take it a little easy, so I'm going to do what he says. Everything is fine. I'll see you at home."

As soon as Jana left the training area, Josh headed over to see Doc.

"Hi Doc, I understand you were a little hard on Jana today."

"Were those her words? I'm just looking out for her health, Josh. Have you really looked at your wife lately?"

"I guess we've been a little busy with the training. She said she feels fine.'

"Well, usually by this time in a pregnancy, I'm telling expecting moms to stop eating so much, because they've gained too much weight, but Jana has lost weight. She was tiny to begin with, but I'm afraid that either she, or the child, isn't getting enough nutrition. She's exhausted, and frankly, she looks like hell. I'm also getting concerned about her blood pressure. She told me that God has special plans for your son, so let's be sure he gets here okay. Sound like a plan?"

"Of course. She just hasn't said anything, so I guess I didn't know about any of this.'

"Well, I've already talked to your mom, and that's why she took Jana off of kitchen duty, but then your industrious little wife simply doubled her time at the training space. We need to see that she slows down. Is it a deal?"

"Yes Sir. She's at home now, and I will see that she stays there, and takes it easy."

"Good, see that you do. Yell if you need me."

• • • • •

Secretly, word was beginning to circulate to all the ARM bases, about the latest actions taken toward Christians in America. They heard about the massacre, of thirty underground church members, and they were shocked to the core. It had become common place, sadly, that Christians around the world would fear for their lives; and be persecuted to death by governments; but the persecution of Christians in the United States, especially to this degree, was a new phenomenon; unless, of course, you worked on a militia base.

The resistance bases were also informed that Cage, he of notorious mountain base fame, had been assigned to Bahram's upper council. And, that many of the generals, from the recently closed PM camps, were now working in the department of interrogation and torture, for the UNGC. That explained the closing of the base on the mountain, and rumors they'd heard about other bases closing, and gave them a little more insight into the council's plans for world governance. After all, why have scattered, secret bases all over the country, when the militia was an everyday fact of life for the ordinary citizen? It certainly made more sense to finance a central location, and send retrieval teams out by chopper; rather than pay to keep dozens of bases operational.

There was still not just cause, in the minds of the council, to bring all of ARM's soldiers out of hiding, to go to battle. Not with their limited resources, and numbers. The most they could hope to achieve now, would be small battles, which would only accomplish the killing off of their own troops. Their hearts broke for the plight of the Christians, at the hands of the UNGC, but for now, all they could do is continue to train, and pray.

At their regular meeting, Chuck brought up the possibility of sending a couple of scouts out into the world, to see how bad things were. With so little communication from the outside, they were forever in the dark, and only received occasional tidbits of information. The motion was put to a vote, and passed unanimously. Josh would choose two of his best scouts, outfit them with supplies for a month, and send them out to gather intelligence for the council. Jack was chosen, and after careful consideration, Seth was picked to accompany him. They would leave in the morning. "Thank you for having faith in us, Sir. We will do you proud."

"I know you will, men. I will see you off, but I want to wish you good luck, safety, and God's blessings. Bring us lots of Intel."

Josh was beginning to feel the weight of the world on his shoulders. He knew the time would come, soon enough, when they would be required to fight, and he hoped he was doing a good enough job training his men. They would be outmanned, out armed, and out positioned. They would have no back up, or replacements, and in many cases, they would be fighting in hand to hand combat, against foe with modern weapons. His biggest concern was that he was sending the troops to a certain, quick death. Once they left this base to fight for their rights, it would be an all out dog fight. The thing was, he knew they had one weapon the enemy didn't have. They had God on their side.

Jana hated being stuck on the sidelines, but she also wanted to give her son every advantage she could. Doc made her circumstances sound pretty serious. Serious enough that she wanted to put her feet up, and spend a little time relaxing. Josh told Mom about the doctor's orders, and all she could say was, "It's about time". She stopped by to see her daughter in law, and told her she would be bringing meals for her and Josh, for awhile.

"I feel like you're all ganging up on me, Mom."

"Well, we are, Dear. Now, rest, and I will see you later."

"Okay, I will rest, but only for the sake of the baby. Once I'm not pregnant anymore, watch out."

"Yes Dear. Just for the sake of the baby. I love you."

"I love you too, Mom."

• • • • • •

Even after two showers, he couldn't get the smell of burning flesh out of his nostrils. He hadn't slept well last night, and would have to show up at the UNGC today, for a fun filled day of meetings. The woman Amir had sent over still couldn't get his coffee right, and he was in a foul mood. He didn't know if he'd ever find servants who cared about him the way Mrs. Adler, and Sally had, but he could try. A cloud of depression hung over his head, and though he'd had many bouts with depression in his miserable life, this was different. He had so many questions. The thing was, his questions were about Jesus, so he didn't dare ask them. For one thing, if this Jesus died for His believers, and really loved them, how could He let believers, like these two ladies, die for Him? The whole concept was confusing, and there was no safe place to find those answers. He certainly couldn't let Amir know his mind was filled with these blasphemous thoughts.

Again, another meeting with the UNGC, and Cage was becoming even more wary of all the transformations he was seeing in the ever changing government landscape. He didn't have any love for Christians, but he could definitely see the favoritism toward Islam, in every new law which was passed. He didn't know if the council saw it, since Amir was such a master manipulator; but at some point, when Sharia law ruled the land, they would certainly see the direction their laziness and lack of courage had taken them.

Amir lined up a number of cooks and maids, for interview. He would help Cage find the perfect servants for his needs; and place informants in his home, at the same time. He liked Cage, and respected his military aptitude, but he'd become a bit suspicious of his religious loyalty. After the emotional display, during the tribunal the previous day, he wondered if he'd judged the man wrongly. He didn't necessarily expect to find anything amiss, but it never hurt to keep an eye on things. Cage was, after all, a member of his upper council; and any actions by his friend, could reflect poorly on him.

They settled on a rather portly woman, with wispy grey hair, which could not all be tamed by her rather garish head scarf; thick glasses; and a face, perpetually, red as a beet; as his new cook. The maid was younger, and thinner, but didn't appear very bright. However, how intelligent did she necessarily need to be, to wash clothes, and toilets? He would have to see how they worked out. If he could just have a decent cup of coffee again, that would be an improvement.

He spent the rest of the afternoon going over menu choices, with the new cook, Lucy was her name. And telling Anna, the new maid, how he liked his bed turned down, and giving her details about his laundry. He didn't understand why he couldn't shake this dismal feeling. He'd grown up in some very dark circumstances, and spent his life surrounded by evil, but suddenly, nothing made sense. Satan, in a moment of panic, felt he was losing control, and he immediately sent thoughts of suicide into the man's head. If Cage asked too many questions, and became a believer, he would lose him forever; he couldn't let that happen; so his only option was to make sure he died before he could convert. Cage tossed, and turned again, all night. Thoughts of self harm swirling in his psyche, until the sun came creeping through the cracks in his dark, heavy drapes. He simply had to find someone who could give him answers.

· · · · ·

Scott and Becca were blissfully happy. Marriage suited them, and they were good for each other. The children were happy too. The little family ate together at the community kitchen every night, but then they headed home to play games and read stories together. If Scott had known how wonderful marriage could be, he would also have known, long ago, how miserable his first one was. It takes more than one person willing to make sacrifices, to keep a relationship going. And, he could happily say that his sweet wife was the kindest, hardest working, most self sacrificing, most compassionate, and most beautiful woman in the world; but, then, he could be a bit biased.

• • • • •

Jana was miserable, but trying as hard as she could, to be nice to the people who were helping her. Mom was bringing meals, three times a day, and even snacks, whenever she came to check up on her favorite daughter in law. Doc told her to rest, and cut down on her activity, but if he'd waited a couple more weeks, he probably could have kept his advice to himself. Poor Jana's ankles were so swollen, she could barely walk. And her wrists, and hands had swollen up so badly, she wouldn't have been able to teach her students, even if she had permission to do so.

She was finally eating though. Little by little, she was beginning to lose the intensely haggard look, which had concerned the doctor. The bags under eyes had gone from suitcases, to overnight bags, and she'd lost the paleness that frightened her mother in law, just weeks ago. She eagerly awaited her husband's return each evening, so they could eat together, and then, more importantly, so they could sit together, and Josh could rub her feet.

Josh gladly rubbed Jana's feet, and talked to her about how the day's training had gone. She listened with interest, though a bit jealously, and savored every moment of the pampering by her favorite man in the world. He would make a great dad, and she was glad this was their future together. She still wanted to hunt, and train, but she also wanted to be a big part of her son's life, and help him to understand how blessed he was to have this man for a dad.

Have mercy on me, O God, according to your steadfast love; according to your abundant mercy blot out
my transgressions. Wash me thoroughly from my
iniquity, and cleanse me from my sin!

Psalm 51:1-2

CHAPTER 24

If there was a God, He would certainly care about His
people, wouldn't He? If He truly existed, why was this
world such a mess? He had so many questions. He'd
started off his service in DC, with his usual selfish intentions. He would work to create fear in those he was scheduled to lead, as was his practice, and charm those who would
attend to his private needs. His relationship with Mrs. Adler
and Sally, had begun that way. But, he realized now, he'd actually grown to care about them, and he was sure they'd truly
cared about him. He couldn't remember feeling that kindness from any others, ever, in his life. Even his own parents

had held him at arm's length. Why had these women cared? Could it have something to do with this Jesus they prayed to? The questions were eating him alive.

He'd witnessed many torture sessions, more executions than he could number, and more people pleading for their lives than he liked to remember; but there was something so very different this time. This event had moved something in him; something he didn't know existed. These people, going to their deaths singing about their Jesus, had touched a chord in him. How could they die so peacefully, so filled with joy? Joy that was evident on their faces, even as the blaze ate away at their flesh. Who was this Jesus who created a loyalty among His true followers, unlike any he'd ever seen before?

Amir had his Allah, but Cage, who had never had a religious bone in his body, wondered what that meant. He'd never gotten a sense of loyalty toward their God, from any of his Muslim cohorts; only a sense of fear, if they did not worship appropriately, or stepped out of line in any way. He'd also never gotten a feeling that they believed Allah sacrificed for them, so they could be in paradise; or the feeling that their God was going to take care of them, so they would be going to a better place. These Christians truly believed that their Jesus, and His sacrifice for them, was their ticket to heaven. How did any of this make any sense?

• • • • •

Bishop Graham had just approved the entertainment for Sunday's services. It was going to be another great one. He would work on his sermon now, which was usually twenty minutes of fluff, covering these topics: remember to celebrate diversity; listen to your government contacts, and obey their orders; be happy with whatever scraps the authorities decide to dole out; and come back next week. So many thousands had been present for the ghastly display of power, in the DC city square, put on by the UNGC, that everyone was nervous including Nathan. How could he know whether or not those powers in charge, were satisfied with the job he was doing? He surely never received any positive feedback, from anyone who mattered. Little did he know that those powers had singled him out for an even greater honor. One that they would be presenting the following Sunday, right there in his humongous, glitzy church.

• • • • •

"I'm concerned about this water retention, Jana."

"I've been pretty concerned about it too, Doc. I've been doing everything you told me to do; drinking lots of water, keeping my feet up. Nothing seems to help. Sometimes I feel like my skin has gotten so tight, I might pop. And, I've been getting terrible headaches."

"I know how uncomfortable it can be, Jana, but my concerns go much deeper than that. Have you ever heard of preeclampsia?"

"That sounds pretty serious, Doctor Rose."

"It is, Josh."

"What is it, Doc?"

"It's a condition, which can arise in some women, during pregnancy. Your blood pressure was so elevated, during this checkup, and the proteins in your urine, also high, that I believe this is what we're dealing with."

"What can we do? Is this bad for the baby?"

"It can prove to be very bad for the baby, but so far he seems to be doing fine."

"So, what can we do Doctor? Do you have medicine for her?"

"No, Josh, there is no cure for this condition. We caught it early on, so we can keep a daily check on it. However, if things get worse, our only recourse is to deliver the baby early."

"Deliver him? It's not time yet. Isn't that dangerous?"

"Yes, Jana, there is risk involved in a premature delivery; but the danger is even more serious in letting the condition progress. I don't want you to worry. I will be here every day to check on you, so we will be able to catch things if they begin to get out of hand."

"What can I do about the headaches?"

"Ice packs might help. I can't give you any medications, Jana. I'm sorry, but the baby is already at risk. I hope you understand. Just try to rest. Make sure you continue to eat right, and keep drinking plenty of water. I will keep you in my prayers. Call if you need anything. I'll see you tomorrow."

After the doctor left, Josh and Jana turned to each other. "What in the heck is going on?"

"I don't know, Babe. We just have to do everything the doctor says. I'm so sorry you're going through this, but we've always known Satan hates us. It would only stand to reason that he wouldn't want this baby to be born. Remember though, that God already told us He has plans for Alec, so, we just have to follow the doctor's orders, okay?"

"I know God said He has plans for Alec, Josh, but what if He doesn't need me anymore?"

"Don't be silly. Of course He can still use you. We will just do as Doctor Rose says, and he will come to check on you every day. Mom will be by with lunch soon, and I'm going to fill her in, so she will know to keep close tabs on you too. I will be here as much as I can, but I still have troops to train, so I can't be here all the time. I love you, Jana. And, I already love baby Alec, even though I haven't met him yet, so we're going to do everything we can to keep you both around. Do you hear me?"

"Yes, Josh, I hear you. I'm just so uncomfortable, and these headaches are something else."

"I know, Babe. I'll go get you an ice pack, and I'll let Mom know to keep them coming."

"Thanks, Josh. Say hi to everyone at training, and keep an eye on Becca for me. I think she has excellent potential. I love you."

"I love you too, Jana. And, I agree. She does have potential. You've done an excellent job training her, and she misses you. I'll tell her you'd like a visit. I've been telling everyone to let you rest. That's the only reason you haven't been flooded with visitors."

"Okay, I'd like that. But make it a little later, I think I'm going to take a nap after lunch."

"Oh, here's Mom, and something sure smells good."

"Hi, you two. I made chicken noodle soup; and grilled cheese sandwiches, with some of my homemade bread. There's also chocolate chip cookies for dessert, and some apples, and milk for later, how does that sound? Hey, how's our girl?"

"I'll fill you in, Mom. I'm going to pray with Jana, let her eat, and then she's going to rest. I'll meet you in the living room in a few minutes, okay?"

"Alright, Josh. But, don't be too long. Now I have all sorts of worrisome things going through my head."

Josh prayed with Jana, and headed out to the front room where he filled Mom in on all the doctor had related.

"Well, I'm just going to have to stop by more often then, when I know you're over at the training space. Things like this can go south very quickly, Josh. They used to call this condition toxemia, and I had a sister, your aunt, Robin, who died while she was pregnant. I've never talked about it to you, because she passed away long before you were born. I'm telling you that we will not let Satan have his terrible way in this. God's will be done."

"I never knew about your sister, Mom. I'm really sorry. But, that does bring things a little closer to home, so

I agree, stop by often, and just come on in. That way, if she's sleeping, you won't wake her. Doc said that if it gets too bad, we will have to take the baby early. Every week that we can stretch this out, is better for Alec, even if it is miserable for Jana."

"I'm going to let the ladies in the kitchen know too. This way we can get everyone praying. I love you son. You are going to be a terrific dad. And, more than that, Jana will be a great mom. Praise God for His protection, and Grace."

• • • • •

"Sure I'll go by and see her. I only didn't go before because you told me she needed her rest."

"I know, Becca. But, now I think she could use all the moral support she can get. She has a condition called pre-eclampsia, and she has to stay down, until the baby is born."

"Oh, Josh, that's terrible. I had a friend who died of preeclampsia. I didn't know things were that serious with her. Is there anything they can do?"

"No, she just needs rest. I thought she could use some cheering up is all. And, she really likes you."

"Well, I really like her too. I'll stop by later this afternoon. But, I think I'll go pick some flowers first. Flowers tend to cheer a girl up, or at least they always do me."

When Becca stopped by, she was shocked at how swollen Jana's face, hands, and feet looked, but she tried to act nonchalant. "It's okay, Becca. You don't have to act like you don't see me all swollen up like a balloon. Thank you for the flowers. They're beautiful."

"Oh, good. I wasn't sure if I could keep that up much longer. And, you're welcome. I just picked them from the fields. How are you feeling, Jana?"

"I feel terrible, but I'm grateful for your visit. I've been wondering how your practice is coming along?"

"Great. I think I'll be able to give you a run for your money, when you're back out on the field, that is.'

"I'm sure you will, but that might be awhile. And, you'll have to give me a few days, to get back up to par, before you try to demolish me."

"It's a deal, Jana. I can't wait. Well, I have to go pick the kids up, so we can get over to supper. It was good to see you. We will keep you in our prayers."

"Thanks, Becca. I can use all the prayers I can get. I'll be praying for you as well."

The boys were coming along. They'd only been training for an hour a day, but they were putting their hearts into it, a hundred percent, and that made all the difference. Josh knew when the time finally came, to do battle with the enemy, all they would really have is their God, and their faith. Gideon had faced similar odds, so he had to remember who it was that he served.

Chuck watched the training from the upper level, and his son's skill amazed him. How could he have become such an adept warrior? He'd never been in the military, until joining the resistance. And, look at Scott. That young man had moves, which would terrify any opponent, but the only training he'd had, was as a scrappy teenager. Then he recollected watching Jana, over the past weeks, as she plied her talent, and was aware that her skill was truly a gift from God. One that she had shared with her friend, Becca. These young people had been brought together, by the hand of God, for a purpose greater than any he could imagine. Working together, when the time came, they would stand for Christ, and win the day. He had no doubt.

• • • • •

Cage was ordered to attend another execution. A new underground church had been discovered this week, in Chicago, and he was to fly out with Amir this afternoon. The UNGC was trying to make examples of all these congregations, to quash further resistance from the people. "Why couldn't they stay out of sight?" He wondered. "If you have to do this, just learn to stay out of sight. Then you can worship your damn god all you want to."

When he arrived home to organize for the trip, Anna had an overnight bag ready to go, filled with everything he would need for the short journey. And, Lucy prepared a light meal of roasted chicken sandwiches, and fruit salad. Her coffee was certainly better than that of the temporary cook he'd utilized, after the loss of Mrs. Adler. But the house just didn't feel the same. For one thing, the kitchen didn't sparkle anymore, not the way it did before. And, the place didn't seem as warm, without the presence of those two sweet ladies. Lucy's peach pie didn't hold a candle to Mrs. Adler's. He knew he couldn't continue to obsess over the loss of these women. They'd been such a small piece of his life, for such a short time. So, why did it matter so much?

Chicago had changed. As far as Cage was concerned, it was always a dirty, grimy place; but the atmosphere, when they stepped off the plane, was darker somehow. The council would penalize twenty three at this public execution, and the streets were already filling up with gawkers. Those who'd heard of the atrocity, which occurred in DC, and hoped to see something equally gruesome, milled about all around the venue. Cage remembered that feeling, from his previous life. The way another's death, could make him feel so alive. It was a feeling he'd craved for decades, but couldn't fathom now. The feeling of power, which he'd held in his hands over the life, or death, of another human being. How could he have been so callus; and what was happening to him now? He truly must be going soft. And, if Amir got wind of it, he'd be finished.

He and Amir, were asked to go into the jail where the prisoners were being held to see if they could sway any of the minds there. Perhaps they would have someone to show the crowd. Someone who'd chosen life, over death. Someone who would sit in the stands with them, to show those who might choose to rebel, what the reward could be for renouncing this Jesus. They interviewed all twenty three, and not a one was willing to grasp the proverbial rope being thrown to them. Once again, Cage left the jail with a heavy heart. He couldn't understand the dedication, and

love, these people felt toward their Jesus, but he was beginning to wish he had something in his life, which meant so
much to him. One woman had actually looked him in the
eye, and said, "God loves you, General. You can run away
all you want to, but you can't escape love." He'd looked
around, quickly, to see if Amir heard, but it appeared he
was in conversation with another of these annoying Christians. What did she mean by that? What love had he ever
run away from?

"Well, we gave them a chance, no one can say we didn't,
and they turned it down. There's nothing else we can do
for them now."

"Yes, Amir, I know what you're saying, but do you
sense that these extreme measures are accomplishing anything? I feel the situation is becoming more out of hand,
the more we use these drastic procedures. I've never dealt
with people like this before, except back at the mountain
camp, and it seems like you're seeing the same results. Results, which used to confuse me. It seemed to me that the
more I pushed, the harder they pushed back. Is Islam the
same way? Are Allah's followers so devoted to him that they
would give up their lives?"

"Actually, those who are the most dedicated to Allah,

and his prophet, are equally devoted to his truth. They lay their lives down for him every day, in acts of holy Jihad."

This comment confused Cage more. Because, as he thought about it, it seemed followers of Allah were taught to prove their love, for their God, by taking the lives of others, and leaving them with no hope; yet the followers of Jesus were taught to prove their love to Him, by loving others, and giving them hope. He'd never really thought about it like that before, but it left him with even more burning questions.

He knew Bibles were banned around the world, and had been since the creation of the 'World Church'. But, he'd taken Bibles from captured, resistance fighters, daily, so there had to be some around, somewhere. He just knew he had to find a Bible, somewhere, and begin reading, if he was ever going to have any answers to his ongoing dilemma. With this revelation, Satan writhed in pain. He couldn't lose Cage, one of his best and most useful tools. This couldn't be happening, and God smiled.

The sky was overcast, and looked like it might open up at any moment. The wind was high, in the center of the windy city, and all sorts of garbage blew around the streets, in sporadic gusts. A skinny dog ran from human, to human, looking for an act of kindness; until one young man kicked him in the ribs, sending him yelping into the crowd. They sat in the stands, waiting for the execution to begin. This one would be accomplished by hanging. After the hours of cleanup, required in DC, Chicago had opted for a neater way to dispose of their problems. However, no hoods would be used, so that the public could still watch the agony of death on the faces of the doomed.

The twenty three stood on the deck of the hangman's tower, lined up for the gawkers to view. The absolute glee, in the eyes of the witnesses, was disgusting; yet, Cage knew he'd displayed that same delight for many years. The prisoners were bloodied, and bruised, attesting to the treatment they'd received at the hands of their jailers. They were lined up by height, from shortest, to tallest. Cage noticed that one of the prisoners couldn't have been more than fourteen years old. A girl with honey colored hair, matted together by blood, he assumed, from numerous blows to the head. She was a pretty little thing, with her jaw set, and her head held high. He wanted to run to the scaffolding and save her, but he wouldn't have gotten twenty feet, before being shot by one of the many guards around the perimeter of the stage. Then he saw the woman. The one who'd told him of God's love for him, and he gasped. Someone had cut off her left ear, leaving a gaping hole in the side of her head. Yet, the look on her face was one of peaceful, serenity. Why was it that when Muslims went to their death, they went angry, screaming, and taking others with them; but when these Christians died, they did so with grace. He had to know.

The judge, shaking in his boots so hard he could barely walk, approached the condemned, and ask each one to take the opportunity to denounce their faith. For if they did so, their death would be less painful. And, each one, in turn, answered "No". Cage tried to look away, but couldn't. It seemed, to him, that someone should witness these brave deaths, and he did so with tears in his eyes. The condemned, were dropped, one by one. The executioner had been in-structed to wait until each one stopped jerking, on the end of his rope, before sending another one to his maker. This, in order to give the viewers a better show. The young girl, never gave up her resolve, and died, he guessed, as bravely as she'd lived, with one small shoe falling off her foot in her last death throes. So, now, would she be with Jesus, they way they believed? Or was she just dead?

Doctor Bahram watched the entire event, by watching

Cage. He saw him gasp, and he watched his eyes tear up. Was he just going soft, or was he becoming an even bigger danger than that? The girls, who had been placed in his house, hadn't seen anything out of the ordinary, but he would have to keep a close eye on him. Cage had always been known as the toughest general in service, but that wasn't what Amir was seeing lately. And, he couldn't afford any trouble, not if he was going to keep his grueling schedule to accomplish the Islamification of the world, before the coming of the Mahdi.

• • • • •

Emma opened the door quietly. She hadn't heard any noise when she approached their quarters, so she assumed Jana was taking a nap. She'd brought some oatmeal cookies, and milk, for an afternoon snack, and would just leave them, if she wasn't needed.

When she entered, she saw Jana, face down on the floor, and dropped her tray. Running to her daughter in law, she turned her over, and surmised that she wasn't breathing. She ran to the door, and yelled. "Get Doc!" Then she ran back inside and began to give Jana CPR. Praying as she worked, she spoke to God. Breaths, and compressions.

"Lord, you promised us good health, and I'm going to hold you to that." Breaths, and compressions. "You told her that you had plans for Alec." Breaths, and compressions. "Lord, this is my only daughter, and my only grandchild! Please!" Breaths, and compressions. As Doc arrived and took over, Jana began to cough, and, though she hadn't regained consciousness, began to get her color back.

"Emma, listen to me. Run and tell Nancy to get the surgical suite ready. We are going to have to take the baby. It's our only chance to save either one of them. Then go and get Josh. Do you hear me?"

Badly shaken, Emma was holding on by a prayer, but she ran for her daughter, and she ran for her grandbaby. When she'd relayed, to Doc's nurse, the instructions he'd given her, she ran to find her son.

"Mom, what's wrong?

"It's Jana, Josh. I found her on the floor, not breathing. I did CPR, and Doc came. They're taking her into surgery. He said it's the only way to save either of them. Go. Be there for her. I'm going to go get your dad."

"Thanks Mom. I'll see you there."

By the time Josh arrived, panting from the run, Doc, Nancy, and Jana, were already behind the curtain, in the surgical suite. Josh knew the instruments here were not always as sophisticated as they might be back at the hospitals in the cities, but he had faith in God, and he had faith in Doctor Rose. He'd seen the man save his wife from certain death, after the battle on the plateau, with very little by way of equipment. And knew what a skilled surgeon he was. The only question was, had they gotten her there quickly enough.

After what seemed like hours, but was actually only moments, Josh's Mom and Dad arrived, and his mom hugged him tight. They prayed together, and lifted Jana and the baby up to the King of the universe. Soon, they heard Doc's voice. "No, wait on the cord. Rub his back. Here, let me do it. You, keep an eye on Mom." Then, as if almost from a distance, a soft cry, like the coo of a dove; and suddenly, a yell, as loud as the cry of any healthy, newborn babe. "Now, wrap him up, and get back here. Let's concentrate on Mom. I don't know how long she was out, or how long she was without oxygen. Here, cut the cord, let's take care of the placenta, and get her closed up. Jana, Jana, your baby boy is here. He needs you, Mommy. Jana. I don't know, Nancy. We might be too late. Here, little man, I'm going to introduce you to your mom. Alec, this is your mommy.

She's a little sleepy right now, but I'm sure she will be okay. Nancy, put him here. Right here on Mommy's breast."

Jana lay still as the dead, her skin pale as snow. Alec cuddled at her breast, and tried to latch on, without much luck. Then he began to cry. Suddenly, Jana's eyes opened, and she sucked in great gulps of air. When she saw her tiny son, her arms came up, automatically, to encircle his small form, and tears flowed from her eyes. "My sweet baby, I thought I'd lost you forever. Doc, when we were with Jesus, He sent Alec back, and I thought He might be keeping me with him this time. As if perhaps my function here, had only been to bring Alec into the world. But, He told me it wasn't my time yet, and sent me back. That's twice now. He's sent me back twice. He must really still need me here."

"You truly are a miracle, Jana. Of course He needs you here. No one can raise this baby better than you and Josh, for whatever God's plan is. And, you have a fine son. A bit on the scrawny side, but I think you'll have him fattened up in no time. Hey, Dad, Gramma, and Grampa, come see our baby boy."

The fool says in his heart, "There is no God," They are corrupt, doing abominable iniquity; there is none who does good. God looks down from heaven on the children of man to see if there are any who understand, who seek after God.

Psalm 53:1-2

CHAPTER 25

"I don't know what you're talking about. What are you accusing me of, Amir?"

"I'm not accusing you of anything, Cage. I'm only telling you what I see. You are showing weakness. And, you are doing it in places where the council can see. I chose you for a top position in my upper council, so your actions reflect on me. Where you show weakness, I look weak. Do you understand?"

"Yes, I do understand. I apologize. I never meant to place you in a bad position. You know I've always appreciated the leg up, and the fair way you've treated me. What is it that you need me to do?"

"I'm going to send you away for awhile. I think a few weeks abroad, organizing some issues for me, might do you some good. And, help you refocus on the goal."

"Yes, that might be a good thing. I do need to get refocused. But, can you tell me again, what is the goal?"

"The goal, General Cage, is to do exactly what I tell you to do, or to be treated as a traitor. Are we clear?"

"Yes Sir. I'm ready to go, any time, and anywhere, you are ready to send me."

Cage knew his last question probably sounded a bit snide: and he could tell it was taken that way, by the quick dressing down he received from his superior; but the longer he was around Amir, the more confused he became.

He'd initially been told that the goal was to get everyone's focus off religion. To do away with all religions, in order to bring people together around a common theme. A theme of multiculturalism in the 'World Church'. There was supposed to be no more Christian, or Jew, no Muslim, or Buddhist, and so on; only people who were focused on equality. However, as he watched his boss place high ranking Muslims in positions of power, and manipulate laws and bills, to favor Sharia law, he knew that wasn't what was happening.

He didn't know much about Islam. Probably about as much as he knew of Christianity. But, from what he could see, Islam was a religion of hate, and war, and forcing others to submit; where Christianity was a religion of love, and reaching out to invite others in. But, he would go, and he would do as his superior had instructed. He was, after all, a soldier. And if there was one thing he did well, it was to pretend he was following orders.

• • • • •

Scott had taken over many of Josh's duties, in the days prior to and right after, the birth of his baby boy. He didn't mind at all. He loved training the troops, and the new position of authority he'd been given. All he wanted to do was make Josh proud, and give God glory. Becca excelled at her new skill, and was therefore helping to train troops in the art of archery. He stood to the side, and watched her as she moved from soldier, to soldier, giving instructions, and tips. She was amazing, and beautiful. How had he become so blessed? He'd never been happier in his life, and all these thoughts swirled through his mind, as he prepared men for war. He knew, just as Josh did, that wherever they went, they would be outnumbered and out armed, so these men were going to have to be able to use their hands and their wits. They would not be backed up by heavy artillery.

Jack and Seth had just returned from their scouting mission. They'd gone out into regular American communities, and blended in, to get the information they needed. When they returned, the council called an emergency meeting. Josh and Jana were there to hear the news, along with everyone else. "Go ahead, Jack, tell us what you found."

"Well Sirs, and Ladies, of the council. As we believed, the country continues to deteriorate. We managed to move about, in certain communities, to ask questions. We had a few close calls, when authorities began to get suspicious, and even one who wanted to scan our chips. So we had to escape and move quickly. We made it to a number of large cities as well, to get a feel for how government was treating the people. It's gotten pretty bad out there. Food shortages, to the point of starvation in some sectors. Lack of medical care. Shortages of heating fuel, and in some areas, no electricity. Crime rates have gone through the roof. There are a lot of desperate people out there, and no one is listening to them.

"The 'World Church' has gotten pretty powerful, and they're cracking down on Christians who continue to meet in underground churches, more than ever. The sentiment, for the most part, among those we spoke with, is that other religions, though not condoned, are not punished to the degree that Christians are. There have been scores of public executions. We heard about a couple of the larger ones, through the grapevine. But smaller ones of one, to ten, people are a very commonplace, and in some cases, daily thing. We heard reports of, burning at the stake, beheading, shootings, drowning, hangings, and even five members of a Florida church, who were fed to alligators. The UNGC has gotten pretty creative while trying to keep the attention of the masses.

"What we found extremely out of the ordinary, was that every community we spoke to has reported more Muslims being put into positions of power, by the UNGC. Certain people in the communities; who used to think the government was out to do good for its citizens, as they diversified governance; are becoming more frightened by the numbers, and are much worse off than they were before the UNGC took over. Random acts of terror, by those claiming to be funded by ISIS, or other terror organizations, are actively on the rise. There are just lots of folks out there who are pretty fed up. We think the UNGC must have been manipulated into making some of those government appointments, because the council was all about ridding the world of any specific religion, if you recall. Until Doctor Amir Bahram was chosen to head up the UN. We did some investigating on him. He is a Muslim, from an affluent family in Iran, and as far as we were able to research, a 'Twelver". There are some pretty radical characters among the Twelvers.

"We also found there are some wealthier communities; though few and far between; which seemed strange to us, since this new world order was supposed to make everyone equal. Where no one wanted to talk to us, and a few even called the authorities. These folks seemed to have decent houses, food, and electronic devices, which their noses were buried in every second of the day. From the few responses we got in these sectors, we surmised that these individuals are satisfied with government, didn't see the increase in Muslim power, thought the World Church was doing a bang up job, and didn't notice any shortages. We assumed these people were related to, or had done favors for, government entities, and their payoff was to live in higher standards than the regular Joe."

"Wow, Jack, we knew things were falling apart, but I don't believe any of us thought it had gotten that far."

"I know, Josh, we were pretty shocked too. I'll tell you what though, there are lots of people out there who are angry that they allowed the government to dupe them into thinking this takeover by the UNGC would be a good thing. We also found plenty of folks who were upset that they'd allowed the administration to implant them. Everyone knows somebody who has tried to remove a chip, and lost their life, so people are scared to death to try to do anything about it."

"Just so you are all aware, I'm getting closer to a solution about the removal of the chips. I hope to have an answer to that dilemma soon. Then we will be able to take in those who want to escape the government, who have already been implanted."

"That's great news, Doctor Rose. You have been a great blessing to us all. Let us know how that proceeds, and maybe you will be able to train us, so we can rescue more people."

" I sure will, Josh."

"Scott, why don't you fill us in on your progress training the troops."

"Sure thing, Boss. The guys are doing great. I am amazed every day by their progress. We've been focused on hand to hand combat and archery lately. Since we don't have the heavy artillery that we will be going up against, we have to learn ways to gain access, by stealth; and how to overcome with our hands; and our wits. The other guy might have some powerful boom, boom, but when it comes to close fighting, he won't be trained to the degree that our guys are. I think I actually feel a little sorry for the other side, when I watch our men go at it."

"Thanks, Scott. We can see what a great job you're doing, and we appreciate your hard work, and commitment.

"As you all know, we are pretty safe up here in the mountain. So far, no one has ever been able to detect our presence. But, we can't count on that forever. Some of the other ARM locations aren't as well hidden as we are, they are also not as well provisioned as we are, and I believe it's only by the Grace of God that they haven't been discovered yet. At some point, when one of the bases is discovered, we will have to come together to fight. That is what we are preparing for, and will continue to prepare for. I believe, as I'm sure you do, that we are here by God's design, and that His hand of protection covers us. But, I am also prepared to die for my God, my faith, my family, my community, and my country. We will continue to train, for that moment when we are called to stand in the gap, and may God have mercy on our souls."

Josh's statement was met by rousing applause from all present. Jana looked up at him, from her chair, and said, "I would follow you anywhere, Husband. Do you think it's coming soon?"

"I'm not sure when it's coming, Jana; but I know it's coming. I believe what I said about God's protective hand, but I also know that in times of war, we lose soldiers. That's the part I'm particularly conscious of, and I want to make sure they are all as prepared as they can be."

"Who do you think is our biggest enemy, Josh? Do you think it's the government, or are you more concerned about the ramping up of Islam, since we've been gone?"

"I think it's gone way past the government, Jana. If Bahram has been slowly placing Muslims in positions of power, you can bet that his strategy will be a full-fledged holy war. When the administration began stepping on the will of the people, it was simply the greed, and ego, of men; and now that administration has been ousted. But, a war against Islam, is a whole different thing. I don't know how many people understand that this will be a spiritual battle. That there is more at stake here, than who is in charge. So, in answer to your question. I believe our biggest enemy is Satan."

"I know, Josh. But, even though the people in our community get it, how do we spread that understanding to people out there?"

"I don't know, Jana. We might just have to leave that one up to God, He is after all, still in charge of it all. I think we do what we are doing, unless He gives us an open door. Now, let's go get the little man. I miss him."

"Me too. Imagine that."

• • • • •

Stepping off his flight in London, Cage could feel a disquieting in his spirit that he didn't quite understand. He was here to see how the Muslim appointments to Parliament, and other high ranking positions in European countries, had gone over. As he was ushered around the city he noticed the same lack of equal treatment, that he'd witnessed back home. Here, too, there were whole areas of the city, which were considered 'No Go Zones'. Areas where the Muslims who lived there, were free to practice their own form of law, and religion, without interference from the authorities. This made little sense, when, two blocks down the way, he saw the dead bodies of Christians, hanging from poles. Signs decrying their sin, of Christian faith, hung from their necks, as birds plucked the flesh from their faces.

Paris, one of his favorite cities in the world; though he'd not visited in decades; was also riddled with these discrepancies. Hordes of Muslims in designated parts of the city, and dead bodies of Christians, in various states of decay, adorning crosses, poles, and buildings, around the area. Every city he visited, was the same. And when he began to interview citizens, his disdain for the condition of the world grew. He'd thought that perhaps the people didn't see the inconsistencies. As though they were, perhaps, blind to the bias, but that was false. They just didn't have anyone to complain to, and if they did find an outlet for their opinion, they were quickly disposed of. There was no room for independent thought, or discontent, in the new world order.

Most of the people living in the slums and poorer neighborhoods, could make out clearly what was going on. They saw their cities being slowly, but surely, taken over by Muslims and Sharia law. And, clearly, at the hand of the UNGC. It was only in affluent portions of the cities, where people seemed to be blind to all that was going on around them.

Citizens were ready to revolt. They'd had enough. He knew conditions were equally bad in America, but he'd never gotten the chance to begin questioning the people, to hear their individual opinions. He wondered if they too, were ready for revolution. He checked on the appointees, which Amir had listed for him, in each city. They were all firmly well-established in their positions, much to the dismay of the local residents in each sector.

As he stood in the sun, in the outside court, of what used to be the Vatican, a shiver danced up his spine. Vatican City was a ghost town, a city of pigeons, which made his heart feel heavy, though he'd never had any particular love for Catholics. While the city all about was rife with Muslim holdouts; who were free to worship outside of the World Church, with no particular retribution; Christians were murdered in their homes and on the streets. He knew it was only a matter of time, before the people rose up to take back what was rightfully theirs. And, by this point in time, he couldn't say that he blamed them.

Sunday rolled around, and Cage was expected to make an appearance at the local, World Church, outlet. Just the usual show of power from the council's upper echelon. The building was appointed in a similar manner as the churches back in America; with gold, and marble, as far as the eye could see. Again, just as in the churches at home, there were gilded statues, studded with precious jewels, of each UNGC member. The entertainment wasn't nearly as star studded, and the Bishop was not as well spoken, but the message was the same: Be good boys, and girls; listen to your government reps, and do as they tell you to do; worship diversity, and stay away from religion; and, by all means, be responsible members of the community, turning in anyone who seems suspicious, or non conformist.

He could certainly understand why Bishop Graham was being considered for higher honors, if this fellow was an average representation of the world's speakers. Nathan had more speaking talent and charisma, in his little finger, than this fellow could muster from his whole body, and he didn't even like the guy. He'd never been so bored. And, to make matters worse, the church was only about a quarter full. No need for additions, and annexes, here. Where were the people? Hadn't they been 'advised' to attend, just like the pawns in America? This was obviously something that needed investigation.

As he left the church that afternoon, he felt the eyes of the bishop, and every person in attendance, on him. He represented the will of the UNGC, and was their emissary to the people, and he could feel the hatred. No, it wouldn't be very much longer, before the people took matters into their own hands. Oh, it would be a bloodbath. The chips, in their hands, gave the council the power to stop them in their tracks. But, there would come a time, in the not too distant future, when that wouldn't matter.

Human beings can only take so much. He'd experienced that phenomenon in many torture sessions. People who were willing to die for their God, and country, to make a point. He didn't know if he would ever go that far, but he'd seen it done over, and over, and he knew that look in their eyes. A battle was coming.

• • • • •

Amir was keeping an eye on Cage. He had operatives in London, and around the world, sending him reports on the general's activities, and demeanor. So far he was pleased with what he'd heard. Perhaps Cage only needed some time away. Maybe he really could trust him after all. If the rest of his trip continued with these glowing results, he would feel much more comfortable with the man's position, and station.

Cage knew, of course, that he was being watched by

Amir's men. He had many talents, and spotting spies was one of them. He could play the game, until he had an opportunity to get the answers he was after. It made him angry that Bahram felt the need to have him followed, but he probably would have done the same thing, if he'd been in the doctor's position. He did not, however, believe Amir's motivation was the same. This was a man, whose greatest concern was keeping the world ignorant of his eventual, total, Islamic takeover; and Cage was becoming more convinced that this takeover would be a very bad thing indeed.

Upon his return to the United States, he was met at the airport by a limousine. When the door opened, he was surprised to see Amir inside. His friend didn't usually bother himself with mundane chores, like picking someone up from the airport. "Hello, Amir. I'm surprised to see you. I thought we would see each other at tomorrow's meeting."

"I thought about waiting, but I decided to come. I hoped we might have supper together, and go over the particulars of your findings before the council hears them."

"Certainly, if you wish. I am tired from the flight, but I could eat something."

"I know of a nice Italian place just down the street. Well, get in, man. Don't just stand on the sidewalk."

Over an excellent supper of salad, pasta, and a nice burgundy, Cage filled Amir in on all that he'd seen. He didn't bother to share the true results of his interviews. He didn't know why he held that information back, but he thought it might have something to do with the safety of those who'd spoken to him. He believed if he told the doctor how dissatisfied the world's citizens were growing, it might be very bad for them. Amir certainly didn't really care about the well being of those individuals; either in Europe, or in America.

There was a piece of Cage that was beginning to resent the council, and their belief that they knew better than the world's citizens about what was good for them. He was also aware the previous administration had held the same view, and that was, in part, how they'd gotten in this mess to begin with. So much, in his thinking, had begun to change. So far he hadn't done anything treasonous, but some of his thoughts were certainly bordering on that. He still wanted to find a Bible. Now, though, he also wanted to find a Quran. He would like to read them both, and compare. There was no other way to make an informed decision. He knew, without a doubt, that the 'World Church' wasn't the answer.

When the limousine dropped him at the steps leading to his front door, he wished Amir a good night, and entered through the mahogany doors. It was sad, but the house just didn't feel the same, and he was once again enveloped in a cloud of despair. He really missed Mrs. Adler, and Sally. He probably hadn't given Lucy, and Anna, a fair chance, but it just wasn't the same. Something made him want to find out more about the women who had touched his heart. After all, they hadn't just touched his heart; they had actually begun to melt his heart. He needed to know more about who they were. He wanted to meet their friends, well, those who were left after the execution, and find out more about this Jesus who they were willing to die for.

Be merciful to me, O God, be merciful to me, for in you my soul takes refuge; in the shadow of your wings I will take refuge, till the storms of destruction pass by. I cry out to God most high, to God who fulfills His purpose for me. He will send from heaven and save me; He will put to shame him who tramples on me. God will send out His steadfast love and His faithfulness!

Psalm 57:1-3

CHAPTER 26

At the following UNGC meeting, Cage was asked to speak. This was unprecedented. Usually, the information for a meeting was gathered, disseminated through the lower council members, and then presented to the higher council. He filled the council in on his findings, leaving out the negative results of the personal interviews he'd conducted. He also relayed his opinion about the church in Europe. He noticed Graham sitting in the back of the gallery, and assumed he'd been invited by Amir. And, though he wasn't a big fan of the Bishop, he decided to be honest about his thoughts on this subject. "I also found, members of the esteemed council, that the church in Europe is sorely lacking. Attendance was at a minimum, with the building where I attended less than a quarter full for services. And, the speaker was probably the dullest human being I've ever had the misfortune to listen to. Here we have Bishop Graham, who certainly keeps the masses coming back. If I had to give the church where I attended Sunday's services a rating; it would be a D minus. I hope I haven't offended anyone here, but I thought you would want me to be honest."

As he sat down, he looked in the direction of the bishop first, and was greeted by a thankful smile, and then in the direction of the doctor, where he got a wink, and a nod. Well, at least this meeting wouldn't end with his beheading. But, he wondered, how long would it be before that changed.

• • • • •

Alec was already pulling himself up on the furniture. He seemed to be in such a hurry to walk. He was a glorious little boy; with large green eyes like his dad, and the same deep dimple in his chin. He had his mom's auburn hair, fair skin, and beautiful, ear, to ear, smile. He would be tall like Josh, and had grown like a weed, so far. From the looks of things, there was no concern that his pre mature birth would keep him from reaching his full height, and Doc commented on how well he was doing at every checkup. Jana sprang back as well. Once the pregnancy had been brought to an abrupt halt, the day that Alec was born, she'd bounced back almost immediately. So she was once again teaching the troops. After she felt comfortable, she and Becca had their contest, and Jana was still victorious, but Becca was bound and determined to practice until she could best her friend, so that would surely keep Jana on her toes.

Days were spent at the practice field, readying men, and now women, for battle; while Alec hung out with Gramma, and the ladies, in the community kitchen. He was a big hit, everywhere he went, with his sweet temperament, and easygoing way. He was surely his father's son.

Every evening Josh and Jana showered, and met Chuck, Emma, and Alec, at the kitchen for supper. Alec was always thrilled to see Dad and Mom, and reached for them eagerly. They shared time with family, and community, and then they went home to enjoy time together.

Alec would be a strong man. His dad was already wrestling with him on the floor, as he giggled and laughed with glee; but more importantly, they took time to pray with the boy. Each night they spent time in devotions, reading scripture, and prayer. He would be strong spiritually. He would see how important a relationship with Jesus was to his dad, and mom, and Jesus would become important to him. Josh, and Jana had never been so happy.

Emma was the best Gramma any boy could have, and she adored Alec. He was so much like his dad, and having this sweet baby boy around, brought back many wonderful memories. She especially loved to show him off to the other ladies. But, as he grew, the kitchen would no longer be an appropriate place for him. He was curious, and began climbing everything he could reach. There'd already been several close calls. A time was coming, soon, when each adult in the family, would have to stay with him for a day, in rotation, just to keep him out of mischief.

• • • • •

Josh received some great news from Scott. He and Becca, were expecting a baby. They'd just told CJ, and Angel, the previous evening, and the children were thrilled about the prospect of having another sibling. Becca was a bit concerned with how the pregnancy might interfere with her ability to teach the troops, but Doc gave her a green light, as long as she didn't get too crazy. Winter was in full swing, and there wouldn't be any forays out onto the mountain any time soon, so she was confident she would be able to swing back into action, immediately after the birth.

Josh was concerned about the condition of the world, and thought it might be a good idea to keep a better eye on situations going forward. So, he called a special meeting of the council.

"Thanks for agreeing to meet again so soon, everyone. I know we just had our regular weekly meeting, but I've been doing quite a bit of thinking on this subject, and Jana and I have talked, so I thought I would throw this idea out there. We all know how difficult it is to get good intelligence, back, and forth, to the separate ARM facilities.

"We all talked, at a previous meeting, about the very real possibility that one of those bases could be uncovered, at any time, and that we would have to be ready to offer our help in time of battle. Jana and I have come up with, what we think, is a possible solution to the communications issue. Our biggest problem, is the mountain. But, the mountain is also our biggest strength. We propose to take a trip in the spring. And, we're working on some solutions to take with us.

"Each of the bases has an element, which helps to keep them hidden; but in most cases, that same element is what blocks a signal from getting out to the other bases. We believe we can find frequencies that the government isn't monitoring as closely, and use them to our advantage.

"Many years ago, HAM radios were all the rage. Virtually no one uses them anymore. But, we can use that outdated technology, to our advantage. If we put together a network of HAM operators; at different locations, outside of the bases for better reception, but not too terribly far away, so that runners can relay messages, we believe this could be a viable solution."

"But, what if the UNGC does figure out that we are transmitting messages over the airwaves?"

"Good question, Dad. I'm glad you asked. We will use a rotating schedule, which we would change up every week, or so, for the frequency we would be using. Additionally, we would use code, to transmit messages. This is a code we have yet to develop."

"How would the other bases know the frequency of the week, or the codes?"

"Well, and here is where it gets a bit risky. Hold on, Mom, I'll probably answer your questions with my next sentence, so hold off for just a moment, okay? A group of us would have to go from base, to base, and teach them the frequencies, and the codes."

"You didn't answer my question, Josh, but I can probably guess the answer. Are you the leader of this group?"

"Yes, Mom, and Jana would be going with me. That is, if you will care for Alec while we're gone?"

"Of course I would, but how long do you think this will take?"

"We are talking about being gone for several months, Mom."

"I hate the thought of Alec not seeing his mom and dad, for so long. Can't someone else go?"

"Others have their duties here. We will take a small group, which would include Jack, and Seth, if they are willing, since they did such a good job scouting for us before. Scott would stay behind, training troops, and you all know Becca is expecting. Mark would like to sit this one out. Pastor Mike has been keeping pretty busy here. And, correct me if I'm wrong, Pastor, but he hasn't been quite the same since Jana took him out. And, Doc is needed here. He's still working on a solution for the implants. So, I'm sorry, Mom, but Jana, and I are the most qualified."

"Just as I thought. Well, you know that Grampa, and I adore Alec, so of course we will care for him. We all have to make sacrifices for the cause, so he may as well begin to learn that now. We will just have to spend lots of time together, throughout the winter, to make up for the time you'll be gone."

"Thanks for understanding, Mom. And, thanks for your help."

"Your dad, and I wouldn't have it any other way, would we Chuck?"

"No. You just do what you need to do, Josh. We will hold down the fort on this end. But, I agree with your mother. We have to spend all the time together as a family, that we can, before you leave in the spring."

"Yes, Dad, I agree. We'll sit down with you after the meeting, to go over some particulars. And, thanks again, Dad, and Mom. We wouldn't be able to do this without your help."

Cage was going crazy, trying to figure out how to get some of his questions answered. He hadn't been able to locate a Bible, and knew there were probably not many safe places to ask. But, he was willing to try something new. He was abundantly aware that he was being followed, so walking out of his house looking like 'General Cage', was out of the question. He would have to find a better way, and then do some asking around.

He put together a disguise which he thought might do it. A pair of jeans, which he dirtied up, and ripped in a few strategic locations. Though, he would have to be careful. It was cold out there, and he didn't want to have too much skin exposed. A dark, hooded sweatshirt; which so many of the young masses seemed to wear these days; would cover his hair. He'd have to be careful that his military haircut didn't give him away. And, a pair of sunglasses. Or was that too much? He certainly couldn't wear them at night, but they might help in the daytime.

Since he was going to sneak out over the weekend, which was typically a time when Amir didn't seem to require as much of his time, he would not do his usual close, morning shave, which might change the look of his face, just enough. Anyone who knew him, knew he was meticulous in his personal hygiene, and he always shaved. Then, if he left by the back door, and walked around the block before changing direction, he thought he could shake the tail which would otherwise surely follow.

He was so anxious to get out to the streets, he barely slept, which might actually add another layer of authenticity to his guise.

His pattern became: Monday, through Friday, pretend to serve the council and its leader, Doctor Bahram; Saturday, search the streets for answers, and an ever elusive Bible; and finally, Sunday, go to a fake church and worship fake diversity gods to make his boss happy; only to go to bed on Sunday night, to wake up Monday morning and do it all over again.

He couldn't let his household servants know of his clandestine pursuits, having more than a suspicion that they were plants set in place by the council. So, on Friday evening he'd retire to his rooms, and give strict orders that he not be disturbed until Sunday morning. This was a time, he claimed, that he was using to cleanse his body through fasting, and meditation. Lucy didn't mind. It meant she could focus on her own desires, instead of catering to her boss. So far, his ruse hadn't created a problem with Amir, who wondered why he seldom accompanied him to parties anymore. He explained to his friend that he had to walk a fine line, between fun and good health, so the topic was dropped. As long as he continued to do the same stellar job with the council, that he'd been doing since his return from Europe, he would get a pass.

Sundays, in church, were the hardest. Listening to the drivel, that came from the mouth of Bishop Graham; about all the good they, as a church, were doing for the community and the world; when he knew it was all lies, and he was already tired from his Saturday outings, was exhausting.

And, he'd noticed an anomaly, which was particularly disturbing. On several occasions now, he was nearly killed, by the oddest occurrences. One Saturday, he was almost run over, by a fast moving delivery truck, which seemed to come out of nowhere. Only his quick wit, and a fast response, saved his life. Another Saturday, as he walked the streets, a large cement gargoyle fell from the facade of an old building. He'd looked up just in time to leap from the path of certain death. And, yet another close call, was the recent storm, which caused an electric wire to fall, swinging only inches from him as he walked.

Cage thought these were all strange coincidences; but, in fact, they were out and out murder attempts by Satan, the king of lies. Satan saw the direction Cage was headed, and knew the only way to assure he could take the general as his own would be to kill him, while he was still wrapped in all his worldly sin. Satan didn't give up easily. But, God didn't give up easily either. He appointed angels, to watch over Cage, and Satan's attempts had, so far, gone unrealized.

Cages search for truth became an obsession. But, he noticed that most people shied away from him, and treated him with distrust. Even in his false identity, he evidently seemed insincere to them. Then, one day, after weeks of traveling the back streets of the city, Cage met a young man who looked him up and down, and said, "Hey, man, you look like you could use a little Jesus. You wanna come with me?"

The invitation shocked him, because even by mentioning the name of Jesus, the young man put his own life on the line. He was deeply touched by the self sacrificing summons, and followed the man to a building. Inside the dark structure, he could hear small noises, which sounded like the scurrying of rats and other tiny creatures. He couldn't tell where he was, but the man seemed to know the path, and something in his heart told him he could trust the way.

After traveling the length of the building, the young man opened a trap door, and the two descended into a tunnel, pulling the trap door shut behind them. In the tunnel, Cage, who was very tall, was forced to stoop, in order to walk. The path was endless, or so it seemed, until they stepped into a faintly lighted junction, before another equally long tunnel. It was unclear what the purpose of the passageway was. It wasn't for sewage, as there was no evidence of that, and didn't appear to contain cables of any kind. There was dirt on the floor, and graffiti on the walls; with dates that proved decades of secret meetings. And a faint smell he couldn't quite distinguish, which reminded him of his grandmother's closet. The young man turned to say, "Don't worry, almost there." Cage continued to follow, and soon the tunnel began to lighten, as they approached another junction. Turning left at the intersection, they entered a larger area filled with people sitting on blankets and pillows on the floor. It seemed the pair arrived just in time for a nightly worship service.

The service started with singing. The first song, which began, "Draw me close to you", echoed off the tunnel walls, into his heart. They sang song, after song, until Cage's face was wet with tears, as he swayed back and forth, with the music. Then they took turns reading scripture, from a worn Bible. One of the men got up to talk, and he spoke of the Grace of God, the Love of Jesus, and the Truth of His Word, to make men free. When they finished, Cage didn't want to leave. He had so many questions. The man who'd brought him, who went by the name of Brother Todd, and the man who spoke, who answered to Brother James, were willing to answer his questions and they talked for hours. They supplied him with a small, New Testament, and admonished him to hide it, to protect himself. Then, after walking him to a place where he could find his way home, they invited him back, and each gave him a big hug. It was the first time in his life he'd been hugged by a man, and it didn't feel strange at all.

Back home, showered, and in bed, he pulled out his copy of the New Testament, and began to read. He didn't know when he'd fallen asleep, but his rest was deep and he felt better than he'd felt in a very long time. Actually, he felt better than he could remember ever feeling in his entire life. He was beginning to see Truth, for the first time.

His new revelations made it harder to sit through the maddeningly phony church services he must attend, with Amir. They also made it more difficult to sit through

UNGC meetings, without leaping to his feet and shouting that he knew what the doctor was doing. He wanted to ask them all if they were stupid, or just uncaring, as they handed everything they'd ever held dear to a bunch of radical, Muslim extremists. But, he also knew that would get him nothing but the brig. And he couldn't do anything from prison. He would attend more worship services, with his new friends, and find out more of this Jesus. Then he would decide what to do.

• • • • •

His first word was Daddy. No one doubted that it would be. But, before he learned to say Mommy, he said Jesus. Jana couldn't have hurt feelings about that, even if she tried. He was bright, and quick to learn new things. He did everything early, just like when he stood up and walked across the room to his dad. And, when she took him with her to the training field, he carried his own tiny bow and sword. He loved his Papa, and Nana, but didn't want to stay at the kitchen anymore. That would have to change, when they left in the spring; but for now, she would indulge him. He wanted to be where the action was, and she couldn't blame him. But, as tough as he was, he had a tender heart; and when he saw someone hurt, he wanted to comfort the injured party, and kiss the wound. She didn't know how, or why, God had blessed her so much, but she knew she was blessed.

· · · · ·

Doc Rose came to Josh with an excitement in his eyes, which could only mean one thing. He'd found a way to remove the government implants.

"Josh, I've got it. I can't believe how I tripped over the answer. It was a complete accident. But, I figure that all God things look like accidents, at first, don't they?"

"Whoa, Doc, slow down. Are you telling me you know how to remove the chips? You can remove them, without killing the patient?"

"Isn't it great, Josh? Now, we can save more people, and get them out of the mess they're in. This will be life changing."

"Is this something that I'll be able to do, Doc? I don't want to have to take you away from the people here that need you."

"Yes, now that I know how, I can't believe I haven't figured it out long before this. It's actually a fairly simple procedure. I'll be able to show you and Jana, before you leave."

"I can't wait to tell Jana. She left to take Alec over to my mom. She's going to be so excited!"

• • • • •

Cage didn't have a chip. The government hadn't thought it necessary in regard to the upper echelon, to have a way of tracking them, as a way of showing their trust in these officers. But, Cage knew that every person in his church group had a tiny GPS transmitter in his, or her, hand, and that made him nervous. The tunnels were deep, and perhaps it would be difficult to follow the signal, to their location; but if a person was under suspicion, they could be tracked at least as far as the tunnel entrance, and that could be very dangerous for them all. So far, all was well, or at least as far as he knew; but he'd been a soldier for far too long, to stop being vigilant now.

He'd made many new friends in the group. More friends than he'd ever had before. At first, some of the brothers, and sisters, were suspicious of him. He was, after all, a member of the UNGC leader's upper council. It took quite some time, but they were beginning to trust him. He was more comfortable here, than anywhere else. He felt loved here.

A strange and unfamiliar sensation to him. He'd learned about Truth, and Grace, and Love, in this place, and it seemed like home.

He continued to do a great job, for Amir, in order to secure his standing, but felt more of a tugging on his conscious, with each passing week. The height of hypocrisy was that on the one hand, he was learning about Jesus, and becoming friends with His followers; and on the other hand, he was sitting in specially constructed stands, with Amir, in various cities around the country, watching those followers be put to death in a multitude of grizzly ways. It was becoming harder to justify.

• • • • •

Josh made arrangements to head out in the spring. They would go from ARM base, to base, using outside contacts, through the underground church. Their plan was to set up communications networks, using HAM radios, special network and airwave scheduling, and codes, which he and Jana had been spending a great deal of time perfecting. And, now that they had new knowledge of how to remove the government's chips, without killing the host, they intended to pass that knowledge along to every resistance stronghold, and within every group of underground Christians.

• • • • •

Cage sat, again, in Sunday services beside Amir, and wondered how this man justified with Allah and his prophet Mohammed, worshipping anywhere besides a mosque, and with anyone besides other Muslims. The studying he'd been doing, in both the Bible, and the Quran, affirmed his belief, that Islam was a lie; and that the Caliphate they, as fundamentalist Muslims, sought to establish around the world, would be the downfall of civilization as he knew it if allowed to come to fruition.

Certain Surahs (or scriptures), in the Quran, spoke of deceiving the infidels; who amounted to anyone who did not subscribe to Islam, and included any who were not of the same variety of Islam, as the Muslim who was reading the text; and lying to them until such a time as they were in a position to destroy them. He counted one hundred and nine separate verses that spoke of hurting and killing those who did not follow Islam, in the holy book of this so called 'peaceful religion'. A member of the underground church, where he attended, owned a Quran, and had brought it to meetings, to educate the group on the dangers they faced. Cage read it thoroughly, but had already figured a lot of this out on his own as he watched Amir setting his brothers up in positions of power, from which they could exact grave destruction.

He was trying to figure out a way he could be of help, without losing his head over the whole bloody mess. That Saturday night, while in the midst of worship with his friends, he was overcome by a sense of love and purpose, so strong, he could no longer put it off, or ignore it. Right then and there, he turned his own life, and eternity, over to The One who had given His all for him. His friends welcomed him into the family and the Kingdom, with hugs, kisses, and handshakes. Now he was one of them, and Satan screeched in abject agony, as God beamed a great smile.

Once Jesus was on the inside, he knew what he had to do. He could no longer aid and abet the enemy. No longer could he sit and watch as his brothers and sisters in Christ were murdered; and pretend it didn't affect him. He would need to go back to his house, one more time, to retrieve some personal items and clothing, but he had no intention of sitting through another Sunday service, with the doctor. His life would never be the same.

Cage talked, to the congregation, about his plans. He was not implanted, and therefore, not as easy to track. He would act as a guide to those who were seeking sanctuary, or a path to another church. He knew things about the system, which would benefit his efforts; and he could share the Gospel with others he encountered along the way. He also knew it was a dangerous calling he was accepting. But he mourned the years of his life he'd been so deceived, by things that didn't matter, and wanted to save others the pain of that deception. He was more filled with joy and peace, than ever in his life; and he had to share this gift with others.

Back at his house, he snuck in quietly, and filled a back-pack with personal hygiene items and a few changes of cloth-ing. Nothing fancy. He wouldn't need any of that anymore. He left his dress blues, his medals, and all the pomp and circumstance, behind. Again, he was struck over how little of true value, he owned. He reached clear in the back of his side table drawer, behind the box of tissue, and the television remote, and found his New Testament. The one thing he'd decided he couldn't live without. Once his pack was full, he snuck back out the way he'd come in, without Lucy, Anna, or James, being any the wiser. They would not see him again.

Next morning, at Sunday services, Doctor Bahram sat in his usual spot, saving a seat for the General. When the meeting began, and Cage still had not arrived, he got a little worried. That concern, however, turned quickly to anger, when he called Cage's cell phone and got no answer. He sent a guard to Cage's house, who found his room was empty, and his bed not slept in. His government assigned cell phone sat on a nearby table, and showed five missed calls. Now, Amir was not only angry, but furious. He'd trusted this man. Cage knew too many of his secrets to live, unless he was firmly planted on his side of things. Where had he gone? He wanted to kick himself. Why hadn't he kept a better eye on the man?

There was no one to tell, no one to confide in. Cage had been his confidant, his only sounding board, no one else. He was the one man in the world who knew Bahram's ultimate plans. He probably knew more than all the Islamic plants and appointees Amir worked so hard to set up in positions of power. He should have paid more attention to the signs of weakness he'd seen in his so called friend. His rage, which was building by the second, was so encompassing that he knew he couldn't sit through another boring service. Not without wanting to outright kill someone.

He would send out search parties to find the traitor. And, once he found him, there would be no power in heaven, or on earth, that would save him. He would make Cage sorry he ever turned his back on the one true leader of the world.

• • • • •

For the first time in his life, he felt a true purpose. Every thought, every action, everything in his previous life had consistently, and only, revolved around himself. When he looked back now, all he saw were veils of evil, in every direction. But, the evil had lifted, with the single act of opening his heart to the Lord. Formerly, he'd been responsible for his own peace, his own joy; and from all remembrances; he didn't believe he'd ever possessed either of those states of mind. He'd never known the freedom of turning himself over to anything worthwhile. Now, he knew, without question, that Jesus was his source, his peace, his joy, and his reason for being. Doing for others, with a pure heart, just felt good. And, yes, he did it all from a pure heart, which seemed strange to him. Like Paul, he had been a Saul, a persecutor, and murderer, of Christians. So how could his black heart be pure? It was pure, because he'd given it to his Savior, and Jesus lived there now. He was forgiven, and free to love.

He'd always been a go getter, and excellent at everything he did, so now he would apply that same work ethic to spreading the Gospel, and helping those in need. It didn't take long before he'd garnered a reputation in the world of the underground church. His friends nicknamed him Paul, and it stuck. If you were traveling the underground, and needed help, Paul was your man. So, it ended up that even the unredeemable, could be redeemed. God is very good.

• • • • •

Bishop Nathan Graham was to be awarded the Nobel Peace Prize, at a ceremony later this week. Some said they couldn't understand why; since he'd never really had any dealings with any foreign governments, and most certainly hadn't aided in any peace agreements. But the UNGC thought it would give the population at large more respect for the man, and give him more credibility on the world stage.

He was a heck of a public speaker, and the 'World Church' USA had grown considerably under his reign. So, credit should be given, where credit was due. Amir still thought he was an insufferable gas bag; and dreaded the weekly torture of attending his service; but he agreed that the honor would be a high mark for the church.

Keeping the church intact, until the Caliphate could be realized, would be essential to his plan. He realized the rest of the council didn't know his plans, and certainly wouldn't condone them, but they would be brought under subjugation soon enough.

Slowly, but surely, all the elements were shifting into place, for his worldwide coup. He was hearing, secretly, from more Twelver's groups, every week. And he continued to make plans for their coming together. He broke out in goose flesh, every time he thought about the arrival of the Mahdi, that great, and holy, day. This accomplishment would put him in a very special light before Allah.

He had search parties looking for Cage. So far they'd not been able to locate the betrayer. How he could have disappeared so swiftly, and completely, was an amazement to him. But he couldn't stay out of sight forever, and when he did surface for air, Amir's goons would be there to take him down.

• • • • •

Paul actually wasn't lying low at all. His presence was large in the underground church. He made more of a name for himself, as time marched on, but he was different now. Different in many ways. His appearance was changed, for one. Where once he'd worn his hair in a severe military cut, now his dark locks were longer, and wavy, and before long he would be tying them back, to keep them out of his face. Even his eyes were changed. They were softer, and less intense; he just didn't look so crazy anymore. He grew facial hair; a moustache, and beard, of black, flecked with grey. His attire was much more casual too, usually consisting of jeans, and a dark hoodie, but could change if the occasion called for it. And, most importantly, his mouth, and jaw were not as rigid and set, so he had actually learned to smile. And, this wasn't just any smile. This was the smile of one who was lost, and now is found; one who was in chains, and is now set free; one whose heart belongs to Jesus, and is so full, he has to share.

He'd always hated his name, so he liked the idea of a nickname. Most people who met him, these days, didn't even know him as the same sadistic general who sat stone faced as their fellows died in agony. That was a man of a different time.

And, as you would expect, he got very good at his new job. He knew every tunnel, sewer, hidden trap door, and friendly, in a six state area. He could get in, and out of an area as quickly, and quietly, as smoke. No militia, or UN guard, had been able to get within a half mile of the man. It has been said that God takes the ordinary, and makes something extra ordinary of it. This is what Paul was born to do. It just, as is so familiar in many of our lives, took him awhile to figure it out.

• • • • •

Scott knew that Josh would be leaving soon, for his mission to the nation's ARM bases, so he was picking his brain for any additional information, which might be helpful in his own undertaking.

"So, when the troops are flanked, what would you suggest as a defensive maneuver?"

"Well, Scott, it's best to stay out of that kind of position altogether. We are trained, as Christians, not to strike the first blow, and to turn the other cheek, but we have to think differently as soldiers."

"So, how do you keep from getting flanked?"

"You send out rear scouts, as well as forward scouts.

You make sure that you know, at all times, where your enemy is. And, you learn guerilla tactics. We don't have the manpower, or arms, to march up face to face with the enemy. We will be stealthy, and use our wits. You see, usually, when your troops are flanked, if you don't have another battalion of men to wrap around the back of them, you're doomed. We don't have the extra battalion of men, so we must keep our troops out of situations that would mean certain death."

"Do you really think we can win in a skirmish with the militia?"

"We've already won many battles against the militia, Scott. Don't get cold feet on me now. Jana and I are going to establish communications, which will aid in the battles to come; but I really need you here keeping the home fires burning, and getting these men and women in shape. Can you do that for us, Scott?

"You can count on me, Boss. I just hope nothing goes down without you here to lead the way."

"I don't believe it will come to that so soon; but if it did, you would do just fine, Scott. You need to remember that God is on our side. He will lead the battle, and He will win the day. Gideon prevailed with much less than we have;

and so did Jana. Trust God, my friend. So, how has Becca been doing?"

"She's well. Doc says everything is just as it should be. She's anxious to have the baby, though, so she can get back out here."

"Just like Jana was. Thank goodness for their determination. We will need all the willing soldiers we can get. We will be leaving soon; and I know I leave the troops in excellent hands. Let's get together for a meal, and some family time, before Jana and I have to leave."

"Sure thing, Boss. I'd like that."

● ● ● ● ●

"I know it's something they have to do, for the good of all of us, but I'm going to be so sad to see them go. Especially knowing how many months they'll be gone. That's going to be so hard on Alec. He's become so dependent on his daddy, and wants to be with him all the time."

"Calm down, Emma. You know this can't be helped. Of course it will be hard on Alec. It will be hard on all of us. But, it will be hardest on Josh and Jana. They are willing to go through that hardship for us, so we will take care of our grandson, and show him pictures of his dad and mom, so he won't forget. It's sad that we live in a world, where this is necessary, but that is the way of it. We will do what we have to do, just as we always have. Now, aren't we supposed to be planning a feast, to top all feasts? If these kids are going to be gone so long, you have to send them off with food that will give them good dreams for a long time."

"I agree. I want to make a special cake, and have Nancy write, 'Happy trails, and God's blessings', on it. Her penmanship is so much better than mine. My hands have gotten so much more shaky as I've gotten older. I think I'll also roast a turkey, and serve it with the works: dressing; mashed potatoes, with gravy; green beans, corn, homemade biscuits, and relishes. You know what I really miss?"

"No, I don't. What do you miss, my dear?"

"I miss cranberries. We grow so many fruits, and vegetables here, but we don't grow cranberries, or pineapple. And, wouldn't it be lovely to have grapes?"

"The vineyards are coming along. The men told me will have a small harvest, of concords, next season."

"That will be lovely. But we'll probably never have cranberries, will we?"

"Dear, the sheer size of the land needed for a bog, would be impossible. I'm sorry, but we'll never have cranberries.

At least not while we live in this cavern."

"Well, then, we shall win the war; and then we will have cranberries."

"It sounds like a lovely feast, Emma. And, they will be fine. Josh and Jana are very good at what they do. They will be back before we know it."

"I pray that you're right, Chuck. They have a little boy who needs them."

• • • • •

Amir heard, through the grapevine, that his wayward general was most likely still in the area. And, he ramped up his search teams to ferret out the traitor.

Paul, who was often in another state, these days; guiding run away Christians to new hiding places; dropped by his old underground church location, to surprise his friends. The scene he walked in to was disturbing. Several of the girls were crying, and no one seemed to be in charge of the situation.

"Hey, hey, why are you girls crying? What's going on?"

"Oh, Paul, we're so happy to see you. Haven't you heard? Brother Todd and Brother James have been captured, along with fifteen of our friends. They're being held at the courthouse, until the execution on Friday. What are we going to do?"

The news hit him so hard, he had a difficult time catching his breath. These men who'd brought him to knowledge of Jesus, who'd acted as his spiritual fathers, were going to be killed. He'd known, since he came to this crazy underground world, what a dangerous place it was. And, he'd seen others, that he deeply cared about, put to death. But the thought of these two pillars of strength, being cut to the ground, was hard to take. He sat down, hard, and put his arms around the shoulders of the two crying girls.

"I'll tell you what we're going to do. We're going to keep fighting. We're going to keep sharing the Gospel. And, we're going to continue the work God has given us to do, just like Brother Todd, and Brother James, would want us to do. I, for one, am not giving up."

"Then we won't give up either. Just tell us what to do."

And, just like that, Paul became the new leader of the DC chapter, of the underground Christian church. Becoming a local leader meant he wasn't on the road as often, but he was still getting the opportunity to witness to plenty of unbelievers, and was helping to grow the Kingdom of Christ. The men, on his mountain militia base, would have fallen over in shock, if they could see him now.

On the day of the execution of his dear friends, he and two of the girls from the church, mixed in with the crowd. He was disgusted by the vitriol, coming from the mouths of the gawkers; and especially disgusted to remember how he used to be the same. He wanted to stay at a safe distance, from the stands, which had been erected for Doctor Bahram, and his aides. But close enough to catch the eye of his friends, if that was possible. When the prisoners were escorted to the square, his breath caught in his throat. They'd been especially brutalized, by their jailers, and one of the young girls was limping so badly, she had to be half carried to her spot on the square. He saw no burning posts, or drowning pools, and no squad of machine gun wielding soldiers. Instead, there was a lone executioner, holding a broadsword. So, this was to be execution by beheading.

He wanted to rush out, and defend his brothers and sisters, as he watched the captives violently probed. One by one they were lashed, and given the chance to renounce Jesus. But, the result was just as he knew, in his heart, it would be; not a one denounced Christ. One at a time, the Christians were led to a block, forced to kneel, and place their neck on the surface of the block. One by one, he watched them meet their Creator, with a smile on their lips. Their heads, dripping with blood, were held up for the crowd to see, and the people cheered. Then, those heads, along with their lifeless bodies, were cast into a nearby garbage dumpster, saturated with gasoline, and set ablaze. As Brother James, was led to the block, he caught Paul's eye and gave a small nod. Paul smiled, what he hoped was an encouraging smile at him, as tears clouded his eyes and he nodded back. His life was extinguished as quick as a downward stroke. Then, as Todd made his way to the sword, their eyes locked, and a message of brotherly love, as old as the Gospel itself, passed between them. This was the man who had first dared to tell him he looked like he needed Jesus. The world would be a poorer place, for losing him.

As the executioner brought down his sword, to take Todd's head, the job remained undone. It seemed that too many heads had been taken that day, and his sword was dull. As Todd's body twitched, and kicked, the executioner hacked, and sawed, at his victim's neck, to accomplish his gory task. And, with four more heads to take, the scene became one of carnage, unlike many had ever seen. Quite like the burning at the stake fiasco, completed in this very square, this senseless act of butchery led to women fainting in the streets, random vomiting, and a big mess to clean up. Paul was rocked to the core. He'd watched these men that he loved, go bravely to meet their maker, as Amir sat stone faced through it all. How could he have ever respected that man? What had he seen in this Muslim terrorist monster?

He knew the plans Amir had for the world. And, he had seen, firsthand, the steps being taken to complete them. There had to be a way to warn the people, and those in power, of the doctor's evil, before it was too late, but how?

Paul had, since his mentor's death, inherited his Bible. And, as the new leader of the church, he spent many hours studying. He'd already memorized most of the scriptures of the New Testament, but now he had access to the prophetic books of the Old Testament, and he began to study those. He was shocked, as he read, by the similarities between those prophetic scriptures, and the current world situation. And, saw many more parallels as he reread the book of Revelation. He imagined that Amir could very well be the antichrist spoken of in those passages. And, he was out to stop the decimation of the world's Christians.

• • • • • •

Josh and Jana, were ready to leave. They'd spent the past

couple of weeks enjoying time with family, and friends; sharing meals with loved ones; and especially, spending as much time with Alec as possible. He was an amazing child, and was growing so fast. They knew they would miss many things while they were gone, but they trusted Papa, and Nana, with the safety of their child, and had already instructed them to take as many pictures as possible. Alec acted as though he actually understood Daddy and Mommy had to go away for the good of the people. He didn't cry, when they held him and hugged him goodbye. And, he didn't cry when his dad handed him to his gramma.

Emma was surprised at his maturity, and thankful for the fact that her job was made easier, by his gentle and easy going nature. Now, they would get through these months of absence, together, until Josh and Jana's return.

The two travelers were taking with them, hope, for the people of the world. They had the answer to the removal of the implants; and that formula was much less complicated than ever imagined, as long as you knew the exact order, in which to proceed. They'd developed a new communications route, and code, which would put all the bases in direct contact with each other for the first time since the world had flipped upside down. And, they would be better able to assess the true numbers of soldiers, and arms, available to them. They also planned to assess the readiness of those available troops, and implement training programs, to get the resistance armies up to speed for the coming battles. A great deal was riding on the success of their travels.

It would be imperative that they make good time, and get the mechanical, and electronic, pieces of the operation up and running, post haste. They knew from previous, life, and death, marches; that they worked better together, than apart, and they were both very good at what they did. It would be good to be out on the mountain, together, again; but more than that, it would be good to get things going in the direction of success, for the resistance movement.

Their first day out on the mountain was peaceful. Still high enough in the peaks, that they didn't have to worry about being seen by militia choppers; they talked, and sang, as they hiked. With Cage, and the PM base gone from the heights, their trip down the behemoth would likely be uneventful, but they still wouldn't let down their guard.

Along the way, Jana bagged a couple of healthy looking rabbits, and field dressed them, on the spot. "You know, you are never quite as sexy to me, as when you are field dressing our supper, my beautiful wife."

"Why, thank you, Husband. You're not too bad your-self."

"What do you say we find a cave, and call it a night? It's beginning to get dark, and I'll collect fire wood if you'll fill the canteens, and cooking pots."

"Good idea. Be sure to cut some pine boughs for the entrance. I still have nightmares about wolves outside my door all night."

"Yeah, I remember you telling me about that. I usually do that anyway, because I've had a few run-ins with critters on this mountain."

"I didn't know about that. You've never told me about your animal stories. Perhaps you'd like to share those while we eat supper?"

"Sure. They aren't as good as yours, but I can give you what I've got."

They went about readying their cave for the night. Josh started their fire, and Jana prepared the rabbits. She pulled out some grain, and dried fruit, from her pack, and made a delicious mash to accompany the roasted hare. While supper was cooking, they read and prayed together. Then, while they ate, Josh regaled Jana with stories of slaying dragons, and fighting mountain wolves. They chatted, and laughed, until the fire died down; then they added a few small logs, and drifted off to sleep in each other's arms.

As they traveled, farther down the mountain, they could see evidence that Spring was on the move. Unlike the heights where their base was located, the lower elevations began to see a decrease in the amount of accumulated snow. This time of year was especially dangerous, due to melting, and the possibility of avalanches. As they descended even further, they saw signs of green buds on trees, and bits of grass springing up through empty patches in the snow. After several more days of hiking, they were getting low enough on the mount, to see patches of crocus, yellow, and purple, against the stark white.

Soon enough they were on flat ground. Josh chose the dryer path, around the turkey foot grass, as the spring thaw would surely create a bog in that area. He had no desire to slog through freezing water once again. He'd told Jana about that fiasco, and she was all for the non direct route, if it would keep them on dry ground.

They arrived at the edge of the forest, and looked at each other. "I haven't been back in this forest, since that day I was running from the PM, with bullets flying around me."

"Well, you're still one up on me, Babe. I've never been in this forest at all. I got on the mountain the easy way, via militia chopper."

"Okay, we'll just take it slow. I don't know if they patrol this area, or if they've implemented any traps, since this is one of the common routes used by runaways."

"Alright, how about this. Going forward, we will communicate by hand signals. The same ones we've taught the troops. It will give us some good practice, and assure that we're not making any unnecessary noise."

"Good idea, Josh. I knew I married you for a reason. Let's stay low, and keep our eyes open for any signs of booby traps."

Going slow, it took them several days to navigate the trees, but they managed to avoid the many traps, which were obviously set by inexperienced troops, and they got to the other side of the woods unscathed. As they stepped out of the cover of the trees, they saw that their favorite park had been used at some time as a staging point for militia. It was empty of troops now, probably due to the closing of the mountain base. But, when they noticed the damage done to trees, and some of their favorite recreational areas, it made them sad.

This war was causing so much harm, to so many things. Jana looked for 'their bench', and finally located the spot where it had been. The bench was broken, and tossed to one side, but she could still see the depression in the dirt, where she'd dug the plastic container filled with secrets from the earth. It seemed very long ago. The park was so beautiful then, with fall colors decorating the trees, and wild asters springing up any place where a bit of sun peeked through. Spring was trying its best to rise above the devastation.

She saw tiny leaves peeking from branches, of the trees which remained, creating light green halos all around the damaged wood. There were baby bunnies and squirrels scampering about, and running to hide under abandoned equipment, as soon as they realized they had company. Patches of new, green grass, made a valiant attempt to re-gain its territory; and here and there, small areas of fern; or colorful columbine, and bleeding heart, made their mighty stand. At some point, nature would do her clever work, and most of the damage would be covered up by vines, and new growth; but until then, Jana wanted to remember the place where her husband dropped to one knee and pro-posed to her, the way it was.

O God, you are my God; earnestly I seek you; my soul thirsts for you; my flesh faints for you, as in a dry and weary land where there is no water. So I have looked upon you in the sanctuary, beholding your power and glory. Because your steadfast love is better than life, my lips will praise you. So I will bless you as long as I live; in your Name I will lift up my hands.

Psalm 63:1-4

CHAPTER 27

Paul picked up another nickname. Government officials were calling him 'The Ghost'. It seemed every time they got close, he'd disappear. He'd moved the church's meeting place, almost weekly, since the deaths of Brother Todd and Brother James. Some might call him paranoid, but he knew there were moles in the underground church, and he meant to keep his community safe. There was no other explanation for some of the recent captures, than subversion. Most likely it was someone new to the fold each time, but he wouldn't allow himself to become so suspicious that he didn't share the Gospel with every person he met along the way.

He wasn't proud of his past, but he also knew God had forgiven him; so it wasn't hard for him, now that he understood that sacrifice, to extend the love to others. He was such a different fellow; kind, compassionate, understanding, and forgiving, that he wouldn't have known himself. But, he wouldn't be so foolish as to allow just anyone to walk into the midst of people he'd sworn to protect. He had talents, which had served him well, and helped to keep his people safe.

One of his many talents was the ability to read people. On a day, just a couple of months after the death of Todd, and James, the girls brought a fresh face into the fold. He was a bit suspicious, when the young man wouldn't look him in the eye, but the girls were sure he was okay. Usually he announced at each meeting, where the next gathering would take place, but he decided to do something different that week. He allowed the young man to believe the next assembly would be at the same location, then he contacted his members later, and gave them the new address, urging them, just for this week, not to share the information with anyone.

On Saturday afternoon, just a couple of hours before their normal meeting time, he arrived and hid himself. He witnessed the arrival of the young man, and saw him directing operatives, for the UN forces, to hiding places where they would be safe from discovery. They were to wait until all the congregants had arrived, before jumping out from their respective hiding places, to capture the members of the church. He hated the fact that he'd been correct. And, he hated that he couldn't come out of hiding to give that young fellow what he deserved. But, he was grateful to God for the insight he'd been given, and that he'd been able to thwart their plan.

Once he arrived, late, to the new meeting place, he filled the others in on the insidious plan, which had almost taken their lives. He didn't want them to stop sharing the Gospel, or to stop inviting new people to attend worship services, but, instead, gave them pointers on how to read people a little better. He knew God was covering them all.

• • • • •

Doctor Bahram was becoming more angry every day,

that his troops had not uncovered the whereabouts of Cage. Though he hadn't shared, with anyone, the extent of information the traitor held. Since it would also lay bare the deception he was perpetrating on the people of the world. They continued to ask after the general. General Cage had been highly esteemed in the halls of the UNGC, and that was due, in part, to the level of trust Amir had placed in him. Therefore, it was unthinkable, to most of them, that he would betray them this way. Obviously, the doctor couldn't share all his secrets, so the council members were only aware that the general had absconded with top secret materials. No one, not even Amir, knew the general was heading up the underground church in their district, and that he'd been present for many of the executions that took place in the square.

Amir had, recently, placed another of his Muslim brothers in a place of high security. Little, by little, and bit, by bit, he was achieving his goal. Pretty soon he would call for Islam to rise. They would establish a worldwide Caliphate, and the Mahdi would come to lead them into global peace. He was sure his war on Christianity, and any other religion that got in his way, was a just one. He was also sure that the members of the 'World Church' would back him. After all, their extreme socialist views were similar to those of Sharia law. He would help them to see the sense of his plan, once it was accomplished. And once they rose up together, and defeated their enemy, he would require that they, also, submit to Islam.

· · · · ·

Josh and Jana arrived at the first of their ARM base stopovers. Josh was once again stumped as to why they had not yet been discovered. It must be the protective hand of God. There was no other explanation. He was also plagued by the lack he saw there. They subsisted on the military rations they'd procured from closed PM camps, and the limited hunting they were able to do in their area. There was no comparison to the life of plenty his people lived on the mountain. And, he felt guilty for allowing their suffering to go on for so long, before preparing their armies to fight back. He also knew, though, that his base couldn't handle this many additional numbers, so he kept his mouth shut, and did what he came to do.

Within four days, they'd worked with electricians on base, to build a basic HAM radio setup; plus they taught three key members of the base elder's council the code they would be using to transmit messages, and gave them a schedule of the rotating band waves they would utilize. Their first transmission was back to their own home base. They let Josh's parents know they were fine, and asked about Alec. "We're so glad you're okay, Son. We've all been praying for you."

"Thank you, Dad. And, thank you for taking care of our little guy. We will call you from each base, as we set up the radio equipment, so you'll be able to track our progress. We love you."

"And, we love the two of you. I'll let your mom know you're doing well. Perhaps next time she can come say a few words?"

"I'd like that. Give Alec a big hug from Daddy and Mommy. We will see you soon. God bless you."

"God bless, and God speed to the two of you, Josh. Come back to us as soon as you are able."

While they were there, they took care of an item, which was of utmost importance. They taught the base's doctor, and two aides, the procedure for removing government implanted chips.

They spent an additional two days working with all the men and women on base, who might be likely candidates to become soldiers of war. They labored to teach them methods of hand to hand combat, that would likely save their lives, and the lives of their children. Jana worked with a couple of artisans, to make bows, and arrows; watching closely to see that they mastered her methods perfectly. They would be left with the task of making enough weapons to outfit an army. The base had some arms, and ammunition, but much like their own situation, the government's confiscation of guns, before the forced implants, had left little by way of firepower.

Once there were weapons to work with, Jana spent some time showing a couple of the more athletic soldiers in the group, the fine art of archery. True, it was a crash course, but they caught on quickly. Now they would be able to teach others. At the same time, Josh worked on teaching the basics of swordsmanship; and the use of a pole, as a weapon; to as many willing bodies as possible, in the short time available to them. They urged elders of the base, to have the soldiers train at least two hours a day, to get their defenses in shape, for the battles to come. On the seventh day, they rested, and worshipped, with their new friends.

They left the base confident that they'd done all they could in so short a period of time.

"Do you think they'll be okay?"

"All we can do is trust God, Jana. Heck, I can't believe no one has found them yet. I mean, for crying out loud. Their base is hardly hidden at all. And, let's face it, they have a lot of resolve, more than many others would have; living in conditions like that, and surviving; when we have so much. I'd say that any group who shows so much determination, will work hard and fight hard. So, yeah, I think they'll do just fine. And, we have to remember who is on our side."

"Yep, God is on our side. We'll keep them in prayer. We gave them a lot of information to process, and I think they looked very hopeful when we left, don't you?"

"I do. Hope is so important. And, now they will be able to communicate with their brothers and sisters in the resistance. I think that will go a long way to bolstering their confidence."

"Good, now, on to the next destination. Where to husband?"

As they traveled the land, sometimes their route was through lesser populated areas of the countryside, where, as long as they were careful, they could be a little more relaxed. But, more often than not, because this trip was about educating the people, they were in more densely occupied towns, and cities.

Wanting to connect with the underground churches in each area proved to be a logistical nightmare, but had to be done, in order to pass along the new much needed method of removing implant devices. In each city, they ran the risk of being caught by government operatives, posing as Christians. But, Josh had a sixth sense about these things, he was sure due to God's protective hand, and they were successful in reaching the correct contacts. At each stop, they passed along the medical information necessary to free people from the grip of their implants, and rallied them for battle.

• • • • •

The UNGC was suddenly seeing a strange phenomenon, in various places around the country. It must be noted that, when the GHO implanted the American people, and eventually, the world; each chip was given a specific serial number, and tracked on a universal computer system. For all this time, those tracking devices have been automatically registering themselves, every day, as the global system reboots at midnight, Eastern time. If a serial number went dark, it usually followed that this person was found to have died. In the case of mass executions, the number of prisoners who were eliminated, would show up on the next day's reboot as dark serial numbers. But, something odd was happening lately. Whole groups, first small ones and eventually larger ones were going dark, without a record of death. That simply could not be. It was widely known, that to disconnect one's implant, meant certain death.

Amir demanded that the doctor, who had created the original chip, be brought to him.

"Explain to me, Doctor, how this chip works."

"Yes Sir. When the chip is implanted, it is dialed in to the body's own electrical system, if you will. Since each person's system, is slightly different, we allow the computer to implement the set point. If the implant is altered, in any way, due for instance, to attempted removal, the set point is altered, and the body's system attacks the host's heart, and brain, killing them instantly. We actually have the power to alter that set point from our office, and have been directed to do that on occasion by the previous administration, in order to kill a targeted host."

"Is there any way to work around that set point, Doctor?"

"Well, of course, Sir. We had to create a work around.

The administration, who was in power at the time, wanted a way to reverse, in case there was someone accidentally implanted, or a case where someone's tracking should be turned off for various reasons. But, you needn't worry about that, Sir. It would be impossible for any lay person to figure out the procedure to remove an active implant."

"Well, Doctor, someone has figured out your impossible procedure. We are seeing implant serial numbers going dark all over the place."

"I, I assure you, Doctor Bahram, there is no way....."

"Take him out and get rid of him. We have no need of him anymore. Not if the average person can now remove their own chip."

"But, Sir, I beg of you."

"Get rid of him. I told you to go! You, yes you! Find me someone who has the knowledge to find the names, connected to serial numbers, of recently deactivated chips. We are going to track these people down. They didn't die from removing the chip, so we will make them examples. People will know that if you remove your implant, we will know, and you will pay."

What Amir didn't count on, was that resistance leaders knew the government kept track of all personal information belonging to each recipient of their chip. So, before they removed any implant device, they conferred closely with the host, to see if they were willing to give up the life they knew, for one of hiding out in the nearest ARM base, or underground church, until such time as a revolution to overthrow the UNGC could be arranged. They didn't have to do any convincing. Most Americans were adamantly opposed to all things government, after the living conditions they'd endured throughout the past few years.

So, when council's troops kicked down the doors, of those citizens accused of illegally removing their devices, they found only empty hovels.

• • • • •

Josh and Jana were making their way around the country. As they went, they shared important information with elders and base councils along the way. These people, who routinely located government runaways, and often had to turn them away; due to the GPS systems in their implants; could now take them in and save their lives. Assimilation of information, into the resistance community, was going well. Each base they'd visited had a variety of talents available to them. They worked with electricians, to build HAM radio transmitters and receivers; with communications workers, to share wavelength, and frequency, schedules, and codes; and likely soldiers, to train for the upcoming battles. Everyone had a role, and the morale and excitement at ARM's bases all over the country was revitalized to a degree that had not been witnessed since the mass exodus of free thinking Americans began.

When their travels led them to underground churches, they still had significant information to share. Due to their clandestine activities and need to roam, churches didn't set up communications devices. After all, to move them would be a monumental task. But, the couple could teach them the process of removing unwanted implant devices; and they could work with congregation members on their hand to hand combat and self defense skills, so they were duly welcomed wherever they went.

As Josh and Jana, ventured into churches in the Midwest, Eastern, and North Atlantic states, they began to hear a name mentioned, over and over, and they sincerely hoped they would have an opportunity to meet this Paul, who was spoken of so highly. Finally, on a particular weekend, when they were in the DC area, they were invited to a service, where Paul was scheduled to speak. It was a beautiful, summer day, and promised to be a beautiful evening, with clear skies and warm, breezy weather. The service would take place outside, in a wooded area, filled with native wild flowers and butterflies. As the congregation of this certain church was becoming very large they hadn't yet found an indoor venue, which could accommodate their numbers.

The couple arrived, and began to mingle. Many faces were new, but they'd met some of these brothers and sisters in their dealings with the local churches. They spent their time, until services were set to begin, chatting and hugging their new friends. The forested area, chosen for worship, was surrounded by mature trees, which gave a protected feeling to the space. The canopy, created by leafy branches, offered privacy, but also let in just enough light to produce an intimate space for gathering. Someone had arranged old tarps and blankets on the ground, for seating.

One young man, with long, red hair, pulled back in a braid, and a bright red goatee, had brought a well worn guitar; and a delicate looking young lady, with blond hair, and huge brown eyes, unpacked a flute. The two began playing some well known Christian tunes, and those listening started to sing along. They were singing, reading scripture, and enjoying a time of worship; when rustling, at the edge of the tree line, indicated that their guest speaker had arrived.

As their leader entered the space, Josh looked up into his face, and leapt up to do battle. Jana, whose instincts kicked in one second later than her husband's, followed close behind. Several men, close to the couple, jumped up to stand between Josh, and the man they knew, only as Paul. "What are you doing here? Do any of you people know who this man is?"

"I'm sorry, Josh. If I'd known you would be here today, I would have asked our elders to prepare you for what has to be one of the biggest shocks of your life. The people here know that I have led a very sordid past; and that I was one of the worst persecutors of Christians who ever lived; which is why, when I came to know Christ as my Lord, and Savior, they nicknamed me Paul."

"I, I'm sorry, for my reaction. You do look different, but I still knew who you were, as soon as I saw your face. If you remember, the last time I saw you, you were threatening to rip the child from my wife's womb, and torture her in front of me."

"Yes. And, to be honest with you, I don't know if I

could ever forgive me, if I were you. I guess that has to be between you, and the Lord. I know it doesn't help much, but I'm not that person anymore. Jesus has brought a peace into my life that I never knew existed. And now I spend my time, underground, sharing the Gospel. I am now a fugitive, with a very large price on my head."

Throughout Paul's speech, Josh, breathing hard, began to loosen his grip on the sword at his side; and Jana's hand, finally, let go of the knife sheathed on her thigh. Both were still visibly shaken. The men; who'd separated them from the object of their fear; helped them sit back down, and brought them bottles of water, to calm them.

Josh was having a hard time comprehending the impossibility of what he was seeing. Cage, here, and a follower of Jesus no less. Now he'd seen it all. And, for anyone watching, this was absolute proof that God still did miracles. Jana just shook her head. This made little sense. But, she was sure, neither did Saul's conversion make sense, to those he had persecuted in the New Testament church. This was crazy, but the more she thought about it, it was also one of the greatest things she'd ever witnessed. This was the one man in the world, she'd been sure was beyond redemption; and here he was, a leader in the church. God really did have a marvelous sense of humor.

The three sat for hours; after services were over, and everyone else had cleared out. Talking about how amazing God was; how much their lives had changed; and little Alec, the blessing, who was thankfully not ripped from Jana's womb. Paul also told them about the time he'd spent with Amir; the death of his friends, and how it sent him in search of answers. And, he began to fill them in on Amir's plans for taking over the world, with an Islamic Caliphate to make way for the Mahdi.

"I didn't have any idea his ideas were so insidious."

"I know, Josh. I didn't either, at first. He trusted me a great deal, so I was privy to many of his appointments and plans, and sometimes I couldn't believe what was right in front of my own face."

"I thought the administration's strategies, when they insisted every American be implanted, were insane. I knew we couldn't just sit around and accept a government that had gone rogue; but I never imagined things had gone so far. Until we began this tour to the ARM encampments, we were very out of touch. I'm glad we're back out here, before all is lost."

"Do you really think there is anything to be done about

it at this point, Josh?"

"Yes we do. We serve a mighty God, and He has put you in our path, so you could make us aware of the state of the world, and the aggression of Islam. So, tell us everything you know."

"Well, I think the real change began when the UN got involved. Then, the previous plans the president had for complete control of the US became hijacked by a more universal strategy. The UN Global Council decided everyone in the world needed a chip, just like the citizens of America, to give them more leverage over the population. I don't believe the council ever meant to see the world become an Islamic state. That came about by their desire to be politically correct. Like the rest of the world, they were so afraid of offending anyone, that they handed over control of the globe to a terrorist. We are all so careful, not to be accused of profiling. We want the world to think we're open and accepting. Well, we've accepted evil, right in through the front door because of it.

"They chose Dr. Amir Bahram as head of council, in part, due to a sense of obligation, because society told them it was the right thing to do. I mean, how long did we listen to the lie that Islam is a peaceful religion, and that we were all worshipping the same God, as terrorists blew up the planet? They were told that Muslims had been treated unfairly, and that we should do something to give them more confidence in our government.

"People from the left told us Muslims were our friends. Things got to a place, long ago, where folks were afraid to speak the truth, for fear of being accused of racism, and bigotry. So they handed over the most influential position on the globe, to a Muslim who was ready to use that power for the bringing about of a worldwide coup. He suddenly had power to change the world, in whatever way he deemed fit, and he's been doing that ever since. Amir has been placing Muslim extremists, his Islamic brothers, in positions of power, all over the world, since he was placed in office. They are planning a global takeover, which will put in place an Islamic Caliphate.

"I don't know if anyone else on the council has figured out his plan, but they don't have the power to override his orders in any case. Most of them were kept in the dark. I knew what he was doing, because I was his confidant. And, honestly, I didn't care one way, or another, at the time, because I didn't worship anything. What difference could it possibly make to a man with no god, which god the rest of the world followed? Now I know the difference, but I'm a fugitive. Who in government, with any kind of influence, would listen to me?"

"So, we are probably more informed than the UNGC, at this point, correct?"

"Yes, I would say you are."

"Well, Paul, it's still hard to call you that, you know?"

"Yes, I'm sure it is."

"I believe, with this information, we can make a huge difference. We told you that we've been setting up a communications network with the other ARM bases. We also told you that we've been training soldiers."

"Yes, and as I was traveling around the world for Amir, I had the opportunity to talk to citizens of every country. People all over the globe are fed up with their plight. The UNGC is woefully under informed about the condition of their people, or the shaky ground on which they stand. Now that we know how to remove their implants, and set them free, I believe many of them would join together with us to battle the evil of Islam. We do have a common goal."

"Then we are going to need you to set up some sort of communications chain, kind of a pony express, if you will, with the other underground churches, so that we can stay in touch. It needs to be a chain, which can withstand missing links, in case someone is captured. Can you do that?"

"I believe I can. I can also see that others know the procedure for removing the implant devices, and make sure that everyone who comes to us gets a few lessons in hand to hand combat, and self defense. We will begin to get our hands on things, which can be used as weapons. That's something we didn't do before, because our sole focus was on sharing the Gospel. Now, though, I believe it's okay to teach the people who come to us that it's fine to fight for their God, their country, and for what they believe. I am confident we can be a formidable force."

"I agree, Paul. It's going to be a long, hard battle. We will surely be outmanned, out armed, and lacking in many things; but the one thing we can be assured of, is that God will be our source. With him on our side, we can do anything."

God shall arise, His enemies shall be scattered; and those who hate Him shall flee before Him! As smoke is driven away, so you shall drive them away; as wax melts before fire, so the wicked shall perish before God! But the righteous shall be glad; they shall exult before God; they shall be jubilant with joy!

Psalm 68:1-3

CHAPTER 28

Josh was amazed that he could feel so close to a man who'd spent the last few years trying to kill him. They embraced, and promised to spend more time together, when they came back through DC. Jana cried, in part for having to say goodbye to such a wonderful new friend, and in part because she was so astonished at God's Grace and never ending surprises. As they departed, she had a pain in her heart that she couldn't understand.

"Did you ever imagine you'd be sorry to say goodbye

to Cage?"

"Well, to Cage, no; but to Paul, yes. I'm flabbergasted at the difference in the man. God is so good; and I know this already; but I am still overwhelmed by His great Love, each time I am confronted by it. Aren't you, Jana?"

"Absolutely. I can't wait to see him again. Now that I know how intelligent a man he is, I find him to be a joy to talk to. I'm so glad God brought him into the light."

"Well, we'll be sure to come back through, after we stop at the other base on our list and the churches who've contacted us. We'll be more relaxed when we know our original duties have been accomplished."

"I'm sure you're right. Well, where to now, Husband?"

• • • • •

Amir continued to rule with an iron fist, so the other council members left most decisions to him. As long as it looked like he had everything under control, they didn't have to get their own hands dirty.

He'd recently placed another Muslim brother in a highly sought after position, and some of the council members were beginning to get suspicious and worried. But they didn't say a word. It was better not to rock the boat. And, the execution of Christians continued.

The doctor still had troops out there, nationwide, kicking in doors, hauling in members of underground churches and searching for Cage. Every day, when they came back empty handed, he raged, and gave orders for more deaths. It was a frightening time to be a Christian.

• • • • •

Nathan Graham knew how popular he'd become, and on the occasions that he went out in public, he was sure to wear as much of his holy regalia as he was able. Like a peacock, in full mating mode, he strutted about seeing who he could impress with his medals, and important looking fluff. Amir was sickened by the attention the man garnered, but he stayed out of the way. As long as the people's attention was clearly set on the bishop, he could secretly accomplish much more. There would come a day, when the doctor would need the help of this annoying idiot. To convince his congregants, and yes, the congregations of the globe, that the Caliphate was the best plan for the world. Oh, he was sure the bishop would balk at first. But, if he understood that his very life depended on swaying the entire earth, in favor of Islam, he would relent readily enough. So, Amir didn't step in the way of his self congratulatory existence; at least not yet.

• • • • •

Paul continued traveling the underground circuit, and sharing the Gospel with every soul he encountered; in spite of the fact that the number of troops searching for him had doubled. He refused to stop doing, what he knew God called him to do, no matter the risk. His friends, and congregation, begged him to lay low for awhile, but he wouldn't hear of it.

"If the brother, who brought me to my first meeting, had laid low because there might be risk in the going, I wouldn't be here today. I have to go. If I can bring even one more to the knowledge of God's Grace through Jesus, then how can I ever be satisfied to simply sit back?"

While he was speaking at a gathering in a nearby town, he was spotted. Troops quietly surrounded the building. The captain of the guard patted himself on the back. This might mean a huge promotion for him. As the meeting disbursed, and Paul left the building, he, and every person who'd attended, was apprehended. He pleaded with the soldiers to let the others go. "You don't want them. You know he'll be satisfied if you have me. Just let them go. I beg of you." It was a valiant attempt, but the troops were deaf to his pleas. When Amir found out he'd been captured, he flew to the holding cell to see for himself.

"So, Paul is it? I had no idea the locals esteemed you so much. We've been calling you 'The Ghost', for quite some time. Are your friends aware that you used to sit with me, and watch, as they were put to death?"

"Yes they are. I've not spared them the awful truth, and yet they choose to love me anyway. Why don't you let the others go, Amir? You don't want them. It was me you were after."

"Actually, you know how much I detest Christians, General. You, above all, know more about me than anyone. I trusted you with my thoughts and plans. You were my confidant. I can't believe how easy it was for you to turn on me. And you. You have become one of them? I can't imagine what you are thinking. You know what is happening, which direction the world is going. Why would you choose the worst path? "

"I chose the path that was right for me. I met Jesus, and He changed my life."

"Jesus! I'm sick of that name! Because you were my

friend, I will give you one chance to deny that name. If you don't, General, I will see that you suffer. I will watch while you beg for death, and then I will see you suffer even more."

"I know you won't understand, Amir, but I could never deny Christ. He is everything to me. You see, when I do leave this place, I have a home with Him. That's something I never really had before. Jesus has been more than a brother to me, and I will die with His Name on my lips."

"Guards! Watch him. If anything happens to him, you will pay with your lives. Do you understand me?"

"Yes Sir. Don't worry Sir."

"And, send your captain to me. We will schedule the execution for Friday. I want to be sure to have a large crowd present for this one."

$$\bullet \ \bullet \ \bullet \ \bullet \ \bullet$$

When Josh and Jana, completed their work at the last base on their list, they headed for DC. They planned to spend a little time with their friend before heading back to the mountain.

All the radio equipment, at every base, was up and running; and they'd had an opportunity to speak with loved ones at home on several occasions. Alec was doing great, and went crazy when he heard Dad's and Mom's voices. He was getting so big, and his vocabulary had expanded so much, that it was hard to believe they were talking to a child who was not quite two years old.

Scott and Becca had their baby a week ago. It was a girl, and they'd named her Elizabeth. They sounded excited as they filled their friends in on every detail. Six pounds, and seven ounces; nineteen inches long (she would be petite like her mom); big hazel eyes; and lots of curly hair, the color of corn silk. Alec was enamored with her, and her brother, and sister, wouldn't leave her alone. Becca was already chomping at the bit, to get back to training the troops; and they couldn't wait for their dear friends to be home.

Josh told Scott about their old nemesis, Cage. He couldn't believe what he was hearing, about the complete conversion of a man who'd been so feared by so many. "Now, there's a guy who I'd never have thought would even want to know the Lord. But, I'd imagine there were a lot of folks who'd say the same thing about me. Well, God bless him. When you see him again, give him my best, and tell him "Welcome to the family", from me."

"We will. We miss you all so much. We're going to swing

by DC, for a short visit, and then we'll be heading home."

Once they arrived in the city, they caught wind of the buzz immediately. They contacted Paul's home church, and were met with cries of anguish. The people there didn't know what to do without their leader. Josh and Jana, were beside themselves. They wanted to help, but couldn't come up with a way. Paul was under heavy guard, and allowed no prisoners. They were heartbroken. They talked about trying to break him out, but his congregation told them he wouldn't want that. "He would tell us to go on. Share the Gospel with everyone you meet. He wouldn't want anyone else captured, trying to save him. But, we know that he would like you to stay, and be there with him as he goes to meet the Lord."

"Oh, Josh, I don't know."

"Jana, this is what he would want. He's our friend, and more than that, he is a brother in Christ. This is something that would be important to him. To know that there are others carrying on his work, after he is gone."

So, plans were made, to house the couple, until Friday's spectacle.

On Thursday evening there were people all over DC, and throughout the underground church circuit, many states away, celebrating the life of their brother, Paul. Church services were taking place in tunnels, fields, warehouses, attics, and basements. And those services were centered on exactly what Paul would want; the Love, Truth, and Grace of Jesus. They were remembering the life of a man, who had come from the deepest pit, to the light, and love of Christ, and who had dedicated the rest of his life, to sharing that love with others. He had truly become the hands, and feet of Jesus.

Morning came, and the mood was somber. Jana dreaded the thought of what she would see in the city square. It was one thing to see the bodies of the dead, when they were your enemies, and were killed in times of battle. And, completely another, seeing those you love and care about, tortured, and slaughtered like animals.

Jana was deeply aware, that for these past months, she, and Josh, had been preparing their brothers and sisters, for a battle unlike any other. They would be fighting for their lives; the right to worship their God; and for the country they loved. They would be fighting an enemy, who didn't believe they had even the right to exist; who outnumbered them, and had access to weapons, and ammunition, they couldn't dream of. The enemy was ruthless, and had a powerful ally in Satan. But, they had a more powerful friend in God, who would be their shield, and buckler. They would fight, because the enemy had given them no other choice; and they would take back that which belonged to them; their world, and their dignity.

It was settled, they would be there for their friend; as they should be, as he would want them to be; but then they would travel home. Soon, they would be back. And, when they came, they would be leading troops to war.

• • • • •

The crowds were massive. Gawkers loved these events, and this one was touted to be a doozey. Amir was seated snugly in the stands, with a self-righteous look on his face. Next to him sat his new political ally, annoying as he was, Bishop Nathan Graham. Also, in attendance, were Paul's brothers and sisters in Christ. Many from the underground churches, in a six state radius; all disguised; would witness an event which would forever touch their lives.

The day was overcast, though it hadn't begun to rain just yet. A city of cement, grey, and lifeless, filled with the best, and worst of humanity. In the center of the square stood thirty three large metal brackets, which looked like supports. Laying on the ground before each bracket, was what appeared to be a wooden cross. So, this would be a mass death, by crucifixion. Amir had thought it fitting, that these rebels for Jesus Christ should die in like manner.

Josh and Jana arrived with members of Paul's church, and hid in plain sight. Neither of them wanted to be there, to see their friend tortured and killed, but they hoped to catch his eye, and give him the knowledge, through their presence, that his work would not be forgotten or forsaken.

He'd brought so many to the foot of the cross. How appropriate then, that the cross would be his way back home. Josh stood stone faced, and Jana tried very hard not to cry. How ironic, that this man who'd been a thorn in their side, the bane of their existence, for so long, could be so dear to them now.

The prisoners were led out single file. They were all badly beaten, and covered with bloody lacerations and bruises. Paul, especially, looked beaten half to death. As he came, he walked with his head held high, and caught the eyes of Josh, Jana, and his church members. He gave a slight nod, in recognition of their presence. The judge stepped forward, on shaky legs, and read to them, a list of their crimes: Practicing a banned religion; leading others down an illicit path; causing division in the determined order; alluding capture; and, removal of governmentally placed implantation devices. The punishment for each of these offences was death.

After they heard the charges, they were each given a chance to renounce the name of Jesus. For if they did so, their death would be quick. Every prisoner declined the opportunity. They were each led to their individual crosses, and forced to lay upon the beam of wood. Thirty two of the prisoners were tied, hand and foot, to their cross. Those crosses were lifted, and placed in their metal brace.

When it came to Paul, his hands and feet were nailed to his cross. He tried very hard, not to scream, but the pain was too great. With each blow of the hammer, he cried out in agony, and Amir smiled. When he was securely affixed to the cross, it was lifted, and placed in its metal bracket.

The captives began to sing, "Onward Christian soldiers......", and Dr. Bahram's face twisted up in anger. He flashed a sign, to the captain of the guard, and the man signaled to his soldiers. Two of the troops made their way to a container, and pulled out sledge hammers. Walking to the last row of captives, with one soldier on each end of the row, they stood, ready for further instructions.

As the rebels continued to sing, the Captain gave another sign, and the troops raised their hammers, to smash the legs of two of the prisoners. Those prisoners, whose legs were broken, could no longer support their own weight. The crowd roared their approval, and Josh and Jana were appalled at what they witnessed. Now, with the weight of their own bodies, pulling at their arms, those captives struggled to breathe, and their singing was cut short. As the other Christians continued to sing, the soldiers were instructed to swing the hammers again, and as two more fought for breath, their singing stopped. Again, as loud approval from the gawkers filled the square, Josh and Jana shook their heads in utter dismay.

The prisoners continued to sing, as the victims were cut short, two, by two, until there was only Paul remaining. The throng began to chant, "Kill the Christian", over, and over. And, Jana's eyes filled with tears, as Paul's eyes again met hers. Some of his followers were openly weeping, and she feared for their safety, if they were discovered.

Paul, who had continued to sing, despite many warnings, saw the soldier walking toward him wielding the hammer. Meanwhile, most of his fellow prisoners had died from suffocation behind him, one, by one. He looked toward the heavens and cried, "Praise God in all the earth. Lord, into thy hands, I commit my spirit." At that second, a bolt of lightning flashed from the sky, and hit him directly in his chest, beating his enemies to the task. With that he was gone to meet his creator, and the audience stood with mouths open. They turned, looking into each other's faces. Searching for an answer, where there was none.

The mood had changed. Slowly, and quietly, the masses disbursed. Each to his own life. Some would go to the Bishop's church on Sunday, some would go on sharing the Gospel, and make a way without Paul. Some would seek out answers, the way Cage had done, and the kingdom would grow. Amir left the square angry. The spectacle, which he'd designed to warn Christians, seemed to have backfired in his face. Well, his perfect plan, for the coming of the Mahdi, was almost in place, and he was sure he would ultimately win, so he'd take this in stride.

• • • • •

Josh and Jana said goodbye to their new friends, and admonished them to continue in Paul's good work, for the sake of the kingdom. They hugged and cried, and promised their brothers, and sisters, that they would see them again. All who were there knew, that the next time they would meet, would be to do battle for the Lord.

As they left the city, with their heads held high, and their hearts full, in spite of the evil Bahram, they held hands. "It's coming soon, isn't it?"

"Yes, Jana, very soon. And we must be prepared."

"I believe there will be millions who will rally with us."

"I know you're right. And we must be prepared to lead them."

"Where to now, husband?"

"Let's go home, Wife. I miss our boy."

"Yes, so do I. I'm right behind you."

www.ingramcontent.com/pod-product-compliance
Lightning Source LLC
Chambersburg PA
CBHW071424190726

48292CB00001B/100